THE BIG DIG

The letter was a hundred-and-twenty-five years old and the cache of Spanish gold it pinpointed under the streets of downtown Los Angeles was worth more than a million dollars.

For UCLA professors Arthur McDowell and Steve Sussman it was the get-rich-quick chance of a lifetime, and they were determined to take it. But . . .

McDowell
hadn't counted on his partner's girl walking nude into his shower and his life . . .

and
Sussman
hadn't counted on his partner's lust or the blue Mustang tailing them . . .

and
Nobody
had counted on murder. . . .

Books by David Westheimer

SUMMER ON THE WATER
THE MAGIC FALLACY
WATCHING OUT FOR DULIE
THIS TIME NEXT YEAR
VON RYAN'S EXPRESS
MY SWEET CHARLIE
SONG OF THE YOUNG SENTRY
LIGHTER THAN A FEATHER
OVER THE EDGE
GOING PUBLIC
THE OLMEC HEAD
THE AVILA GOLD

THE
AVILA GOLD

David Westheimer

BALLANTINE BOOKS • NEW YORK

Library of Congress Catalog Card Number: 74-18568

ISBN 0-345-24807-4-175

This edition published by arrangement with G. P. Putnam's Sons, New York

Manufactured in the United States of America

First Ballantine Books Edition: May, 1976

For Regina

THE
AVILA GOLD

1

ARTHUR MCDOWELL lay sleeping in a net hammock swung between two large avocado trees in his backyard. It was a big backyard for that neighborhood, large enough for the swimming pool McDowell would have liked but could not afford. There were other trees in the yard, an orange, a lime, a magnolia and a banana that bore fruit which never reached maturity because the Southern California climate was not right for it.

McDowell was a thickset man of over six feet and two hundred pounds. He did not bear the weight well. Too much of it was in his belly and jowls, yet he was not unpleasant-looking. At forty-three, his hair showed hardly a trace of gray, though there was a bald spot on top of his head the size of a small ice-cream saucer. Everywhere else his fair hair was so luxuriant that had he wished he could have combed it over the bald spot and revealed no trace of scalp. It had never occurred to him to do this. His complexion was ruddy, and he had an open, honest face which even in sleep looked good-natured. A copy of Dana's *Two Years Before the Mast* lay open, facedown, on his chest. The chest bulged with muscle and fat beneath his sweat shirt, which was stenciled with the letters UCLA. It was early afternoon in May, and sunny, but cool enough for the sweat shirt.

Because of McDowell's bulk and the sweat shirt, a stranger might have thought him a former athlete now going to fat, perhaps a sports coach of one sort or another. But he was not. Arthur McDowell was a professor of history at the university.

He shifted position in the hammock. The book, dislodged, fell to the ground. The fall was almost soundless, but the movement of the book across his chest awakened him. He opened his eyes, which were light brown with fair lashes, and yawned, stretching thick arms. He retrieved the book, found his place and be-

1

gan rereading the California section, which he enjoyed doing from time to time.

The back door of the stucco bungalow opened, and Florence McDowell emerged. She was a tall woman of thirty-eight, a bit heavy but, unlike her husband, not actually fat. She was a contented-looking woman, attractive enough, with brown hair that did not look as if it had received professional attention lately.

"Chet Heaps called," she said. "But I didn't want to wake you. You looked so comfortable."

"I always look comfortable," McDowell said. "What did he want?"

"Special Collection's got a new acquisition. He thought you might be interested. He said you could have first look."

McDowell grunted to a sitting position and planted his stained canvas shoes on the ground.

"First look, huh? That means he wants me to go through it and tell him if it's anything. What's he got?"

"He didn't say. He said call him if you're interested."

"Another free afternoon shot," McDowell said with feigned resignation.

Actually, he welcomed an opportunity to examine new acquisitions in his field before they were catalogued and scattered through the archives. He sat in the hammock scratching his stomach for a few moments after Florence went back into the house. He marked his place in *Two Years Before the Mast* with a fallen avocado leaf and went inside.

Florence was in the kitchen with her head inside a cabinet. She was putting in new contact paper. He paused in passing and took a handful of her comfortable bottom.

"Your new diet's working, feels like," he said.

"Really?" she said from inside the cabinet, pleased. "I weighed a little heavy this morning."

"Scale must be wrong," said McDowell.

"Are you going to call Heaps?" Florence asked.

"Might as well. If it sounds like anything, maybe I'll run over to the research library."

"Don't be late," Florence said, emerging from the

cabinet. "I'm trying a soybean meat loaf tonight, and I don't want it drying out in the oven."

"Oh, Lord. Soybean."

"It wouldn't hurt you to lose a few pounds, Arthur."

He had heard that before and, while not denying the truth of it, avoided any serious attempt to get his weight down.

He went into the room he called his library and dug the telephone from a huddle of books and periodicals. Heaps had just got in a box of old Hispano-California documents. It was, Heaps said, the gift of an elderly Bel Air couple who were discarding some of their impedimenta preparatory to moving from the family mansion to a small, twenty-four-hour security condominium in La Jolla. The wife, Heaps said, could trace her roots back to the days of the early rancheros. All the material was in Spanish, which Heaps could not read. However, one of the items appeared to be a diary or journal, with the first entry 1811.

"I'll be over and have a look," McDowell said.

He liked having first crack at things that had not passed through the hands of another scholar. There was always that possibility of turning up a new bit of information to add to what was known about the life and times of early Californians. Over the years he had published several well-regarded papers discussing virgin material passing through his hands into Special Collections. He was not a particularly vain man, but he was aware the greater his reputation became in his field, the more material would find its way to the university, through either donations of collections or grants for purchases.

McDowell changed into a sports shirt, clean slacks and loafers. When he went to the kitchen to tell Florence he was leaving, she reminded him once more not to be late for dinner. Assuring her he would not be, he went out to his car. It was a seven-year-old racing green TR4. There was not much clearance between the steering wheel and his belly. His students said Professor McDowell did not drive his little car, he wore it.

He had bought the Triumph from a professor in the English Department who had brought it back from a sabbatical in London. McDowell had had it for three years now. It was his first sports car, a fortieth birthday present to himself and his only personal extravagance in all the years he had been married, excluding the occasional rare book he found irresistible. But those, he explained to his wife, and with some justification, were investments, not extravagances.

When he squeezed under the wheel, he felt, paradoxically, slimmer, though he really did not care one way or the other whether he was fat or thin. He enjoyed eating and disliked exercise, except for his regular tennis game with Steven Sussman from the Department of Engineering and Applied Science, and if the penalty for that was being overweight, he suffered it willingly.

As he drove away, he looked back at his house. The lawn was shaggy. Mr. Kuwahara, the thirty-five-dollar a month gardener, had not come last week. McDowell did not take that amiss. He and Mr. Kuwahara had an understanding. Because McDowell was a college professor, and one of Mr. Kuwahara's sons had been a student of his, Mr. Kuwahara kept the McDowell yard for thirty-five dollars instead of the fifty dollars he normally charged for a yard that size. And because Mr. Kuwahara respected educated men and knocked fifteen dollars off the going rate, McDowell was unperturbed when Mr. Kuwahara was a few days late. Some of the neighbors did their own yards, but McDowell did not even own a lawn mower.

The McDowells lived in one of the few remaining one-family houses in that block of Darlington Avenue in a part of West Los Angeles ten minutes from the UCLA campus. It was an area which for years had been in the process of being devoured by apartment buildings. One by one, homeowners were selling out to the multi-unit developers. McDowell had received more than one offer for his property. Though a substantial profit was involved, he and his wife had rejected them with a minimum of deliberation. The old stucco bungalow was comfortable, it was close to his work, and they could never buy a comparable home for less than twice what they had paid for it twelve years ago when Robert was born.

4

McDowell drove east to Barrington and, at the stop sign, studied the traffic. When the traffic on Barrington was heavy, he turned right, to Wilshire, and approached the campus through Westwood. When it was light, he turned left across both lanes and took Sunset to the rear of the campus. Today the traffic was light.

Sunset skirted Bel Air, where lived, or had lived, the couple who had given UCLA the papers McDowell was on his way to examine. Bel Air was an area of hills, greenery and imposing homes, redolent of money, with winding roads among which it was easy to get lost. McDowell wondered if that was not deliberate, to discourage sightseers.

Inside the campus, he took Circle Drive to the parking lot, for which he had a permit. He slipped his blue key card into the slot, retrieved it, drove past the lifted barrier and found a parking place. He climbed out of his little car and gazed lingeringly at the Gypsy Wagon. The Gypsy Wagon was a lunch stand behind Rolfe Hall and only a few paces from the low steps leading up to the broad courtyard in front of the research library. If Florence was going to be on a health and diet kick for dinner tonight, it might be wise to fortify himself. The Gypsy Wagon dispensed what he considered the best chili dogs in town.

But Florence would be disappointed if he failed to do justice to her soybean concoction. And it was so seldom she asked him to make such a sacrifice. Usually, when she was caught up in a new diet, she prepared her meals separately and did not inflict them on him and Robert. He sighed and walked quickly past the Gypsy Wagon and its line of waiting students.

One of McDowell's students was on duty at an exit check station in the library, his nose buried in a book.

"That doesn't look like assigned reading to me, Slotkin," McDowell said.

The young man looked up, startled, and grinned when he saw the speaker. He held up the book so McDowell could read the title. It was one of the new best sellers filled, or so McDowell had heard, with detailed sexual activity.

"Is that what you waste your time on when you're

5

supposed to be wallowing in nineteenth-century California?" McDowell demanded.

"It's not wasted time, Dr. McDowell," Slotkin replied. "It's like, you know, a manual of instruction. And I'm only reading the dirty parts."

"That's different," said McDowell. "Carry on."

He went down the steps to Special Collections on the A level. He moved from case to case in the display area to see if there was anything new, but the displays had not been changed since his last visit. The graduate student who worked part time as a typist hailed him.

"Dr. McDowell, Mr. Heaps is expecting you."

She rose when McDowell approached her desk. That pleased him. They did not always stand up for a professor. And she was well shaped, too, something that had not shown to advantage when she was sitting down. He hoped that was one of the reasons she had gotten up. Just because a man had let himself get a trifle heavy did not mean a pretty girl shouldn't angle for an appreciative glance from him.

"Go right on in," she said, fingering a button at her shirt collar.

So she had noticed he'd noticed, McDowell thought. That was nice. They'd both had a little innocent pleasure from her figure.

Heap walked across the office to shake hands when McDowell entered. He was a thin man in old-fashioned austere metal-rimmed glasses. McDowell always thought of him as one of Special Collections' permanent displays. McDowell looked at a large cardboard box on the floor. DEL MONTE PEACHES was printed on the side.

"That it?" he asked.

"That's it," Heaps said.

"Hell of a way to treat valuable documents," McDowell said with a smile. "What if a potential donor was to barge in and see the shoddy way you store material?"

"That's the way it came in. The old boy brought it in himself. Said he was glad to get all that old rubbish out of the house."

"I don't suppose that'll keep him from expecting an inflated appraisal for his tax return."

"As a matter of fact, he said he had another batch he was thinking about giving Cal State San Diego when he moved down to La Jolla. If UCLA is insufficiently impressed by this lot."

"Well," McDowell said, rubbing his chin, "if the stuff's not too bad, I'll see what I can do. Within reason."

Heaps took a small leatherbound volume from his desk and handed to to McDowell.

"This is the diary," he said. "Or what I think is a diary."

The leather was dried out, cracked and mottled. It shouldn't be like that, McDowell thought with a trace of annoyance. The owners should have had enough pride of possession, if not appreciation for a piece of history, to take better care of it. He looked at the first page. No name or other identification. It started off with January 1, 1811. A continuation of a previous diary or diaries, he thought, wondering hungrily if they were in the lot the donor was holding ransom for a generous appraisal. He skimmed the opening entry. It was an account of some sort of party written in a gushy, girlish style but with flair and an eye for detail. If it was a fair sample of the contents, the diary promised to be good reading as well as valuable source material.

"It's a diary, all right," McDowell said. "Are you sure it's the only one in the box?"

Heaps nodded.

"Too bad," said McDowell.

He put the diary in the box with the other material, a grab bag of faded documents, old books and clothbound ledgers.

"Can you have it taken over to my office?" he asked. "I'd like to get started this afternoon."

"Certainly," said Heaps. He went to the door. "Andrea," he said, "will you come in the office?"

The graduate student came in wearing a yellow pencil like an ornament in her red hair. "Yes, sir?" she said.

7

"Will you take this box over to Dr. McDowell's office in Bunche," Heaps said.

"That box looks heavy," McDowell protested.

"I don't mind," the girl said.

McDowell wavered. After all, Bunche Hall was practically next door to the research library and she was a healthy, robust youngster. But it wouldn't be right to let a girl carry the box for him, even a large, strong girl. Heaps should be ashamed of himself asking her.

"Never mind," McDowell said. "I'll manage."

He picked up the box easily. Despite his indolence, he was a powerful man. A hell of a note, he thought, as he climbed the steps. He was doing Heaps a favor and giving up a free afternoon, and Heaps couldn't even take the trouble to scare up a male student to carry a box to his office. McDowell put the box on the counter at the check stand where his student was on duty. The student's job was to see that books passing his station were properly checked out and that no one was trying to sneak one out in a bag or briefcase. He did not look in the cardboard box.

McDowell waited just beyond the check station, eyeing the library patrons passing through it. When he saw what he was waiting for, a large, empty-handed young man, he stopped his victim with a touch on the arm.

"Excuse me," he said briskly. "I'm Dr. McDowell. I wonder if I could ask a favor?"

"Uh, yes, sir," the young man said uncertainly.

"Would you mind carrying that to my office for me?" Mc Dowell said, nodding toward the cardboard box. "It's just across the way in Bunche."

"Yes, sir," the young man said, apparently relieved that was all that was being asked of him.

Slotkin, McDowell's student, glanced up covertly from his novel and grinned. McDowell's distaste for physical activity was notorious. The young man scooped up the box. McDowell held the glass door open for him and followed him out. They walked across the courtyard side by side.

"What field are you in?" McDowell asked.

"Phys Ed."

"I should have guessed from your size. Are you engaged in sports?"

The young man looked at McDowell suspiciously, as if he thought he were being put on.

"Yes, sir," he said. "Track, wrestling and football. I play defensive end. All-American last year."

"Of course," said McDowell, as if he now recognized his benefactor. An All-American defensive end, and an obliging one, deserved at least that. McDowell did not follow sports.

At Bunche, McDowell unlocked his office and opened the door for the All-American and gestured for him to put the box on his desk.

"Thank you very much," McDowell said. "I'm looking forward to seeing you play against Southern Cal next year."

"I'm a senior," the young man said. "I graduate next month."

"Oh, that's right," said McDowell.

The young man turned to go. McDowell cleared his throat.

"I'd like to show my appreciation for your help," he said. "Let me treat you to something at the Gypsy Wagon."

"Oh, no, sir," the young man said, embarrassed. "It's not, you know, necessary."

"I insist," said McDowell, getting out his wallet. "How about a chili dog? And you may as well bring me one, and a large Coke."

He forced money on the reluctant athlete and began taking things out of the box. After a moment of indecision, the young man left, closing the door very quietly behind him.

In addition to the diary, the box contained correspondence, old books in deplorable condition, accounts ledgers, receipts, bills of sale, a baptismal certificate and other items, none apparently under a hundred and twenty years old. McDowell was winnowing through the material when the young man returned with his chili dog and drink. He gave McDowell his change and left hastily. McDowell cleared a space on his desk and devoted himself to the chili dog. The young man had neglected to bring a plastic spoon, and

McDowell was compelled to forgo the delectable sauce that always slopped over into the cardboard container. It was with regret that he wrapped the container and its precious contents in paper napkins and dropped it in his wastebasket.

He returned to the documents. They appeared to be largely household and business accounts from a rancho in the vicinity of El Pueblo de Nuestra Señora la Reina de Los Angeles, as Los Angeles was known at that period. A cursory examination revealed little exceptional. He put everything back in the box except the diary and a letter that, because its seal was unbroken, appeared never to have been opened. He laid the letter aside and dipped into the diary. The handwriting was almost childish, but the letters were carefully formed, and he was able to read it without difficulty.

As he read, he formed a mental image of the diarist. Young, romantic, naive, enthusiastic. And, of course, a ravishing black-eyed beauty. She magnified everyday matters on the rancho and in El Pueblo and described less common events with the air of one watching history in the making. Which in a sense she was, McDowell thought, though not to the degree she imagined. The diarist was an orphan living with a prosperous aunt and uncle. Some of the things she described were reminiscent of the little tales in Ana Begue Packman's *Leather Dollars,* a collection compiled by Mrs. Packman from stories told to her by a great-aunt. The diarist's accounts, however, were firsthand and in greater detail. She wrote of balls, horse races, fiestas, local gossip, household affairs, food and visits to other ranchos and El Pueblo.

Occasionally she touched on matters with which McDowell had some familiarity, making him feel as if he were being transported backward in time. She wrote of a visit to the rancho by Lieutenant Francisco Maria Ruiz, whom McDowell knew to have been acting commandant of the company of Spanish soldiers at San Diego. She described her emotions at learning of the death at San Gabriel of Father Francis Dometz, who, her uncle had informed her, was the last surviving companion of Junipero Serra in the district. Of this event she wrote, "As soon as I gained the privacy of my own room I shed tears of sorrow even though I know the good fathers at San Gabriel do not often find it in their hearts to minister to El Pueblo de Los Angeles."

McDowell made notes as he read. "Is this the Father Panto later poisoned by his cook at San Diego Mission?" "She refers to the death of her father in Santa Barbara. A clue to her identity? Check archives."

It should not be too difficult, he thought, to obtain a grant covering the expenses of publishing an annotated translation. Almost any university press would be delighted to bring it out. The phone rang. He picked up the receiver, annoyed at the interruption. It was Florence.

"Do you know what time it is?" she asked calmly.

"Three, the last time I looked at my watch," he replied.

"That was almost three hours ago, Arthur. The meat loaf's ready to come out of the oven and Bobby is starving."

Robert was always starving, and looked it, all knees and elbows, ribs that showed and shoulder blades like wings. McDowell had looked the same at twelve. Whoever would have expected him to grow into a size 44 portly? he wondered.

"Tell him to hang on," McDowell said. "I'm on my way."

He retrieved a used manila envelope from his wastebasket and put the diary in it. As he was leaving, his glance fell on the sealed letter he had put aside. He stuck that in the envelope with the diary. The next day, Friday, would be a busy one, so if possible, he would finish skimming through the diary tonight. He might even get to the letter as well.

The soybean meat loaf was only a partial success. McDowell was glad he had fortified himself with the chili dog. Robert, who could eat anything, had two large portions. After dinner, McDowell and his son worked the Los Angeles *Times* crossword puzzle from the morning's paper. They did this every evening. Some men played catch with their sons. McDowell

11

worked crossword puzzles with his son. He believed children should play with children.

The puzzle finished, McDowell retired to the library with the diary. After an hour he was nearing the end. Florence thrust her head in the door and asked if he wanted a cup of Sanka.

"Thanks," said McDowell, marking his place with a forefinger. "Any cookies left?"

With Robert's appetite, there sometimes weren't.

"You didn't like the meat loaf," Florence said.

"I ate it, didn't I?"

"Not very much."

"I'm watching," McDowell said. "I'd like to keep my weight down where it is."

"Sure you would," said Florence. "When you come to bed, put that shirt in the laundry hamper. It's got chili spots all over it."

McDowell grinned at her departing back. She brought only two cookies with his mug of Sanka.

"Am I being punished?" he asked.

"You can have more if you want," she said. "But you really should cut down on sweets. You don't want to get diabetes."

"You don't get diabetes from eating sweets."

"I know they say that," Florence said.

McDowell made do with two cookies and finished the diary with his coffee. He was not as confident as he had been about its prospects for publication. After a while there was a sameness to it. He put the diary aside and went to the living room. Florence was needlepointing, and Robert was doing homework. They were both also watching television. How they managed that was a mystery to McDowell. He stood in the doorway looking at the TV screen. He seldom watched television except for crime dramas and news. If the set was on, he would pause in passage and watch a few minutes. If something caught his fancy, he would join the family circle.

"Any good?" he asked from the doorway.

"Yes," said Robert. "But you won't like it."

McDowell accepted his son's judgment and returned to the library and the letter he had brought back with the diary. He examined it front and back,

12

wondering why it had never been opened. Misplaced, then forgotten, he thought. On the front, written in mannered script now faded to a rusty brown, was: "For the Hand of Don Estevan Ruiz Cedillo." The name was unknown to McDowell. He would have known it had Don Estevan been anyone of historical importance.

The sealing wax was brittle with age, cracked and checked with fragments missing. The impression was circular and shallow. He played the beam of the desk lamp directly on it. He could make out reversed letters and numbers on two sides and on the bottom of the circumference. At the left was R. I TE.PS H, on the right, G.D.VI O AC and at the bottom 09 1. The device in the center appeared to be a portrait bust, though it was difficult to be sure because of the condition of the wax.

He picked up a letter opener to pry away the seal but thought better of it. The brittle wax would shatter beyond reconstruction and he wished to preserve the seal. Its circular shape, serrated perimeter and center device suggested something familiar, but he could not recall having seen such a seal before. He got a razor blade from the bathroom and sliced carefully around the seal. Because of his large, clumsy fingers, the blade at some points cut through the several thicknesses of heavy paper and into the top of his desk. This caused him no great concern. It was already so blemished new marks were inconsequential. He lifted out the seal and the portion of letter to which it was affixed. He put it aside, smoothed the open letter on his desk and fitted the piece in again, written side up. The letter was dated Sonora, February 14. There was no year.

Compadre, [it read]. After five weeks, with God's help, I am safely arrived here. It has been a long and difficult journey because, as you understand only too well, a patriot who fought successfully against the wretched Gillespie and later against others who supported the invaders scarcely could travel openly, though it pleases me to report I was dealt with most kindly by such compatriots, and they are not few, as still bear in their hearts allegiance to our revered flag. Also, I was delayed for some days by an illness which came from having taken of tainted beef. It was given me wholesome at the rancho of Don Pedro A., but I fear it spoiled along the way.

But these matters and my reasons for having departed in such haste are things of the past. What is important is that by the grace of the Virgin we may still salvage some benefit from the calamity which has befallen us and our country. As you know only too well, I was unable to return to my house before the arrival of the Americans and you are also aware of the reasons why I could not do so after they resumed possession. I have no desire ever again to see the place where God granted me such contentment now that it is in the hands of the usurpers from the North. But there is a possession of mine which I am most anxious to retrieve, and for which endeavor I earnestly request your assistance, as one old friend of another. I am aware there has been a change for the worse in your fortunes in these weeks of occupation —ill tidings travel swiftly—and therefore in friendship and understanding I propose to you an equal share.

As you may recall, after my return from Chino following the victory with Varela at the rancho where Carlos fell, I hinted to you that I had acquired something of great value. How it came into the possession of Williams, or, if not Williams, another of his compatriots, I know not. Nevertheless, it was in one of his outbuildings, concealed among hides. Fortunately, I was alone when I came upon it and contrived to keep my discovery secret by wrapping it in hides. To give you an idea of its substance, may I tell you it took most of my strength to raise it into the cart. You can well understand why I did not seek assistance in this endeavor.

As you know, good friend, upon returning home, after but a few days I was obliged to set out again once more to accompany Garfias to Santa Barbara. Being unwilling to leave unprotected that which I had so carefully fetched back, and you, my friend, by the

14

will of God being absent on business of your own at the time, and having no other on whom I could rely, I set about finding a place of concealment. To this end, I took it late at night to the home of Doña Encarnación and let it down into the well in the rear courtyard, where it still must lie, for had it been found there is certain to have been much talk.

What I beg of you is this. If the situation is now stable, and if it is not as soon as it becomes so, and if the American commander is not once more quartered in the house of Doña Encarnación, go to the well at an hour when you may do so in utter secrecy, talking with you a length of rope and a grappling hook and secure that which I deposited there in my haste. I recommend to you to take with you one who is strong and trustworthy to assist you for, as I have earlier related, the box is quite heavy. Then you must find a way, with God's help, to bring the box and yourself to Sonora, where we will make division of its contents.

If you have any doubts as to the worth of this business, I call your attention to the seal of this missive and assure you it is indicative of what you may expect to find upon successful completion of your mission.

God be with you, old friend and companion. I await your arrival in Sonora with what patience I can muster.

Diego del C.

McDowell sat back in the chair and worked his shoulders, stiff from hunching over first the diary and then the letter. He stretched, yawned and rubbed his eyes. They were fatigued from reading so many handwritten pages in faded ink, and in a language which, though he knew it well, was still not his mother tongue. There were elements of an interesting little puzzle in the letter but because it was a puzzle long overtaken by the years and because he was surfeited with the great drafts of trivia he had gulped down in the past few hours, McDowell did not dwell on it.

When he went to bed, Florence was watching the

news on the old black and white portable. McDowell propped himself against the headboard and watched with her. After the weathercast, which was near the end, he got up and turned off the set and the bedroom light. Someday, when he could afford it, he intended buying a color set with a remote control like the one in the living room.

"What were you reading so long?" Florence asked from the darkness beside him.

"An old diary in Heaps' latest collection of junk," he replied. "I may be able to get an article or two out of it."

"That's nice," Florence said.

Her hand slipped under the waistband of his pajamas and down. He suppressed a grunt. He was always ticklish at first contact.

"The yard looks awful," Florence said. "I want you to speak to Mr. Kuwahara. He only comes when he feels like it."

"I will," McDowell promised.

He turned to her and began groping almost automatically. After seventeen years of marriage almost everything was a habit. He felt the ripples just above her hips. She had been on the new diet a week or more, but he could detect no change.

"Your new diet's working," he said. "You've lost right here."

"Really?" Florence said, pleased.

"I don't want to be too hard on him, though," McDowell said. "We'd never get another gardener half as good for twice what we pay him. And I like the old guy."

"That feels good," Florence said comfortably.

"So does that," McDowell said.

"Don't forget to remind him he hasn't done the back flower beds in a month," Florence said.

"Has it really been that long?"

McDowell made an adjustment in his position, and Florence gathered him in.

"Maybe not a month," she said. "But at least three weeks."

Then they stopped talking for a while. At what

16

should have been a critical moment, McDowell abruptly found his mind wandering.

Who were Don Estevan Ruiz Cedillo and Diego del C. and where was the house of Doña Encarnación and just what the devil had been in that box?

2

McDOWELL had a 10 A.M. class Friday. When there was nothing urgent to be done at the office, he slept as late as possible, leaving just enough time for break-fast and traffic. Barrington was always clotted from San Vicente to Sunset, and when he went through Westwood, Wilshire was impossible. This morning, however, he awoke at seven and could not doze off again because of a middling sense of urgency. There was something he had intended doing before class.

Florence was already up and out of the room. She was an early riser. Robert was, too. When McDowell was his age, he'd had to be dragged out of bed mornings to get to school on time. Still did, he thought. Then why couldn't he go back to sleep? It was that letter, of course. He wanted to read it again. He slipped on his broken-back house shoes and padded to the kitchen. Florence was poaching her butterless eggs and sipping black coffee.

"I thought your class wasn't until ten," she said.

"How about a couple of those things for me?" Mc-Dowell asked, nodding at the egg carton. "But use butter. And an English muffin if there's one left."

He opened the refrigerator and got the orange juice. He held the bottle to his lips and took seven deep swallows.

"Can't you use a glass?" Florence said.

McDowell nodded amiably, took three more swallows and put the bottle back. He went out to the front yard to get the *Times,* not bothering to put on a robe. He did not think his baggy pajamas would lower the moral or esthetic tone of the neighborhood. Robert was in the kitchen, dressed, when he returned with the paper.

"I thought your class wasn't until ten, Dad," Robert said.

McDowell put aside the classified section, which contained the puzzle, handed Robert the sports section and gave the View section to Florence. He sat down at the kitchen table and read the first-page headlines. While he was skimming the inside-page news summaries, he heard the refrigerator door open. He looked up. Robert was lifting the orange juice bottle to his lips.

"Use a glass," McDowell said, looking at Florence for approval.

Robert poured a glass root beer mug full of juice and brought it to the table. Both he and his father read their sections of the paper while they had their bacon and eggs. After a while Florence looked at the kitchen clock and said, "Time for school."

Both McDowell and Robert looked up from their papers.

"I'm talking to Bobby," she said.

McDowell shaved and dressed, except for coat and tie, before tackling the letter again. The name of the writer, Diego del C., and the intended recipient, Don Estevan Ruiz Cedillo, still rang no bells. But Gillespie, the first name mentioned in the letter, did. It provided a clue to the time and the place. A Captain Archibald Gillespie had been left in charge of El Pueblo de Los Angeles when Stockton and Frémont pulled out in 1846. The locals had rebelled against his repressive measures and driven him out, restoring Los Angeles temporarily to Mexican control. This was obviously the Gillespie of the letter. And Diego del C. had been one of those driving out the occupying force. That meant the letter had been written after 1846.

The name Varela, in the next paragraph, was also known to McDowell. Sérbulo Varela had led the attack on Gillespie's command. "As you may recall, after my return from Chino following the victory with Varela at the rancho where Carlos fell. . . ." That was too obscure even for McDowell, though the name Williams, in the next sentence, did arouse vague stirrings of memory. At any rate, Diego del C. had found

18

something valuable on the Williams rancho and later dropped it down somebody's well. There it was in the next paragraph: "the home of Doña Encarnación. . . ." The name Doña Encarnación also seemed familiar, but McDowell could not quite place it. He saw that if he wished to pursue the matter further, he would have to run over to the research library.

He put the letter and diary in his briefcase, donned his coat and tie and drove to the campus. He reached the research library a little before nine, took the self-service elevator to the third-floor stacks and walked unerringly to the shelves holding Bancroft's venerable *History of California*. He found Volume V, which covered the events of 1846 and took it to a study area.

He checked the index for the appropriate chapter and leafed through the pages with practiced speed. There it was. On September 27, 1846, Varela and his men had taken the rancho of one Isaac Williams at Chino. ". . . The rancho where Carlos fell . . ." the letter had said. Bancroft even identified Carlos. A Carlos Ballesteros had been killed in the fight for the rancho.

McDowell put the book aside and returned to the letter. Don Diego had taken the box of valuables found at the rancho to "the home of Doña Encarnación and let it down into the well. . . ." Doña Encarnación, he thought. Doña Encarnación. He read further. ". . . and if the American commander is not once again quartered in the house of Doña Encarnación. . . ." ". . . once again quartered. . . ." That was the key. It should have occurred to him on his first reading of the letter, but he had been too bloated with the effusions of the diary to concentrate. When Commodore Stockton and Major Frémont took Los Angeles on August 13, 1846, Stockton found one of the houses unoccupied, the owner having fled, and requisitioned it for his headquarters. It had been the Avila house. And the Doña Encarnación of the letter was Doña Encarnación Avila, widow of Francisco Avila, who had built the house in 1818 or thereabout. A house which was, interestingly enough, still stand-

19

ing, much restored. The Avila Adobe on Olvera Street. Olvera was no longer actually a street but rather a block-long stretch of Mexican shops and restaurants almost always aswarm with tourists.

There was no well at the Avila Adobe now. McDowell did not recall ever seeing a reference to there having been one. As he remembered, the residents of early Los Angeles had obtained water from the Zanja Madre, the Mother Ditch. But if Don Diego said there was a well, there obviously had been one.

McDowell rested his chin on his palms and looked down at the letter. He wondered who eventually had retrieved the box. Not Don Estevan Ruiz Cedillo. The letter obviously had never reached him. Perhaps Diego del C. himself. Or Doña Encarnación. Or a servant, or some lucky American who had reoccupied Los Angeles in January, 1847, with Commodore Stockton and General Kearny. But it had been so long ago it did not really matter.

He read the penultimate paragraph. ". . . I call your attention to the seal of this missive and assure you it is indicative of what you may expect to find. . . ." He lifted out the seal and studied it. The letters and numbers told him nothing except that the impression had not been made by a conventional seal. They were reversed. With a seal, the design was reversed on the seal itself so that the impression would not be.

The circular shape, the portrait bust and the arrangement of letters and numbers suggested a coin. ". . . it is indicative of what you may expect to find . . ." The impression had been made by a coin, and from the box Don Diego had found. What better way to convince his friend, Ruiz, the box was worth going after?

McDowell wrote down the numbers and letters in normal, unreversed position. On the left side they now read CA O. IV. D.G. and on the right, H SP.ET I R. At the bottom, obviously a date, 1 90. The box had been found in 1846 so the date was 1790 or earlier. Don Diego had found himself a box of coins, so many of them it had taxed his strength to pick it up. He wondered if they were gold or silver coins, not that it mattered one way or the other at this late date. Coinage was outside his area of interest, and he could not tell from the seal if the coin was gold or silver, or even the denomination. Somewhere in the stacks there should be a book that could tell him.

He looked at his watch. Almost ten. It would have to wait. Monday, perhaps, if he had the time and the subject still held his interest. He took the Bancroft back to its place in the stacks. Despite his laziness in other matters, he never left books lying around on the tables as so many others did. Too often, finding a book he wanted missing from its place, he had gone to the check-out desk to put a hold on it only to learn it had not been checked out, only left in a study area.

He had a staff meeting immediately following his class and after-lunch separate appointments with two students, one of whom tried to cajole him into reconsidering the grade on a paper and the other seeking advice on the subject for a master's thesis.

Heaps phoned while McDowell was talking with the latter, wanting to know if he had finished itemizing the contents of the box.

"Not yet," McDowell replied. "I got stuck into the diary and read the whole darn thing."

"That good, eh?" Heaps said. "Is it publishable?"

"I thought so at first. But now I'm not so sure."

"Anything else of particular interest?"

"Afraid not," McDowell said. "But don't worry. Your donor should get an appraisal that'll keep him happy."

After he hung up and turned back to the student he was advising, McDowell realized he had neglected to mention the letter. But then there was no reason he should have. Though it posed a little puzzle to be solved for his own amusement, it was not an important or unusual item. If it had been written by a famous personage of the day it might be worth something for the signature alone. But a Diego del C.? McDowell did not even know who he was.

He sent the student on his way charged with a desire to plunge into research over the coming summer vacation, cleaned up a week's accumulation of correspondence and began itemizing the contents of the cardboard box. His mind wandered back to the seal.

21

Why wait until Monday? If he did, it would be nagging at him the entire weekend. It should take but a few minutes to identify the coin, and then he could put the whole thing out of his mind. He finished the list, made a generous but supportable appraisal, signed his name to it, put the diary in the box with the other material and phoned Heaps to send over and pick it up. He'd keep the letter until he'd checked out the seal. The letter was not on the itemized list. Since he had not put it in the box with the other things, he had forgotten to list it. No matter. He could add it later for Heaps' records before everything went into the archives. The value was not enough to change his appraisal appreciably.

He considered calling the library and having some coin books sent over. But the research library was on the way to the parking lot, and he might as well stop off there on his way to the car. He fixed the seal in place with clear plastic tape, put the letter in his pocket and stuffed some papers he intended looking at over the weekend in his briefcase.

The card catalogue listed several books on coins. He wrote down the author, title and file numbers of a selection of them. Among them were Friedberg's *Gold Coins of the World* and Hobson's *Historic Gold Coins of the World*. He would begin with gold coins, he thought, and work down. The Hobson book was not among the other CJ113's in the third floor stacks, but he found the Friedberg and took it to a desk. He fished the letter out of his pocket and laid it down, seal side up, then turned to the Mexico section. The Spaniards had begun minting coins in Mexico City in the seventeenth century.

There was nothing resembling the seal among the first entries. He turned the page and skimmed the two columns of photographs and type. He found what he was looking for near the end of the second column. In the center was a portrait bust of a man with a prominent Roman nose and beneath it a date, 1790. At the left of the bust was CAROL.IV.D.G. and at the right, HISP.ET IND.R., neatly filling in the missing spaces of the seal's 1 90, CA O .IV.D.G. H SP .ET I .R.

22

It was a gold piece from the reign of Charles IV, 1788-1808. The 1790's had been minted in denominations of eight, four and one escudos. The denominations were on the reverse side. Two denominations were illustrated, the 1790 eight and a variant 1800 two. McDowell compared the seal with the illustrations. It was smaller than the eight-escudo piece and larger than the two-. It could only be a four-escudo coin. In 1958, when that particular edition of *Gold Coins of the World* had been published, the four-escudo piece was valued at $300. Probably worth a lot more than that now, McDowell thought, not that it mattered. In Don Diego's day four gold escudos must have had great purchasing power. If the coin used as a seal had indeed been indicative of the contents of the box, the person who eventually brought it out of the well had come into a fortune.

Now that he had satisfied his curiosity, McDowell had no further interest in the letter. On his way out of the library he stopped by Special Collections to return it. Special Collections was closed. It closed at five, before the research library. Monday would be soon enough, McDowell thought. He'd return it then and add it to the itemized list at the same time.

That night he took his family to dinner and a double feature in Santa Monica. Dinner was fish-and-chips at the Mucky Duck. Florence's diet banned potatoes and anything fried, so she had her dinner at home before they left. Salad, four ounces of cheese and a piece of fruit. At the movie, she refused to taste even one kernel of the tub of buttered popcorn McDowell and Robert kept passing between them. After the show, however, when they went to Clancy Muldoon's for ice cream, she weakened and had a small single cone, but of sherbet, not ice cream.

"Sherbet has fewer calories," she explained.

Saturday morning McDowell had the house to himself. Florence was out checking Ohrbach's and a sale at the May Company and Robert was swimming in the pool of an apartment house down the street, where a school chum lived. McDowell settled down in the library with the papers he had brought home and a bag of macaroons. He counted the macaroons before eating them. He had a pact with Robert that Robert was to get half. The pact covered all sweets brought into the McDowell home except those Robert bought with his own money. Robert seldom bought any with his own money. He preferred investing in gadgets.

McDowell was interrupted in the midst of his work by the sound of an insistent automobile horn. It was Steve Sussman's Mercedes. They had an eleven thirty tennis date. McDowell had let the time slip away from him, as he always did when he worked. The horn sounded again, a series of beeps. Sussman was playing a tune and would insist on McDowell's trying to identify it. McDowell went to the front door and called out, " 'The Last Time I Saw Paris.' "

" 'Your Cheating Heart,' damn it," Sussman called back. He was from Texas and listened almost exclusively to country music. Not that he had been all that fond of it back home, he had once explained to Mc-Dowell, but because now that he was away he wanted to maintain contact with his roots.

McDowell stepped out on the porch.

"You're not gonna play looking like that?" Sussman demanded. "They'll run you off the court for indecent exposure."

McDowell knew Sussman meant the comfortable belly hanging over the waistband of his disreputable Bermuda shorts but took no offense. Sussman only insulted people he liked. With others he might be ironic, but seldom impolite.

While McDowell was changing into his tennis clothes, he could hear Sussman playing country tunes on the horn. A voice, sounding as if it came from the apartment house across the street, shouted, "For Christ's sake, man!" and Sussman's voice shouted back, "Sorry, amigo." The horn fell silent.

McDowell joined Sussman in the white Mercedes, as usual parked in front of the house facing in the wrong direction. The Mercedes was a model that cost nine or ten thousand dollars new and had been only two years old when Sussman bought it. Pretty high living for an assistant professor McDowell had thought at the time. The radio came on when Sussman started the engine. It was tuned to KLAC, a country music station.

"Can't you get something else?" McDowell demanded.

"Sure," said Sussman. "Soon's this one's over. Barbara Fairchild's 'Teddy Bear.' Haven't heard it in maybe a year."

The Mercedes shot away from the curb. Sussman did not bother to pull over to the right until a car loomed up ahead. When the record ended, Sussman punched a button and got rock music. He played a two-handed accompaniment on the steering wheel.

"That's even worse," McDowell said.

"There ain't no satisfying some folks," Sussman said, turning the radio off.

McDowell leaned back luxuriously in the leather bucket seat. The Mercedes made his battered old Triumph look like two cents, but he still preferred the TR4. And it was all paid for, unlike Sussman's car.

Sussman was just under six feet, an inch shorter than McDowell, and as dark and lean as McDowell was fair and pudgy. He had thick black curly hair, heavy black eyebrows, black eyes and an evil black mustache. His teeth were large and very white, making his smile startling.

Their unlikely friendship had begun a couple of years earlier at an interdepartmental meeting. They had been standing close together while an administrator made a boring speech full of platitudes. Sussman had muttered, "Bullshit," under his breath in Spanish, and McDowell, chuckling, had said, "You're so right," in the same language and asked him if he were in the Department of Languages.

"No," Sussman had replied. "Engineering and Applied Science."

"Chicano?" McDowell had asked.

Sussman had grinned, those white teeth flashing.

"Name's Sussman," he said. "German Jew on my granddaddy's side, plain American Jew on my mother's. That's Tex-Mex I was talking."

After that they occasionally had lunch together and then, at Sussman's instigation, had drifted into a weekly tennis game, tennis being the only physical activity that had even the faintest attraction for Mc-Dowell. Sussman came over for dinner on the infrequent occasions when he had an urge for home cooking and family life. Florence liked him and thought him wildly handsome but did not approve of his still being a bachelor at thirty-one. Robert adored him because he always brought complex gadgets and boxes of See's candy and fought phony kung fu bouts with him, neither of them knowing anything about the art except what they had seen in the movies and on television.

When McDowell and Sussman got to the UCLA courts, a couple of girls, strangers to both of them, wanted to play mixed doubles. Girls reacted that way to Sussman.

"Sorry, girls," Sussman said. "But my old dad is giving me a lesson today."

"No shit," said one of the girls.

McDowell resisted the urge to scowl. It was old-fashioned of him he knew, but he did not like women using that sort of language.

"Aren't you Mr. Sussman?" the other girl asked.

"That's right," Sussman replied.

"You used to take out Corinne Martorelli."

"Martorelli, Martorelli," Sussman said with a covert glance at McDowell. "The name sounds familiar."

McDowell smiled. Miss Martorelli must have been a student of Sussman's at one time. There were rumors, never substantiated, that Sussman occasionally slept with his prettier students, but no one had ever accused him of sweetening their grades in return, so why not? Let he that was without lust cast the first aspersion.

"It should," the girl said.

Before she left with her friend, she said, "I'm Peggy Barnett. I'm in the student directory. Okay?"

Sussman did not reply. McDowell had a feeling he would have if he had been alone.

They played two sets, with Sussman running him all over the court as usual. McDowell took two games in the first set and one in the second. His record for two sets was seven games on a day when Sussman was recovering from an overactive night.

McDowell lay flat on his back with eyes closed, sweating and puffing. Sussman sat beside him chewing a blade of grass and breathing normally.

"When you get through gasping, how about lunch?" Sussman asked.

"You're going to kill me one of these days," McDowell said, sitting up. "Run me to death. Where for lunch?"

"How about the Farmer's Market? I've got to pick up some cigars across the street at Wittner's."

Wittner's was on the west side of Fairfax Avenue. It was a long, narrowish shop with tiers of boxed cigars in a case running almost its full length. While Sussman was buying two boxes of Ornelas No. #5's McDowell looked hungrily at a display of Barling pipes in the locked cases across from the cigars. When he learned what they cost, he lost interest.

Sussman paid for his cigars with a twenty, a single and some change. And they were small boxes.

Outside, McDowell asked, "How many cigars in a box?"

"Twenty-five. Why?"

"That's forty cents a cigar. How can an assistant professor afford forty-cent cigars?"

"I've got a couple of nice things going for me. One, I'm single. Two, I don't pay my bills."

In the Farmer's Market, McDowell wanted Mexican food.

"Hell, if I'd known that, I'd have taken you to El Coyote," Sussman said. "What you eat here is crab louie."

McDowell loaded up on Mexican food at Castillo's and Sussman got crab louie at the seafood stall. The Farmer's Market, as usual on Saturdays, was crowded, and they had to wait for a table.

"So what you been doing all week?" Sussman asked.

"The usual. Oh, I did find an interesting letter in a box of old documents Special Collections got in."

"Yeah?" Sussman said indifferently.

A couple finished dawdling over coffee, and Sussman made a dash for the table they were vacating.

27

McDowell followed at a more leisurely pace. They sat down and started eating.

"Written in eighteen forty-seven and never been opened," McDowell said between bites of chili relleno.

"What was?"

"The letter. Fellow who wrote it said he'd found a box of goodies in a raid on a rancho. And then dumped it down a well at the Avila Adobe. That restored house on Olvera."

"The taquitos are pretty good down there," Sussman said. "But none of the other stuff can compare with El Coyote."

"The box had at least one gold coin in it. Don Diego, the one who wrote the letter, used a gold four-escudo piece to mark the wax seal. Checked it out in the library yesterday."

"That's where you were. I tried to get you at the office and nobody answered."

McDowell finished the last bit of refried beans and said, "I wonder who wound up with it?"

"Wound up with what?" Sussman demanded.

"The box Don Diego put down the well. He wrote the letter from Sonora to a friend in Los Angeles. Wanted the friend to get the box for him."

"So his friend got it."

"I don't believe Cedillo, that was the friend's name, ever got the letter. I told you, the seal wasn't broken."

"After all these years, what difference does it make who got the box?"

"None," McDowell admitted.

"Wish it had been me. I could use a few escudos."

"Who couldn't? Only hitch is, if it had been you, you'd have been dead about a hundred years by now."

Back at home, McDowell spent the rest of the afternoon in the hammock dozing over *Two Years Before the Mast*. In the evening he and Florence went to a friend's house for dinner, followed by word games. McDowell liked words but not games, so the evening was a mixed success for him and he saw to it that they left at midnight.

It was after two in the morning when the bedside phone rang. McDowell stabbed for it, knocking the receiver from its cradle. While he was fumbling for it,

Florence turned on the light and said anxiously, "Who is it at this time in the morning?"

"Don't know," McDowell growled, putting the receiver to his ear.

"Mac?" Sussman's agitated voice demanded. "Mac?"

McDowell's annoyance turned to concern.

"Steve," he said, "are you all right?"

"It's Steven?" Florence said. "What's wrong?"

"I've been lying here all night thinking," said Sussman.

"You called me at this hour to tell me that?"

"Tell you what?" Florence demanded.

"You know that box you were talking about?" Sussman said.

"What about it?"

"Is he drunk?" said Florence.

Sussman's voice was urgent.

"What if it's still there?" he said.

3

AT after two in the morning McDowell was in no mood to discuss crackpot ideas, particularly with Florence at his elbow adding to the confusion. To get rid of Sussman, he agreed to meet him later in the day and hear him out. Sussman suggested the Sculpture Garden at nine. McDowell consented to be picked up at home at ten.

"He is drunk, isn't he?" Florence said when McDowell hung up.

"Yes," said McDowell, in no mood for prolonged explanations.

"That isn't like Steven," Florence said.

"No," said McDowell, closing his eyes. "It isn't."

Sussman's horn sounded outside at a quarter to ten, before McDowell had finished even Section I of the enormous Sunday Los Angeles *Times*. Sussman was really serious about this, he thought, arriving early instead of his usual ten minutes late. And to give merely

29

a few impatient toots of the horn instead of playing an unrecognizable tune.

"Isn't that Steven's horn?" Florence said. "Ask him to come in for a cup of coffee. And I'll make him breakfast if he hasn't eaten yet."

"He won't come in," McDowell said, putting the paper aside and getting up.

"Is he mad at us or something?" Robert said.

"No. He's got something on his mind."

"It's not a girl again, is it?" Florence demanded. "If he was married, he wouldn't be going through these things all the time."

"It's not a girl," said McDowell. "It's another one of his nutty ideas."

"If it's another new stock, don't you dare agree to put any money in with him," Florence said.

"It's not a stock deal."

Often, when Sussman read about a new process or design in an engineering magazine, he would invest in the company involved if he happened to be in funds, wanting to be in on the ground floor. He invariably let McDowell in on his good thing. McDowell had invested only once, a hundred and fifty dollars he could not afford, and which he lost.

Sussman began speaking before McDowell shut the car door behind him.

"Really," he said. "What if it's still there?"

"What's still where?" McDowell replied, straight-faced.

"God damn it, Mac, I'm serious!"

He pulled away from the curb, on the wrong side of the street, as usual.

"Watch where you're driving," McDowell said. "Look, there's no way it could still be there. I told you, he put it down the well in eighteen forty-six. That's almost a hundred and thirty years ago."

"But you don't know that anyone ever got it," Sussman persisted. "Right?"

"There's not even a well there anymore," McDowell said.

"Oh," said Sussman weakly.

"I've been through the Avila Adobe and in the rear

patio. Nothing but solid ground. I'm not even positive there was ever a well there."

"The letter said there was," Sussman said with a little more spirit. "And this what's-his-name claims he dropped a treasure chest in it. Right?"

"Diego del C. So there was a well. But it was so long ago it doesn't matter now."

They were crossing San Vicente, heading toward Sunset.

"Can you imagine what something like that would be worth today?" Sussman said.

"Certainly. I can imagine what the cargo of a sunken Spanish galleon would be worth today, too, but I don't find it anything to get excited about personally."

"I'm not talking about sunken treasure. I'm talking about something right here in town, for God's sake."

"Get it through your head, Steve, it's not right here in town. Not anymore. It was put there in eighteen forty-six, for Pete's sake."

Sussman set his jaw and concentrated on his driving, zipping around the curves of Sunset Drive, slowing only when he turned into the campus. He parked the Mercedes by McGowan Hall and headed for the Sculpture Garden without waiting for McDowell. McDowell caught up with him as he strode past the reflection pool with the abstract metal fountain in the middle.

"Not so fast," McDowell said. "This is Sunday, the day of rest."

Sussman thrust his hands in his pockets and slackened his pace. McDowell clasped his hands behind him and strolled along a step behind. Sussman stopped to glare at the David Smith "Cubi-XX" sitting on the lawn.

"I don't like it either," McDowell said.

"Don't like what?" Sussman demanded irritably, as if McDowell were intruding on his thoughts.

"That so-called piece of sculpture."

"I like it," Sussman said. "You said there's no well behind the Avila Adobe now. Any idea when it was filled in?"

31

McDowell shook his head. Sussman grabbed his arm.

"Then it's all the more reason!" Sussman cried.

McDowell stared at him. A dog ran up and began jumping playfully at McDowell, as dogs often did. Sussman started to say something but remained silent until the dog's owner retrieved his pet and led it away. Students often brought their dogs to romp in the Sculpture Garden. There were several of them there now, coursing about and ecstatically sniffing the spoor of their colleagues. There were also a number of students in the Sculpture Garden, some studying, others sitting and talking or lying on the grass to bask in the sun, and a couple who, but for a few thicknesses of cloth, would have been making love.

"This place is like Grand Central Market," Sussman complained.

"You picked it," McDowell replied.

Sussman walked on, motioning McDowell to follow.

"Suppose no one ever came for the box and then the well got filled in," he said. "Then, unless what's-his-name, this Diego dude, dug it up, it'd still be there. Right?"

McDowell shrugged.

"I mean if it was buried, there'd be no chance of anyone just stumbling onto it," Sussman continued.

"True," said McDowell. "But it's more likely someone took it out long before the well was filled in."

"Jesus! I don't think you want to believe it could still be there."

They were passing Gerhard Marcks' "Maja," a larger-than-life metal nude. McDowell slowed to look at it, as he always did. There was a body, he thought. Not big in the chest but big enough, and solidly built. Very much the way Florence had been when young, except that Florence's chest was more imposing. A girl wearing shorts, braless in a halter top, walked past and, observing the direction of McDowell's gaze, smiled. McDowell smiled back.

"I don't know much about art, but I know what I like," he said.

She stopped smiling, embarrassed at being caught watching him, and increased her pace. Sussman contemplated her retreating bottom, which was clearly defined in the tight shorts.

"Haven't you any imagination?" he demanded.

"Those shorts don't leave much to the imagination."

"I'm not talking about asses and you know it. You know what I'm talking about."

"It's not that I don't want to believe, Steve. Honestly. I just don't think it's possible. It's not as if the box were dropped in the ocean or hidden off in the hills. Even in those days the pueblo of Los Angeles was a lively place. And the Avila house was occupied for years after eighteen forty-six. Someone had to find that box. Getting water, cleaning the well."

"But suppose when the water table fell or it started silting up, nothing was done?" Sussman said. "What if they just let it fall into disuse? Couldn't they have gotten water somewhere else?"

"The Mother Ditch. Ran right in front of the house. And there was a brick viaduct bringing water from the mountains."

"Then they could have gotten along without a well. It could have been filled in any time with the chest still in it, right?"

McDowell did not miss the fact that Sussman was saying "chest," as in "treasure chest," now instead of "box."

"Maybe, but not very likely," he said.

"At least I'm making progress," said Sussman. "From not possible to not very likely. I think it's worth having a look."

"Having a look? How?"

"With a metal detector."

"You're really serious about this, aren't you, Steve?"

"Damn right I'm serious."

"All right," said McDowell reluctantly. "If it'll make you happy, I'll find out who to ask and see if you can get in there with a metal detector."

"That's the last thing we want," Sussman said.

McDowell was baffled and showed it.

"We don't want to advertise," Sussman said. "What if we locate something?"

"We inform the officials, naturally."

33

"Jesus H. Christ! Why do you think I'm willing to go to all the trouble?"

They had walked past the grassy knoll that dominated the Sculpture Garden and arrived at the Hepworth "Oval Form" and the free-form concrete rest area. In places the concrete shapes were benchlike and fitted with wooden planks for seats. A student was studying there.

McDowell stared at Sussman. "Are you telling me your idea is to—"

"Come on," Sussman interrupted with a cautionary look at the student.

He took McDowell's arm and led him out of earshot.

"That's crazy," McDowell protested.

"What's so crazy? What if it's still there? Nobody knows about it but us. And it could be worth hundreds of thousands."

Sussman gave McDowell an anxious look.

"You haven't told anyone else about this, have you?"

"No. But if you think I'd go along with anything like that—"

Sussman raised a placating hand.

"Look," he said. "Just let me handle this my own way. If nothing's there, nothing's lost. And if something is there, well, then we'll talk about it."

"There's no way you can get back there without getting permission," McDowell said. "The house is kept locked and there's always a crowd milling around out front. And you can't get in from the back because there's a high wall."

"We could go over the wall."

"It's in plain sight of Alameda Street."

"We could go over at night."

"Not me. Either we get official permission or we forget about it."

"Unh-unh," Sussman said firmly, shaking his head. "Let me think a minute."

He began walking swiftly, with McDowell tagging along behind. When he stopped, it was so abruptly that McDowell barged into him.

"What we'll do," Sussman said, "is find an excuse

34

to get in there. Like we're from the city. The Department of Water and Power."

"You're crazy, you know that?"

"We'll say we're trying to locate an old conduit."

"Count me out."

"No way. You're the one found out about it. We're in this together."

"Not me."

"Aw, come on, Mac. Wouldn't you like a little excitement in that dull life of yours?"

"No."

"I'll put it another way. As a favor to a friend."

"I'd be too nervous," McDowell said. "I'd ruin it for you."

"As a favor to a friend?" Sussman repeated coaxingly. "You won't have to open your mouth. I'll do the talking."

McDowell sighed. Sussman was his best friend despite the difference in age and temperament. If he refused, Sussman would think he'd let him down. And perhaps he was being a fuddy-duddy. He did not think of his life as dull, but it was true he had done nothing ever faintly daring in years. And what Sussman proposed wasn't actually risky. Just hare-brained. Had he become such a stuffed shirt he was afraid to do something unconventional?

"All right," he said reluctantly.

Sussman clapped him on the back.

"Good old Mac," he said. "I knew you'd do it."

"That's more than I did," McDowell said wryly.

"Now don't say anything to Florence about this," Sussman cautioned.

"I was just about to ask you that."

"Here's what we'll do . . ." Sussman began.

"Can't we sit down?" McDowell implored. "All this walking up and down is killing me."

They sat on the grass behind the "Maja." Sussman said he would get coveralls and work shoes for McDowell. He already had some of his own, having occasion to use them in his work from time to time.

"I'll get a metal detector from the department," he said. "They've got 'em. We'll go to the Olvera Street information office and I'll give 'em this story about

35

looking for the conduit. No sweat. First we'll check the street behind the Avila Adobe to make it look good, and then we'll tell the dude in charge we've got to check the rear patio, too."

"You've got the makings of a master criminal," McDowell said, trying for a light touch but not achieving it.

His stomach knotted at the thought of what he had agreed to do. He wanted to back out, but it was too late. Sussman would never forgive him.

Neither McDowell nor Sussman had afternoon classes Monday. Sussman had an afternoon lab, but he did not have to be on campus for it. He had graduate students to supervise the lab and answer questions. Sussman hurried McDowell through lunch and led him to a van he had borrowed.

"It doesn't have Department of Water and Power on it, but it beats driving up in a Mercedes," he explained.

"Are you sure you still want to go through with this?" McDowell asked hopefully.

"You won't have to say a word," Sussman said. "I'll handle everything. Just stand around and look dumb." He grinned. "That shouldn't be too hard for you, should it?"

McDowell smiled weakly.

Sussman parked the van in the big lot at Main and Macy, across the street from the Olvera Street complex of shops and restaurants and just north of the Plaza Catholic Church. They climbed in back of the van to change into their overalls. McDowell's fit snugly.

"Sorry about that," said Sussman, who appeared tense but in high spirits. "They were the biggest I could find."

"The shoes are comfortable, though," McDowell said, wriggling his toes. "I didn't know work shoes were so comfortable."

They really were, but McDowell had only brought up the subject to prolong the moment before he had to venture out.

"It's the last," Sussman said. "They make 'em room-

36

ier than your ordinary shoe. Here, you carry this. It'll give you something to do with your hands."

He gave McDowell a metal clipboard and a mechanical pencil. Several sheets of paper gridded in blue and red were clipped to the board. The top sheet had markings on it.

"Window dressing," Sussman explained. "Makes it look like we've been checking out other locations." He picked up a rodlike device with a metal frame at either end and said, "Let's go."

McDowell's stomach churned. The coveralls felt tighter than ever, and sweat popped out under his arms. He wondered how he had ever let Sussman talk him into such a scheme.

They took the Main Street crosswalk to the entrance of Olvera Street. The Plaza Mexican Methodist Church was on one side of the entrance, a tortilla shop on the other. In between was a memorial cross. Sussman paused at the cross, then motioned for McDowell to follow him into Olvera.

It was like a bazaar. There was a row of booths down the middle, and on each side other booths interspersed with more substantial shops and restaurants. The tile-surfaced aisles between the booths were swarming with sightseers. What if he saw someone he knew? McDowell wondered. How could he explain the way he was dressed, and the clipboard, and Sussman walking ahead of him with a metal detector? It wasn't merely that they were doing something ludicrous. They also looked ludicrous.

Sussman led the way, saying, "Excuse us, please," and "Coming through," in a confident voice.

They pushed between booths displaying curios, jewelry, hand-embroidered work shirts and Mexican blouses, cactus candy and other sweets—McDowell did not even feel an urge for leche quemada, "burned milk," one of his favorite candies—past the old, no longer used three-story Metropolitan Transportation Authority powerhouse to the Avila Adobe. The Avila Adobe was a long one-story structure, its adobe walls whitewashed, the open wooden shutters at the windows freshly stained. A chain at the top of the plank

37

steps barred admission to the porch running the length of the front.

Sussman stopped in front of it and said, "Let's sharpen our act."

McDowell looked at him blankly, conscious that many of the sightseers were staring at them. He felt himself blushing.

"Could you clear out this area, please?" Sussman said. "We're running a survey. City business."

The tourists moved back grudgingly. Sussman began passing the metal detector over the tiles, moving slowly along the passage between the Avila Adobe and the sales booths. From time to time he called out cryptic numbers. McDowell trailed behind, feeling foolish. Sussman looked back at him, frowned and joined him to whisper, "Write something on the fucking clipboard when I call a number, for Christ's sake."

"Oh," said McDowell.

He began writing down the numbers Sussman called out.

After a couple of passes with the metal detector, Sussman said, "All finished here, Obromski."

Obromski, McDowell thought. Where did Sussman dig up that name? He felt more ridiculous than ever. Now he even had an alias.

"Where's the office?" Sussman asked.

McDowell made a helpless gesture.

"Somewhere around here," he said. "I've never actually been to it. Just talked on the phone."

Sussman looked at him, shaking his head.

Just beyond the Avila Adobe was a larger building of Spanish design but of much more recent origin.

"That looks official," McDowell said helpfully.

They went through the broad tile-floored entrance into the cavernous interior. On the left was the San Antonio Winery and Gift Shop and on the right a profusion of racks and showcases laden with articles of the sort on sale outside. Inside, away from the crowd, McDowell felt slightly less ill at ease. No one was staring at him, just at Sussman and his metal detector.

"I don't see anything that looks like an office," Sussman said. "Ask somebody."

"You said I wouldn't have to open my mouth," McDowell reminded him.

Sussman leaned the metal detector against the wall and went into the Craftsmen Center across from the wineshop to ask a clerk. When he returned, he said, "The office entrance is around the back."

They went to the truncated street behind Olvera. Across Alameda, bustling with traffic, loomed the Union Station.

"Not exactly private, is it?" Sussman said.

Behind Olvera, nothing had been done to recreate the Hispano-California origins as had been done for the façades. The large building housing the winery and Craftsmen Center and, in the rear, the offices of El Pueblo de Los Angeles, Inc., was, however, sparkling white and of Mexican design. Beyond it was a high brick wall of flat dun-colored bricks with ornamental metal grillwork on top. The rear patio of the Avila Adobe lay behind the wall. Past the wall was the mellow old red brick of the abandoned powerhouse.

The receptionist in the office, a neatly groomed chicana, gave them a warm, pleasant smile when they entered. McDowell wondered if everyone got such a smile or if it was in response to Sussman's charm.

"Miss, we're from the city," Sussman said. "Department of Water and Power. Can I talk to the boss about getting in there behind that Avila Adobe place?"

He did not sound at all like an assistant professor, McDowell thought admiringly. Sussman certainly knew how to get into the spirit of things. He only hoped Sussman would not complicate matters by trying to date the girl.

"Just one moment, please," the girl said.

She had a marked Spanish accent, which surprised McDowell a little. Olvera Street, though all the shop people and restaurateurs were chicano, was prop Mexican, not the real thing, and he had expected anyone working in the office to sound plain Angeleno. He wondered if they hired people with accents to preserve the flavor of the area.

The dark girl returned with a dark man.

"Yes," he said, "what may I do for you?"

39

He had a trace of an accent, also, but of the sort McDowell had heard from native-born Angelenos whose parents spoke Spanish at home.

McDowell could feel the sweat popping out in his armpits again. His hands were clammy and seemed to belong to someone else. He put the clipboard under his arm and thrust his hands into the pockets of the coveralls to get them out of the way.

"Why, uh," Sussman began. "Why. . . ."

He gave McDowell a covert, imploring look.

He's lost his nerve, too, McDowell thought in panic. How do we get out of this?

"Yes?" the man asked patiently.

McDowell cleared his throat. Just pretend you're talking to a class, he told himself.

"Why, yes," he found himself saying with scarcely a tremor. "We're from the Department of Water and Power. We're trying to locate an old underground conduit supposed to be around here somewhere. Right, Obromski?"

"Right," Sussman said, finding his voice. "We think it runs under the Avila Adobe. We just checked out the front, and now we got to check the back and the patio."

"I see," said the man. "How may I assist you?"

"Like I said," Sussman said briskly. "We got to get in the back to take readings. How do we get in?"

"I'll get the keys," the man said.

While he was doing so, Sussman moved next to McDowell and whispered, "You did great."

When they went outside, Sussman asked the man if he minded waiting until they ran a quick check of the street side of the wall. He donned the earphones of the metal detector and began making deliberate passes over the sidewalk. McDowell walked beside him, pencil poised over the clipboard. Sussman did not call out any numbers, so he had nothing to do.

"Nothing out here," Sussman said, removing the earphones. "You want to know what I think, I think the supervisor is all wet about that conduit." He looked apologetically at the man from the office. "But we gotta check out the whole deal anyway or he'll send us back sure as hell."

40

McDowell felt more relaxed now. It had started when he came to Sussman's rescue back in the office. But he still felt silly. It was like wearing a costume to a party where everyone else was in regular clothes.

The man unlocked the gate and accompanied them up a flight of steps that started parallel to the wall and then turned at a right angle. There was a grape arbor with a beehive oven in it at one side of the patio. The rest of the back was barren dirt. Except for the crowd sounds from Olvera Street and the hum of Alameda Street traffic the patio had a curious remoteness from contemporary Los Angeles. It was like stepping back into the past.

Sussman put the metal detector down and, taking the clipboard from McDowell, paced off the dimensions of the patio, diagramming the shape and writing down the measurements on a fresh sheet of grid paper. He divided the diagram into a series of numbered and lettered squares. After returning the clipboard to McDowell, he slipped on the earphones of the metal detector and began a methodical survey of the patio, walking up and down in carefully spaced straight lines. He did so in silence, McDowell tagging along, feeling both useless and silly. After a series of passes with the detector, Sussman asked for the gridded diagram. He studied it for a moment, then returned the clipboard.

They were in the patio for twenty minutes or so, during which the man from the office waited patiently. McDowell would have preferred that he left them to go about their charade alone. The longer it went on, the sillier he felt. The man seemed interested in what they were doing and convinced of its legitimacy. Sussman muttered an expletive and removed the earphones.

"I could have told 'em it wasn't here," he said. "Half a day shot all to hell."

"I'm very sorry," the man said.

You think you're sorry, McDowell thought. Sussman's probably crushed. As for himself, he was relieved. He had never believed the box could still be there and now that Sussman knew it, too, Sussman would stop nagging him about it. He hoped Sussman

41

wouldn't tell anyone about their escapade. Later on it might seem amusing, but not now.

"Well, Steve," he said later as they walked past the Biscailuz Building behind the Plaza Mexican Methodist Church, "I hope you're satisfied."

Sussman did not reply. He appeared lost in thought, or was it depression? McDowell had not expected him to take it so hard. He'd warned Sussman how unlikely it was for the box to still be there. And he was not even sure the well had been in the place they had explored. The Avila property might once have extended much farther back, and the well site could have been beyond the wall. But he certainly wasn't going to mention that to Sussman. Sussman would want to check halfway to Union Station, and he had had enough of this nonsense.

"I'll buy you a drink, and we'll have a good laugh and forget about it," he coaxed. "You knew there wasn't really much chance of finding anything. Cheer up."

"I'm fine," Sussman said in an unexpectedly cheerful tone.

Sussman wasn't taking it that hard after all, McDowell thought. He was being a good sport about it. McDowell was relieved.

They stowed the metal detector in the back of the van and got out of their coveralls.

"Let me see that clipboard a minute before I forget," Sussman said.

McDowell handed it to him. Sussman made a mark on the diagram and tossed the clipboard carelessly into the back of the van. When they drove out of the parking lot he turned on the radio and dialed the country music station. The vocalist sang a while in English, then in Spanish. Sussman sang along with him, language for language.

"Johnny Rodriguez," he said. "He's from Texas."

Sussman switched off the radio and looked at McDowell.

"Something's there," he said.

4

THEY sat in the bar at El Coyote drinking margaritas and scooping up guacamole on toasted tortilla wedges. McDowell drank at parties but seldom in bars and almost never in the afternoon. He was on his second drink and beginning to feel weightless. Sussman, a far more experienced drinker, was on his third and seemingly unaffected. He was buoyant, but not from margaritas. He had been so since informing McDowell he had found a strong indication of metal under the rear patio of the Avila Adobe. It had been his idea to come to El Coyote to celebrate.

McDowell hadn't wanted to.

"There's nothing to celebrate," he had protested. "And if I go home smelling like a distillery, next thing you know I'll have to tell Florence about the whole silly stunt."

"Hey," said Sussman. "We agreed not to tell Florence."

"What makes you so sure it's Don Diego's box down there?" McDowell demanded. "Can that detector tell one metal from another?"

"No," Sussman said.

"Then it could be an iron gas main or something like that, couldn't it?"

"Nope. The indication was confined to one small area. A pipe would have run all across the yard."

"A piece of pipe, then. Or scrap iron. When they stopped using the well, they could have dumped all sorts of things in it."

"I'm not saying you're wrong," Sussman had replied with irritating tolerance. "All I'm saying is the indication is in a spot where the well could have been."

After that, he had turned the radio on again and, by increasing the volume, indicated to McDowell that for the time being he did not wish to continue the discussion. He spoke only once more during the twenty-minute drive from downtown Los Angeles to El Coyote, on Beverly Boulevard west of La Brea. That was when the radio played "Old Dogs, Children and Watermelon Wine."

"Must be my day," he had said. "First I strike gold and then they play my favorite old Tom T. Hall record."

"You didn't strike gold and who is Tom T. Hall?"

Sussman did not answer. He appeared bemused either by the song or visions of buried treasure.

Now, as they sat at the bar eating guacamole and drinking margaritas, McDowell said, "There's one way to find out what's down there. If we don't mind being made to appear idiotic."

"How?" said Sussman, instantly alert.

"I can go to the El Pueblo people, and if they're crazy enough to believe there's something valuable down there, they'll excavate."

Sussman chewed and swallowed a tortilla chip, his eyes on McDowell's face. He sighed and shook his head.

"You still don't understand, do you, Mac?" he said.

"Don't understand what?"

"Like I said yesterday, the last thing we want is any officials getting into the act. Or anybody else. If the gold is there, it's ours."

"But it's not," McDowell objected.

The effect of the two margaritas was rapidly draining away. Sussman was being so maddeningly unreasonable. First in jumping to the conclusion he had found a box of gold, or whatever it was in Don Diego's box, that was last heard of nearly one hundred and thirty years ago. Second in assuming that if he had found it, it was his. Or rather theirs, as Sussman had put it.

"Now what?" Sussman asked with what McDowell thought was calculated obtuseness. "Not there? Or not ours?"

"Both."

"Let's hypothesize," Sussman said. "Something is down there. Some official digs it up. Who gets it?"

"I'm not sure," McDowell said. "The city, I suppose. Or the state. There's been controversy for years over just who should run the restored area. What does it matter, anyhow?"

Sussman looked away and addressed an unseen presence. "What does it matter, he says?" He turned back to McDowell. "Who has more right to it, you or a flock of bureaucrats?"

"Me? What right do I have to it?"

"Who found out about the goddamn box? You or them?"

"Even the letter's not mine," McDowell protested. "If you want to base the claim on that, the box belongs to UCLA."

"Now that's the stupidest thing you've said all day," Sussman said angrily.

He raised his voice in his anger. The bar had begun filling up, and people were looking at them.

"Don't talk so loud," McDowell said stiffly. "I was merely pointing out how illogical it is to say I have any claim on the box."

He didn't mind a little needling from Sussman, but now Sussman was being positively insulting, and he did not intend putting up with it.

Surprisingly, Sussman grinned and patted him amicably on the shoulder.

"Sounds like you're admitting the chest may be there," Sussman said.

McDowell shook his head helplessly. How could he stay angry with Sussman?

"I'm not admitting anything," he protested more mildly. "We're just hypothesizing, remember?"

"You're right," Sussman said agreeably. "It's ridiculous for us to sit here snapping at each other over a hypothesis. Like a couple of prissy academicians."

McDowell looked at his watch.

"It's almost six," he said. "I'd better be getting home to dinner."

"Let's eat here,' Sussman said. "We can start working things out over a mess of green corn tamales."

"Spoken like a true bachelor. You know what would happen if I ate out after Florence had gone to the trouble of making dinner for me? And there's nothing to work out."

Sussman made a placating gesture.

"All right," he said. "All right. Just promise me one thing. You won't make up your mind before I have time to give it some thought and you won't go spouting off to any officials."

"That's two things," McDowell said. "But I promise."

He did not want to get Sussman fired up again. Perhaps after sleeping on it, Sussman would realize it was all a pipe dream and would be willing to drop the matter. Or at least acknowledge the alleged box was no concern of theirs but of a legally authorized agency of the city or state.

Sussman was quiet and unresponsive on the drive to McDowell's house. McDowell did not know if it signified Sussman was still put out with him for his attitude or simply bemused by dreams of buried treasure.

When he got out of the Mercedes, McDowell said, "Why don't you have dinner with us?"

"Even a bachelor knows you don't spring unannounced guests for dinner," Sussman said with a grin. "And I've got a date for dinner. See you tomorrow, okay?"

"Yes," said McDowell. "I'll see you tomorrow."

And by tomorrow he hoped Sussman would have gotten any crazy ideas out of his system.

"There you are," Florence said when McDowell came into the kitchen. "I called your office half a dozen times. You should let me know when you're going to be late." She sniffed the air, cocked her head and looked at him inquiringly. "You haven't been drinking, have you?"

"Steve Sussman asked me to have a drink with him."

"That's what kept you. Girl trouble again, I know it. We've simply got to find a nice, quiet girl for him so he can quit all this nonsense."

"Did you ever stop to think Steve might not want to quit all this nonsense?" McDowell replied, relieved that he had not had to invent an explanation for his tardiness.

"It's not what he wants that's important, Arthur. It's what's best for him that should concern you."

"You're absolutely right, dear."

McDowell did not have much appetite for dinner, which was unlike him. All that guacamole, he thought,

46

and reaction to that ridiculous masquerade. And Sussman's stubbornness. He had been a fool to let Sussman talk him into going to Olvera Street. But now that he had gone, if there actually was something in the ground behind the Avila Adobe, it was his duty to inform the El Pueblo State Historic Park people. It wasn't likely to be Don Diego's box, but it might very well be some significant artifacts. As he recalled reading somewhere, they had found several quite interesting items back in the late twenties when they'd first begun excavating Olvera Street preparatory to restoring the area.

"It's more serious than his usual girl trouble this time, isn't it?" Florence said.

"What are you talking about?" McDowell demanded, aware he was being unduly irritable.

"Steven. What he wanted to talk to you about. You're so preoccupied. And touchy. Is he in any sort of trouble?"

"No. It's his imagination." Which was true. "I think I straightened him out." Which he hoped he had.

The crossword puzzle took his mind off the events of the afternoon, and he was able to get a good deal of work done afterward when he retired to his library. His appetite returning in full cry, he consumed an enormous sandwich and a can of Florence's diet soda before going to bed.

He went to bed resolved to tell Florence the whole bizarre story, but she was asleep by the time he retired. In the morning it no longer seemed like a good idea. He had promised Sussman not to say anything, and besides, what would she think if he told her about pretending to be a workman from the Department of Water and Power and playing the fool all over Olvera Street?

At noon, Sussman rushed him through lunch and hustled him off to the grassy expanse at the Janss Steps. Hooking his arm through McDowell's to keep him moving along at his side, he said, "I think I've got our next step worked out."

"What next step?" McDowell asked warily.

"After I left you, I realized what's making you so

47

mulish is you don't believe it's the chest down there. If I can just prove it to you. . . ."

He was still tugging McDowell along by the elbow. McDowell did not like being tugged along by the elbow, even by such a friend as Sussman, or rather, under the circumstances, especially by such a friend as Sussman. He interrupted his friend by jerking away and saying in an uncharacteristically harsh voice, "Steve, I don't want to hear another word about it. Not one more damn word."

Sussman was taken aback by McDowell's strong reaction, but only momentarily.

"Watch that temper, Mac," he said. "Portly dudes are candidates for heart failure. And they're supposed to be jolly."

"I am jolly, damn it!" McDowell cried. "It's just that you and your—"

He became aware students were staring at them and continued in a lower tone. "It's just that you've got this obsession and insist that I share it. And I'm not going to."

"Do me a favor," Sussman coaxed. "Just listen a minute. Then make up your mind."

"All right," McDowell said. "But quit pulling me around like a dog on a leash. I listen better when I'm sitting down."

"We'll sit," Sussman said quickly. "I forget how much energy it takes you to move all that mass."

He hunkered down cowboy-style, his muscular rump resting on a heel, while McDowell sat on the grass and tried several positions before settling down.

"Comfy?" Sussman asked.

"Screw you," said McDowell, who normally did not speak in such terms.

"Supposing I could prove that what we located yesterday was a chest of gold coins? Would it change your mind?"

"Prove it? How?"

"I'll need your help."

"Oh, no."

"Jesus, you're impossible," said Sussman. "I never figured you for one of those old faculty farts."

"You've overwhelmed me with your charm," Mc-

48

Dowell said. "Tell me how you intend to prove wealth beyond my wildest dreams lies waiting behind the Avila Adobe."

"We'll go back and probe for it," Sussman said.

No, we won't, McDowell thought, but he did not say it aloud.

"I'll get a mine auger, and we'll bore until we hit what's down there," Sussman continued. "Then we'll take a core sample to see what we hit."

"That's the craziest thing I ever heard of."

"You're starting again," Sussman warned.

"All right, Steve. All right. How could you do all that without anyone knowing about it?"

"That's better. We go over the wall. At night."

"Hey, Steve, come on!"

"I mean it. Nothing to it. I'll get a scaling ladder. The kind firemen use."

"You won't get me on one of those things," Mc-Dowell said, regretting the statement immediately because Sussman might take it to mean he intended to participate.

"So I'll get a stepladder."

Sussman hurried on before McDowell could explain he had no intention of going over the wall by any means.

"I'll get hold of an auger that'll take us down as far as we have to go. With two of us on the cross-bar it should give us enough muscle for a deep bore."

"Am I supposed to know what you're talking about?" McDowell asked helplessly.

"You don't have to know. When the time comes, I'll show you what to do."

McDowell heaved himself to his feet and brushed the grass from the seat of his pants.

"Steve," he said gently and with regret, "don't lose your temper and don't call me an old fart even if you think I am, but I really don't want any part of it."

Sussman sprang to his feet and seized McDowell's elbow. McDowell stared at the clutching hand, and Sussman let go immediately.

"But why?" Sussman demanded. "There's no risk involved. We can get in and out with no one knowing.

And we'd know once and for all what's down there. Wouldn't you like to know?"

"Of course I would. It would be a fantastic find. Historically. But it's not our place to do it."

Sussman's jaw tightened. McDowell could see he was struggling to keep his temper.

"Then we ought to make it our place," Sussman said, his voice controlled but raspy. "Can't we for God's sake for once in our lives do something a little bit offbeat?"

"I'd say it's more than a little offbeat."

"All right. Then a whole lot offbeat, damn it. That makes it even better."

"What if we went over the wall and a watchman caught us?" McDowell said patiently. "Think how ridiculous we'd look."

"Are you that afraid of looking ridiculous?" Sussman asked quietly.

"It also happens to be illegal."

"Illegal," Sussman said with a snort. "Trespassing, maybe. That's no kind of rap."

McDowell smiled despite himself. Sussman using cop-show jargon.

"You weakening?" Sussman asked hopefully.

"Let's go back to work," McDowell said, shaking his head. "I've got a stack of paper work a foot high on my desk."

"I'm trying to take you away from all that. But okay. I guess I'll just have to go it alone. I just hope I'll be able to bore deep enough without help."

"Steve, why don't you just drop it?"

"You know I can't do that. Damn it, Mac, don't you realize you're the one who turned me on to this?"

"I wish I hadn't."

They were walking through Royce Hall among a stream of students.

"Maybe I'll get some strong kid to come along," Sussman said musingly. "I wonder who I could trust to keep his mouth shut?"

"You're determined to go, whatever, aren't you?" McDowell said, foreboding clutching at his chest. He knew what was coming and dreaded it.

"Yes."

McDowell sighed heavily. "All right," he said. "I'll go with you."

"What did you say?" Sussman asked incredulously.

"But on one condition."

"Anything."

"Whatever's down there, if it's valuable or of historical importance, we let the proper authorities know about it."

"Aw now, Mac."

"Take it or leave it."

They were past Rolfe Hall now, and McDowell could smell the aroma of chili dogs and frying hamburgers wafting from the Gypsy Wagon. It was too soon after lunch, however, for him to feel any real yearnings. Sussman put his hands in his pockets and stared thoughtfully at McDowell.

"Tell you what," he said. "We'll see what's down there and let you decide. Whatever you say goes. Okay?"

"Okay. It's a deal."

McDowell did not sleep at all well that night. He had vivid images of climbing over the back wall of the Avila Adobe and performing strenuously with some cumbersome device brought along by Sussman and in the midst of his exertions being surprised by an evil-tempered night watchman. He imagined the watchman shooting first and asking questions afterward. That, he realized, was a little melodramatic. What was more likely was that they'd be hauled off to jail, booked and fingerprinted. He could visualize Florence's being roused in the middle of the night to come down and bail him out or whatever one had to do in cases like that. And he could see his photograph, looking sheepish, in the morning *Times*. He hoped similar thoughts were keeping Sussman awake, though he knew it was not likely.

Sussman phoned in the morning while McDowell was still at breakfast and asked McDowell to meet him for coffee at the Student Union before classes. McDowell wondered if that was a good or a bad sign, hoping it meant Sussman wanted to tell him he'd changed his mind.

When he saw Sussman, he decided it was a good

sign. Sussman did not look as if he'd had a good night either.

"I had one hell of a time getting to sleep last night," Sussman said. "How about you?"

"Me, too," said McDowell, thinking, good, with Sussman having second thoughts it should not be difficult to persuade him to give up his plan.

"All I could think about was all those coins just sitting there waiting," Sussman said. "Big ones, little ones, a whole chest full of 'em, just sitting there. I can't wait to find out if we're right. Can you?"

"Frankly, yes," said McDowell, disappointed.

"It'll be a couple of days before we can do it," Sussman said. "The department doesn't have everything we need. I'll have to get some of it fabricated."

"I can wait."

It was almost a week before Sussman announced he was getting the required equipment, a period during which McDowell alternated between anxiety and optimism, hoping a delay might dampen Sussman's enthusiasm. Because he was not sleeping well and was frequently preoccupied, Florence asked him if something was bothering him. He told her no, just the usual end-of-quarter workload.

Sussman came to his office with a problem.

"I'm getting the auger made," he said. "Off campus. The only thing is, it's fifty-five bucks. And I'm a little tight till payday. I'll give you my half the first of the month. Okay?"

"I'll have to give you a check," McDowell said reluctantly. "I don't carry around that kind of cash."

He had not realized there would be expenses involved. Fifty-five dollars was no fortune, but on the other hand, it was more than he could afford to put out casually and without even mentioning it to Florence. It wasn't that she'd ask him about it when she went through the canceled checks—they had a joint account—it was just that it was her money, too. Actually, though, it would be only twenty-seven fifty because he would be getting half of it back from Sussman. On the rare occasions when Sussman borrowed money he always paid it back promptly, usually under protest from McDowell. Sussman was such an inveterate tab grabber McDowell felt in his debt.

When he gave Sussman the check, he lost all hope of the plan's collapsing. The fact that they were investing money in it made everything painfully concrete.

"When will it be ready?" McDowell asked.

"You're getting anxious, aren't you?" Sussman said. "That's a good sign."

"Just anxious to get it over with."

"Tomorrow afternoon," Sussman said. "We go tomorrow night."

McDowell buried himself in work that night and, when he went to bed, took one of Florence's Seconals. He knew that without it he would be tossing all night. He did not tell her he had taken the sleeping pill, and seeking to relieve the tensions she was aware had been plaguing him, she came to bed bare and mildly aggressive. Mr. Kuwahara having put the yard in first-class shape and there being no other pressing household matters, they were not distracted by small talk, and despite drowsiness and a troubled mind, McDowell responded with verve. This is how it must be with soldiers who know they're going into battle the next day, he thought. It had been his opinion that anxiety stifled sex drive, but apparently the threat of danger stimulated it.

"That was gorgeous," Florence said with a low chuckle.

It was a family joke. Years ago they'd heard a television commercial that said, "Give your loved one a gorgeous Gruen for Christmas," and had thought it an hilarious double entendre.

"I needed that," McDowell replied drowsily.

"Obviously," said Florence. "I'm better now that I've lost those four pounds, don't you think?"

McDowell's answer was a light snore.

5

McDOWELL'S stomach was so fluttery in the morning
that he took a Librium. It helped but did not entirely
dispel his sense of foreboding. When he left for school,
he took the bottle with him. He got through his morning class with unexpected ease, and a tranquilizer before lunch left him reasonably relaxed. Sussman suggested they have lunch off campus. They went to
Mario's in Westwood Village, though McDowell protested he was not hungry enough for Italian food. Even
though he was tranquilized, thoughts of the night's
business affected his appetite.

"So eat a salad," Sussman said.

The salad proved insufficient, and McDowell ordered the veal Milanese as well, though normally he
did not spend that much for lunches. Sussman also ate
heartily, the spaghetti alla Amatriciana, and drank
half a liter of wine with it. McDowell passed on the
wine. Between it and the tranquilizers he did not think
he would be able to get through the day.

"How do you eat like that and stay so thin?" Mc-
Dowell asked.

"Frequent applications of sex and a rampant me-
tabolism," Sussman said. "The probe's ready. I'm
picking it up this afternoon."

"Then it's still on for tonight?" McDowell said, his
heart sinking.

"I'll pick you up about eleven," Sussman said. "We
don't want to go over the wall until everything's quiet.
I drove down there last night, and by midnight there's
nobody around but the winos. If there's a watchman,
I didn't see him."

"Eleven?" McDowell demanded. "How'll I explain
leaving at eleven to Florence?"

"Tell her I've got a couple of hot numbers," Sussman said with a grin. "So I'll pick you up about eight
and we'll see a movie."

"I've got to do better than that. What if she wants
to see the movie, too?"

"Tell her it's a porno. Say we're going bowling or something. Mac, you're not one of those husbands who can't get out at night."

"I know. But I've never lied to her about where I go."

"Tell you what. I'll lie to her. I'll call you about seven thirty and say I need you to fill in for a poker game. Somebody dropped out at the last minute."

"I don't play poker, and Florence knows it."

"For Christ's sake, Mac, quit stalling! Tell her you're doing it as a favor to me. She'll buy that. It's not as if you really need an excuse anyway. And you know it. There's not another couple on campus with a relationship like yours and Florence's."

"All right," McDowell said. "No point in getting so vehement." He looked thoughtfully at Sussman. "You're nervous, too, aren't you?"

"Not nervous. Excited. Tonight could change our lives."

"That's what worries me," McDowell said soberly. Then the significance of Sussman's words sank in.

"Just a minute," he said. "You said if we found something, we'd report it. We stick to that or it's all off."

"I said I'd leave the final decision up to you, and I will."

"Just so that's strictly understood."

Sussman grabbed the check when the waiter put it on the table.

"It's Dutch," McDowell protested. "I thought you were broke."

"I've still got my credit cards."

McDowell got through the day with the help of another tranquilizer and at home managed to present a fairly calm front except that he gave an involuntary start each time the phone rang. He let Florence answer all calls. When Sussman phoned, she would hear the story they had agreed upon directly from his friend and he would not have to tell any elaborate lies.

When the phone rang promptly at seven thirty, he heard Florence say, "Why, hello, Steven, why haven't we seen you lately?" There was a considerable pause, and then she called out, "Arthur, it's Steven Sussman. He wants to know if you'll play poker tonight. He says it's an emergency."

"It must be," McDowell replied. "He knows I'm no poker player. Tell him all right," he added with a reluctance that did not have to be feigned.

Florence hung up and said, "He'll pick you up in half an hour. And he said not to worry. He'll stake you for helping him out."

Instead of honking, Sussman, looking insouciant in blue loafers, maroon velour jumpsuit and balloon-sleeved white alpaca cardigan, came in the house to apologize to Florence for taking her husband away on such short notice.

"I'll see he doesn't draw to any bobtail flushes or inside straights," Sussman promised. "And if he starts to bet into a lock, I'll kick him under the table."

"That's an absolutely stunning jumpsuit," Florence said, not having understood a word. "Arthur, you've got to get one. Was it terribly expensive, Steven?"

"I'd look like a beached whale in it, and you know it," McDowell said.

He was nonplussed by Sussman's garb. Knowing he would be climbing ladders and working in the dirt of the patio, he had put on the ancient gray Daks no longer fit for company, the UCLA sweat shirt and his tennis shoes. He had been under the impression that was the proper dress for poker as well as for surreptitious trespass.

"Should I change?" he asked.

"You're fine," said Sussman. "The other dudes are slobs, too."

"I think Arthur looks very nice," Florence said tartly. "In his own way."

"Just jiving," Sussman said. "Matter of fact, I'm overdressed for the occasion, and Mac is just right. Only reason I got myself up like this is I knew I'd be seeing you, Flo."

He seemed in no hurry to leave, explaining the game would not be starting for another half hour. He helped Robert with a model plane, McDowell being absolutely useless at such things, and discussed with him the high points of the UCLA basketball season,

56

another area in which McDowell did not share expertise with his son. And while doing so, he continued to charm Florence. McDowell admired the ease and genuine sincerity with which Sussman captivated his family. If Sussman ever gets married, Florence is going to be sorry, he thought. Sussman's wife will be getting all this attention.

Even McDowell was affected by Sussman's ebullience. He hardly thought about what lay ahead until they were driving away.

"You're not going dressed like that?" he asked.

"I thought we might kill a few hours at the Horn," Sussman replied.

The Horn was a pleasant night spot on Wilshire in Santa Monica with lively, informal entertainment, generally singing and good-natured clowning. McDowell and Florence had been Sussman's guests there and had enjoyed themselves immensely.

"I'm not going there dressed like this," McDowell said.

And not without Florence, he thought. It wouldn't be fair, and besides, she enjoyed a night out so much half the fun was watching her have a good time.

"Just a thought," Sussman said. "We'll go to my place. Got to go there anyhow to change and pick up the van. I borrowed it again."

Sussman lived in a big apartment complex in the Brentwood area on Sunset. It was occupied mostly by singles. "Swinging singles," according to the rental brochure. His one-bedroom apartment came furnished. Only the king-size water bed, the color television set and the expensive stereo system were his own. The apartment was unusually clean and orderly for a bachelor's pad. Sussman shared a once-a-week maid with several other tenants, and between her visits one or another of the girls in the building saw to it that his breakfast dishes were washed, his clothes put away and the bed made.

Sussman fitted a cartridge into the stereo.

"I want to hear this," he said. "I'm gonna turn you on to country music yet."

"Old Dogs, Children and Watermelon Wine," the

song that had entranced Sussman the day they visited Olvera Street, filled the tidy living room.

"Put the tape together myself," Sussman explained. "My favorites from Tom T. Hall, Waylon Jennings and Dolly Parton. And a couple of Sammi Smith's."

"This one's not too bad," McDowell admitted.

"Grows on you."

Sussman disappeared into the bedroom.

"Make yourself a drink," he called. "You know where it is."

"Better not," McDowell replied. "I've been taking tranquilizers."

Sussman appeared in the bedroom door in jockey shorts and an orange T-shirt, grinning.

"And I thought you were being so cool because you finally dug what we're doing," he said.

Tom T. Hall was singing "The Year That Clayton Delaney Died" when Sussman returned to the living room dressed much the same as McDowell.

"You know, he's not bad," McDowell said.

"A storyteller is what he really is," Sussman said, going to the tiny portable bar and pouring scotch in a glass. "I hope there's ice."

He went into the kitchen, and McDowell heard him say, "Good girl. She remembered to fill the trays."

He came back and settled himself in an easy chair.

"So you're dropping downers," he said. "To tell the truth, I'm kind of uptight myself."

McDowell was pleased to learn that. Sussman's seeming insouciance had made him feel stuffy as well as timid.

"Couldn't tell it," he said.

"It doesn't show on me the way it does on you. And I expect I've been in more tight situations than you have."

"You know something strange, Steve?" McDowell said thoughtfully. "I don't think I've been in a tight situation since my PhD orals. Except possibly financially. And then not really tight."

"How do you stand it?" Sussman demanded. He held up his hand for silence before McDowell could answer. "Dolly Parton."

A woman with a high, childish and, McDowell

thought, somewhat unpleasant voice was singing something about her Tennessee mountain home.

"This is the part I like best," Sussman said. "Listen."

The childish voice sang of "playing with June bugs on a string."

"Right there," Sussman cried. "Reminds me of my daddy."

McDowell smiled. A grown man, a sophisticated grown man, calling his father his daddy.

"When I was just a little kid, he taught me how to do that. You catch a June bug, see, and tie a thread to its leg. Then let him fly around at the end of it."

"Sounds fabulous," McDowell said dryly.

"Well, it is. When you're five or six years old. Didn't you ever do it?"

"I don't even know what a June bug is. I don't think we had them in Santa Barbara."

Around ten, a party started in the next apartment and began getting louder. Pounding rock music, which McDowell truly detested, laughter and girls' voices. Sussman rose and rapped on the wall. Minutes later the door opened and a ravishing black girl entered without knocking. She was wearing faded jeans and a man's shirt with the tail out. Wavy hair hung down to her shoulders. She was barefoot, with beige-painted toenails.

"Hey, Stevie, come on over," she said. "We can use another man." She looked at McDowell and said, "Hi. Make it two men. You're cute, for a fatty."

"What are you people smoking over there?" Sussman demanded.

"You name it, we're smokin' it," she said. "Come on, man, shake ass."

"Not tonight, darlin'," Sussman said. "Mac, this is Marcie. Marcie, Dr. McDowell."

"Doctor?" Marcie said, showing interest. "Hey, man, I got like, you know, this little swelling in my groin. Maybe you can take a look."

She reached under her shirttail as if for a zipper.

"I'm sure he'd love to," Sussman said. "But he's not that kind of doctor. He's a professor."

"Cool," said Marcie, bringing her hand out from

under the shirttail. "You dudes change your mind about the party, you know where it's at."

She left.

"I hope I didn't spoil anything for you," Sussman said with a grin. "Marcie's got the neatest little groin in the building. Or so they say."

"This kind of thing go on all the time?" McDowell asked.

" 'Fraid so. Shocking, ain't it?"

Around eleven thirty Sussman looked at his watch. "About time to go, I reckon," he said.

McDowell went to the kitchen for a glass of water to wash down a Librium.

They went down to the van, the noise of the party following them all the way to the street. The end of the ladder stuck out of the back several feet. The van doors were tied in a partially closed position with rope. McDowell felt numb, for which he was grateful. Sussman stayed just below the speed limit on the freeway, which was considerably slower than he normally drove.

When he got to Macy Street, he circled around the far end of Olvera to the short street behind the Avila Adobe. He double-parked the van behind some vehicles parked at the curb.

"You can't do that," McDowell protested. "What if a patrol car comes along and sees us double-parked?"

"There won't be any patrol car. This dead-ends. And it's not even a real street. Come on."

He got out and untied the rope holding the back doors together.

"Take the ladder," he ordered. "I'll bring the auger."

The ladder was aluminum, and light, but it made an appalling rasping noise when McDowell dragged it across the metal floor of the van.

"Not that way, for Christ's sake," Sussman whispered urgently. "Pick it up."

McDowell looked fearfully across the dark plaza. There was no sign of life. There was traffic over on Alameda, but it was unlikely drivers would notice any activity from there. He breathed more easily. He waited with the ladder sitting lengthwise on the pavement, propped against his leg, while Sussman climbed into the van for the auger. There was a clanking noise and Sussman muttered, "Shit!" I should have wrapped the pieces separately." He emerged carrying a canvas bag about five feet long and nearly a foot in diameter. He cradled it tenderly in his arms, like a baby.

"This damn thing's heavy," he said. "You take it. You're stronger than me."

"Not so loud," McDowell whispered, reaching for the bag.

The ladder toppled flat with a clatter.

"Jesus!' said Sussman. "Did you have to do that?"

"I didn't do it on purpose," McDowell said testily.

They peered anxiously into the darkness, fearful the noise would bring someone running, but there was only silence. Sussman reached into the van and brought out the metal detector. He carried it to the base of the wall behind the Avila Adobe and came back for the ladder, which he leaned upright against the wall. Then he picked up the metal detector and climbed to the top with it. He stood there straddling the metal grillwork. McDowell stood on the sidewalk looking up at him and cradling the canvas bag as Sussman had done.

"Come on, for Christ's sake," Sussman whispered.

McDowell put a foot tentatively on the first step of the ladder. It was not going to be easy climbing up with the cumbersome bag in his arms. He leaned forward and lifted his crooked arms until his elbow rested on the highest step he could reach, then cautiously placed the other foot on the bottom step. Then he repeated the process.

"This is taking too long," Sussman said. "See if you can hand it up to me."

McDowell worked the bag into an upright position and pushed it toward Sussman, who reached down. Sussman was just about to grasp the bag when his face froze into shock and a startled gasp escaped him. At the same time McDowell felt a tugging at his trouser leg and a voice said, "Hey, buddy."

McDowell went rigid. He looked down over his shoulder. There was just enough light to see the speaker was not a policeman. He was cadaverous and unshaved, with an undershirt showing under a shapeless suit coat.

"Hey, buddy," he said again.

"Beat it!" Sussman grated.

"Ain' talkin' to you," the man said. "Talkin' to him. Hey, buddy, you got twelve cents? I got 'nough for carfare 'cept for twelve cents."

"Go away," McDowell said desperately, trying to pull his trouser leg from the clutching hand.

The canvas bag was growing heavier by the moment, and he was starting to sweat.

"Take the bag, damn it!" McDowell muttered to Sussman, who was staring down at him.

"What I want with no bag?" the man demanded. "Twelve cents. All I want is a lousy twelve cents."

Sussman hauled the bag to the top of the wall and said, "Get rid of him before he attracts attention, for God's sake!"

McDowell felt in his pocket for a coin and handed it down to the man.

"Now beat it," Sussman said.

The man held the coin close to his face.

"Ain' but two bits," he complained.

"You only wanted twelve cents," McDowell said angrily.

"Give him more, damn it!" Sussman said. "Don't stand there arguing with the son of a bitch."

Pressing his stomach against the ladder, McDowell reached into his back pocket, got out his wallet and removed a bill. After assuring himself it was only a single, he handed it down to the man.

"Jesus, green!" the man said. "God bless you, buddy."

He lurched off into the shadows.

"Oh, God!" Sussman gasped.

Strange muffled sounds escaped him.

"What's the matter?" McDowell cried. "You all right?"

"I can't stand it," Sussman groaned.

The muffled sounds were swallowed laughter.

"What's so funny?" McDowell demanded, aggrieved. "That could have ruined everything."

"Come on," Sussman said. "Let's get out of sight."

McDowell joined him on top of the wall, straddling the grillwork awkwardly. They pulled up the ladder, being careful not to let it scrape against the bricks, and let it down on the other side. Sussman climbed down, taking the metal detector with him.

"Hand down the bag," he said briskly.

The ludicrous incident had apparently broken the tension for him. No so for McDowell. Still shaken, he leaned down and passed the bag to Sussman. When he was safely down the ladder and behind the shelter of the wall, he gulped down another Librium. It was darker on this side of the wall, for which he was grateful.

They climbed the steps up to the patio. Sussman took a folded paper from his pants pocket and studied it in the thin beam of a penlight. It was the diagram on which he had marked the location of the metal indication on their previous visit. He snapped off the light and moved into the patio with the metal detector. Donning the earphones, he began moving the detector over the ground, holding it close to the surface. He shifted it back and forth in an increasingly narrow range.

"Here," he said. "The strongest return is right here." He ground his heel into the dirt to mark the precise spot and said, "Bring me the bag."

Sussman undid the drawstrings at the top of the bag and began taking out four-foot lengths of pipe. He placed them side by side on the ground. Reaching deep into the bag, he produced three smaller objects, in the darkness unidentifiable by McDowell, and laid them beside the pipes. Switching on the penlight, he selected two of the pipes. One of them was fitted in the middle with a collar and a square protrusion. The end of the second pipe was crimped into a square for five or six inches of its length. Sussman fitted the protrusion into the squared-off pipe end and set it in place by tapping the second pipe smartly against the ground. He picked up one of the three smaller objects and screwed it into the end of the second pipe. It looked to McDowell like a long, fat drill.

Taking hold of the pipe forming the handle, Sussman set the drill in the spot he had marked with his heel and began screwing it into the ground.

"Need some help?" McDowell asked.

He felt helpless and vulnerable just standing around.

"Not yet," Sussman replied.

He screwed the auger into the ground a couple of feet, then withdrew it. He thrust the bit end at McDowell, saying, "Hold this."

McDowell wound his hands around the bit. It was gritty with soil. If he'd known he'd be doing this, he would have brought gloves. Sussman should have told him. Sussman picked up another of the smaller objects on the ground and clamped it on the pipe above the bit. It was a pipe wrench. The bit twisted in McDowell's hands.

"Tighter," Sussman ordered.

McDowell tightened his grip. Sussman turned the pipe until the bit came free in McDowell's hands. Sussman screwed a second length of pipe into the first and screwed the bit into the end of that. He thrust the bit into the bore hole and went back to work.

After a third length of pipe had been added and he made a few turns he grunted and said, "It's getting harder. Grab an end."

With McDowell at one end of the handle and Sussman at the other, the auger ate steadily into the ground.

"How deep do we have to go?" McDowell whispered.

"Don't know. If I knew the surface area of what we're after, I could make a rough estimate from the strength of the return. But I don't."

At about twelve feet the drill encountered resistance.

"This may be it," Sussman whispered. "Let's go down another couple of turns and then bring it up."

They heaved at the handle, and suddenly it twisted more easily.

"We broke through something," Sussman said. "Let's pull up."

They raised the pipe assembly until the bit emerged

64

from the hole. The handle towered above their heads at the other end.

"Hold it there," said Sussman.

He squatted and shone the penlight on the auger. "Nothing," he said, disappointed. "Just a shiny patch along the side. Must have scraped past a rock."

Three four-foot lengths of pipe and part of a fifth were in the ground when the drill again encountered resistance. This time it took less muscle to push through, but only for part of a turn. The auger refused to budge. Sussman ordered McDowell to stop pulling.

"We'll snap off the handle," he said. "Haul up."

There was excitement in his voice. McDowell was infected by it despite the tranquilizers he had taken. They brought the auger out of the hole. The assembly was now so long and unwieldy McDowell could not hold it in a vertical position.

"Lay it flat," Sussman said.

While they were doing so, they heard footsteps on the other side of the wall. The end of the assembly fell the last few inches and struck the ground with a muffled thump. They froze.

The footsteps stopped, and a voice cried, "Anybody in there?"

McDowell dared not breathe. He could sense the stiffness in Sussman's body next to his.

"I said is anybody in there!" the voice demanded.

There were scraping noises, as if the speaker were trying to leap for a handhold. The wall was much too high for that, however.

"Fuckin' rats," the voice said.

The footsteps started up again, receding.

McDowell took a deep, shuddering breath. Sussman did the same. Neither spoke for several minutes. McDowell felt his thighs cramping from the strain of crouching.

"I think we're okay now," Sussman whispered. "He thought it was rats."

He snapped on the penlight.

"Don't do that!" McDowell whispered.

"It won't show over the wall. Besides, he's gone."

Sussman played the light over the end of the bit. "Look," he said.

McDowell looked. He saw nothing of any significance. The grooves of the bit were caked with dirt to within an inch or so of the tip. Then there was a narrow band of a different hue and texture.

"I can't see anything," he said.

Sussman rolled a pinch of the bottom substance between thumb and forefinger.

"It could be rotted wood," he said. "And look at this!"

The light shone on the very tip of the bit. A minuscule fragment of metal clung to it.

"Is it gold?" McDowell whispered, his throat suddenly dry.

"I don't know," Sussman said. "Looks like it, though."

He took out his handkerchief and picked off the fragment with it, folded the handkerchief and put it back in his pocket.

"Let's get the bit off," he said.

They removed the bit with the pipe wrench and replaced it with the third smaller object Sussman had taken from the bag. It was a core sampler, a tubelike affair with an opening along one side. They raised the trembling, awkward length of the pipe assembly and lowered it into the bore hole.

"I'm not sure we can bring anything up with this, but it's worth a try," Sussman said.

When the assembly would go no further, they began turning the handle. It rotated easily but went no deeper.

"Put some weight on it," Sussman said.

McDowell pushed down while Sussman turned the handle. It penetrated a couple of inches and then began turning easily again without going deeper.

"It's no use," Sussman said wearily. "We've hit something solid. Feels like rock. Let's bring her up."

He sounded discouraged. In a way, McDowell was glad. Now maybe Sussman would stop pestering him. The speck of metal on the end of the drill had probably been nothing.

They pulled up the assembly and began taking it

apart with the pipe wrench. Sussman replaced it in the canvas bag piece by piece as it was disassembled. Fifty-five dollars wasted, McDowell thought. Not wasted, really, if it meant Sussman would get off his back now. Everything but the last length of pipe and the core sampler had gone into the bag when Sussman stuck his finger in the end of the sampler.

"Something's in here!" he exclaimed.

"What is it?"

"Can't tell. It's stuck tight."

Sussman shone the penlight in the end of the core sampler. McDowell peered past his arm. He could see nothing.

"It's a coin!" Sussman cried. "By God, I think it's a coin!"

"Not so loud," McDowell begged. "What kind of coin?"

"I can't see. It's up in there. But it's a coin, all right."

"Let me try," McDowell said.

He took the core sampler from Sussman and thrust a finger into the opening at the side. He crooked the finger around the object within and tried to pry it out. It would not budge. It had a serrated edge that bit into McDowell's finger.

"Why didn't I bring some pliers?" Sussman groaned in frustration.

"Let's go," McDowell said nervously. "The watchman may come back."

"Okay. We've screwed around here too long already."

McDowell could not have agreed more fervently.

Sussman went up the ladder until he could just see over the top.

"Coast's clear," he said. "Come on."

McDowell handed him the metal detector and the bag. Sussman put them on top of the wall and climbed to the top himself. McDowell was mounting the ladder when Sussman said, "Oh, shit! I forgot to cover the bore hole."

Sussman backed down the ladder and pushed past McDowell. McDowell climbed up until he could see over the wall. He could hear Sussman stamping and

67

scraping back in the patio. It sounded fearfully loud. He peered anxiously over the wall. Then Sussman was scrambling up the ladder, saying, "Let's get outta here."

They pulled up the ladder and let it down to the sidewalk. When everything was stowed in the van, instead of starting the engine, Sussman got out his penlight and shone it into the core sampler.

"Let's go!" McDowell urged. "Let's go!"

"I'm trying to see if it's gold, damn it."

"Later. Let's get out of here."

Several times along the way Sussman wanted to stop, but McDowell insisted they get off the streets without delay. They went to Sussman's apartment. It was after three when they got there. The party next door was over. In the kitchen, Sussman took a fold-up tool kit out of a drawer and selected a pair of long-nosed pliers. Padding its jaws with McDowell's handkerchief, he took a firm hold on the wedged coin and worked it free. He removed the coin, still swathed in the handkerchief, and let it lay in his palm a moment. Then very deliberately, while McDowell looked on breathlessly, he drew back a fold of the handkerchief.

There, gleaming dully against the white cotton, was an eight-escudo Mexican gold piece dated 1823.

6

"I knew it!" Sussman cried exultantly. "I knew it! Didn't I tell you it was there?"

McDowell could say nothing. The gold piece in Sussman's hand seemed unreal to him. Yet because it was there, the letter of Diego del C. was transformed from a historical trifle to a living document and Don Diego to a real person who had found, and lost, a fortune. It was as if a direct line had been opened to a past he had studied and taught but never actually touched. He took the coin from Sussman and turned it over in his hand. It was cool and heavy.

"Eighteen twenty-three," he said tonelessly. "The first year of the Mexican republic."

"Don't be so demonstrative," Sussman said. "It's bad for your heart. I need a drink."

McDowell followed him to the living room and accepted a large straight scotch without protest. He no longer felt the effect of the tranquilizers and, in fact, had forgotten all about them.

Sussman collapsed in a chair, took a long pull at his drink, gave a sigh and said, "Ahhh, that's better." He looked over at McDowell, who was staring into his glass. "Hey, you all right, Mac?"

"Fine," said McDowell without looking up.

"You nodding off? Maybe you ought to not drink on top of all those pills."

"I'm fine, Steve. Really, I'm fine."

"Finally got to you, didn't it? Finding the gold?"

McDowell stared thoughtfully at his friend.

"Yes," he said at last. "I suppose it did."

"Good," said Sussman. "I know it's late, but I think we ought to talk about our next move. I'm too up to sleep anyhow. Aren't you?"

"What do you mean, our next move?"

"How to get the rest of the stuff."

"Not so fast, Steve. We had an agreement. If it was there, the next step was up to me."

Sussman looked at him quizzically.

"So?" Sussman said.

"So I say the next step is to report what we found."

Sussman leaped to his feet, crying, "Report it! Report it, for Christ's sake! There's a fortune down there, you dumb son of a bitch!"

"It's not our fortune," McDowell said doggedly.

"Whose is it then? Of all the. . . . If it's not ours, whose is it? Just tell me in language simple enough for a dumbass engineer like me to understand. I mean, no history lecture, no civics lesson. Just why it belongs to somebody else when it's you who found out about it and us who went to the trouble to check it out."

"It wasn't ours when it was lost, it's not on our property, and we were trespassing when we found it. Is that simple enough for a dumbass engineer?"

Sussman shook his head angrily and gave the living room couch a vicious kick. It seemed to relieve him.

"You're right," he said, surprisingly. "It's not ours. So we steal it. Who are we stealing from? This Diego dude? He's dead. And he stole it to begin with. And the dude he stole it from probably stole it from somebody else. Right?"

"I don't question that. An ordinary ranchero wouldn't have had a fortune like that. It had to be one of the old Spanish families, with wealth that went back generations. Someone like—"

"No history lessons, please," Sussman interrupted. "Tell you what. We don't make any decisions tonight. Okay? Let's think about it a couple days and then we decide. Is that asking so much?"

"If it'll make you happy. But I already know the answer, Steve."

"It's agreed, then. We don't do anything either way for a couple of days."

They shook hands on it. McDowell left the coin with Sussman when Sussman drove him home. He did not want to take the chance of Florence's seeing it. Too many explanations.

Florence woke up when he got into bed.

"What time is it?" she mumbled. "For goodness sakes, it's four o'clock." She sat up and ran her fingers through her hair. "Did you win?"

"Win?" McDowell replied blankly.

"You lost then," Florence said. "How much? I thought Steven was going to stake you."

"Oh," McDowell said, remembering at last that he was supposed to have been playing poker. It seemed so long ago. "He did. I suppose you could say I broke even."

All during breakfast he expected a call from Sussman. It never came. After class he waited in his office for Sussman to phone or come by. Sussman did not, nor did McDowell see him when he went to lunch. After lunch he phoned Sussman's office. Sussman was not there. He had not been in all day. He had called in sick.

McDowell did not believe Sussman was actually ill. Was Sussman avoiding him? And doing something

70

rash? McDowell was troubled. Not so much because Sussman might be doing something rash. It was Sussman's nature to be rash. But because it smelled of duplicity and duplicity was not Sussman's nature. Yet could you really be sure of anyone when a lot of money was involved? Yes, he decided. You could if that someone were Sussman. Sussman would never go back on his word to a friend, and they had agreed to do nothing about the find at the Avila Adobe without discussing it.

Sussman phoned him early in the afternoon, sounding cheerful and excited.

"I tried to get hold of you," McDowell said accusingly.

"I've been busy," Sussman said without apology. "You free?"

"Come on over."

Sussman came to McDowell's office carrying a brown paper bag from which he produced two cans of beer. He pulled the caps and handed a can to McDowell. McDowell accepted it, took a swallow and said, "What's on your mind?"

Sussman pulled a chair close and put his feet on McDowell's desk.

"Been doing some research," he said.

McDowell studied him suspiciously but said nothing.

"Don't you want to hear about it, ole buddy?" Sussman said.

"I'm listening, ole buddy."

"I weighed the gold piece. Just a shade under one ounce. Avoirdupois."

"Avoirdupois?"

"Yeah. Gold's normally weighed in troy ounces. A troy ounce weighs more than a regular ounce but a troy pound weighs less."

"Fascinating," said McDowell.

"Only twelve ounces to the troy pound instead of sixteen," Sussman continued, unfazed. "I thought it would make it simpler for you if I put everything into avoirdupois ounces and pounds."

"So far it's not working out that way. What are you getting at?"

"Stick around. So the coin weighs an ounce. The one used as a seal on the letter was four escudos, right?"

McDowell nodded, mystified and wary.

"We'll say it weighs half an ounce, okay? You said the chest was so heavy Diego had trouble picking it up. Even if he was just a ninety-eight-pound weakling it would have to weigh sixty, seventy-five pounds, okay? Let's be conservative. Say it's fifty pounds of gold pieces, plus the weight of the box."

"Avoirdupois, of course," McDowell said dryly, sensing what Sussman was getting at.

"Now, we have fifty pounds of eight and four escudos weighing one ounce and a half ounce respectively."

"Who has?" McDowell interposed.

"They also minted two- and one-escudo pieces. I looked it up. But to simplify the arithmetic let's say eights and fours. And we knew for sure there were eights and fours. Say half and half. Fifty pounds means twelve hundred gold pieces."

"Twelve hundred?" McDowell said, impressed despite himself.

"Any idea what old gold coins are worth today?"

McDowell shook his head and finished his beer. Without being conscious of what he was doing, he crushed the can in his fist, took the top and bottom between thumb and forefinger and bent it double before tossing it into his wastebasket.

"You got a grip on you like a gorilla," Sussman said. "Let me tell you what one of 'em's worth. The one we found last night. I went to a coin dealer today."

"You sold it?" McDowell cried, half rising from his chair.

"I didn't even show it to him. Just described it. Told him my old uncle wanted one for his collection and I was asking around for the old gent."

"What did he say?" McDowell asked, settling back.

Sussman took his feet off the desk, picked up the legal pad on which McDowell made notes, turned to a fresh page and scrawled something across the length of the page. He held the pad up for McDowell to read. Written on the pad in large numbers was the figure 1,700. McDowell leaned back in his chair with his mouth open. Sussman grinned triumphantly.

"Shakes you, don't it?" he said.

"Seventeen hundred dollars?" McDowell said softly. "For one coin? I don't believe it."

"Of course, I gave you the good news first. Now the bad news. The other one, the one used to mark the seal, it's only worth six fifty."

"Six dollars and fifty cents?" McDowell said. "That sounds awfully low, with gold prices what they are."

"Six hundred and fifty dollars," Sussman said.

McDowell rose and strode around his office. He thrust his hands in his pockets and took them out again. He clasped them behind his back and then let them hang. The contents of the chest could be worth a million dollars. He had not dreamed it could be so much. He had not really thought about what the coins might be worth in dollars, only in historical significance. Displayed in a museum, with a note about how they came to be found. The Sussman-McDowell Escudos, perhaps. Sussman's name first because Sussman's vision and expertise showed they were there. But now the sheer magnitude of the find forced him to think in terms of dollars.

"I've never seen you like this," Sussman said. "Is it something I said?"

McDowell shook his head impatiently and kept pacing. He did not want to talk just yet. He did not know if he could, coherently. The thought of so much wealth had a bludgeoning effect. He was numb and confused. Money had never meant a great deal to him before, he thought ruefully, very possibly because he had never had occasion to consider a great deal of it. Now there was a fortune involved. And so much he could do with it. A new television set for the bedroom, with remote control; the swimming pool they'd been wanting since Robert learned to swim; enough to spend his next sabbatical anywhere in the world with a tutor for Robert if there was no suitable school. He laughed without mirth, causing Sussman to look at him curiously. What was he thinking about, a new TV set, a new swimming pool? That much money meant a whole new way of life. He could teach only the courses he wished, or not at all, if it pleased him. A new home with a real library, not an extra bedroom called a library, and a collection to fill it, not bits and pieces painfully scrounged. A cook and housekeeper for Florence. A vacation house on the beach or in the mountains. Robert liked the beach, but Florence liked the mountains. Maybe they could have both.

Yet he found it more comfortable to think about little things, things to grace his and his family's way of life, not change it. Because he was content with his life as it was. It was a good life. Was that the reason he was hesitating now, that he was afraid of change, not that he thought it dishonest to take something that was not his? Was it so dishonest, really? A fortune was there for the taking. A fortune which, as Sussman said, did not belong to anyone. It merely happened to be on public property. If they had stumbled on it up in the hills somewhere, would he be so scrupulous? Certainly not. Finders keepers. How different, after all, was this? Not all that much. Except that where it lay now it was more difficult to get at.

For the first time, he realized, he was thinking about the problems involved, not the morality of it. Before, he had been thinking of it as a simple choice between taking or leaving the gold. But taking it was not all that simple. The chest was almost sixteen feet in the earth. He felt a surge of crushing anxiety. What if they couldn't get at it, if that great fortune was destined to sit there just out of their reach? He stopped in mid-stride and looked over at Sussman.

"But how do we get it out?" he demanded.

Sussman grinned, relieved.

"I thought you'd never ask," he said.

McDowell sat down behind his desk and waited.

"We can't go in there and just dig it up, that's for sure," Sussman said.

"I know that. How do we do it?"

"We'll have to tunnel."

"Tunnel?"

"Shouldn't be too hard. The soil in that area is sand, gravels and silt, I think. You know that red brick building next to the Avila Adobe?"

McDowell nodded.

"It's an abandoned powerhouse. I called the El Pueblo de Los Angeles office this morning and they told me."

"You've certainly been busy," McDowell said. "Considering you weren't supposed to do anything until we talked it over."

"I really didn't *do* anything," Sussman protested. "I just asked a few questions here and there. Anyhow, if we can get in there, it's just a few yards to the chest. Only a few nights' work."

"How do we get in there?"

"I haven't figured that out yet. I wanted to wait until I was sure it was all right with you," Sussman added righteously. "I'll check it out tomorrow. Right now I've got to go home and get some sleep. I haven't been to bed yet."

Sussman's news the next day was disappointing. The old powerhouse was rented out for storage space, part of it to the La Noche Buena Restaurant, a small structure in front of the red brick building.

"When I found that out I told 'em I was interested in leasing some of the space and they took me through it," he said. "Mostly just a lot of open space. Absolutely nowhere in it we'd have a prayer of working."

"It's all off then," McDowell said, disappointed but also a little relieved. Despite his need for sleep, he'd had a bad night, torn between thoughts of a fortune in gold pieces and the risks of getting it. It probably was not intended he should ever get easy wealth, he thought, or wealth of any kind, for that matter.

"What are you saying, Mac?" Sussman demanded.

"It just won't be quite as easy as we thought."

He explained it would now be necessary to look around and find another site from which to start a tunnel.

"There must be someplace around there we can rent," he said.

"I doubt it," McDowell replied. "I've never seen any empty shops on Olvera Street."

Sussman looked thoughtful.

"Wasn't there an office building on the other side of the powerhouse?" he asked.

"The Biscailuz Building."

"Maybe we can rent space in the basement. It'd be perfect. Wouldn't even have to sink a shaft. Just break through the wall and start tunneling. It's a little farther than the powerhouse, but what the hell, considering what's at the other end."

"It's getting more and more complicated," McDowell said.

"Life's complicated, amigo. That's what makes it so much fun. Besides, you could use the exercise." He grinned wickedly at McDowell. "I'm gonna work your fat ass off. Whatd'ya think of that?"

"Not much," McDowell admitted.

"Well, I better get moving if I'm gonna check out the Biscailuz Building."

"Want me to tag along?" McDowell asked reluctantly, feeling he should make some sort of contribution. Sussman was doing everything, and he felt guilty about that. The least he could do was offer to help.

"Why not?" Sussman disappointed him by saying. "You look so fuckin' honest. Me, I look like a con artist."

"I'll go along with that," McDowell said.

Before visiting the building, they fortified themselves with taquitos at La Noche Buena, the tiny restaurant in front of the powerhouse. The little kitchen was within arm's length of their table.

"You can look into the kitchen from the powerhouse," Sussman said. "The smell of frying tortillas like to drove me crazy."

The Biscailuz Building was around the corner next to the Plaza Mexican Methodist Church and faced the plaza. The Spanish motif had been preserved in its design. The Indian Folklore Shop occupied one end of its covered patio and part of the basement. There was an elevator to the basement, but they took the stairs. They found nothing in the basement but smooth walls and two locked doors, both blank and obviously not office doors.

"Doesn't look like any office space down here," Sussman said, disappointed. "I guess we'll have to keep looking."

76

"I haven't got all day," said McDowell, looking at his watch. "I've got some work to clean up."

"Me, too," Sussman replied. "Let's just take a quick walk around the block and see what we can see."

They went outside and looked south, toward the broad leafy plaza with its walks and a kiosk in the center. Across the plaza was another group of restored buildings, one of them the old firehouse. They went around the corner, toward the powerhouse and the rear of Olvera Street. On that, the east side, was a parking lot and then Alameda Street. At the end of the Olvera block, to the north, was more open space, triangular, where Alameda and Main Street intersected at an angle. They turned west on Macy, which bounded the far end of Olvera, and walked to Main. There was nothing on the far corner of Macy and Main but a Shell service station and, behind the station, on North Spring Street, a string of low, dismal buildings. To the south on Main, across from the other side of the Olvera Street complex, was the big parking lot extending back to North Spring. Beyond the parking lot on Main was the venerable Plaza Catholic Church.

"Come on," said Sussman, going south on Main.

Across the plaza was the old Pico House, still being restored. On the other side of Main, beyond the church, was the padlocked La Esperanza Bakery and the rear of a municipal building.

"Esperanza," McDowell murmured. "Hope. I wonder if we could work from there? It's a long way from the Avila Adobe, though."

Sussman shook his head.

"It's got to be somewhere we can set up a legitimate-looking front," he said.

McDowell looked at his watch.

"Say, I really do have to be getting back," he said.

Back in the parking lot, in Sussman's Mercedes, he said, "It doesn't look too good, does it, Steve?"

"Don't be so anxious to give up," Sussman replied.

He sounded less confident than he had when they began their search. They turned left on Macy, heading for the approach to the freeway. Sussman drove slowly past the North Spring intersection. He looked up North Spring at the buildings they had seen behind the Shell station. McDowell followed his gaze. Two- and three-story buildings on both sides. Mexican and Chinese restaurants, a Chinese movie theater, nondescript shops.

Sussman drove on, looking thoughtful.

Heading back to the campus on the freeway, Sussman said, "It'll have to be from there. North Spring Street."

"But it must be a couple of blocks from the Avila Adobe," McDowell protested. "And I didn't see anything for rent."

"I thought I saw a place near the corner."

"I didn't see it."

"It was there. Let's go back."

"I've got work to do."

"Okay. I'll drop you off and go back myself."

"If you'll wait until tomorrow. . . ."

"Got to find out today. If I don't, I'll be up all night wondering."

By the time McDowell was back in his office the afternoon was almost gone. He plunged into the work he had let accumulate. It helped take his mind off the afternoon's disappointments. When he got home, Florence told him Sussman had phoned.

"He said he called your office first," she said. "He must have just missed you." She gave him a searching look. "What's going on with you and Steven?" she asked. "You've been thick as thieves lately."

Her choice of words made McDowell wince inwardly.

"It can't be girl trouble," she said. "Not that much. Even with Steven. He's not trying to talk you into another sure thing, is he?"

"No," said McDowell.

"I hope not. He's terribly bright, but somehow none of his schemes ever comes to anything."

McDowell winced again.

"He said he'd call back," Florence said.

"Where was he?" McDowell asked casually.

It wouldn't do to sound too eager. Florence was already wondering what they were up to. If they went into this thing, it was going to be terribly difficult to

78

keep it from her. But he would have to. She would be horrified. And disappointed in him.

"He didn't say," Florence replied. "He said he'd call back."

Sussman did, during dinner. McDowell was pleased with the timing. Florence would not be able to hear their conversation from the kitchen.

"I found a place," Sussman said exultantly. "I found a fucking place."

McDowell wondered why Sussman always used that word when he was angry or excited.

"You didn't!" he exclaimed.

His feelings were ambivalent. If Sussman had found a place, it meant they could translate speculation into action. But it also meant they were really going to do it.

"Who didn't what?" Florence asked from the library door. "Your dinner's getting cold."

"It's Steve," McDowell said. "He, uh, he got an offer from Rice."

He felt terrible lying to Florence. He had been evasive a few times in their long marriage, but he could not recall ever having told her an outright lie before.

"Is he taking it?" she asked.

"That's what he wanted to talk about," McDowell said. "He's not sure."

The second lie was as difficult as the first. Was it Scott who had said it? McDowell wondered. "Oh, what a tangled web we weave,/when first we practise to deceive!" Scott or Shakespeare. He'd look it up in Bartlett after dinner. He'd have quite a web to weave before this was over.

"I hope not," Florence said. "Not unless it's an associate professorship. Though he is young to expect that, maybe."

"You pass out or something?" Sussman demanded.

"Florence just came in," McDowell said. "I was telling her about the offer from Rice."

"The offer from Rice? Are you. . . . Oh."

"Tell him you'll call back," Florence said. "Unless you like cold broccoli."

"I'll call you back after dinner," McDowell said.

"Why don't you come over instead?" Sussman said.

"We can talk more freely here. There's a lot to talk about."

"Be right there," McDowell said to Florence. As soon as she left, he said, "I don't think I'd better. She's already wondering what's going on."

"Tell her we've fallen in love," Sussman said. "You know, we've really got to think of something to tell her. Once we get into this thing you'll have a lot of explaining to do."

"I know," McDowell said ruefully.

That was an aspect he had not considered when he first agreed to join Sussman in going after Don Diego's hoard.

Robert appeared at the door munching on a chicken leg.

"Mom says are you coming or not?" he said.

"Coming," said McDowell. "Coming. You know your mother doesn't like you eating all over the house. I'll call you back, Steve."

He returned to the kitchen. Florence had put his plate in the oven to keep the food warm. McDowell's feeling of guilt increased. She was so thoughtful, and here he was, wondering how to deceive her.

"Is it a good offer?" Florence said. "Is he excited about it?"

"Not exactly," McDowell replied, picking up a piece of chicken. "I have a feeling he's not going to accept."

"Isn't it an unusual time of the year to be approached?" Florence said.

"I hadn't really thought about it."

"Rice is his alma mater, isn't it?"

"Yes."

"I suppose the department just learned of an opening coming up and they thought of Steven right away," Florence said. "You want Cool Whip on your jello?"

"Yes," McDowell and Robert said together.

He was relieved that Florence had provided her own explanation to her question. Maybe that was the way to handle her. Not answer unless he had to and hope she would beat him to the explanation. She was good at that.

After the crossword puzzle, on which McDowell found it hard to concentrate, and after a few minutes of familial harmony in the living room, he went to his library and phoned Sussman. A woman's voice answered.

"Sussman apartment," it said. "Mr. Sussman is out. If you wish to leave a message, wait until. . . ."

Damn it, McDowell thought angrily, of all times for Steve to be out. He could be so irresponsible. Then Sussman's voice interrupted the announcement.

"Gloria, will you stop that shit? I'm expecting an important call."

"Who's calling, please?" the woman's voice asked.

So it wasn't a recording, just one of Sussman's girls being cute.

"Tell him Mac."

"And what is the nature of your call, Mac?"

There was a muffled scream, followed by a giggle, and she said, "You let go of that, and I'll let go of the phone."

"Get back in the kitchen and finish those dishes," said Sussman's voice. "Mac, you still there?"

"Can we talk?" McDowell said doubtfully.

"Sure. I sent Gloria to the kitchen. She won't hear anything with the dishwasher on."

"Dad," said Robert.

He was standing in the door with the handle of a See's caramel sucker sticking out of his mouth. McDowell put his hand over the mouthpiece of the phone and looked at his son, hiding his annoyance at the interruption.

"Something you like's coming up on television," Robert said.

He tossed a sucker to McDowell. McDowell made a stab for it but was late in closing his fingers, his catching coordination was not good, and it fell to the floor.

"Thanks, son," he said. "Be there in a minute. Steve? I'm back on."

"We've got a place," Sussman said. "Perfect. First door, just two doors from the corner of North Spring and Macy. And a basement."

"Isn't that a long way from where we want to go?"

"We've got all summer."

"We've got a trip to Canada planned for July," McDowell protested. "Can we finish by then?"

"Make it next summer," Sussman replied. "Then you can buy Canada."

"Robert's really been looking forward to it. Can't it wait until we get back?"

"Wait? With the chest just sitting there? We've got to grab the space while we can. And finish before the fall quarter starts. It's too late to put in for leaves of absence."

"Why do we have to finish before the quarter starts?"

"Because digging a tunnel is a full-time job. Unless you want to take forever."

"All right," McDowell said reluctantly. "I don't know how I'll explain it to Robert and Florence. Especially Florence."

"We'll think of something." There was a long pause. "There's just one problem."

"Yes?"

"The space is six hundred a month. On a year's lease. And they want the first and last month in advance."

"That's twelve hundred dollars!"

"Sure is. And we'll need more to get started. Lots more. You got any bread?"

"Not to spare. What will we do?"

"We'll think of something. Gloria, get your ass back in the kitchen! Look, I gave 'em a five-hundred-dollar deposit. Postdated check. You got five hundred I can have to cover it?"

"I could take it out of savings," McDowell said reluctantly.

"Fine. Let me have it tomorrow. And we'll talk about how to finance the rest. Okay?"

"All right."

McDowell stared at the phone for a while after he hung up. Was this going to be just another one of Sussman's sure things?

McDOWELL and Sussman were both tied up all morning and unable to meet until lunch. They went to Jason's, just off campus in the Village, for falafel—pita bread stuffed with vegetables and chickpea puree. McDowell had a side order of french fried onions as well. While they ate, Sussman went over the figures he had assembled the night before. He estimated that before they were done they would have to invest as much as seven thousand dollars in the project.

"Seven thousand dollars!" McDowell exclaimed. "Where'll we get that kind of money?"

"Don't get uptight. We'll find a way. That's no investment at all when you consider the return."

It sounded remarkably like other statements Sussman had made in the past, and McDowell told him so.

"This is different. This isn't speculative. We know the stuff is there," Sussman said.

Sussman estimated they would need the North Spring Street premises for about three months. That included the time it would take to set up a cover business as well as the actual tunneling. That meant twenty-four hundred dollars for rent alone, counting the last month in advance they would forfeit.

"We could stall the landlord the last month and stiff him for the rent," Sussman said, "but that's low. And besides, he might start looking for us."

A truck for hauling away the tunnel material would cost another fifteen hundred to two thousand dollars. Five hundred or more to fix up the office in some semblance of a going concern. Another couple of thousand for tools, lumber for shoring, ventilating and lighting equipment, furniture for the dummy office. And a fund to cover unforeseen expenses Sussman said were sure to crop up.

"I've been thinking we should be in the duct and ventilator business," Sussman said. "Means a bigger investment than if we go into something like insurance or real estate where we don't need any special equipment, but it's a better cover. I mean, it won't look so peculiar when we haul stuff in and out and saw up lumber in the basement and carry on in general."

"Sounds logical," McDowell said dubiously. "But it's beginning to sound as if even seven thousand won't be enough. How can we get our hands on that kind of money?"

"I can raise forty-five hundred."

"Forty-five hundred? Where will you get forty-five hundred dollars?"

"I'm gonna sell my car. Already have an offer that'll net me that over what I still owe on it."

"Sell your car? You love that car, Steve."

"I love girls. The car I only like. When this is all over, I'll buy one twice as mean. Now, how much can you raise?"

The five-hundred-dollar withdrawal for Sussman had left thirty-one hundred dollars in the McDowell savings account. The joint checking account fluctuated between a low of one hundred dollars and a high of eight hundred or so. McDowell did not know exactly where it stood at the moment. That was Florence's department. She was better than he at keeping the balance straight. Except for the equity in his house and a few shares of public utility stock, and Robert's inviolable college fund account, that was it.

"The only cash I've got is a little over three thousand at Brentwood Savings," McDowell said. "But I can't—"

"Get me twenty-five hundred," Sussman interrupted. "That's our seven thousand right there."

"Just a minute. Those are Florence's savings, too."

"She'll get it back a thousand times over."

"But what will I tell her?"

"Don't tell her anything."

"She'll find out the first time she makes a deposit."

"You make the deposits."

McDowell sighed. After all, Sussman was putting up forty-five hundred dollars in addition to doing all the planning.

"All right," he said. "But what if we find out seven thousand's not enough?"

84

"We'll cross the bridges when we come to 'em."

"I've never operated that way."

"You'll learn. Just stick with old Sussman."

"We could always sell the eight-escudo piece," Mc-
Dowell said, realizing that in so doing he was aban-
doning all reservations about its ownership.

"If we have to. But let's hang on to it for as long
as we can. If just for sentimental reasons."

They agreed to do nothing until the quarter ended
except lease the office. They would be free after that,
and it was only a few days until exams were over and
grades given.

Sussman took their money and opened a checking
account under an assumed name. James Ferguson.

"Name of an old-time governor of Texas," he explained. "Pa Ferguson. He got himself impeached."

"I think that's appropriate," McDowell said. "Considering the nature of our enterprise."

"So he ran his wife. Ma Ferguson. She won, too."

Sussman signed the lease with the same name. Afterward, around eight o'clock at night, he came to take
McDowell to inspect the premises. He came on the
motorcycle he had bought to replace the Mercedes,
wearing a black leather jacket, goggles and a crash
helmet. Robert was impressed. Sussman insisted on
taking him for a ride around the block over Florence's
objections.

"Whatever made you buy a motorcycle when you've
got a perfectly darling car?" she demanded. "Don't
you know how dangerous they are?"

"Bob ride his bike?" Sussman asked.

"What?"

"Does Bob ride his bicycle?"

Of course he rides his bicycle. What's that got to
do with anything?"

"Bicycle's the most dangerous vehicle there is, Flo.
Except maybe a tricycle. Didn't you know that?"

Florence looked at him skeptically.

"Are you making fun of me, Steven?" she said.

"No, ma'am. You can look up the statistics."

After Sussman brought Robert back from his ride,
McDowell drove him to North Spring Street in the

TR4. He felt a little guilty about keeping it when Sussman had sold his Mercedes to raise money.

The office was sandwiched in between two restaurants. One, the Sonora #2, was Mexican. The other, the Glorious Dragon, was Chinese. Neither looked as if it catered to gourmets.

"A choice of restaurants right next door," Sussman said. "And if that's not enough, there's more on both sides of the street. And Olvera Street's just over there with a choice of more Mexican, and Chinatown's a couple of blocks thataway with more restaurants than Peking. And if you eat sloppy, we've got a Chinese laundry two doors away."

Across the street was a Chinese gift shop, closed for the night. Next to it was the Chinese movie house with the marquee and posters in Chinese. The façade was severe, with no visible foyer. The theater was of more recent vintage than the other structures, except for the little Chinese hotel next to it, and its spanking clean paint made it and the hotel look strikingly out of place in the neighborhood.

"And we get tired of digging," Sussman continued expansively, "we've got entertainment." He waved an arm at the theater. "And not just movies. Couple of the restaurants have music, and there's a nightclub. Dance till dawn if that's your bag."

McDowell did not respond. He found the neighborhood depressing and thought it would probably be even more so by day, when the squalor was more evident.

The deep, narrow store Sussman had leased had previously been occupied by a Chinese tailor. His sign was still painted on the dirt-encrusted plate-glass window that shared the width of the shopfront with the door.

"Welcome to the new home of the North Spring Street Vent and Duct Company," Sussman said, unlocking the door and pushing it open.

The electricity had not yet been turned on, and they had to use flashlights. Sussman probed the interior with the beam of his flashlight and motioned for McDowell to precede him. Where the floor was visible beneath the dirt, newspapers and debris, it was rough and splintery.

"We're paying six hundred a month for this?" Mc-Dowell said incredulously.

"You want a fancy address, you have to pay for it. And don't forget, it includes a basement."

"What's that smell?"

"Piss and Sweet Lucy."

"Sweet Lucy?"

"Cheap wine. Winos crash here. Get in through the back window. The landlord promised to put in new glass. And we'll put a metal grate over it."

"When the decorators get through, you won't recognize it. I'm having it done in Ming whore-house. Don't look so miserable, for Christ's sake. I've arranged for a crew to come in and clear out the crud. Come on down in the basement. That's what I'm proud of."

The steps, naked fissured wood on concrete and without a handrail, plunged down steeply from a narrow opening at the side of the shop about a third of the way back.

"Watch your step and stay next to the wall," Sussman said, lighting the way with his flashlight.

Downstairs the smell of wine and urine was even stronger, and mixed with the odor of vomit. McDowell tried to breathe as shallowly as possible. The fetid air was palpable as mist. The flashlight played over a bundle of rags in a corner. McDowell let out a gasp. It was a human body. Sussman strolled over and knelt beside it.

"Hey, man," he said, shaking the corpse's shoulder.

The corpse groaned and muttered querulously.

"After tonight you gotta find someplace else to crash. Okay, pal? You mobile?"

The derelict struggled to sit up. Sussman tucked the flashlight under an arm and hauled him to his feet, leaning him against the wall.

"Here's a couple of bucks," he said. "Go buy yourself a jug. And tell your friends this hotel's out of business."

The man tottered toward McDowell and steadied himself by grabbing McDowell's arm. McDowell pulled away in distaste and was immediately ashamed of himself for doing so.

"You can't stay here," the man said. "You heard my frien'. Beat it, bum."

Sussman laughed.

"Takes one to know one, Mac," he said.

He shone the flashlight on the stairs to light the man's way. The man stumbled up them, coming perilously close to the edge but never quite falling over. When he was gone, Sussman played the light over the rear of the basement. The back wall was brick, with a long, narrow horizontal window at the top.

"The basement ceiling's about eighteen inches above ground," Sussman said. "And the floor's nearly seven feet below the surface. Gives us a seven-foot start on the shaft. Means we won't have to dig so deep before we start digging laterally."

"Marvelous," McDowell said despondently, looking at the scabby brick and the riffles of dirt on the concrete floor.

"Cheer up, Mac. Once we get it all cleaned up and aired out it'll be just like home."

The quarter ended. The morning after, McDowell put on his tennis clothes and went to Sussman's apartment. Sussman had maps from the Substructure Section of the Los Angeles Department of Public Works and from the Department of Building and Safety, as well as a bore report from the Geology and Soil Engineering Section of the DPW. The substructure map showed the location and dimensions of all known underground lines and drains, power vaults, manhole covers and the like, the Department of Building and Safety map lot numbers, property lines and other surface information. The bore report described subsurface strata.

Sussman pinpointed the location of their office and the Avila Adobe on the surface map and marked them on the substructure map with a fine draftsman's pen. He was most painstaking, using a magnifying glass and a long rule, with closely spaced markings.

"Accuracy's critical," he explained, looking up from the table on which he was working. "We need the exact bearing and distance from the start of the dig to the chest. We don't want to end up in some taco joint."

He drew a tiny circle inside the Avila Adobe property line.

"Diego's chest," he said. "This could be a couple of feet off. I don't have an exact reference point to measure from."

"What if we miss it?" McDowell asked.

"If we hit it right on the money. . . ." Sussman paused and grinned. "No pun intended. If we hit right on the money the first shot, I'll be surprised as hell. When I think we're close, I'll have to get a surface reference for the final adjustment."

Sussman drew a line from the southeast corner of their premises, which was at the back of the basement, to the circle, then measured the distance with a brass rule.

"Fourteen and one-eighth inches at thirty-three and a third feet to the inch," he said. He made some figures on a scratch-pad. "Just over four hundred seventy feet."

"Is that all?" McDowell said, pleased.

He had expected it to be more. It had seemed so much farther when they walked it. But of course they'd had to walk about two-thirds the length of Olvera to Macy and then up Macy and around the corner to North Spring. This was a straight line.

Sussman leaned back, ran a hand through his thick black hair and looked solemnly at McDowell.

"Once we start digging you'll find it plenty far enough," he said. "Of course, if you'd like to start from Chinatown to make it more challenging. . . ."

He drew a line extending the southern edge of the office, which was at right angles to North Spring Street on the map, so that he could measure the angle of its intersection with the line to the Avila Adobe. He used the largest protractor McDowell had ever seen to measure the angle. It had a sliding scale along the arc for measuring fractions of degrees.

"Hundred sixteen and two-tenths degrees," Sussman said. "I'll have to check and make sure our wall is exactly ninety degrees to North Spring like I've got it drawn here before I'll know if it's an exact bearing.

But we've got a hell of a lot to do before that." He got up and stretched. "How about a beer?"

While they drank from the cans, he went over the bore report for McDowell's benefit. From zero to six feet, the subsurface comprised silty to medium coarse sand, gravel, brick fragments and concrete rubble four to six inches in diameter.

"The fragments and rubble are fill," Sussman said. "Under the fill, from six to twelve feet, more sand, gravel and cobbles. Cobbles are rocks. Shouldn't give us any trouble unless they're in a hard matrix. But the bore report doesn't indicate that."

At twelve feet, the bore encountered reddish brown silty clay.

"Shale," Sussman said. "Bedrock."

"Bedrock?" McDowell demanded. How are we going to get through rock?"

"We aren't. Twelve feet's as deep as we go. We tunnel down to the shale and then go laterally. Gives us a firm, even floor, if we're lucky."

"But we hit the chest below fifteen feet," McDowell protested. A thought struck him. "And we didn't hit any bedrock, did we?"

"Nope."

"Then how could it start at twelve feet?"

"We made our probe in a well site. It was dug down into the shale."

"How could they get water out of solid rock?"

"It's not all that solid. The bore report shows lenses in the shale water could have seeped through."

It took the better part of a week to get the premises into the shape Sussman wanted. He had a floor-to-ceiling partition constructed across the shop at the head of the steps. There were two doors in it, one opening directly to the steps and the other into the back part of the shop. Then he had the carpenters close off the steps from the rest of the basement with another floor-to-ceiling partition, with a second door at the bottom. Both doors could be bolted from the inside.

"We don't want anybody wandering down into the basement," he told McDowell. "This way we'll have three locked doors between our shaft and the street."

90

The ground floor and basement windows were given thick coats of white paint and the latter covered with heavy steel mesh to keep out overnight guests. An electrician was brought in to install additional power outlets in the basement and a sign painter to letter NORTH SPRING VENT AND DUCT COMPANY on the plate-glass window facing the street.

All this came to more than eleven hundred dollars.

"With the rent, we've already spent twenty-three hundred dollars, and we haven't even started yet," McDowell said, worried.

"Don't get so uptight," Sussman said blithely. "When did you start getting so nervous about bread anyhow?"

"When I started seeing the way you spend it."

"Better get used to it, amigo. Like you said, we haven't even started yet."

Sussman bought the van next, for sixteen hundred and fifty dollars, a 1970 eight-cylinder Ford, explaining it was needed right away to transport other purchases. He could have bought an older, cheaper model, and McDowell thought he should have but Sussman insisted that they buy a reliable vehicle that could carry heavy loads.

"Sand and gravel weigh," he said.

Next came the office furniture. A desk, chairs, filing cabinets, typewriter, checkwriter, in and out basket and all the other things they could recall seeing in of-fices. They bought everything secondhand. Sussman agreed to used furniture only because he thought it looked more convincing than new. When the office was furnished Sussman stood in the doorway and studied it with a critical eye.

"Something doesn't look right," he said.

He sat down in a swivel chair and rotated slowly.

"Bare walls," he said. "No papers on the desk. No clutter at all."

They hung an advertising calendar on a wall, put a few forms and other papers on the desk and some empty boxes of various sizes on top of the filing cabi-nets and on the floor against the wall.

"I'll say this for you, Steve," said McDowell, "you

think of everything. Are you sure you're not a professional con man?"

"Just a gifted amateur." Sussman tugged at his chin. "You know, Mac, it still doesn't look right. I don't know what it is, but something's missing."

"Looks perfect to me."

"What does a regular office have this one doesn't?" Sussman mused.

McDowell surveyed the office. What *did* other offices have this one did not? He thought of his own office. Desk, chair, typewriter, telephone, filing cabinet. A telephone. That was it.

"No telephone," he said.

"That's it!" Sussman said. "Whoever saw a business without a phone?"

"We'll get one installed."

"Nope. I'll get one and make it look like it's installed. I'd just as soon not have us listed in the phone book."

"We could have an unlisted number," McDowell said.

"Whoever heard of a business with an unlisted number?" Sussman demanded.

And then Sussman bought tools. Chisels, hammers, sledgehammers, pinch bars, short-handled picks and shovels, a power saw, T square, miter square, a vise and a power drill. He bought a workbench, sawhorse, nails of various sizes, cloth bags for dirt, reels of insulated wire, light bulbs and protective wire cages for them, eight-inch plastic ducting, rope and heavy twine. He bought lumber for shoring, two-by-tens and three-by-tens, chiefly, but smaller sizes as well. He bought steel-toed work shoes, coveralls, hard hats, goggles and heavy work gloves. When the buying stopped, he had spent five thousand of their seven thousand dollars.

During the week and a half it took to do all this, McDowell found it increasingly awkward to explain his daily absences. As usual, Florence did not ask particularly probing questions, but he thought it would be unnatural not to volunteer anything. He was going to the research library, he was visiting friends, he was hunting down rare documents he'd gotten wind of, he had to go to Santa Barbara to see one of his graduate students who needed advice on independent summer study and could not come to Los Angeles because he'd broken his leg. The last was an invention of Sussman's who was exceptionally clever at such things, and the only excuse that created a problem. Robert wanted to go along for the ride, and Florence suggested they make a family outing of it.

"It's been ages since we've been to Santa Barbara, and we could have lunch on the pier," she said.

"That would be great, but—"

But what? he thought furiously.

"You promised Jack Torres you'd take him to lunch, didn't you?" Florence said. "You're always doing things like that for your students. And he'd feel uncomfortable if the whole family was there. That's it, isn't it?"

McDowell nodded, grateful she was so understanding in her misunderstanding.

"Bobby, you'll just have to go to Santa Barbara some other time," Florence said.

"Aw, Mom," said Robert, "I never get to go anywhere anymore."

"How can you say that?" Florence demanded. "When we're going all the way to Vancouver next month."

McDowell swallowed. Next month he would be burrowing toward Olvera Street. Unless he left it to Sussman to do it all himself for the three weeks they had planned to be gone. That would hardly be fair, and it was important that they finish the job as soon as possible. The longer it took, the greater the chance there was of something going wrong. Sussman would have to help him think of an excuse to get him out of the Canada trip.

After all the supplies were purchased, Sussman brought a surveyor's transit and rod to the shop. He hung a light from the office partition on an extension cord so that it dangled flush against the south wall at eye level. With McDowell at his heels carrying the rod, he went outside and set up his transit. He sighted through the window at the light. He had been obliged to scrape a clear space in the window paint to do so.

"Too much light," he said, annoyed. "I've got to get a can of black spray paint."

"What are we doing?" McDowell said, mystified. "Or isn't it polite to ask?"

"Getting a base line," Sussman said, which explained nothing to McDowell. "But the light source is too big."

Sussman sprayed the light bulb with black paint, then wiped away enough to permit a pinpoint of light to escape. He went back outside and set up his transit a few feet from the curb at a distance he measured carefully with a tape measure. He sighted into the shop again, muttering, "That's more like it." After making a few minor adjustments in the position of the tripod, he sent McDowell north on Spring to find a manhole cover he said would be there.

"Put the end of the rod in the hole in the center and hold the rod absolutely straight," Sussman said. "I'll signal you if it's not straight. Wave my right hand, tilt to the right. My left hand, the other way. Okay?"

He appeared to be enjoying himself. McDowell was not. He had no idea what was going on, and he did not like standing out in the street with cars whizzing by. After he positioned the rod to suit Sussman, Sussman folded the tripod and went into the shop, taking the transit with him. McDowell felt foolish standing out in the street all by himself holding onto a pole stuck in a manhole cover. To make matters worse, the sun was pouring down and he was sweating. After a few minutes, when Sussman came out of the shop and yelled, "What the hell are you doing out there?" he felt even more foolish.

Back inside the shop, Sussman showed him on the substructure map what they had been up to. He had determined the exact angle the south wall made with the curb line.

"Ninety degrees exactly," Sussman said. "That means our base line, the line here"—he pointed to the line representing the south wall—"is true as drawn. Which means our base angle, the bearing from the point from where we start the dig to the chest, is a hundred sixteen and two-tenths degrees, as originally measured. Understand?"

"If you say so. When do we start digging?"

"Soon. After all the trouble I had arguing you into joining up, I never expected you'd be so itchy to start."

"I want to get it over with. I'm running out of things to tell Florence, and we haven't even begun."

And he was anxious to get it over with because once it was done, he would not have to worry about something going wrong. Fortunately Sussman exuded confidence, and for those periods when he was with Sussman he felt more confident.

Sussman spent the rest of the day jotting down figures and trotting back and forth between the office and the basement. After a few hours of this, McDowell got the unsettling notion Sussman was stalling.

"What are you figuring now?" he demanded at last. "We already know everything we have to. And we've got all the equipment we need with enough left over to open a surplus store."

Sussman grinned sheepishly. "To tell the truth," he said, "I'm a little nervous."

"You're nervous? You're supposed to be in charge. How do you think that makes me feel?"

"The thing is, I know the theory cold, but I've never actually done this before."

"You sound like a bride on her wedding night," McDowell said. "Look, I'm a virgin at this business, too. What say we just fumble around together and see what happens?"

"Right," said Sussman. "We'll start first thing in the morning."

On the way to Sussman's apartment—they were in McDowell's Triumph and he had to give Sussman a lift—McDowell found himself thinking more about the need for a plausible explanation of his daylong absences than for the labors that lay ahead. As much as he despised physical activity, slaving in a tunnel did not seem as intimidating as facing a puzzled Florence every morning and evening. He discussed his problem with Sussman.

"Give me a minute to think about it," Sussman said. "I'm a past master at telling the tale."

He was smoking one of his forty-cent Ornelas and looking very rakish. If anyone could think of an acceptable lie, McDowell thought, it was Sussman. Sussman looked like such a jaunty conniver you had either to believe everything he said or nothing. For his part, McDowell had always believed everything and never had cause to regret it. Except in the case of the bad investment, and Sussman had believed in that himself.

"How's this?" Sussman said after a moment's thought. "I've bought a run-down old house up in one of the canyons and you're helping me get it in shape to resell at a profit."

"I don't know," McDowell said dubiously. "Florence knows how hard it is to get me to do anything involving hard work. And I'm really lousy at telling complicated lies."

"You won't have to. I'll handle it."

He phoned that night and asked to speak with Florence. McDowell managed to overhear but little of her end of the conversation. Robert was attempting to explain to him the operation of a model internal-combustion engine Robert was assembling, and McDowell always made it a point to be attentive when his son was discussing a project. All he heard was Florence saying, pleased, "Then that means you're not taking the offer from Rice."

After she hung up, she brought him a platter of peanut-butter cookies without being asked and, while he was munching on one of them, said, "Arthur, now don't say no until you've heard me out."

"No," said McDowell.

That was always the sensible answer when Florence prefaced a request that way.

"Steven's put every cent he has into an old house up in one of the canyons," she said, undeterred. "He thinks he can put it in shape and clean up the grounds and make some money. You didn't tell me the reason he's driving that awful motorcycle is that he sold his car to get the down payment."

"I, uh, I thought he'd be embarrassed if he knew you knew," McDowell said.

That Sussman. He was a genius.

"Steven embarrassed?" Florence said with a laugh. "Be that as it may, he asked me if I'd persuade you to help him."

"Me?"

"He knows how you detest physical work. Really, Arthur, you should give him a hand. He can't afford to hire anyone and if he has to do it alone he can't finish before the fall quarter. And you're the only one he feels close enough to to ask. I think that's nice, Steven thinking of you as his best friend when he's so much younger."

"You really think I should?" McDowell said, resisting an urge to protest he was not that much older than Sussman. "What about our trip to Canada next month?"

"You can take time off for that. I really think as his best friend you should pitch in and help. And the exercise will do you good."

McDowell sighed convincingly. "All right," he said. "If you really think I should."

Florence kissed him on top of his head where there wasn't any hair. "You're such a dear," she said.

That made him feel terrible despite the fact he was now free to work in the tunnel every day without awkward explanations at home, at least until it came time for the vacation trip.

"Tell him I'm dying to see it," Florence said.

McDowell looked at her blankly.

"Steven's house," she said. "I hope he made a good buy. For once."

"I 'll tell him," McDowell said.

If she got insistent about seeing the house, Sussman was going to have to come up with a good excuse why she couldn't.

The next morning, a Wednesday, they put up a CLOSED sign, locked the office door and went down to the basement. Sussman bolted both doors behind them. With the additional power outlets and new ceiling lights the basement was well lit. They had put the stacks of lumber, the plastic ducts, the workbench and their other purchases at the street end of the basement, leaving the back part clear. Sussman plugged the radio he had brought downstairs into an outlet and turned the dial to KLAC, the country music station. It was a new, expensive-looking radio.

"That's some radio," McDowell said, "even if it

happens to be playing crummy music at the moment."

"Glad you like it," Sussman said, unbuttoning his shirt. "It's half yours. James Ferguson bought it."

Sussman took off his shirt, pants and shoes and got into coveralls and work shoes. McDowell followed suit. Using a plank as a guide, Sussman chalked off a six-by-six-foot square on the basement floor with one side the south wall and another the back wall. He fetched a sledgehammer and a long chisel from the pile at the front of the basement and said, "You want to hold or hit?"

McDowell looked at the chalked square.

"Isn't that a pretty big hole?" he asked.

"We'll need room to move around in. You hold the chisel. I don't know if I trust you with the sledgehammer."

He put on gloves and goggles and picked up the hammer. McDowell put on gloves, goggles and a hard hat.

Sussman grinned.

"Don't you trust me, amigo?" he said.

He showed McDowell how to hold the chisel and began banging away at it with heavy blows of the sledgehammer. McDowell winced each time the hammer fell. He felt the vibrations from the chisel all the way to his shoulder and said so.

"Don't hold it so tight," Sussman advised.

It was slow grueling work. McDowell's muscles began protesting. He ached from neck to calf. He tried different positions, crouching, sitting, kneeling. After an hour they had made but little progress and were streaming with sweat. They peeled down to their shorts.

After a while Sussman, panting, said, "This won't get it. Let's try the drill."

He got the electric drill, fitted a heavy-duty bit and attacked the concrete again. Progress was still slow, but faster than with hammer and chisel, and with much less effort. At times McDowell had nothing to do but watch. Because the basement was completely sealed off, the air grew humid and stifling. McDowell found it hard to breathe. It was like being in a steam room.

"Don't you think it's awfully close in here?" he said.

Sussman gave him a compassionate look. "If you think this is close," he said, "wait till you start working in the tunnel."

8

IT took a long, arduous day to break through six square feet of concrete floor using the electric drill, chisels and sledgehammer. McDowell's hands began to tingle and then to burn as if he had held them in a fire. He had to stop and rest at increasingly shorter intervals. Even Sussman fell victim to fatigue as the day wore on. The narrow, airless basement grew increasingly humid with their sweat. They took time out to fetch gallons of water in plastic jugs from a nearby Chinese market with naked ducks dangling by their snakelike necks behind the meat counter. Sussman also bought salt pills, which he insisted they take to prevent heat prostration.

"Heat prostration would be welcome if it meant I could stop working," McDowell said wearily.

They had to suspend operations for a day, for which McDowell was grateful, while an exhaust fan was installed in the basement window. Working conditions had become too intolerable in the airless basement. McDowell had wanted an air conditioner, but Sussman said it did not circulate enough air. Sussman constructed a wooden pallet from two-by-tens to cover the hole in the floor while the installers were there. They piled equipment on the pallet and hid the rubble behind the stack of lumber.

They spent three full, muscle wracking days digging the six-by-six hole down to the shale, five feet below the floor. The tools Sussman had bought for working in the tunnel were unsatisfactory for ordinary digging, and he had to buy picks and shovels with longer handles. They put the rubble, sand, gravel and stones in bags and stowed the bags in a corner to be disposed of later.

McDowell was a mass of aches. He could scarcely

move without groaning. His hands were so stiff and tender he could not make a fist. Sussman was not a great deal better off.

"We'll get used to it when we get in shape," Sussman said without conviction.

McDowell found that fatigue stifled his appetite. All he could take at lunch was a thick milk shake, which cooled as it nourished and partially slaked his ever-present thirst. At home, he asked for salads, canned tuna and fruit and drank soft drinks by the quart.

"Maybe I should start working for Steven, too," Florence said. "I've never seen anything like what you're doing for appetite control. And think of the calories you must be burning up."

"It's much too hard for a woman," McDowell said, alarmed.

"You don't really think I was serious, do you?" Florence said. "Why aren't you tanning? Out in the broiling sun all day."

"We've been working inside. We'll get to the yard later."

He told Sussman about that and Sussman bought a sun lamp.

"Spend a few minutes under it every break," he said.

"But I don't tan," McDowell protested. "I burn."

"Then burn, ole buddy. Unless you can think of something real good to tell Flo."

"And another thing," McDowell said. "Florence keeps asking when she's going to get to see the house."

"Tell her, tell her as soon as we get it cleaned up enough to look like something."

The nearly seven yards of excavated material made an imposing pile of filled sacks.

"I didn't realize it would be so much," McDowell said.

"This is nothing," Sussman replied. "We've still got four hundred seventy feet of tunnel to excavate."

They loaded as many sacks as they could into the van and went looking for a place to dump them. Carrying the sacks up the steep steps was not as hard as digging, but it was hard enough. McDowell was better at it than Sussman because he was strong. He winded

100

more easily than Sussman, however, and had to rest more frequently.

"I can see one thing," Sussman said. "We've got to get heavy-duty springs and shocks for the van if we expect it to take this kind of punishment."

"That makes two of us," McDowell said. "Me and the van."

"I'm afraid we can't modify you, Mac. You'll just have to fight it until your stamina builds up."

They were unable to find a suitable disposal site in the hills of North Hollywood or beyond Beverly Hills and, after a search of several hours, had to settle for a place off Mulholland Drive a mile or so from the San Diego Freeway off ramp. It was farther from North Spring Street than their homes were.

It took three trips to dispose of the material. They had to empty the sacks over the side of the ravine to which they backed the van. It would have been too conspicuous to dump sacks and all. They worked until well beyond their usual quitting time. Sussman was eager to dispose of all the material from the hole and make a clean start the next morning when they started tunneling.

"Don't you think you're overdoing it?" Florence asked when McDowell came in and collapsed on the living-room couch.

"That Sussman is a fucking slave driver," McDowell said.

His language startled Florence, and McDowell, too, when he realized what he had said. He was picking up Sussman's way of speaking. He wondered if he would be talking with a Texas accent before it was over. Already he had noticed country tunes running through his head. And except with rare exceptions he didn't even like them.

"By the way," McDowell added. "He wants to wait until we've got things cleaned up a little before you see the house."

He came to bed wearing only his pajama bottoms. He was pink to the waist from the sun lamp, and the tops chafed his tender skin.

"You poor darling," Florence said. "Just lie there and I'll get the suntan oil."

She began applying the oil and working it into his skin with gentle strokes. Apparently this had an effect on her because she drew off the pajama bottoms and began applying the oil in places that had not been exposed to the sun lamp.

"I'll turn off the light," she said a little breathlessly.

When she rejoined him in bed, she had taken off her gown. Knowing what was expected of him, McDowell fondled her. He felt absolutely nothing. He was simply too tired.

"You're exhausted, aren't you?" Florence said understandingly. "My poor darling."

She tried to help him prepare himself, but although he did feel a spark, it was not enough.

"I'm sorry, Florence," he said, feeling inadequate.

It was the first time in their marriage anything like this had happened. He wondered if it was only exhaustion that had made him impotent or if guilt also had something to do with it. He wasn't old enough for this to be happening to him. Perhaps he should tell her the whole story. But he couldn't do that. Not unless he talked it over with Sussman first. He owed that much to his friend. This was undoubtedly only temporary, anyhow. Once he grew accustomed to demanding physical labor he'd be all right. Maybe even better than ever because he'd be in good shape. And on weekends, when he was rested, he'd certainly be himself again. Unless that goddamn Sussman intended working on Saturdays and Sundays, too.

"It's all right, lover," Florence said, giving his shoulder a reassuring pat. "You're just tired."

"I'll make up for it over the weekend," he said, kissing her good night.

The next morning, June 21, they began the tunnel. Sussman had bought several big sheets of plywood. One he placed upright in the hole against the south wall, fastening it with pegs driven into holes drilled into the brick. He floored the hole with another sheet. Then he cut a two-foot strip from a third sheet and sawed one end at a carefully measured angle.

"Seventy-three and eight-tenths degrees," he said as he ripped away with the power saw. "The supplementary angle to our base angle. It's our guide to line up the tunnel in the right direction."

McDowell, as usual, had no idea what he was talking about but did not ask questions. Sussman was in charge of the technicalities. He was only common labor.

Sussman lay the plywood strip on the plywood floor covering and slid it flush against the plywood forming the south side of the hole. The end of the strip cut at an angle pointed toward the back wall. Sussman nailed it firmly in place with its length flush against the sheet of plywood pegged to the south wall. This done, he sawed two lengths of two-by-ten, one of them two feet long, the other two and a half feet. Using the shorter piece as a guide, he scratched a groove at the back of the hole four feet above the plywood flooring and parallel to it. He marked off the bottom entrance of the tunnel entrance with the longer piece. Then he scratched lines connecting the ends of the bottom markings with those of the top groove.

"Have a look," Sussman said. "And bring me a piece of two-by-four."

McDowell did as he was told.

"This is our tunnel," Sussman said, pointing at the marks he had made at the back of the hole. "Four feet high, two feet wide at the top and two and a half feet wide at the bottom. We make sure we maintain just those dimensions by checking with these hunks of two-by-ten as we go along."

He slid the length of two-by-four flush against the slanted end of the plywood strip nailed to the floor.

"And we line up the tunnel at the correct angle with this," he said. "The plywood guide keeps it pointing at exactly the right angle. As we go in, we push the two-by-four into the hole, keeping it against the guide. We just dig alongside it."

"I had no idea it would be so complicated," McDowell said, impressed. "I thought we just started digging."

"That way we could end up in Pomona. For every degree we're off we'd be over eight feet off at the end of the tunnel. Even this way's not all that accurate. But when we get in a ways I can check it with the transit. The two-by-four deal is just to get us started in the general direction. Once we really get in there, we'll adjust as we go along."

McDowell looked at the marks outlining the tunnel entrance. He had envisioned something larger, something a man could stand up in.

"Is that going to be big enough to work in?" he asked.

"I thought about making it smaller," Sussman said. "The bigger it is, the more dirt we have to move. But if it was any smaller we'd have to work lying down. And that could get to be a real drag. Come on," he continued, climbing out of the hole.

He got out nimbly, putting his palms flat on the concrete floor and then, with a bound, springing straight up and bringing both feet to the floor between his hands. McDowell struggled up behind him, having to hook an elbow and knee over the edge to manage it.

"Maybe we'll put in an escalator," Sussman said with a grin.

He opened a cardboard box he had brought with him that morning. From it he produced two plastic tulip glasses and a split of Hans Korbel champagne, the latter sealed in an insulated bag to hold the chill. He removed the seal, thumbed out the cork and, with a flourish, poured the foaming wine into the tulip glasses. He handed a glass to McDowell.

"To the Avila gold," Sussman said, lifting his glass in a toast.

They touched rims and drank. Plastic wineglasses did not make a satisfactory clink.

"Domestic, I'm afraid," Sussman said, holding his glass to the light. "But with a certain California impudence, wouldn't you say?"

"If there's anything I can't stand, it's a smartass young wine," McDowell replied, thinking, we can't be acting this silly on one glass of wine. It's because it's really about to happen. We're really going after the gold.

Sussman threw his glass against the wall. It fell to the floor unbroken.

"Damn," he said. "I shouldn't have been so cheap and got real glass."

McDowell threw his glass against the wall and then trod both under his heel.

"Just like a Jewish wedding," Sussman said. "The groom breaks the glass that way."

"What do I use?" McDowell said. "Pick or shovel?"

"Choose your weapon," Sussman said.

They climbed into the hole, and Sussman said, "You take the first lick. You're the one who found out about the chest, so you get to break ground. Just stay in the lines."

It was not too difficult at first. McDowell had only to bend to attack the soil, and where it did not yield easily to the shovel the pick was effective. But after he had gouged a foot or so into the sand gravel and stones and had to reach inside, it was more difficult. While he dug, Sussman sawed lengths of three- and two-by-ten boards. He turned up the volume of the radio so he could hear the music above the screech of the saw. McDowell thought his skull would crack. If this was going to be a regular thing, he'd have to get earplugs.

After twenty minutes or so he straightened with a groan, removed his gloves and blew on his smarting palms. Sussman stopped sawing and came over to the hole.

"Pretty good going," he said. "But it'll get harder when we get inside and have to kneel."

"Don't say that," McDowell protested. "It's bad enough this way."

"Want me to spell you? I've got enough shoring to last a while."

McDowell nodded gratefully. He was so weary Sussman had to help him out of the hole.

"How about that escalator you promised me?" McDowell said.

"Sit down and catch your breath," said Sussman. "Then get your ass back in the hole and start filling sacks. We've got to get the material out as we go along."

They alternated after that at digging and filling sacks. The one digging would push the dirt back along

105

the shale floor and the one in back would shovel it into sacks.

"We're gonna need us some rakes," Sussman said. "So we can reach in and pull the stuff out."

When they were in three feet, Sussman put in the first shoring at the tunnel entrance. He had McDowell watch so he would be able to do it, too. He held a two-foot length of three-by-ten against the ceiling of the tunnel and wedged it in place with lengths of two-by-ten flush against either side of the excavation. Then he wedged another length of two-by-ten between the side pieces up against the ceiling piece. He knocked it in place with a few blows of a hammer and nailed it to the ceiling piece.

"It's called a spreader," he said, wiping the sweat from his face. He lifted his goggles and wiped them as well. "I didn't know it would be so fucking hard driving nails straight up."

McDowell reminded himself not to pick up that word from Sussman again. Not that he found it offensive under the circumstances; he just did not want to get in the habit of using it at home.

As they dug, Sussman checked the top and bottom dimensions with the two lengths of planking he had cut earlier. As the excavation lengthened, he pushed the two-by-four into the hole along the shale floor for a guide, holding it against the cut end of the strip of plywood nailed to flooring.

They kept at it until four o'clock, skipping lunch. By then McDowell was utterly exhausted, and even Sussman was tired enough to agree they had done enough for one day.

"We've still got to get rid of the tunnel material, though," he said.

They had tunneled almost four feet, and he was pleased with their progress, though McDowell was not. He had expected it to go more quickly.

"Not even a full day," Sussman said cheerfully. "Once we get into the swing of it we should knock off ten, twelve feet a day. We could be to the chest by the first week in August."

"What if I can't get out of the Canada trip?" said McDowell.

"You'll have to. We'll think of something."

They were able to get most of the sacks into the van. Sussman said that after a while they would let the sacks pile up for a couple of days while they were getting heavyduty springs and shocks installed. And they would need light in the tunnel to work by. The last foot they'd had to work by flashlight.

"And another thing," he said. "We can't keep carrying sacks out the door. We're supposed to be in the vent and duct business. We'll have to use cardboard boxes."

McDowell followed the van in his car and left the TR4 parked in Sussman's space at Sussman's apartment building when they went to dump the sacks off Mulholland Drive. He came back to Sussman's place to shower. They had worked in shorts and were covered with grime from head to toe. Even if he was supposed to be clearing land with Sussman, Mc-Dowell did not think he would be able to explain all that dirt to Florence.

At home, he made ready for bed right after a light dinner, too tired even to work the crossword puzzle with Robert.

"Aren't you going to take a shower?" Florence asked. "Oh, you've already cleaned up. Is the hot water on at the house you and Steven are renovating?"

"Yes," he said, wondering how long Florence would continue answering her own questions.

He did not hear Florence come to bed. When he woke up in the morning, she was sleeping peacefully on her side of the bed. He was stiff and sore all over. He eased out of bed, trying not to groan. He looked down at his wife. She looked so pretty lying there with her eyes closed, a half-smile on her lips. He felt a wave of tenderness and guilt. Perhaps he should tell her what he was really doing. But what if she should object and try to persuade him to report the find? Now that he and Sussman had gone this far he had no intention of doing that. If Florence knew they were after the chest and was firmly against it, he'd really have a situation with her.

He looked at his watch. It was early, not yet six.

He had slept more than nine hours and, though he ached, felt rested. He went quietly to Robert's room and looked in on his son. Robert was sleeping. He seldom got up before eight now that school was out. McDowell went quietly back to the bedroom and closed the door. Robert never came into the bedroom without knocking when the door was closed. McDowell got out of his pajamas and eased into bed next to Florence. That was the least he could do, he thought. She murmured something unintelligible and, drowsily, turned to press against him.

Sussman phoned at eight. He was taking the van in for new rear springs and shocks and wanted McDowell to pick him up at the garage.

"You sound mighty chipper this morning," Sussman said. "I thought after the workout you had yesterday you'd be a bear."

McDowell did not explain he was in such a good mood because he had both eased his conscience a bit and discovered his impotence was purely temporary.

Sussman strung a light to the back of the tunnel before they began digging that morning. He suspended the wire from a hook screwed into the spreader of the shoring. It was a good thing one of them was clever with his hands McDowell thought.

Without the excitement of the first day to stimulate him and plagued by lingering aches and pains, McDowell found digging in the tunnel a torment. Stiff in every joint and muscle, he could not find a comfortable position in which to dig. When he knelt, pebbles ground into his knees, and the hard shale was numbing, though not numbing enough to deaden the shooting pains in his kneecaps. When he sat with his legs folded, his legs stiffened so that he could not straighten them without using his hands. He tried crouching, but that was the worst of all. The top of his hard hat butted against the ceiling, his thighs cramped, and the small of his back hurt.

Dirt showered down on his bare skin, mixed with sweat and made him itch, especially his armpits. Grit worked its way under the waistband of his shorts and dug into the tender flesh of his waist. Some of it drifted all the way down to his crotch, and though it was not painful, it was maddeningly uncomfortable.

And, as the tunnel lengthened and light from the basement no longer filtered in, and he was working only by the light from a naked bulb in a protective wire cage, he felt he was deep in the bowels of the earth instead of only a few feet under downtown Los Angeles. He discovered he had claustrophobia. Enclosed places had never disturbed him before, but this was different. He felt as if the walls were closing in and the ceiling were pressing down. The constriction of the tunnel seemed to be squeezing all the air out, and it was an effort to breathe. At first it was so real he thought the earth was actually bulging inward from some sullen outside force, and he had to reassure himself by measuring the width of the tunnel with the lengths of plank Sussman had cut to check dimensions. Even then, though logic told him the walls were firmly in place, instinct insisted they were closing in.

When he could stand it no longer, he dropped his shovel and scrambled on hands and knees toward the mouth of the tunnel. Sussman was working a few feet behind him, filling sacks. McDowell squeezed past him without a word, knocking Sussman over. When he emerged, he stood erect in the entrance hole, panting, his hands pressed down on the concrete floor of the basement to confirm that here was solidity, his head thrown back and his eyes fixed on the ceiling, seeking as much space as possible.

Sussman burst out of the tunnel crying, "Mac, what's the matter?"

"I got frightened," McDowell said sheepishly. "Claustrophobia."

"Christ!" said Sussman. "That's all we need. A miner with claustrophobia. You scared the crap out of me. I thought you were having some kind of attack."

"I'll be all right," McDowell said. "I'll just have to get accustomed to it. Maybe I ought to go back in right now just to prove to myself I can."

"No. Rest a few minutes and pull yourself together. I remember once in Houston, a horse threw this dude at the stables I used. He got right back on the horse because that's what you're supposed to do or you'll lose your nerve, right? The fucking horse threw him again, and he broke both his arms."

"I suppose there's a moral in there somewhere," McDowell said. "But I've got to get back in the tunnel eventually."

"I'll dig awhile and push the dirt back far enough for you to reach in with the rake. Okay?"

They did this until Sussman had to stop for rest. McDowell clenched his teeth and crawled back into the tunnel.

"If it starts getting bad, come on out," Sussman said.

It was bad, but McDowell fought it, determined not to give in to an illusion. It was the only way, he knew. Stick it out long enough for it to sink in that the walls were not moving and let logic take over from instinct. He concentrated on what he was doing, watching the shovel push into the harsh mixture of sand and gravel, following the pebbles as they fell, watching the point of the pick drive among the cobbles, thinking of the pain in his muscles and the numbness in his hands as he dug and shoved mounds of material back toward Sussman. Before, he had tried to ignore the pain. Now he clung to it. Sussman helped him along by talking to him and, when conversation lagged, singing snatches of country songs. His voice was awful, and McDowell told him so, snappishly.

"That's a good sign," Sussman said. "Shows you're thinking about something besides being buried alive."

"You have to put it that way, you son of a bitch?" McDowell cried.

"That's good! Get sore at me. Let that adrenalin pump. Best antidote there is for fear. You fat, yellow bastard. You bald-headed turd."

McDowell began laughing. He could not help it. And he was grateful he could not help it. For the moment that crazy Sussman had taken his mind off all that suffocating earth pressing in around him. But the light mood quickly drained away, and terror began gnawing at him again. It filled his throat and climbed his chest. He could breathe only in great, unsatisfying gulps, but he forced himself to keep working doggedly. He worked until he knew he absolutely must leave the tunnel, like a diver going up for air. But this time he did not panic. He backed out carefully and said, "Excuse me," when he squeezed past Sussman.

Sussman joined him in the entrance hole.

"Doing better?" he asked.

McDowell nodded, breathing deeply.

"Some," he said when he caught his breath. "I felt like I was suffocating."

"It'll help to get some fresh air back there. We're gonna have to run a duct in sooner or later anyhow, and we might as well start right away."

The rest of the day Sussman did the digging and McDowell filled sacks. Because of the interruptions and the fact Sussman ran into several large rocks that had to be pried out with a pinch bar, they made less progress than they had anticipated. And the deeper Sussman dug, the longer it took to remove the material.

"We'll have to do something about that," Sussman said. "We need some way of loading up and hauling the stuff out with a rope. And that way you won't even have to come in the tunnel. I'll load it at my end and you can pull it out. I'll have another rope at my end to pull it back."

"Great idea," said McDowell. "Except about you doing all the digging. I'm going to do my share if it kills me."

"Stout fella," said Sussman.

"Fat yellow bastard," McDowell replied.

They looked at each other and began laughing.

That night McDowell had a nightmare. He dreamed he was buried alive. He was in a coffin. There was no air, but somehow he did not suffocate. He drew in great drafts of nothingness that clawed furrily within his chest. He beat with his hands and kicked with his feet against the unyielding metal of the coffin. Taunting music filtered down to him from the surface far above. Guitars, banjos and a harmonica playing a maddening, vaguely familiar tune. McDowell screamed and screamed, knowing as he screamed there were no ears to hear it.

"Arthur," said Florence's voice. "Arthur."

A hand was shaking his shoulder.

111

"Arthur," Florence said again anxiously. "You were groaning so in your sleep. Are you all right?"

McDowell breathed deeply of real air, gloriously relieved to find himself safe in his own bed.

"Yes," he said. "I'm sorry I woke you."

"Were you dreaming? What were you dreaming?"

"I don't remember."

He did not want to tell her he had dreamed of being buried alive. It was too close to what he was doing with his days.

"It must have been a nightmare, darling," Florence said. "Usually when you have a nightmare, you remember it. Vividly."

"I never have nightmares," McDowell said.

"I know. I didn't mean you. I meant people who do have nightmares. Does something hurt then?"

Everything hurts, McDowell thought. My arms, my legs, my back, my joints.

"No," he said. "Let's try to go back to sleep."

"I'll make you some warm milk with honey." Florence said. "That ought to relax you."

Warm milk and honey was Florence's latest elixir and soporific. She was so good to him, McDowell thought guiltily. He was deceiving her shamefully, and here she was offering to get out of bed in the middle of the night and bring him milk and honey. But at least he was not deceiving her with a woman. And never had. That was something to cling to when the guilt grew too oppressive.

"You know something, sweetheart?" he said. "You're a wonderful woman."

"And you're a wonderful man, darling. I think Steven must be working you too hard. That's why you were groaning so. He ought to be ashamed of himself."

"Oh, no," McDowell said quickly, wondering if he had talked in his sleep and said something to indicate what he and Sussman had really been doing. "It was probably a nightmare, and I just can't remember it. Did I say anything?" he added casually.

"No. Just those terrible groans. Are you sure you don't want hot milk and honey?"

"I'm fine now. Really I am. Go back to sleep, sweetheart."

Florence drifted off at once. He had been able to do that, too, when he had a clear conscience and before he learned about claustrophobia, McDowell thought grimly. He dreaded falling asleep again, afraid the nightmare would recur. But when sleep came at last, it was dreamless.

He did not have to face the terrors of the tunnel the next day. It was spent doing other things. Though Sussman had promised a bonus for quick service, the van was not ready first thing in the morning as promised. Sussman took advantage of the wait to hunt down and buy something he called a squirrel-cage vacuum pump.

"A vacuum pump?" McDowell said. "I have enough trouble breathing down there as it is."

"It pulls the stale air out and fresh air pours in to replace it," Sussman explained.

"I sincerely hope so," said McDowell.

The van still not being ready, they toured supermarkets getting cardboard boxes out of refuse bins to replace the sacks in which they had been hauling material from the tunnel. The TR4 would not hold many, and they made repeated trips back to the van to store them in the back. When, at last, the van was ready, McDowell drove to North Spring Street and waited.

Sussman came in with a child's coaster wagon as well as the vacuum pump. He removed the handle and drilled a hole in the rear end of the wagon bed.

"For the rope to pull it back into the tunnel with," he said. "We'll need two ropes to pull it out, one on each side of the front axle. The front axle turns, and it takes two ropes to guide it when it's loaded."

"You think of everything, don't you?" said McDowell.

Sussman spent the rest of the afternoon installing the vacuum pump in the basement window while McDowell emptied sacks of sand, gravel and stones into cardboard boxes.

"Not so full," Sussman cautioned when he saw that McDowell was filling them to the top. "That stuff's heavy. We'll never get 'em up the steps the way you're filling 'em up."

He had cut a circle in the window with a glass cutter. First he had been obliged to cut a hole in the steel mesh with heavy snips he had bought for the purpose. He vented the squirrel cage to the hole with a length of plastic ducting and sealed the ducting in with masking tape. He linked up more ducting to the other squirrel cage connection, turned on the pump and disappeared into the tunnel, dragging the plastic tubing behind him.

"Works like a charm," he said when he emerged. "Even cools things off a little back there. Want to check it out?"

"All right," McDowell said reluctantly.

The tunnel seemed to narrow as he crawled back into it. He remembered his nightmare. And he realized why he had heard music in it. Country music. Sussman's radio was going full blast back in the basement. He crawled all the way to the end of the tunnel fighting his terror. He felt a gentle stir of air around him. There was no sense of suffocation. It helped. It did not prevent him from feeling he was immovably encased in a shroud of earth, but it helped. He could beat this thing, he told himself. He forced himself to sit still at the end of the tunnel, breathing easily. He touched the right wall with one hand, the left wall with the other. He reached up and touched the ceiling with both hands. See, he told himself, space. Not much space, but enough.

"What were you doing back there?" Sussman demanded when he emerged. "I was about to come in after you. I thought you'd passed out or something."

"It wasn't as bad as yesterday. I think I'm going to be all right."

"Just don't rush it," said Sussman.

After they dumped the material in the ravine, they went back to Sussman's apartment. McDowell did not take a shower. He was no more dirty and sweaty than he might have been had he been working at Sussman's imaginary house. Sussman opened a couple of beers, and they sat at the kitchen table relaxing.

"This manual labor's been playing hell with my social life," Sussman complained. "The last couple of nights I've been just too damn tired to get interested."

"I'm glad," said McDowell. "I thought it was just me had that problem."

"I've been thinking," Sussman said. "Getting it with a pick and shovel is a real drag. What we need is an electric hammer. I could kick my ass for not thinking about it before.'

"Electric hammer?"

"Like one of those jackhammers you see 'em digging up streets with. Except that it's not as powerful and works off electricity instead of a compressor. Only one thing."

"Yes?"

"They don't give 'em away and we're running low on bread."

"So soon?"

Sussman nodded.

McDowell looked glumly into his beer. They'd just begun and were already running out of money. Where would they get more?

9

As it happened, there was enough in the James Ferguson account to buy the electric hammer, leaving a balance of somewhat less than seven hundred dollars. Seven hundred dollars was only a hundred dollars more than the rent that would be coming due in another week. Sussman did not share McDowell's anxiety about the state of their funds.

"We pay the rent, we've got a whole month to worry about next month," he said.

"What if we have to buy other things? What if there's an emergency?"

"Master Charge."

"We're not going to run up bills we can't pay."

"Mac, we're sitting on maybe a million dollars. When we get it, we pay off."

"What if something happens? What if we don't get—"

"Don't talk like that, for Christ's sake," Sussman

interrupted. "You want to jinx us? Nothing's gonna happen."

"We pay as we go," McDowell said firmly.

"Okay. So where do we get the bread? Take a second trust on your house?"

"We can sell the eight escudos."

"Sell it? It's our good-luck piece."

"If it is, it hasn't been working. It doesn't make any sense to let it sit there when we need money."

Sussman at last agreed. They flipped the gold piece to see who would have to sell it, and McDowell lost. When he got home, he looked up the names of coin dealers in the yellow pages of the western section phone directory. Several dealers had ads in addition to their listings. The one that appealed to him most was Franz Ulrich, Numismatica. The advertisement said Franz Ulrich specialized in gold coins.

In the morning, before going to North Spring Street, McDowell went to the coin shop. It was in Beverly Hills. He wore his best suit, one he'd fought through the crowd to buy at Carroll's semi-annual sale on a Saturday morning a year earlier. He had gone at Florence's insistence. Most of his clothing Florence bought at Ohrbach's and brought home for him to try on. She knew his sizes, her taste was better than his, and he detested shopping for anything except rare books and mixed chocolates at See's. He wore a button-down shirt and a tie Florence selected for him after vetoing his first choice. He told her he was getting all dressed up because he had a meeting with a professor from Berkeley. He would be going from the meeting to Sussman's canyon house, he said.

Franz Ulrich was talking on the telephone when McDowell came hesitantly into his shop. Though a buzzer sounded when McDowell stepped through the door, the man did not look up to acknowledge his presence. McDowell waited patiently a moment, then perceiving Ulrich was in an extensive discussion with someone about a collection in which Ulrich was professing to show interest only as a favor to the person on the other end of the line, began looking at the coins on display in showcases. One section was devoted exclusively to gold coins. McDowell concentrated on

116

them. They were in plastic containers, singly and in sets. The prices of some were extraordinary. McDowell took heart. Seventeen hundred dollars no longer seemed such an outlandish price to expect for his eight-escudo piece.

A voice behind him said, "What can I do for you?"

The disinterested tone belied the courtesy of the words. McDowell cleared his throat uncomfortably. He had never sold anything before that he could recall, not since his long-past college days when he sold his old textbooks every year.

"Mr. Ulrich?" he said.

"Yes?"

Ulrich was as tall as McDowell, older and slimmer but with a small paunch. He was in his shirt sleeves. His tie was knotted in the symmetrical way McDowell could never achieve. His belt buckle appeared to be of gold, though McDowell could not be sure of that.

"I've—I've got a gold coin I'm interested in selling," McDowell said, his throat dry.

He hated that dryness. Why should he be intimidated by this man? People never intimidated him. It had to be because he had something he wanted to sell and the role was foreign to him.

Ulrich looked up at the ceiling as if for solace. There was an expression of distasteful resignation on his face.

"No one wants to buy these days," Ulrich said. "You all want to sell."

McDowell was tempted to leave at once. Who does he think he is, the snotty so-and-so? But, he thought, it's just a ploy. He wants to get me on the defensive and skin me. McDowell's diffidence turned to anger. He knew nothing about gold coins or selling them, but that did not mean he had to put up with arrogance and condescension. He stared a moment into Ulrich's face. Ulrich had a long nose, perfectly flat at the tip. The sixty-year-old face was smooth, with here and there a broken capillary that spoke of good living. The gray eyebrows were shaggy; the gray hair was just a little rumpled. The face had the suggestion of a sneer, or was it merely disinterest?

Ulrich stared back at him unabashed.

"Do you buy gold coins or don't you?" McDowell said.

"That depends, my friend."

"Depends on what?"

"The coin, and what you want for it."

"I thought they had list prices."

"They do and they do not," Ulrich said with a gesture. "Suppose you show me the coin."

McDowell took it out of his pocket and unwrapped the tissue in which he had put it. Ulrich held out his hand. Instead of giving the coin to him, McDowell placed it carefully on the glass top of a show case. He began to feel nervous again. He knew absolutely nothing about gold coins. Perhaps Sussman had been wrong about the value of the eight-escudo piece. And perhaps Ulrich would want to know where he'd got it and why he wanted to sell it. He kept watching Ulrich's face. The faintest widening of Ulrich's eyes indicated interest. He picked the coin up and looked carelessly at both sides.

"Very good," he said at last.

McDowell was surprised. He had not expected Ulrich to admit that. Perhaps he had misjudged the man. First impressions were not always correct.

"Yes," said Ulrich disparagingly. "Very good is the best I can say for it."

"What do you mean very good is the best you can say for it?" McDowell said. "Very good is very good, isn't it?"

The dealer looked at him thoughtfully.

"You're not a collector," he said.

It was not a question.

"Not exactly," McDowell replied. "What's that got to do with it?"

"If you were a collector, you would know that very good is not so good, my friend."

McDowell wished Ulrich would not call him, "my friend." He did not feel like a friend of Ulrich's.

"Very good, fine, very fine, extra fine," Ulrich said. "That's how it goes."

"Oh," said McDowell, feeling stupid and at the same instant realizing it was Ulrich's intention to make him feel so. "It looks extra fine to me. As good as new."

"Look? See these scratches?" Ulrich demanded, presenting the coin to view. "And the reeding around the edge is marred in two places."

The scratches must have come from the pliers, despite the protective handkerchief, and the marks on the sides were where the coin had been jammed into the core sampler, McDowell thought. He hoped they did not tell Ulrich that.

"Would you mind telling me where you got it?" Ulrich said. "It's a rare item. A relatively rare item," he corrected himself. "A hooked neck eagle."

What the devil was a hooked neck eagle? McDowell wondered.

"It's been in the family," he said.

If Ulrich admitted it was rare, it might be worth as much as seventeen hundred dollars after all.

Ulrich went to the back of the shop and returned with a large book. It was *Gold Coins of the World*, the same book McDowell had seen at the research library, but it appeared to be a more recent edition. Ulrich turned directly to the page he wanted. He looked at it a moment and closed the book.

"You've found me in a generous mood," he said. "Nine hundred dollars."

"Nine hundred dollars? It's worth seventeen hundred."

"Not to me, my friend." Ulrich's face arranged itself into what was obviously intended to be a frank smile. "If I were selling, perhaps," he said. "But not buying."

"No thanks," said McDowell.

He was not normally one to bargain, except for a manuscript, where he had expertise, not even in Tijuana, where Florence would haggle for twenty minutes over the price of a clay pot. But this was too much to stomach. He picked up the coin and began folding it in the tissue. Ulrich smiled again, a smile no more ingratiating than the first one.

"Eleven hundred," he said. "And that's my absolute limit. Take it or leave it. I'm very busy."

Eleven hundred dollars was a lot of money, Mc-

Dowell thought. And he did not want to go from dealer to dealer trying to get a better price. It would not do to have every dealer in town know he had an old eight-escudo piece to sell. Someone might start wondering where it came from.

"All right," he said. "But you're a thief."

Ulrich smiled again. And this time it was genuine. "Your name, sir?" he said.

"My name?"

"I never make out checks to cash. My accountant doesn't like it."

"I'd rather have cash, if you don't mind," Mc-Dowell said uncomfortably.

He had not anticipated being paid by check. The last thing he wished was to be connected with the eight-escudo piece.

"I'm afraid I don't pay cash," Ulrich said, not sounding regretful at all. "Not for transactions this size."

"All right, then," McDowell said. "James Ferguson."

He was pleased with himself for having thought of it. It would pose no problem for Sussman to endorse the check and put it in their account. And Ulrich would never know from whom he had bought the coin.

Ulrich gave him a check for eleven hundred dollars and said routinely, "It's been a pleasure doing business with you, Mr. Ferguson. If you have any other coins of similar interest. . . ."

"I don't," McDowell said quickly.

As he drove away, he saw Ulrich standing in front of his shop. Had the coin dealer followed him outside? He was getting paranoid, McDowell thought. The man had no doubt stepped outside for a breath of air. It must be tiring to spend all day every day in a little shop. Not as bad as spending it in a tunnel, though, he thought ruefully.

The door of the shop was locked when he got to North Spring Street, and he did not have a key. He and Sussman always came together, and Sussman kept the key. They always kept the door locked. Mc-Dowell banged on the door until he thought he'd better stop before attracting attention. In fact, Mr. Less, from the Chinese market a few doors down the street, was looking his way with his hands tucked under his white apron. McDowell nodded to him and stopped pounding. There wasn't much point in pounding on the door anyhow. Even if Sussman wasn't in the tunnel, there were three doors between the basement and the street and Sussman always had the radio on.

He went around the corner to North Main, skirted the service station and went to the back of the shop. There was only vacant land at the rear of that block of buildings. The ventilating fan was going at one side of the narrow basement window and warm air was gushing from the squirrel-cage vent at the other. McDowell could hear the radio and Sussman's voice, singing a country tune, "Hold your sweet lips a little closer to the phone."

"Steve," McDowell called. "Steve."

When there was no answer, he took a coin out of his pocket and rapped fiercely on the window glass. The singing stopped abruptly.

"Steve," he said. "It's me. I'm locked out."

"I'll open up," Sussman replied.

Sussman was waiting for him at the front door. Sussman locked it behind them, and they hurried downstairs.

"Sell it?" Sussman asked.

McDowell nodded.

"How much you get?"

McDowell got the check out of his wallet. Sussman wiped a dirty hand on his shorts and took it from him.

"Jesus Christ!" he exploded. "Is this all you got? Never send a boy to do a man's job."

Everything boiled over in McDowell. Ulrich's arrogance, getting rooked and now this.

"If you don't like it, you can kiss my ass, Sussman," he snapped. "If you thought you could do better, why didn't you go?"

Sussman was taken aback by the uncharacteristic outburst.

"Hey, man," he said. "Hey. Don't get so uptight. I'm sorry. Okay?"

"Okay," McDowell said grudgingly.

He took off his suit and hung it up.

"I've gone two feet," Sussman said. "And moved the material to the entrance hole for you. That electric hammer's just what the doctor ordered."

"Great," said McDowell, stripping to his shorts. "Why don't I do the digging today and you stick to boxing the material?"

"You don't have to pamper me, Steve," McDowell said, still smarting. "I'll do my share of the digging."

"Anything you say."

Sussman had fastened ropes to both ends of the wagon. It made getting the material out much easier. When it was filled, the man in the tunnel would give a shout and the outside man would haul away on his ropes. After it was emptied, the inside man pulled it back.

They changed duties every twenty-five minutes and took a ten-minute break every hour. McDowell was never really comfortable during his shift in the tunnel but was learning to cope with his fear. He found the electric hammer awkward to handle at first. His arms grew weary, and the vibrations jarred his upper body. Once he acquired the knack, however, it proved much easier than pick and shovel. And much more efficient.

With the electric hammer and the wagon they did almost seven feet that day despite having to knock off early to make two trips to Mulholland to dispose of tunnel material. There was enough for a third trip if they had elected to take time.

"Looks like getting rid of the material is gonna be our biggest problem," Sussman said. "Not the digging. It sure eats into our working day."

"Maybe one of us should take off and dump it when we have a load," McDowell said. "We really don't need both of us to do it."

It was the first time he had made a suggestion about improving their efficiency.

"It would speed things up some," Sussman conceded. "What we really need. . . ."

Instead of finishing, he shook his head.

"What do we really need?" McDowell asked.

"If we had someone taking care of that end of the

deal we could both concentrate on the tunnel. But no way. He'd have to know something wasn't kosher." Sussman looked thoughtful. "We could let it accumulate and get rid of it on weekends."

"No," said McDowell. "It's bad enough I go off all day every weekday. I've got a family to consider. And we've got to rest sometime. I don't know about you, but I couldn't work like this seven days a week."

"I guess you're right. It was just a thought. You know what I'm gonna do tomorrow? Not a goddamn thing. I'm just gonna lay around the pool all day and get up my strength for tomorrow night."

The next day was Saturday.

"I wish I could," McDowell said enviously. "Florence probably's got something planned. Saturday's her day and Sunday's Robert's."

"It must be a joy to be so well organized," Sussman said with a grin.

"Rub it in. Your turn'll come someday."

He wasn't angry with Sussman about the coin sale anymore. Who could stay angry with Sussman?

"No way," Sussman replied. "How'll I know the chick's not marrying me for my money?"

At breakfast Saturday morning Florence said, "Today would be a good day to see the house."

"Who wants to see some old house?" Robert demanded. "Why can't we go to the beach? The waves are up."

McDowell was grateful for the interruption.

"He's right," McDowell said. "It is a great day for the beach."

"We'll go to the beach Sunday," Florence said. "Bob, you don't have to go to the house with us if you don't want to."

"It's really not much to see yet," McDowell said.

"Not much to see yet? When you've been slaving away on it all this time?"

"It's only been a week. There's so much it needs."

"But I want to see it. Even if it's in a mess. All the better. Before and after. I'll come back and see it again when it's all done."

"I don't know if Steve would like that. I mean with it looking the way it does."

"Call him and ask him then."

Sussman's phone rang six times. He couldn't already be down at the pool, McDowell thought. It was only a little past nine. He'd pretend he was talking to Sussman.

"Steve," he said. "It's me. Florence said she'd like—"

"Hello," Sussman interrupted grumpily. "Hello, for God's sake."

"—to have a look at the house today," McDowell went on bravely.

"A look at the house? What goddamn house?"

"That's right," McDowell said. "I told her it didn't look like anything yet, but she wants to see it all the same."

"Oh," said Sussman. "Florence wants to see the house."

There was silence for a moment.

"Look, I can't think," Sussman said. "I'm still half asleep. What'll we do?"

"All right, if you feel that way about it," McDowell said. "I'm sure she'll understand."

He hung up and turned to Florence with an apologetic shrug.

"He said he'd rather you waited until you can get a better idea of what he's trying to do with it," he said. "I told him you'd understand."

"You should have let me ask him," said Florence. "Oh, well. I suppose I can wait until we get back from Canada."

She settled for a drive to Redondo Beach to have lunch at Tony's on the pier. This appealed to Robert no more than a visit to a vacant house. He made arrangements to spend the day with a friend.

McDowell and Sussman made excellent progress in the tunnel the first part of the week. They worked until they had a van load; then first McDowell and next Sussman would go off to Mulholland to dispose of it while the other remained and worked.

When they were some thirty-five feet along, Sussman called a halt while he checked the angle with the transit. He painted a narrow vertical white line on the plywood panel forming the south wall of the entrance hole, made some painstaking measurements with T square and rule and, after McDowell swept it clean for him, made some mysterious marks on the plywood floor of the hole. He removed the transit from its tripod and fixed it to the plywood floor, then sent McDowell to the end of the tunnel with a flashlight blacked out except for a tiny opening in the center.

McDowell crouched at the end of the tunnel aiming the flashlight toward the entrance. Sussman shouted instructions.

"Higher, Just a frog hair more. Good. A little left. Too much, too much! Right. Now left just a hair. Cool! You can come out now."

Sussman was at the workbench with the substructure map and protractor when McDowell joined him.

"We're pretty damn good operators, amigo," Sussman said. "Less than two degrees off."

"I thought that two-by-four and the plywood guide angle were supposed to keep us on the right track."

"It's not all that accurate. But it was accurate enough. Two degrees is nothing to correct. We just have to bear a little to the right to be back on the money."

By late Friday afternoon they had burrowed forty-six feet. McDowell was taking his trick in the tunnel. He heard a steady rumbling above him and dirt began to shower down. He was a couple of feet beyond the last shoring. Cave-in, he thought instantly, scrambling backward in blind panic. He bumped into the wagon, turned around, squirmed over it and hustled as fast as he could toward the entrance on hands and knees. Despite the hard hat, his head rang from beating against the spreaders and his knuckles were skinned from scraping the side planking. He burst out of the tunnel, shouting, "Cave-in!"

"Christ!" Sussman cried. "Is it bad?"

"I didn't hang around to find out," said McDowell, gasping for breath "I heard a rumbling and stuff started coming down."

"I better have a look."

"Don't go in there, Steve! You could get killed."

"Did any of the shoring give?"

"Not while I was back there."

"Maybe it's just at the end then. I'll be careful."

Sussman got a flashlight and ducked into the tunnel. He popped out again immediately.

"The light's still on back there," he said. "Couldn't have been much of a cave-in."

He went back into the tunnel. He was gone several minutes. He emerged looking thoughtful.

"Well?" said McDowell.

Instead of answering, Sussman climbed out of the hole and went to the substructure map. He made a measurement with his dividers. When he turned back to McDowell, he was grinning.

"That was traffic, you dumb bastard," he said. "We've reached Macy Street."

"How was I to know?" McDowell said sheepishly. "It sounded like a cave-in to me."

"I'd have been shook, too," Sussman said. "Coming unexpected that way. There'll be more of it until we get across." He studied the substructure map. "We'll reduce the intervals between shoring while we're under the street. There's lots of vibration from the traffic."

"Sorry I panicked, Steve."

"Forget it. It's my fault, anyhow. I should have anticipated it and warned you. I'm supposed to be the engineer on this project."

McDowell looked at the tunnel and sighed.

"Then it's once more into the breech, I suppose?" he said.

Now that the worst was over, he realized how fatigued he was. The past few days his muscles had no longer complained, but the exhausting work had had a cumulative effect. Every morning he had awakened a little more tired. Thank God it was Friday.

"Nope," said Sussman. "We're both bushed. It's about quitting time, anyhow. Let's dump the last load and call it a day."

On the way back to Sussman's apartment, McDowell said, "It's already July, you know."

"Yeah," Sussman replied. "And we've still got four hundred twenty, thirty feet to go. The farther in we go, the longer it's gonna take us to move the material

126

out. Slow us up. We'll be lucky to do six, seven feet a day. Means sixty, seventy working days. It could put us into October. And the start of the fall quarter."

They exchanged glum looks.

"If we just had another man," Sussman said wistfully. "It'd make all the difference in the world. I'll just have to find a better way to move the material."

"I was really thinking about something else when I said it was already July," McDowell said. "Have you forgotten I'm supposed to be taking off for Canada in a couple of weeks?"

"Oh, Christ! I forgot all about that. That'll really put us behind. Mac, you've got to get out of it."

"How? Florence has already got the maps from the auto club, and she and Robert are planning the side trips."

"Let's cool it a few days. We'll think of something."

After dinner that night Florence said, "Arthur, have you seen our savings account passbook?"

McDowell's heart sank.

"No," he said. "Why?"

"I've got to transfer some money to the checking account."

"You do?"

"Everything's coming due at once. The auto insurance, the mortgage payment, the dentist's bill of Bobby's. And we'll need seven hundred and fifty dollars in traveler's checks."

"What do we want with seven hundred and fifty dollars in traveler's checks?"

"For the trip."

"Oh. Well, keep looking. You'll find out where you put it sooner or later."

He had, of course, hidden the passbook to keep her from learning he had withdrawn almost everything. He spent a miserable weekend wondering how he was going to explain why there was only a few hundred dollars left. And even if he did stumble on a convincing story, which was patently impossible, where was he going to get the money to pay the bills she said were coming due? There was still money in the James Ferguson account. Over a thousand. He'd have to get

Sussman to get it for him. Then he could at least stall Florence for another week or so.

Monday was July Fourth, but McDowell and Sussman did not take a holiday from the tunnel. Florence had agreed it was foolish to go anywhere over the Fourth when everything would be so crowded, and besides, they would soon be taking a full vacation trip.

McDowell wasted no time in telling Sussman he had to have money from the James Ferguson account. A thousand, if they had that much.

"That'll just about wipe us out," Sussman complained.

"Can you come up with a better idea?" McDowell demanded.

"Yeah. Tell her the trip's off. You've changed your mind."

"Spoken like a true bachelor."

"Okay, but if you go, there's no way we'll reach the chest before the fall quarter."

"All right. I'll start hinting we may not be able to go. But I'll still need the money. We've got bills to pay."

"I'll get the thousand for you on the way from the dump tomorrow," Sussman promised.

Tuesday, when he returned from his run to Mulholland he brought McDowell a cashier's check for a thousand dollars. McDowell deposited it in the checking account after his own run to Mulholland. That night he told Florence he'd found the passbook and transferred a thousand to the checking account.

"But let's wait a few days on those traveler's checks," he said.

"You always leave everything to the last minute, Arthur," Florence protested.

"I'm not sure we can make the trip," McDowell said cautiously.

Florence gave him an incredulous look. "Not make the trip?"

"Uh, I've been meaning to talk with you about that. You see, Steve. . . ."

"Steven? What has he got to do with our trip?"

"He, he thinks he has a buyer at a heck of a price if we can get the house and landscaping finished by,

128

by the middle of next month and, well, he can't do it without my help."

"I never heard of anything so ridiculous in my life," Florence said. "Let him hire someone to help him. I think it's just awful the way he's had you slaving away helping him. I never dreamed he was like that."

"I'll tell him," McDowell said, backing down. "I'll tell him he'll have to get someone else. But, Florence, he's not like that. I volunteered. He said he'd hire someone to replace me. But I happen to know he can't afford to."

"That's his problem," Florence said.

"Yes," said McDowell. "Yes. I suppose it is."

Wednesday, when McDowell told Sussman there seemed to be no way he could get out of going to Canada, Sussman took it with more grace than McDowell had expected.

"If you can't, you can't," he said philosophically. "I may be a bachelor, but I understand your family comes first. And one thing I don't want is for Florence to be sore at me. Y'all are my family out here."

Sussman showered first when they went to his apartment to clean up after work. He had to go to a cocktail party in Encino. He went off, leaving the apartment to McDowell. McDowell was luxuriating in a cascade of hot water when there came a rapping on the shower door, a female voice cried, "Surprise," and the door slid open.

Standing there was a naked young woman. Though her tousled mop of hair was wheaten, her pubic hair was dark. She had long, slender legs, a flat stomach and breasts that appeared to be taking aim at him. Her lovely oval face wore a look of surprise. McDowell observed all this in the instant before he turned away in confusion, hiding his crotch.

"Who're you?" she demanded. "I thought it was Steve."

"Steve's not here," McDowell mumbled, his face hot. "I'm Mac."

He looked back at her over his shoulder, taking care to keep his eyes on her face.

"So you're Mac," she said, unabashed. "I talked to you on the phone once. I'm Gloria."

129

"Pleased to meet you," McDowell said. "Now, if you don't mind. . . ."

He started to slide the glass door shut, but she grasped the edge.

"When's he coming back?" she said.

"He's gone for the evening."

"Shit," said Gloria, stamping her foot childishly.

It made her breasts bounce, a sight McDowell could not avoid even though he was trying to keep his eyes fixed higher up.

"Would you mind letting go of the door?" he said. "You're getting water all over the floor."

"Would you believe it?' Gloria said. "You're embarrassed, aren't you, Mac?"

"As a matter of fact, I am."

"There's nothing to be embarrassed about. You're a little heavy, maybe, but you've got good shoulders. And all those muscles."

McDowell had lost ten pounds since going to work in the basement, and his muscles had toned up. Despite his embarrassment, he thought of that now and was grateful for it.

"Everything considered, you don't, you know, look too bad," said Gloria, not releasing the door. "What the hell, as long as I've gone to this much trouble already. . . ."

She stepped in the shower and slid the door shut behind her.

"Hey!" McDowell cried. "What do yo think you're doing? Get out of here."

He really did not want her to, but he was a married man. And she was Steve's present girl.

"You're not gay, are you?" she demanded.

She reached around and felt him.

"No," she said with a laugh. "You're not gay."

When they were dressed, Gloria said, "I'll bet that's the first time you ever balled in the shower."

"You'd win," McDowell said.

He was pleased with himself, but also desolated. She was lovely, she was much experienced, and he apparently had acquitted himself quite well. But he had also been unfaithful to Florence for the first time.

"You're strong as a bull," she said. "Do you lift weights?"

"No," McDowell said modestly.

"You picked me up like I was a feather."

"It's because you don't weigh a good deal," McDowell said. "You're very slim. You really have a beautiful body."

"I know. Look, Mac," she continued, not looking directly at him. "Like, you know, you're not going to say anything to Steve about this, are you?"

"I was just going to ask that of you."

"Cool."

She stopped at the door and said, "See you around then."

"Yes," said McDowell. "See you around."

He drove home slowly, in turmoil, dreading having to face Florence. He had been lying to her for weeks now. About working on a house with Sussman when he was actually engaged in a criminal act, about their savings, which in a real sense he had stolen because they were half hers, and now this. Most of all, this. He could not deny to himself that it had been a heady experience, enormously good for his ego, but it was the first time he had been unfaithful to Florence. He had looked, and he had imagined, but he had never acted.

He walked in the door of his home feeling like a stranger. He was not the same man who had left that morning. There was a wall between him and Florence now, a wall of guilt and deception. She was so good and so trusting, and he was such a bastard. He would have to make it up to her the best he could. And he would begin by going through with the trip to Canada. The Avila gold would just have to wait.

His somber mood seemed to infect Florence. She was very quiet all evening and seldom looked directly at him. It was only when he unexpectedly glanced her way that he would find her eyes on him. Had she guessed, he wondered?

After dinner, when the three of them sat in the living room, Robert watching television and assembling some sort of machine, McDowell pretending to read and Florence at her needlepoint, it seemed to Mc-

Dowell there was a brooding tension in the air. Or was he only imagining it because he was so tense himself? And was it also his imagination that Florence seemed to be waiting for them to be alone?

After Robert went to bed they remained in the living room, still silent, Florence needlepointing, McDowell with his book. He felt something akin to his claustrophobia in the tunnel. The walls were closing in on him. At last Florence put down her needlepoint and looked at him long and sadly.

"Arthur," she said in a low, hurt voice. "We've got to talk."

"What about?" he asked, his voice just as low, and shaky.

"You've been deceiving me," she said.

Oh, God, she knew! She had read it in his face.

"Sweetheart," he said brokenly, going to her.

He put his head in her lap. To his surprise, she did not pull away. What a dear, wonderful girl she was. He did not deserve her.

"Sweetheart," he said again, his voice muffled in her lap. "I'm sorry. What else can I say?"

"I went to Brentwood Savings today," she said. "You've been behaving so strangely about the passbook."

McDowell raised his head and looked at her. What the devil was she talking about?

"And there was only a few hundred dollars left in the account," she said. "You drew out all the rest."

"Oh, that," McDowell said, vastly relieved.

"What do you mean, 'Oh, that'?" Florence demanded, her tone for the first time displaying irritation.

"Nothing," McDowell said quickly, getting to his feet and sitting down beside her. "I mean I can explain everything."

The time had come when he had to tell her about the tunnel and the Avila gold. It seemed little enough when there was something so much worse she did not even dream of.

"You don't have to," Florence said. "I've already guessed."

"You mean you know what we've been doing and

you never said a word?" he demanded, gaping at her.

"No. Not until I found our savings gone. It isn't only Steven who bought the house, is it? You're in it, too, aren't you? You took the money and went in with him. And that's why you've kept driving yourself day in, day out, isn't it?"

"Yes," McDowell said eagerly, feeling like a condemned man who had just been reprieved.

"Oh, Arthur," she murmured, starting to cry. "Why did you have to do it behind my back? If you wanted to go in with him that badly, I wouldn't have stood in your way."

"I know you wouldn't, sweetheart," McDowell said, starting to cry a little, too. "I'm sorry. I can't tell you how sorry I am."

He was ashamed of his tears. They were crocodile tears. Not that he wasn't truly repentant because he was. But he was seizing on her goodness and innocence to deceive her more. What kind of monster had he become since he'd got a smell of the Avila gold? He felt a great urge to tell her everything. Not about Gloria but everything else.

Instead, he said, "I'll never do anything like that again. And we'll go on our trip, and I'll make it all up to you."

When they went to bed, Florence, flushed with forgiveness, was amorous. But once again McDowell failed her. His hasty encounter with Gloria had not sapped him, for he was quite a virile man. It was because he was too torn by everything that had happened the past few hours to respond. Infidelity, Florence's goodness, deceit compounding deceit.

"That's all right, darling," Florence said with gentle understanding. "You've had an exhausting day."

And that, to McDowell, was the most painful thing of all that had been said and done that day.

10

MᶜDowELL felt awkward with Sussman in the morning. He'd screwed Sussman's girl. True, Sussman's girls were always temporary, but all the same there was an element of betrayal in it. Gloria had thought so, too, asking him not to tell Sussman. And if a girl who obviously attached no importance to a casual tumble felt that way, it was a betrayal. It would not happen again. That would help make things right and in time he would forget about it.

"What the hell's eating you?" Sussman demanded as they were getting into their coveralls.

They had decided it was better to steam in coveralls than strip to shorts and be coated with a slime of grit and sweat.

"Florence found out about the savings account," McDowell said, glad he had so ready an explanation for his mood.

"Oh, Lord. Did she hit the ceiling?"

"She was very calm about it. Calm, but hurt."

"Damn, Mac, I'm sorry."

"The way it turned out, it's not all bad. She thinks I took the money to go in with you on the house."

"She does?" Sussman said admiringly. "Mac, you're getting to be one clever son of a bitch."

"Oh, it was her idea, not mine. Before I could get a word out, she came up with it on her own."

"Well, if you can't be clever, it's good to be lucky, my daddy always said."

They were working more efficiently now, particularly at installing the shoring. McDowell had learned how to do it, and when it was his trick in the tunnel, Sussman no longer had to drop everything and come back to put in the planks. But it was taking them longer to crawl to the end of the lengthening tunnel and back and to bring out the material. Both had knee problems from the hard, grit-covered shale. Sussman bought them basketball knee pads, which were a great help.

"There must be a better way to get the material out," Sussman said. "We've got to mechanize. I wonder where we can find something small enough to operate in the tunnel?"

McDowell remembered a little electric car Robert had had when he was younger. A wildly extravagant Christmas present when McDowell had a windfall from an article picked up by *Reader's Digest*. It had gone four or five miles an hour and was powerful enough to move McDowell's weight. He wondered if they still had it. It had been several years since Robert had played with it. McDowell could not recall seeing it around. It might be in the garage under the other junk. He mentioned the car to Sussman. Sussman was enthusiastic.

"We could hitch the wagon to it," he said. "And use it to get back and forth in the tunnel. Are you sure it'll fit?"

"I think so. As I remember, it was only a couple of feet wide. We might have to get pretty low to clear the ceiling, though."

"Beats crawling like a worm."

Florence said they had given the car away more than a year ago to a young niece in Santa Barbara.

"Whatever made you think about that after all this time?" she asked.

"I don't know. It just popped into my head."

Sussman said they would have to buy one. There was almost nothing left in the James Ferguson account. McDowell drew enough out of the joint checking account to pay for it. By the time Florence went over the canceled checks he hoped to have an explanation.

By lying flat, they were able to ride the car in and out of the tunnel. It did not eliminate the crawling entirely, however. The man bringing out a load of material had to crawl back to the tunnel end, and the man returning the empty wagon had to crawl back to the basement. Sussman promised to devise a method of getting it back and forth without a driver.

McDowell's fat was melting away, and his muscles growing rock hard. None of his trousers fit anymore, and his jackets were too big in the waist. Florence was proud of him and a little envious.

135

"You've lost more in less than a month than I've ever done in three," she said. "And you look simply marvelous."

Gloria had thought he looked pretty good, too.

Gloria.

He had been thinking about her often despite every effort not to. She had been so supple, so adept. And so complimentary. His showers in Sussman's apartment were ordeals of lust. They always made him think about her. In the tunnel, though, it helped to think about Gloria. It took his mind off the arduous business at hand. There were times when Sussman came back to relieve him that McDowell found it hard to believe twenty-five minutes had passed. But as he crawled back through the tunnel, his aching body always told him he had, indeed, been slaving for almost half an hour.

The unremitting work, the confinement, the necessity for deceit aroused in McDowell an increasing sense of isolation, both physical and spiritual. He saw almost no one but Sussman and had little time for his family. And when he was with Florence and Robert, he was too tired to give as much of himself as before. The thought of the fortune at the end of the tunnel did not temper his sense of isolation. It was too far away, days and weeks of grubbing in the earth, and he was not even positive sometimes that it was actually there. It was something he and Sussman had dreamed.

And he grew edgy from hard work and constant association with Sussman. Sussman was affected similarly but to a lesser degree. McDowell did not realize how strained their relationship had become until they had a blowup on Friday.

He was working in the tunnel. Sussman had taken out a load of material and was slow in returning the wagon and electric car. Material piled up behind McDowell until he had to stop digging. He called for Sussman at the top of his voice but got no answer. Probably had the damn radio turned up so loud he couldn't hear anything else, McDowell thought angrily. What was Sussman doing, anyhow? Didn't he know the material had to be cleared away as they went along? He crawled back toward the entrance, fuming.

136

As he neared it, he could hear the power saw over the noise of the radio. Sussman was sawing planks when he emerged.

"What the fuck you expect me to do with the dirt?" McDowell cried, surprising even himself with his vehemence.

Sussman whirled and looked at him, tight-faced.

"Shove it up your ass, why don't you?" he said. "I'm getting some shoring ready."

"Why didn't you tell me before? I could have been resting instead of piling material all over the floor I've got to shovel up again."

They were both embarrassed by the outburst when they cooled off but did not apologize. McDowell thought it would only point up the unpleasantness if he did. They were careful to be agreeable the rest of the day.

That afternoon Sussman took a reading with the transit and made a minor adjustment in the tunnel angle. Then he measured the distance they had dug.

"Seventy-six feet," he said.

"Is that all?" McDowell said with a groan.

It seemed as if they had dug miles.

"We're just under four hundred feet from the chest," Sussman said. "Say with the electric car we can make seven feet a day, that's about fifty-seven working days. Say eleven weeks. And that's if we don't run into any unexpected delays."

"Eleven weeks? Oh, Christ."

It was a phrase McDowell did not normally use. Just one more thing he had picked up from Sussman, he thought.

"Twelve or more if you go screwing off to Canada and leave me on my own. It puts us into October for sure."

"You think I want to go to Canada?" McDowell snapped. "I'm as anxious to get this over with as you are. I already feel as if I've spent half my life in that tunnel."

"Sorry, Mac," Sussman said. "I know you'd get out of it if you could. And I'm sorry I've been such a bastard lately."

"I've been the bastard," McDowell said. "I'm not accustomed to working like this."

"Who is?"

"We've got the weekend coming up. That's something."

Sussman looked at McDowell speculatively.

"About the weekend," he said. "Would you consider working tomorrow?"

"Steve, enough's enough."

"Not digging. I've figured out a way to get the car and wagon back and forth by themselves. It'll take maybe half a day to set it up, and I hate to take the time out from the tunnel."

"All right," said McDowell.

The thought of losing even half a day was unbearable. He had never dreamed it would take so long to dig four hundred and seventy feet. If his body could stand it, he would even be willing to work seven days a week to get it over with. And the longer it took, the more money they would need. The rent would be due again in three weeks, and they did not have enough money left in the James Ferguson account to cover even that. And there was only about five hundred dollars left in his savings account.

"Will it be all right with Florence?" Sussman asked.

"I think so. Now that she thinks we've got our savings tied up in your alleged house she shouldn't object to my working on a Saturday."

Florence agreed so readily that McDowell thought it an appropriate moment to suggest they postpone the Canada vacation until next year.

"Florence," he said, "I want to ask you something. And don't get upset. I wouldn't ask if it wasn't important to me."

"Of course," said Florence.

"I'd rather not take the trip right now."

"What? When we've been planning it for months? Bobby would be heartbroken. I don't care what you say, the house is simply not that important. It won't hurt Steven to carry on by himself for a week or two."

"It's not just the house. It's the money, too."

"The money? We have enough in the checking account. Or have you been into that, too?"

And before he knew it, McDowell was telling her everything. The pressure of weeks of deceit, of having been unfaithful to her, of a raging impatience to finish the tunnel and be done with both the lies and the digging, forced it out. He told her about the letter, about the night visit to the Avila Adobe, the coin and the tunnel. As the words tumbled out, Florence's face became a taut, inscrutable mask. I shouldn't have told her, he thought in panic. It's all over. She won't let me rest until I promise to give it up. What can I tell Sussman?

"Don't you see, sweetheart?" he said desperately. "It could be worth a million dollars. Think what it means to us. What we could do for little Robert."

Florence pressed her palms against her cheeks and stared at him as if wondering who this stranger might be. Is she going to get hysterical? McDowell wondered frantically. Is she going to scream and tear her face?

"Did you say a million dollars?" she said at last in a stifled voice.

McDowell nodded dumbly.

"And you've kept it from me all this time!" Florence demanded, her voice rising. "You should be ashamed of yourself. I've been worried sick about you losing everything in some harebrained scheme with Steven when we're virtually rich."

Now it was McDowell who stared.

"You're not disgusted with me?" he said incredulously.

"Disgusted? Heavens, no. Why should I be disgusted with you?"

"I thought. . . . Because it's. . . . Damn it, it's not . . . it's not legal. What we're doing."

"It's not as if you were hurting anyone," Florence said. A troubled look crossed her face. "Arthur, is it terribly dangerous being down there in the ground like that?"

"Oh, no," McDowell said, still shaken. "It's all shored up. Steve knows about that sort of thing."

"How much is he getting?"

"Half."

"Half? You discovered it, Arthur. Without you,

139

there'd be nothing." She sighed. "You never were a businessman."

"Steve's the driving force," McDowell protested, thinking, this really can't be happening. All the weeks I've been frightened to death Florence would find out. He was lightheaded with relief and beginning to appreciate the humor of the situation.

"He had to talk me into it," he continued. "And he was the one who knew how to find out if it was actually down there and did all the planning. I couldn't have done a thing without Steve."

"You're right," Florence admitted. "Steven certainly does deserve an equal share. The thought of all that money made me greedy for a minute. I hope you don't think I'm terrible."

"Oh, no," McDowell said quickly. "Not at all. Do you forgive me for not telling you?"

"Certainly. It was sweet of you to want to spare me knowing about it. Since you thought I'd be upset. But promise me one thing. Promise me you'll never deceive me again. You're someone I don't know when you do that."

"I promise."

McDowell felt physically lighter, as if he had laid down a great burden. If only he did not have Sussman's girl on his conscience, he would be completely at peace. Even that, he realized, was not nearly so important as he had imagined. He had meant nothing to the girl, nor she to him. Other married men did it all the time without anyone being hurt. The only reason it had been so traumatic for him was that it had ruined his perfect record of fidelity. Now that he knew how upsetting it could be he would never do anything like that again. The bond between him and Florence was, if anything, strengthened by the escapade. Of course, if Florence ever found out about it, that would be another story entirely.

"I wish there was something I could do to help," Florence said.

"I can see you down in that tunnel," McDowell said with a fond smile.

"I know I couldn't do that, Arthur. But there must be *something*."

McDowell knew she meant it. But what was there for her to do? It was grinding toil that took muscle and stamina.

"You could make our lunch," he said.

After the first few days they had stopped going to the neighboring restaurants. Not only was it a lot of trouble to get cleaned up, but also Sussman said it was better not to get too well acquainted in the neighborhood. They had been picking up hamburgers, hot dogs, tacos or burritos at fast food stands, seldom going to the same one two days running. McDowell had not minded that. He was always too weary to eat much or to care what he ate.

"Wonderful," said Florence. "I'll start planning some beautiful menus for you and Steven."

"Just sandwiches, please," McDowell said. "Anything more would be wasted on us. You'd think we'd be ravenous, but we aren't."

"I'm sure you know best," Florence said, disappointed.

When he picked up Sussman Saturday morning, he brought along a brown bag of sandwiches and cookies and a gallon Thermos of lemonade.

"Compliments of Florence," he said.

"You mean she not only let you off on Saturday but even fixed you a lunch?"

"Us a lunch," McDowell said. "Steve, I told her about the tunnel. It just all came out."

"You told her? You shouldn't have done that, Mac."

"Look, she's my wife, for Pete's sake. She had to find out sooner or later. And she's got as much at stake in this as I have."

"Wasn't she sore?" Sussman said. "Didn't she raise hell?"

"She made our lunch, didn't she? You know something, Steve? The only thing she was mad about was that I didn't let her in on it from the start. I never realized Florence was that interested in being rich."

"All women are that interested, amigo. Why should they be different from us men?"

Sussman's device for making the car self-operating was simple. It required only a line of two-by-ten

141

planks laid end to end up the middle of the shale floor to keep the car on course.

"When it starts to go off, the inside of the front wheel hits the side of the plank and straightens it out," Sussman explained.

He had bought a small bit and a special fitting for their electric drill. He drilled holes through the planks into the shale and then, with the special fitting, screwed square-headed bolts into the holes. It took only a few hours to lay a line of two-by-tens to the end of the tunnel. After they were down, Sussman went to the tunnel entrance and sent the car and wagon back to McDowell. It arrived without a hitch.

Before calling it a day, they made a test run with a load of material. McDowell sent the car back to Sussman, who filled the wagon with material and returned it. Again, it performed perfectly.

"This calls for a celebration," Sussman said. "You and Flo got anything on for tonight?"

"No. I've been too tired to go out nights. Even weekends."

"It's on then. How about dinner and the Horn?"

"Great. We'll pick you up at your place."

Florence was delighted with the idea.

"It seems like forever since we had a night out," she said.

Sussman was waiting out front when they arrived. Gloria was with him. McDowell felt acutely uncomfortable. It had not occurred to him Sussman would be bringing her. He wondered how he was going to get through the evening. He hoped Gloria would not let anything drop. And that he would be able to conceal his own uneasiness.

Gloria was wearing tight slacks and a knit top that poked out at the nipples. Sussman should not have let her dress like that, McDowell thought with a flash of irritation, knowing she was going out with Florence. Sussman opened the rear door of the station wagon and climbed in behind his date.

"Gloria, say hi to Florence and Arthur McDowell," he said.

"Hi," said Gloria.

"Flo and Mac, Gloria Stavros," Sussman said.

"How nice to meet you, Gloria," Florence said.

"Hello, Gloria," said McDowell, hoping he had achieved the proper tone.

"So you're Mac," Gloria said. "I've heard so much about you from Steve I almost think I already know you."

At Sussman's suggestion they went to El Coyote. McDowell worked hard to react to Gloria's presence the way any normal man would to a girl he'd just met with her endowments and who also happened to be his best friend's girlfriend. Gloria was perfectly at ease, conversing unselfconsciously with both McDowell and Florence, leaning with her chest against Sussman's arm, toying with his hand and once, to McDowell's discomfort, nibbling his ear. When she did that, McDowell felt Florence's foot nudging his under the table.

Later at the Horn after a couple of drinks on top of the margaritas at El Coyote, Gloria became more amorous, discomfiting Sussman not in the least but embarrassing McDowell. He could tell it made Florence uncomfortable, too. McDowell's embarrassment edged into irritation. Did she have to behave like that in front of Florence? Then he thought, am I put out because she's behaving like that in front of Florence or in front of me? Am I jealous? The thought was absurd. Whenever he saw any couple nuzzling like that in public, he had the same mingling of emotions. Embarrassment, irritation at being subjected to the spectacle and, yes, envy. Envy of the young man who would most certainly be in bed with the girl before the evening was over. No, he told himself firmly, it wasn't Sussman specifically he was jealous of. It was merely his old-fashioned prudery.

After they dropped Sussman and Gloria off at Sussman's apartment, neither McDowell nor Florence spoke for a while. McDowell was wondering if they were already in the hay. Gloria was so great in the shower she must be really fabulous in bed. To hell with that, he thought. Florence was all the woman he needed or wanted. More, in fact, now that he was always so bushed from working in the tunnel. He reached over and patted Florence's knee. She put her hand on his.

"She was darling, wasn't she?" Florence said.

"Yes," McDowell said casually. "I suppose she was."

"But a little . . . common, don't you think?"

"Well. . . ."

"I hope Steven isn't serious about her. It's all right sleeping with a girl like that, and she is fun, but I hope he isn't thinking about *marrying* her. Has he said anything to you?"

"No. He's never even mentioned her."

"Good. Then it can't be serious. I hope you don't think I'm being catty, Arthur. I'm sure she's a perfectly fine person in her own way. She just isn't right for Steven. He's so intelligent."

"No," said McDowell. "I don't think you're being catty."

"Do you want me to tell Bob the trip's postponed?"

"What? Oh, the Canada trip. No, I'll break it to him."

McDowell was relieved that Florence had dropped the subject of Gloria so abruptly.

Later, while making love to Florence, he found himself thinking of Sussman and Gloria in bed. He was more annoyed than ashamed. He concentrated on what he was doing, apparently to good effect, because Florence murmured, "I'm going to have to get you smashed more often."

Robert took the news about the trip hard but accepted McDowell's explanation that he was simply too busy to leave town just then. Next vacation, McDowell promised, they would take the entire summer off and go to Alaska or Europe, whichever Robert preferred.

"Could we go to Alaska *and* Europe?" Robert said, brightening.

"If that's what you'd like."

"It's a deal," said Robert.

He'd handled that pretty well, too, McDowell thought.

11

Sussman said they needed walkie-talkies so they could communicate between the basement and the back of the lengthening tunnel. McDowell thought it an excellent idea. With a walkie-talkie he would not feel so isolated when he was underground. Florence offered to get the money from their savings account and buy the equipment for them if Sussman would tell her exactly what he wanted and where to get it.

"Then you wouldn't have to take time off from the tunnel," she said. "And I can feel as if I'm helping, even if it's only a little."

When McDowell came home from work Tuesday—it was strange, he thought, how he considered it a job he went to now that Florence knew what was going on—Florence told him a Mr. Ulrich had tried to reach him several times.

"Franz Ulrich?" McDowell said, alarmed.

"He didn't give his first name. Who's Franz Ulrich?"

It must be the coin dealer, McDowell thought. How did Ulrich get his real name? And what did he want? It had to have something to do with the hooked necked eagle. How much did Ulrich know, if anything?

"Arthur," Florence said, "is something the matter?"

"He's the dealer I sold the coin to. How the devil did he find out who I was?"

"Maybe you should call him," Florence said anxiously. "He left his home number the last time he called and you still weren't here yet."

McDowell returned the call with Florence hovering at his elbow.

"Mr. Ulrich?" he said cautiously. "Franz Ulrich?"

"Correct," Ulrich replied. "To whom am I speaking?"

"Did you call 555-1345 and leave your number?" McDowell asked, still unwilling to give his name.

"Ah," said Ulrich. "Professor McDowell. Or do you prefer to be called James Ferguson?"

"I don't know what you're talking about."

"Oh, come now, Professor. The little car you drove away in was registered in your name."

"I lent it to a friend."

"Lent what to a friend?" Florence whispered. "What does he want?"

McDowell waved her away impatiently.

"Please, Professor," Ulrich said with a chuckle. "I went to UCLA and got an excellent description of you."

"What is it you want?" McDowell asked, realizing it was useless to pretend any longer.

"Frankly, I'm a bit curious about why you gave an assumed name. Even intrigued, one might say."

"That's my business," McDowell said.

"What's your business?" Florence whispered.

"I'd like to have a chat with you," said Ulrich.

"No," McDowell said.

"It might be to our mutual advantage," Ulrich said.

"I doubt that seriously."

"Why don't we have lunch tomorrow?" Ulrich said, unperturbed.

Perhaps he should, McDowell thought, to find out what Ulrich wanted, and what he knew or suspected.

"All right," he said.

"Excellent."

Ulrich suggested the Café Swiss on Rodeo.

"It's convenient, and I like the dining patio," he said. "Let's say noon, shall we? Any later there's a wait for a table."

"Very well," McDowell said, hanging up without saying good bye.

Florence was as indignant as she was alarmed when he told her what Ulrich had said.

"If he thinks he can muscle in on us, he's in for a big surprise," she said fiercely. "When you see him, you tell him in no uncertain terms we don't want anything to do with him."

McDowell called Sussman and told him about the conversation.

"I wonder how much he knows?" Sussman said, worried. "Maybe I ought to go with you. I'll know how to handle the son of a bitch."

"Don't be stupid!" McDowell snapped, resenting the insinuation he could not cope with the situation. "You want him to know there are two of us involved?"

"You're right," said Sussman. "Sorry. But look, Mac, don't let him pry anything out of you."

McDowell went to North Spring Street in the morning and put in a couple of hours' work before going home to clean up and change clothes. Sussman warned him again to be on his guard. When Florence did the same, McDowell glowered at her. He was fed up with their lack of confidence in his discretion.

Ulrich, who had been so unpleasant in his shop, could not have been more cordial.

"Delighted to see you, Professor," he said.

"Exactly what's on your mind, Mr. Ulrich?" McDowell demanded.

"We haven't even sat down yet," Ulrich protested.

The hostess conducted them to a table under a large umbrella in the walled-off patio at the rear of the café.

"Shall we have a drink, a bite of lunch, a little wine and then a nice little chat?" Ulrich said.

"I don't drink at lunch, I'm not hungry, and I don't feel particularly talkative," McDowell said.

He was being deliberately antagonistic to hide his anxiety. And it was not difficult to be antagonistic. Ulrich was being so charming it put his teeth on edge. What did the man know? McDowell wondered. What demands was he going to make?

When the waitress came to take their drink order, McDowell shook his head and Ulrich said, "I'd like a—"

"No drinks," McDowell interrupted. "Just bring the menu."

"Patience is not one of your more outstanding qualities, Professor," Ulrich said dryly. "I noticed that at our previous meeting."

In the past, McDowell had been a very patient man. It had only been since he started digging like a mole that he had changed, McDowell realized. But even before he changed, he would have found it hard to be patient with Ulrich. The son of a bitch was playing cat and mouse with him. Why couldn't he come out with it and say what was on his mind?

McDowell scanned the menu without interest. Wednesday's luncheon special was an open-face hot roast veal sandwich.

"I'll have the special," he said. "And iced tea."

"Why not one of their Swiss *specialités?*" Ulrich coaxed. He pronounced it "spece-e-alitays" in a most irritating manner. "And a bottle of the Neufchâtel?"

"You've got another half hour of my time," McDowell said. "Let's get on with it. What do you want?"

After the waitress left with their orders, Ulrich said, "When you came to my shop there was something . . . interesting about your manner. You were nervous. Defensive."

"You made me nervous. Are you always such a boor with your customers?"

"If I think it makes for a better bargain," Ulrich said, unabashed. "So I took your license number. Imagine my surprise when I discovered it was registered to Arthur McDowell, not James Ferguson. And I began to wonder. Why would a solid citizen, a professor of history no less, sell me an unusual coin under an assumed name?" He looked into McDowell's eyes. "Why?"

"I was selling it for James Ferguson."

"But you said it had been in your family."

"Did I? What of it?"

"I'm wondering if Mr. Ferguson has other coins he might like to dispose of through you."

"That was the only one."

"How can you be so sure?"

"Because he said so."

When the waitress brought their orders, McDowell discovered he had an appetite after all. The roast veal was excellent. Ulrich only picked at his food.

"If there were other coins, he might find me more generous," Ulrich said. "I am with regular customers, you know."

"There aren't."

"Would you mind telling me how you became involved?" Ulrich asked carefully.

He's wondering if there really is a James Ferguson

148

or if I was selling the gold piece for myself, McDowell thought.

"It's obvious, isn't it?" he said. "My field is Hispano-California history. Ferguson assumed I'd know something about old Mexican coins."

"He made quite a mistake, didn't he?" Ulrich said with a smile.

"Yes," McDowell said, thinking, he believed me.

"If your friend should ever tell you he has more Mexican gold, I'll still be interested," Ulrich said.

"I'll keep that in mind."

McDowell was in high spirits driving downtown. He found himself whistling a tune. It was one of Sussman's many favorites. "Release Me," as sung by Johnny Rodriguez. He stopped at the first convenient phone booth and called Florence. He had promised to do that.

"False alarm," he said cheerfully. "He thought my friend Ferguson might have more coins he could swindle me out of."

"Are you sure?" Florence said. "You know how gullible you are."

"Of course I'm sure," McDowell retorted.

He'd handled it exactly right. Why should she think he could not?

"I didn't mean gullible," Florence apologized. "I meant trusting. Oh, you went off without the walkie-talkies. Do you want me to bring them?"

"No. We keep the door locked and couldn't hear you if you knocked."

"Darn. I'm dying to see the tunnel."

"We'll give you a tour some Saturday," McDowell promised.

Sussman confessed he had accomplished less than usual during McDowell's absence.

"I was too uptight thinking about what that Ulrich dude had on his mind," he said.

McDowell told him what had been said in as great detail as he could recall.

"You blew it," Sussman said.

"What do you mean, I blew it?" McDowell demanded.

First Florence and now Sussman doubting him.

"You should have stuck him for a more expensive lunch," Sussman said, grinning. "Really, you did a hell of a job. I'm glad it was you dealing with him instead of me. I get hotheaded when I think somebody's trying to screw me."

McDowell felt a subtle change in their relationship. Before when there was a crisis, it had always been in connection with the work and Sussman had handled it. But this crisis, potentially more serious than any previous, he had taken care of. And better, Sussman had volunteered, than Sussman himself might have.

They began using the walkie-talkie Thursday. The tunnel man used it to inform the basement man a load was on its way out and the basement man would alert the tunnel man when the car and empty wagon was coming his way. When shoring was needed, the man in the tunnel called the outside man, who put the precut planks in the wagon and sent them back to him. The time saved enabled them to dig an extra half foot that day.

They found a note in the door when they locked up for the evening. It said simply, "Call Mr. Bevins at 626-9271 between 9 A.M. and 5 P.M."

"What the hell does this mean?" Sussman said, worried.

"Maybe he wants some ductwork," McDowell said.

"A customer is the last thing we need."

Though it was a few minutes after five, McDowell found a phone booth and called the number. Everyone was gone for the day, but the switchboard operator told him he was calling the Tax and Permit Division of the city Clerk's office.

"I wonder what the hell he wants?" Sussman said.

"Maybe we need a permit to operate a business," McDowell replied.

"Oh, Jesus. I wonder if they'll come in and look around?"

"I'll call in the morning and find out."

McDowell noticed they were both taking it for granted that he would handle Mr. Bevins. It pleased him. There was now a clear division of duties. Sussman was the troubleshooter in the basement, and he was the one for outside problems.

150

They usually began tunneling at eight thirty. Friday morning McDowell occupied himself in the basement for half an hour instead of taking his trick in the tunnel. He wanted to remain clean on the chance he would have to go to City Hall. He phoned Bevins from a booth promptly at nine. Bevins told him the North Spring Street Vent and Duct Company needed a permit to do business. And, he asked with some asperity, just how long had he been operating without one? McDowell explained he had just gone in business and had not known a permit was required. Bevins was skeptical.

"What kind of businessman are you, Mr.—?" he demanded.

"Atkinson," McDowell said. "Mr. Atkinson."

Atkinson was Florence's maiden name and the first alias that came to his mind.

"Anyone in business should know you need a city permit, Mr. Atkinson. And you pay a tax on gross receipts. You do keep sales records, I hope."

"To tell the truth, Mr. Bevins, I haven't had any sales. Yet. I just went in business."

"I can see why you didn't know you needed a permit," Bevins said. He sounded almost sympathetic. "If you come in today and pick one up, I'll see there's no penalty."

Before going to City Hall, McDowell went back to the basement to tell the anxiously waiting Sussman about his conversation with Bevins. He took what money Sussman had in his wallet.

The permit was not expensive, and between Sussman's money and his own he had enough to pay for it in cash. Bevins was more sympathetic than censorious.

"I hope you make it, Mr. Atkinson," he said. "That's not the greatest location in the world for a new business."

"We're finding that out," McDowell said.

When they finished tunneling for the week, Sussman said they had done thirty-two feet.

"Two more than last week," he said, "even though we were short-handed awhile two days. But we've got

151

to do better than that. We're still one hell of a long way from the Avila Adobe."

He showed McDowell where they were on the substructure map, a few feet from the curb line on the far side of Macy Street.

"Is that all we've gone?" McDowell said.

It was less than a quarter of the distance to the chest. To top things off, there was another note in the street door. This one said, "Don't you people want business? You're always closed. Leave a sign or something when you're open." There was no name on the note.

"This is getting to be too goddamn much," Sussman said. "Next thing you know, we'll have to start really making ducts."

"It would be easier than what we're doing," McDowell said.

"What'll we do?" Sussman said. "We can't sit around in the office waiting all day to tell some clown we don't want his business. What would he think, anyway?"

"We'd tell him something like we're filling a big contract and can't take any new business right now. You know, Steve, we really ought to have someone in the office. The longer we're here, the more of this sort of thing we'll get."

"We've got too much to do for one of us to fart around in the office," Sussman protested.

"Let me think about it over the weekend," McDowell said.

He lay awake that night thinking about the problem. Perhaps Sussman could rig up a doorbell that rang in the basement. The outside man could answer it. But that meant showing himself in coveralls caked with tunnel dirt and sand. That would look a bit strange for someone doing what they were supposed to be doing.

"Something's worrying you, isn't it?" Florence said. "Is it that Ulrich man? Did he really know something and you don't want to worry me with it?"

McDowell told her the problem.

"I could do that," Florence said. "I could sit in the office every day."

"You?" McDowell exclaimed, sitting up. "I don't want you getting mixed up in this. What if something happened and we got arrested?"

"Arrested for what?" Florence said. "Is it against the law to dig a tunnel?"

"Probably," McDowell said wryly. "If you don't have a permit."

"Really, Arthur, I could do it."

"What about shopping, and the housework, and Robert? Who'd look after Robert?"

"Bobby is perfectly able to look after himself. He knows how to get his own lunch, and he's hardly ever home during the day anyhow."

"I don't know."

"Let me *contribute*," Florence coaxed. "It needn't be all day. Something like ten to three or four. Then you wouldn't have to interrupt your work for every Tom, Dick and Harry."

"What would you do all that time?" McDowell asked, weakening.

"I could write letters," she said eagerly. "Needlepoint. Catch up on my reading. It would be like a vacation for me. The one we're not taking."

"I suppose we could get a sign that says 'Open ten A.M. to three P.M.,'" McDowell said. "It would explain why no one was in the office before and after those hours."

"You're an absolute darling," Florence said.

Sussman at first protested the arrangement.

"She might let something slip," he said. "She's not experienced at this kind of thing."

"Were we, when we started?" McDowell replied. "She's coming at ten. We'll see how she does today, and if we like her work, we'll keep her on. All right?"

"I know what you're up to," Sussman said. "You think if you give her a job, she'll come across."

A little before ten, McDowell went up to wait for her. She arrived five minutes late, not looking too happy.

"I had to put the station wagon in a parking lot," she said. "It's going to be expensive."

"We'll charge it to the business."

153

"And this neighborhood. You didn't tell me your building was so awful."

"You don't have to do this if you don't want to, sweetheart. It was your own idea."

"I want to. The way you're drudging away in that tunnel, what sort of wife would I be to complain about sitting in an office? Even if it is ugly and dirty." She looked around in distaste. "It's not air-conditioned," she said, as if just realizing it. "Poor dear, it really must be dreadful down in the basement."

She insisted on seeing the tunnel before taking up her station in the office. She was appalled by the dirt and incredible clutter in the basement.

"How do you get anything done?" she asked. "There's hardly room to turn around."

"Wait until you see the tunnel," McDowell replied. "This is like outer space."

He went in first and sent the car back for Florence. When she reached McDowell, she was close to hysteria. She clutched him and buried her face in his shoulder.

"It's so terrifying down here!" she gasped. "How do you stand it?"

"I'll take you back."

The car did not have enough power to move their combined weights. With Florence in it, and McDowell crouched in the wagon, it barely inched along.

"I'll have to send you out alone," he said. "Keep your eyes closed. Then it won't be so bad."

A few minutes later Sussman called him on the walkie-talkie to tell him Florence was a little shaky but in control of herself.

"I'll clean her up and send her upstairs," Sussman said.

Florence's voice came on.

"I'm all right now, Arthur," she said. "I'm sorry I was such a baby."

That Monday McDowell felt really comfortable in the tunnel for the first time. Finding himself able to reassure Florence had helped. And knowing she was upstairs helped even more. He no longer felt a sense of isolation. It was almost like being at home. Except, of course, he'd never worked like this at home. And once the tunnel was finished, he would never work like this anywhere.

There was one problem. Each time someone came into the office, Florence would rush down to report it. Now that she was there, they no longer kept the stair door bolted from the inside. There were more drop-ins than they had anticipated. Panhandlers, solicitors, tourists asking how to get to Chinatown or Olvera Street.

"I gave a dollar for refugee relief," Florence said on one of her visits to the basement. "Was that all right?"

"Yes," said McDowell. "But don't do it again. You'll have fund raisers and panhandlers running out of your ears."

The man who had left the note came by, and Florence hurried down to report she had done exactly as instructed, told him about the big contract that had them tied up for the next two or three months.

"Cool," said Sussman, who was in the basement at the time. "You'll find a raise in your next pay envelope."

Her last visit was at three.

"I'm going home now," she told McDowell. "But I really hate to. It's been so interesting. And I had a delicious lunch at the Glorious Dragon."

"Go," McDowell said quickly. "Robert needs you. Don't forget to lock the door behind you and hang the closed sign on the knob."

When they were loading the van for the last trip to Mulholland, Sussman said hesitantly, "Mac, do you think Flo ought to be running in and out of the basement all day?"

"No. It does disrupt things, doesn't it?"

"I'm glad you agree," Sussman said, relieved. "I wouldn't want to hurt her feelings."

"I'll talk to her about it tonight."

Florence took it well.

"I know I should stay put in the office," she said. "But I was just bursting to tell you everything that happened. And I adore watching you and Steven at work."

"You can come down three times a day," McDowell

said. "When you come to work, before you go to lunch and when you leave for the day."

"Or if there's an emergency," Florence said.

"Naturally."

Tuesday Florence wanted to go on a run to Mulholland with him, saying it was the only part of the operation she had not seen.

"I'm afraid not," McDowell said. "Did you ever stop to think how strange it would look if I had a beautiful, clean woman like you with me while I'm dumping dirt?"

"I'm not beautiful," Florence said fondly. "Except to you."

"Not only beautiful, but modest," McDowell said, patting her bottom. "Oh, hell, I got your slacks dirty."

"Any time," said Florence.

It was fortunate he did not take her. He was dumping a box of material into the ravine, at a different part from that where they had begun because the old site was beginning to look conspicuous, when he was arrested by a voice saying, "Hey, Mac."

He froze. What miserable luck to have someone who knew him catch him at this. How would he explain? He turned slowly, his mind racing. Facing him and looking severe was a uniformed highway patrolman. Oh, God, McDowell thought.

"Yeah?" he said, trying to sound like a laborer, whatever a laborer sounded like. Some of his brightest students over the years had worked summers as manual laborers.

"You got a permit to dump here?"

"A permit?"

Was there anything a man could do these days without a permit?

"That's what I said, Mac. Let's see it."

"You need a permit to dump on private property?"

"Private property?"

"That's what this is. The owner's paying me to fill in this ravine."

The highway patrolman walked to the edge and looked down into the ravine. McDowell thought he looked a terribly long time.

"You've got yourself a lifetime job, Mac," the highway patrolman said at last.

"Okay with me," said McDowell. "As long as he keeps payin'."

He watched the highway patrolman get in his car and drive off. His pulse did not begin slowing down until the car was out of sight. He calmed down on the long drive back to North Spring. He was even a little pleased it had happened. He had been frightened, but he had not panicked. He had handled it exactly right, as he had Ulrich and Bevins. The third-time instinct, or something, had saved him. McDowell felt he could face any future crisis with confidence. And he must instruct Sussman how to behave if Sussman was surprised getting rid of a vanload of tunnel material.

12

THAT week, perhaps cheered on by Florence's presence, they made record progress, thirty-four feet. As usual at the end of the week, Sussman showed McDowell their position on the substructure map. They had crossed Macy and were under the near edge of the big parking lot.

"It's still a long way to the Avila Adobe, isn't it?" McDowell said.

"At least we won't have to put in so much shoring now that we've crossed Macy," Sussman said. He looked at the calendar he'd hung on the wall. July was a superendowed girl wearing bikini bottoms and a seductive smile. He studied August and September, ignoring the half-draped ladies illustrating them. "If we can pick it up to seven feet a day, we'll get there in forty-seven working days. Little over nine weeks. Puts us into the last week of September. You know, Mac, we just might make it before the fall quarter starts. If nothing goes wrong."

He knocked on wood.

"You really think we can do seven feet a day?" McDowell said dubiously.

"We better bust our asses trying if we don't want the fall quarter to catch us."

"Maybe we should work longer hours."

Sussman gave him an incredulous look.

"Since when did you get to be such a glutton for work?" he demanded. "I remember when your fat ass was dragging after two easy sets of tennis."

"I suppose I'm in better shape now."

"You can say that again. This fucking tunnel is building you up while it's tearing me down. Why the hell is that?"

"I don't know. Diet, maybe. Florence is a nutrition nut. And maybe I get more rest than you do."

"You're not just a' bird turdin'. That goddamn Gloria. I'm gonna have to dump her."

McDowell felt a twinge. He hadn't thought much about her lately, and he'd rather not be reminded of her.

The next week they made their thirty-five feet. It put them almost across the tapering northeast corner of the parking lot.

"I knew we could do it," said Sussman. "I just hope we can keep it up."

"I hate to mention it, but we've got a little problem coming up Monday," McDowell said.

Sussman gave him a quizzical look.

"The August rent's due," said McDowell. "And James Ferguson is broke."

"Oh, Jesus. That's right."

"I'll try to scrape it up. We've still got five hundred in the savings account. And there must be something in the checking account. I know there's at least the seven fifty we didn't use to buy travelers' checks for the trip."

"It shouldn't all be on y'all's back," Sussman protested. "I'll try and raise some bread, too."

"I've been thinking," McDowell said.

"Better watch that. It softens the brain."

"We should push a little harder. The longer it takes, the bigger problem money becomes. And I'd really like to get this over with. Wouldn't you?"

"I suppose."

"Let's try a ten-hour day and see how it goes. We can always cut back if we have to."

"You're a fucking slave driver, you know that, Mac?"

They began working at seven thirty Monday morning instead of their former eight thirty.

On her way in, Florence closed out the savings account and withdrew another hundred from the checking account. She brought the six hundred dollars for the rent in cash, as instructed. They had been paying cash for everything so there would be no James Ferguson checks connected with the North Spring Street Vent and Duct Comapny.

"We have just enough to see us through until the fall quarter," Florence told McDowell when she turned over the money. "Will we be all right?"

"By the fall quarter we'll be rolling in wealth," McDowell said cheerfully.

He had not told her they still had to think about the September rent, the big power bills because of the electric hammer, the exhaust fan, the squirrel-cage pump and the tunnel lighting, and money for more lumber and ducting and the new tires Sussman said they needed for the van. Why should both of them worry?

They worked until five thirty instead of four thirty even though it meant hitting peak traffic on the final trip of the day to Mulholland. Though they faded toward the end of the day, they still managed eight feet for their best single day yet.

"If we can keep it up, we'll finish in seven weeks, won't we?" McDowell asked.

"About. But I don't know how many ten-hour days I can put in. My ass is really dragging."

"I was thinking about building up to twelve," McDowell said, half serious.

"Impossible. Nobody could put in twelve hours a day at this kind of work. Not even you."

Sussman was right, of course, McDowell thought. Like Sussman, he was not sure he could even maintain a ten-hour day consistently. If only it was not necessary to make those long trips out to Mulholland two and three times a day. It would mean two or three man-hours saved. An extra foot or two a day. Sussman had once suggested they hire a man for that. But they had agreed it would be impossible to keep him from getting curious about what they were doing. And what would they pay him with?

They did eight feet again Tuesday. Sussman checked the substructure map and said they were getting close to North Main.

"It'll slow us up some," he said. "We'll have to put up more shoring, the way we did under Macy. And look at this."

He showed McDowell the parallel lines on both sides of North Main.

"Water main, telephone lines, power conduit, sewer line, more telephone lines, Western Union lines, signal conduit, another power conduit. There's no indication of their depth, but I don't think they spell trouble. They should all be well above us. The only things that really go down are vaults and catch basins."

Wednesday morning, when McDowell was working in the tunnel, the electric hammer encountered unusual resistance. He put it aside and went to work with a pick and shovel. He had struck an obstruction of some sort. He recalled what Sussman had said about vaults and catch basins. But Sussman had said the substructure map didn't show any. McDowell slipped the light line from its hook in the overhead spreader and held the bulb in its wire cage close to the wall. He scrubbed at the surface with his gloved hand. There was brick under the crust of sand. He called Sussman on the walkie-talkie.

"We've run into a brick wall," he said.

"Cut the crap, Mac."

"I mean it. There's a goddamn brick wall down here."

"Just a minute. I'll check the map."

When Sussman came back on he said, "Nothing on the substructure map. It could be an old foundation. Shit. That's all we need."

"What'll I do?" McDowell asked helplessly.

He did not like the sensation. It had been some time since he had felt helpless.

160

"Sit tight. And send the car back."

McDowell started the car back and stretched out on the floor of the tunnel. At least he was getting a few minutes rest. Sussman brought chisels and a sledgehammer with him.

"It's a brick wall, all right," Sussman said.

"I told you it was a brick wall, damn it."

"It's got a little curve to it. Could be a cistern from the old days. Give me a little room."

McDowell backed off a few feet. Sussman took a firm grip on the sledgehammer and started battering the brick wall. Nothing happened at first, then the old mortar between the bricks gave way. A gush of water shot out, driving Sussman against McDowell.

"Jesus Christ!" Sussman yelled.

For a moment McDowell was petrified with fear. The water was up to his waist. With a cry, he tried to stand erect, forgetting in his panic he was in a tunnel only four feet high. His hard hat smashed against a spreader. He fell backward over the wagon. The steel rim bit into his back. There was water in the wagon. Oh, God, he thought, we're going to drown. Why did I ever tell Sussman about that goddamned letter?

"It's caving in!" Sussman cried. "I'm stuck!"

The light was still burning back in its hook on the spreader. The water had not reached that high. Sussman lay face up, his torso propped on his elbows. He was buried to the waist in mud. His head craned upward, inches above the dark water, his face a mask of mud. Water still poured from the broken wall but in much diminished volume. McDowell stopped his frantic backward scramble and crawled to him through the mud and gravel. His claustrophobia, so long dormant, returned in full cry. He shut his eyes tight against the threatening earth and reached for Sussman. His hands closed on Sussman's shoulders. He pulled, but Sussman did not budge.

"Hurry!" Susman cried.

McDowell opened his eyes and clasped Sussman under the arms, heaving back with all his strength. Sussman came free with a sucking noise, like a cork leaving a bottle. McDowell closed his eyes again and

161

dragged him back, pushing the car and wagon ahead of them, until there was only an inch or so of water at the bottom of the tunnel. Then he huddled into a ball, breathing heavily.

"Thanks," Sussman said. "I needed that."

How could he joke at a time like this? McDowell thought.

"Are you all right?" he said unevenly.

"Just scared shitless."

"Let's get out of here."

"You go. I want to check the carnage."

"You want to be buried alive?" McDowell demanded.

"The shoring's holding. Back this far, anyhow."

"What was it we hit?"

"A cistern, I think. Or a catch basin. Put in so long ago it's not on our map. You go on back. I'll be okay."

McDowell had to push the car and wagon ahead of him. The water had ruined the car's electric motor. He waited for Sussman in the basement. He wanted to be sure Sussman made it out safely, and he was unwilling, in his present state of mind, to go upstairs and tell Florence what had happened. Sussman emerged looking glum.

"Could be worse, I guess," he said. "But we lost about five feet of tunnel. And mud and water for thirty, forty yards back. God knows how long it'll take to clean it up."

"That's all we need." McDowell groaned.

"At least we're alive, amigo. What if it had been a water main?"

Florence paled when McDowell came up to tell her, covered with mud and scum.

"It's all right," he said. "It's all over."

"What in the world happened?"

"We hit a little water."

"Steven. Is he all right?"

McDowell nodded wearily. He had never felt so tired, not even during the worst early days of digging. He did not see how he could face the tunnel again, knowing he must. But not today, he thought. That was too much to ask.

Sussman agreed.

"We've got to let it dry out anyhow," he said. "We'll start off fresh in the morning."

To expedite the drying process, they left the tunnel lights burning for what heat they gave off and let the exhaust fan and squirrel-cage pump run overnight to keep the air circulating. It took all Thursday and Friday to clean up the tunnel, clear away the five blocked feet and put in solid shoring where the ceiling had fallen in next to the cistern wall. They broke a hole in the cistern the same dimensions as the tunnel. Sussman crawled through it with the ceiling light.

"Jesus!" McDowell heard him cry.

"What is it?" McDowell said.

"Come in here."

McDowell crawled through the hole.

"Look," said Sussman. "Over there."

To one side, protruding from the silt of perhaps a hundred years or more, was a huddle of bones and, unmistakably, a human skull.

"God," McDowell whispered.

"What'll we do about it? I can't go by every day and see it lying there."

"I wonder who it was?"

"What does it matter now?" Sussman demanded.

"I suppose I think in footnotes. An occupational disease."

They decided to leave the skeleton where it was but to cover it with material from the tunnel.

"It wasn't that bad a break after all," Sussman said. "Hitting the cistern. It's gonna save us seven feet of digging. And we can stack one hell of a lot of tunnel material against the sides. Save us some trips to Mulholland."

But first, he said, they would have to shore up the cistern. The cistern was just over seven feet high, with a brick top. That meant there was nothing between them and the parking lot but a few feet of earth.

"It's been holding all these years," McDowell protested.

"We're punching through the other side, too. Those two big holes can't help but weaken the walls. You want the parking lot coming down on us?" He shone

163

the light up at the ceiling. "We can shore it up in maybe a half day Monday."

"Why wait until Monday? The last two and a half days have been like a vacation. No heavy digging and hauling."

"Yassuh, boss," Sussman said with a sigh, then, more businesslike: "We'll need some eight-by-eights for the supporting beams. I'll use three-by-ten stuff for crossbeams. And we need a new walkie-talkie, electric hammer and car. The water did 'em in."

"What'll we do for money?"

It was so frustrating, McDowell thought, churning, having to worry about a few dollars when there was a fortune less than three hundred feet away.

"Don't worry about it," Sussman said. "I've got bread."

"You? Where'd you get money?"

"Sold my stereo."

"You sold your stereo!"

"What else did I have? I tried selling my beautiful body, but every chick in the apartment said there was more of that stuff lying around free than they knew what to do with."

"What did Gloria have to say about that?" McDowell said with a laugh.

"Gloria who?" Sussman said, blank-faced.

McDowell wondered if that meant Sussman had dumped her, as he said he intended. If Sussman wasn't seeing her anymore. . . . He put the notion resolutely out of his mind.

Saturday they took out the brick floor of the cistern to preserve the tunnel's level shale bottom. They covered the skeleton with the rubble. Having ample room in which to work, it was not difficult to wedge three-by-tens across the top of the cistern with the eight-by-eights Sussman had bought that morning. That done, Sussman was ready to call it a day.

"We're under the sidewalk on the west side of North Main," he said. "Right at two hundred feet."

"It's not even two o'clock yet," McDowell protested. "Let's punch through the other side before we knock off."

"I liked you better when I had to hold you up after a couple sets of tennis," Sussman growled.

They used the new electric hammer to take out the two-by-four by two-and-a-half-foot section of the far side of the cistern and added the bricks to the pile covering the skeleton. When this was all over, McDowell thought, perhaps he would make a search of old records and documents for a mysterious disappearance. He would have the means and the leisure. It would be challenging to try to identify the owner of those long-hidden bones. Only to satisfy his own curiosity, of course, because he could not tell anyone about it.

The following week they put in five consecutive ten-hour days unmarred by interruptions. Despite being obliged to put in extra shoring because they were under North Main Street, they established another new one-week record. They dug thirty-nine feet, a scant foot short of averaging eight feet a day. They passed under the lines and conduits on the west side of North Main without incident. As Sussman had surmised, none of them was buried deep enough to interfere with their work.

Nevertheless, McDowell was dispirited. By the end of the week he and Sussman were so completely drained physically that he was obliged to confess they could not maintain a ten-hour workday. He agreed reluctantly to cut back to nine.

It had taken them from June 21 to August 12 to dig only a few feet more than halfway to the Avila gold. More than seven weeks. Even considering the unexpected delays they had encountered, and their increased efficiency now, and even if by some chance they could maintain an eight-foot-a-day pace on the nine-hour-a-day schedule, they would still be at it another six weeks. Six long weeks, and that only if they ran smack into the chest, which Sussman had said was unlikely. It would take a surface reference, he had said. That would add more time. And suppose they encountered further obstacles? Another cistern? A forgotten building foundation? It might be seven weeks, or even eight. If the digging dragged out that

165

long, it would definitely put them into the fall quarter and mean working nights and weekends.

They should have realized it was too much to be expected of just two men. Sussman should have, at any rate, because he was an engineer. They should have had three men instead of two even if it meant sharing the gold pieces. A third of the hoard was still a fortune. And they would have had someone to share expenses.

But, McDowell thought, they had come this far alone, and however great the temptation to seek help, it would be foolish to do so now that they were halfway home. They would have to stick it out even though the past seven weeks seemed more like months and the next six stretched out ahead into infinity. He remembered how, as a child, before he developed his interest in scholarship, the remainder of the school year after Christmas vacation had seemed endless. And so, now, did the next six weeks. Or was it seven or even eight?

Sussman apparently entertained similar thoughts. They had planned on a celebration when they reached the halfway mark, but he did not mention it when they parted for the weekend. Nor did McDowell remind him of it. He was in no mood for a celebration. He only hoped a weekend of rest would restore his spirits as well as his body.

Monday morning he lay in bed half an hour longer than he had intended, reluctant to begin a new week in the bowels of the earth. Robert, up earlier than usual, had breakfast with his parents, and McDowell yelled at him for drinking out of the orange juice bottle. Yelling at Robert, or at anyone for that matter, was something McDowell rarely did. And Florence was snappish as well. She was growing disenchanted with sitting alone in the office day after day.

"And all those Mexican and Chinese restaurants for lunch," she complained. "And those delicious almond cookies so cheap at Amay's on New High Street. This morning my weight was up another half pound. That's more than four pounds since I started helping out."

This rather long outburst came after Robert had

left the breakfast table. They had told him she was helping his father with some work, letting him assume it was at the university. They tried never to lie to him unless it was absolutely necessary. He knew all the details of procreation and the definitions of various words he had heard from his schoolmates over the years or overheard in the conversations of adults.

"Maybe you'd like to change places with me," McDowell said irritably. "Look, Florence, it was your idea to watch the office."

"I'm sorry, Arthur," she said contritely. "Complaining when it's you who's working so hard. But those restaurants are so tempting. And it does break up the day to go out to lunch. I'll simply have to resist the temptation."

"I'm the one should apologize," McDowell said, getting up from the table and kissing her forehead. "I've been in such a foul mood the whole weekend." He reached down and put his arms around her. "And don't worry aboout those extra pounds. They make you that much more sexy."

That, they both knew, was stretching things a bit. Except on weekends McDowell had been too weary to touch her for days at a time. Sometimes he wondered if even Gloria Stavros could interest him these days.

He worked grimly Monday, trying not to think about how many similar days lay ahead. What was it the Alcoholics Anonymous people had said in that old JP Miller movie he'd seen on TV, *Days of Wine and Roses?* One day at a time. That was the way he'd have to take it. One day at a time. But it was difficult not to think about the day after, and the day after that, and the weeks after that. For the first time McDowell fully understood how an alcoholic felt contemplating a life without another drink. It simply was not human nature to think in terms of one day at a time.

Sussman called him on the walkie-talkie and said, "Mac, listen to this."

Music came over the receiver. Another of Sussman's damned country favorites. "I Really Don't Want to Know."

167

Stupid song, McDowell thought. And Sussman thought it true and bittersweet. Sussman, of all people. Sussman who went from girl to girl like a stallion. But he heard the song through. It did take his mind off the tunnel. Sussman's voice came on again.

"You know who can really sing the wheels off that?" he demanded. "Andy Williams. Andy fuckin' Williams of all people."

"What's wrong with Andy Williams?" McDowell demanded with more heat than the occasion merited.

Andy Williams happened to be one of his favorite singers. A hell of a lot better than any of those bumpkins Sussman was always insisting he listen to. Except perhaps Tom T. Hall and Ray Price. And Roy Clark. And possibly Waylon Jennings. God, McDowell thought, Sussman not only had sentenced him to life in the mines, but had even corrupted his taste in music.

"Who said anything was wrong with Andy Williams?" Sussman retorted. "You surly bastard. Did I say he sang the wheels off it or didn't I?"

"You said he sang the wheels off it," McDowell acknowledged.

He was behaving like a schoolboy. Yelling at Robert, yelling at Sussman, being sarcastic with Florence. This damned tunnel was changing his whole personality.

"Hey, Steve," he said. "I'm sorry."

He went back to work, thinking he should lose his temper more often. At least it took his mind off the tunnel for a little while.

McDowell went directly home that afternoon. Sussman went to Mulholland to dump a load before going to his apartment. McDowell had showered and changed into clean clothes when Sussman phoned him.

"Mac," he said, agitated, "we've got a problem."

"What kind of problem?"

"James Ferguson got a letter from Franz Ulrich."

"How could that be?"

"It was with my other mail. Where the hell could he have got the address? You didn't. . . ."

"What kind of damn fool do you take me for?" McDowell interrupted. "I'll be right over."

He told Florence he had to see Sussman about a problem coming up in the digging next day, not wanting to alarm her. Sussman met him at the door with the letter and a can of beer.

Dear Mr. Ferguson [the letter said]. Your friend, Professor Arthur McDowell, may or may not have told you of my interest in rare gold coins and of the resources at my disposal to acquire them. And I am wondering if Professor McDowell relayed to you my suggestions some days ago when we had lunch together. On the chance he did not, may I tell you this? I would be most interested in any other coins you may have and assure you of the utmost discretion in any dealings we may have. And, it goes without saying, you will not be displeased with the financial arrangements. I must admit to taking a little advantage of Professor McDowell in my dealing with him. He was obviously unsure of himself, and it is a cruel fact of this business that one makes the best bargain possible. In your case, however, I can assure you of the best possible prices. I am puzzled by your choice of Professor McDowell to dispose of the coin for you. That, of course, is your business, and it is not my nature to pry into the affairs of my customers. If, as I hope, you have other coins, please contact me. My card is enclosed, with my home number as well as my business phone.

"The son of a bitch!" McDowell said.

He was rankled both by Ulrich's persistence and by Ulrich's derogatory remarks about his inadequacy.

"How did he get this address?" Sussman demanded.

"What address did you give the bank for James Ferguson?"

"This address."

"Then he must have got it from the bank. Why didn't you give a fake address to the bank?"

"I had to give 'em a real address. You want the statements going back undeliverable? I guess I could have taken a post office box, but I didn't think about it."

169

"Neither did I," McDowell said.

"How would Ulrich know what bank James Ferguson had an account with anyhow? He couldn't call every bank in L.A."

"You have any canceled checks from the Ferguson account, Steve?"

"Somewhere. Why?"

"Get one."

Sussman rummaged through several drawers and located a bank statement with a few canceled checks. They were all made out to cash.

"You auditing me or something, amigo?" he asked. "You'll find every dime went for our expenses."

"Don't be stupid. I only want to have a look at the back of one of them. You did deposit Ulrich's check in the Ferguson account, didn't you?"

"Yeah. Where else?"

"That's how he identified the bank. Look."

He showed Sussman the back of a canceled check. It was stamped with the name of the bank through which it had passed.

"When Ulrich got his canceled check back, all he had to do was look at the back to find out where it was deposited," McDowell said.

"I guess I goofed. I should have taken it to his bank and cashed it."

"No, you did the right thing, Steve. If you'd gone to his bank they would have wanted identification. You have an ID for James Ferguson?"

"You know something, Mac? You're getting damn shrewd in your old age."

"If Ulrich doesn't get an answer, his next step may be to come here personally. And he'll find Steve Sussman lives at this address, not James Ferguson. Then he'll have both our names. And he'll wonder why you're using an alias and what our connection is."

"That's right," Sussman said, worried. "What'll we do?"

"James Ferguson writes him a letter. Tell him you wish you had more, but that was the only coin you had. I told him that at lunch, and maybe he'll believe it when you corroborate it."

"Corroborate," Sussman said. "You sound just like a college professor."

"And tell him in view of the way things worked out you wish you had brought it in yourself instead of sending me. Tell him the reason you didn't was that you assumed I'd know all about old Mexican coins. That I was supposed to be a leading authority on the period. That supports what I told him, too. It should get him off our backs once and for all."

"Clever, clever."

"You want me to write it for you?"

"I can take care of it, for Christ's sake," Sussman said sharply.

How times have changed, McDowell thought. Only a few weeks ago it was Sussman offering to handle things and him being touchy.

Sussman wrote the letter and they went over it together, agreeing it should serve their purpose admirably.

On Wednesday, Sussman was late getting back from a trip to Mulholland. McDowell came out of the tunnel several times to see if he had returned and for some reason had not checked in by walkie-talkie. Florence came down to the basement, worried.

"Do you think he's had an accident?" she asked.

"He probably stopped for lumber," McDowell said. "We're getting low. Go back upstairs and don't worry."

He left a note by the walkie-talkie asking Sussman to call him as soon as he returned. When at last Sussman did so, his voice was strange.

"Mac," he said, "you better come out here."

McDowell stretched out on the electric car and started it back toward the entrance. What was wrong? he wondered. Had Ulrich or someone found out about the tunnel?

Sussman's nose was puffy; there was a Band-Aid on his forehead and a bruise on his cheek just under the eye.

"What happened to you?" McDowell demanded.

Sussman looked at him a moment before replying. "I totaled the van," he said.

171

13

"TOTALED the van?" McDowell said, aghast.

More time lost, God knew how much. And where was the money coming from for a replacement? He despised himself because these were the first thoughts to spring to mind. He should be worrying about Sussman, not money and lost time.

"Are you all right?" he asked belatedly.

"Just a few cuts and bruises."

On his way back from Mulholland the transmission had gone out on the freeway. Sussman had tried to edge over to the emergency parking lane and a speeding cement truck, attempting to pass on the right side, plowed into the van.

"Was the other driver hurt?" McDowell said. "Was there any police action?"

"No, thank God. The dude was scared shitless. He was speeding and driving with a suspended license. He said if I didn't report it, he'd pay for the van."

"That's something," McDowell said, relieved. "We won't waste a lot of time getting another van."

"At ten bucks a week?" Sussman said bitterly. "That's what he said he could afford."

"Wasn't he insured? Wasn't the company he drives for?"

"What difference does that make? Can you see us trying to collect? Insurance people asking questions. And it would take months to get our money, if ever."

"Where's the van now? Are you sure it's hopeless?"

"It's hopeless, all right. I had it towed to a wrecking yard. Then I hitched a ride to my apartment for my bike and got here as quick as I could."

They sat down on the edge of the entrance hole, their legs dangling, and stared wordlessly into the pit.

"So what do we do for a van?" Sussman said at last.

What was his collection of books and documents worth? McDowell wondered. A few thousand at most. And they were not the sort of thing one could sell overnight. The last time he had looked at the market quotation on their few shares of utilities stock, the shares had been worth eleven or twelve hundred dollars. Not enough for a van. And in less than three weeks the September rent was due. There were Robert's college fund savings bonds. They had bought a twenty-five-dollar bond every month since his birth. Eighteen seventy-five a month for twelve years. Two years' worth were past maturity and drawing extra interest. He would assume the average was twenty-two dollars a bond by now.

"Steve," he said, "what's twenty-two times twelve times twelve?"

Steve was good at doing arithmetic in his head.

"Thirty-one hundred sixty-eight," Sussman said after a moment. "Why?"

"We've got that much in Robert's college fund."

"You wouldn't . . ." Sussman said, shocked.

"Might have to. As a last resort. It's the only way I know to raise quick money. Unless we take a second trust on the house. But that would take time, wouldn't it?"

"You're really antsy to get that chest, aren't you? You've really got gold fever."

"It's not exactly the money," McDowell said, which was true. The gold wasn't real to him yet, nor would it be until it was actually in their hands. "It's knowing I'm going to be down in that tunnel day after day after day. I can't even get away from it at night. Sometimes I dream I'm digging."

"Me, too. So I guess it's Robert's college fund."

"I'll talk to Florence about it tonight. No, right now."

Why waste a whole afternoon? he thought.

"I'll get back in the tunnel," Sussman said. "We can let the material pile up until we have the new van."

"Good idea," McDowell replied, knowing he should have at least asked Sussman if he felt up to the work before agreeing so readily. "Are you sure you're all right?"

"Never felt worse. But I'd rather be down in the hole digging with my back broken than up there asking Florence to part with Bobby's college fund."

173

"She'll understand. Florence is in this as much as we are."

But Sussman proved the better prophet.

"No," Florence said flatly. "Bobby's college fund is one thing we'll never touch. We made a sacred vow we'd never touch it no matter what."

"A sacred vow?" McDowell protested. "I don't remember making a sacred vow. When we got married, we made a sacred vow."

"You know very well what I mean, Arthur."

"But in a couple of months it'll be chicken feed. We'll be able to send Robert to any college in the country. And put him in the best private school before that, if we want to."

"What if the coins aren't there?"

"What do you mean, what if they aren't there? We know they're there. Where do you think the eight escudos came from?"

"Maybe that's all there was."

"But the chest was there, too. We had to drill through it. There was rotted wood on the end of the bit. I told you that."

"I know you did."

"So admit we know they're there."

"All right," Florence snapped. "We know they're there."

"Well then?" McDowell said triumphantly.

"But what if they aren't?"

"Jesus Christ!" McDowell cried, throwing up his hands in defeat. "How about borrowing money on the house then?"

It could mean a long delay. There was just so much room for material in the basement; then they would have to stop digging until they had money for the new van. Every week's delay before the fall semester began would add several weeks of night and weekend work. But what could he do?

"A second mortgage on our house?" Florence said. "The payments are already as much as we can manage, and what—"

"If it's not there," McDowell said, completing the sentence for her.

"You could sell your collection," Florence said helpfully. "Or your little car."

"I've already considered that. The car's not worth much, and it could take weeks to sell off my collection. And it still wouldn't bring enough to make a dent in our expenses."

"You'll think of something," Florence said confidently. "You always do."

"Thanks for the vote of confidence," McDowell said sourly.

He called Sussman on the walkie-talkie when he got back to the basement.

"How'd it go?" Sussman said anxiously.

"You were right," McDowell admitted. "We're in trouble."

While he was waiting for Sussman to come out of the tunnel, McDowell made a reluctant decision. Now was the time to recruit another man. A man with money. A man with money who would also be useful in the tunnel. With three men working they could finish in a month, well before the fall quarter began. And they would not have to drive themselves as hard as they had been doing and worry constantly about money. Totaling the van might prove to have been for the best. It was forcing them to take in someone else, which they should have done weeks ago, when the magnitude of the task had become obvious. They would not have to cut him in for a third, only a small percentage, perhaps just a cash guarantee. They'd discovered the chest, done all the planning and more than half the labor. A cash guarantee should be enough. A few thousand dollars would not make a dent in the Avila gold. All they needed was the right man. Someone reliable, and with money. But who?

Sussman listened patiently to McDowell's proposal, his expression changing gradually from outright rejection to guarded approval.

"And you really think we wouldn't have to cut him in for a third of the action?" he asked when McDowell had finished.

"I told you, he wouldn't be a full partner. He couldn't expect that, now that we're so far along. The way I see it, our only problem is finding someone with money we can trust."

"I know," Sussman said solemnly. "You can't hardly find a man with money you can trust."

"I'm in no mood for jokes," McDowell said, still nursing a residue of exasperation from his encounter with Florence.

"I may know the right man."

"Who?"

"Colonel Pike."

"Colonel Pike?"

The name sounded faintly familiar.

"Bill Pike," said Sussman. "Professor of air science. The Air Force ROTC dude."

McDowell placed him now. A short, wiry man, middle-aged, with crew-cut salt-and-pepper hair. One of the few men on campus, student or faculty, with such a haircut. He carried himself absolutely straight, shoulders back, stomach in, as if to make it abundantly clear he was a military man, not one of your faculty pedants.

"He must be in his fifties," McDowell protested. "What do we want with someone that old? We need a young man who can work along with us."

"He's in tremendous shape. He jogs. Plays handball like a fiend."

"What makes you think a man like that would get himself involved in the sort of thing we're doing? A career officer."

"He'd do it if he thought there was bread in it. And a little excitement."

"How do you know so much about Colonel Pike?"

"I used to take out his daughter. He'd bend my ear fifteen, twenty minutes every time I picked her up. While he was checking me out to see if my shoes were shined and all my buttons buttoned."

"Tell me something, Steve, are there any girls you've missed?"

"A few. But I'm still a young man. And something else about Pike. He's done some tunneling. In World War Two."

"Really?"

"Would I shit you, amigo? You remember that flick

176

The Great Escape? All those prisoners tunneling out of Stalag Something in Germany? He was in on that."

"Why didn't you mention him before?" McDowell said. "Back when we first decided to go after the chest. Think how much help he'd have been."

"Never entered my mind we needed help. Has there been anything I couldn't handle?"

"I didn't mean it that way," McDowell said quickly. Artists were supposed to be temperamental, he knew, but engineers?

"And I hadn't been seeing Henrietta for a while," Sussman continued. "That's his daughter."

"Has he got the cash to lay out?"

"I'd say he's got the first dime he ever earned and two more the dime earned for him."

"If he's so well off, why would he want in on a shady deal like this?"

"To get better off. And for the excitement. Look, I know the dude. That was one thing he was always talking about, how great it was being in World War Two. With the Korean War a close second. And what a pain in the ass it is to be put out to pasture on a college campus. The only reason he hasn't retired and gone into something lively is he keeps hoping there'll be another war and he'll get his star. He thinks it was a conspiracy he didn't get it during Vietnam."

"He told you that?"

"Not in those exact words. But that's the impression I got."

"Call him tonight," McDowell said. "Let's not waste any more time than we have to."

"There's only one thing," Sussman said hesitantly. "We're not exactly what you'd call asshole buddies right now. You know how it is."

"No, I don't. How is it?"

"Henny had marriage on her mind, and I guess he got the impression it was on my mind, too. So when I quit taking her out. . . . "

"So what other candidates do you have for us, Casanova?" McDowell said, disappointed.

"Oh, he'll go for it. Don't worry about that, Mac. Only you'll have to do the talking. But don't worry, I'll tell you how to handle him."

177

"I'll know how to handle him."

"All right," Sussman said placatingly. "All right. I'll call him and set up a meeting."

"Tonight. I want it settled tonight."

"Tonight it is. I sure hope Henny's out on a date."

"I take it the parting wasn't exactly amicable."

"Not exactly."

Florence was not enthusiastic about bringing in an outsider. "After you and Steven have done practically all the work, he wants to step in and reap the profits," she said indignantly.

"You're talking as if he's trying to horn in," McDowell said. "We're making the overtures, for God's sake."

"Just don't let him take advantage of you, Arthur. That's all I ask."

"I promise," McDowell said with a sigh.

He picked Sussman up in the TR4. Pike lived in a good section of Brentwood. His one-story white brick house was on an oversize well-landscaped lot with trees, shrubs and flowers. McDowell wondered how much he had to pay his gardener. A hell of a lot more than the thirty-five dollars he paid Mr. Kuwahara, he thought. The house and grounds gave him pause. Why would a man who could afford that sort of place want to crawl around in a tunnel? For the excitement, Sussman had said. But there was no excitement in digging a tunnel. Just sheer, endless drudgery. But he was overlooking what lay at the end of the tunnel, McDowell realized. A fortune in gold coins. Any man with a spark of adventure in his makeup would be intrigued by buried treasure. Look what it had done to him, a stick-in-the-mud history teacher. And according to Sussman, Pike had a good deal more than a spark of adventure.

A girl answered the doorbell. "Well," she said frostily. "If it isn't the renowned Steven Sussman."

"Hi, Henny," Sussman said amiably.

McDowell admired his suavity.

"This is Professor McDowell," Sussman said.

"I know," Miss Pike replied. "How do you do, Professor. The colonel's in his study. I believe Mr. Sussman knows the way."

She was taller than McDowell had expected, Pike being a rather short man. She was well groomed, unusually so, McDowell thought, for a young woman these days. She was good-looking in a quiet way, not the sort he thought would have appealed to Sussman. The large, round glasses she wore made her no less attractive. At the moment, there was something implacable in the gray eyes behind the glasses. She wore a plain white shirt with short sleeves and a yellow skirt, not too short. McDowell found that a welcome relief from jeans and shirttails. And she had one heck of a figure, though she did not flaunt it. Too bad Sussman had lacked the sense to know a good thing when he saw it. McDowell was sure Florence would have approved of Miss Pike, too.

He wondered if she was always so aloof with strangers or if it was only because he came with Sussman. The latter, no doubt. She appeared too decent to be so curt with a guest in her father's house.

"Looks like she's still sore at me," Sussman said as he led McDowell through a living room and formal dining room done in excellent taste.

Colonel Pike was sitting behind a large carved desk in his study. The top of the desk was bare except for a model of a silver four-engine airplane. A B-17 or B-29, McDowell guessed. He was not familiar with plane types. The colonel rose and came to meet them when they entered the room.

"It's a pleasure to meet you, Professor McDowell," he said, extending his hand. "I'm aware of your studies in California history. Hello, Sussman," he added, his voice losing warmth.

"Colonel," Sussman replied with, McDowell thought, a parody of a military nod. Sussman had better watch that stuff.

Pike shook McDowell's hand but not Sussman's. He waved them to a heavy black couch and returned to his seat behind the desk. The couch was leather and deeply cushioned. McDowell sank into it gratefully as it enfolded and eased his work-weary muscles. When he had money, he would get one like it. It would go well in the real library he intended having in the new house. Pike's chair, he noticed, did not match the couch. It was of wood, ample, glossy and solid. The colonel, he decided, was one of those men who disdained too much ease and comfort. Which was fine. He would not find too much of that in the tunnel.

The colonel looked at him expectantly, appearing quite relaxed for a man sitting at attention. McDowell was too interested in the colonel's study to begin at once, and he was also hoping Pike would speak first and give him an opening. There were maps on the walls, some marked with red and black lines and stuck with pins of various colors and tiny flags; framed photographs, mostly of Colonel Pike in uniform standing by airplanes alone or in the company of men in flying garb, and a large photograph, a full-face view of a very young, grim-faced and unshaved Pike.

Following his gaze, Pike said, "My prisoner of war ID photo. Blown up."

"You should see the print he had it blown up from," Sussman said helpfully. "No bigger than a postage stamp."

"The goons made excellent cameras," Pike said.

"Goons are what the prisoners called Germans," Sussman explained.

"I'm sure Professor McDowell is not interested in that, Sussman," Pike said coldly, his eyes and tone exactly like his daughter's when she had let them in.

"As a matter of fact I find it very interesting," McDowell said, his eyes straying to an almost life-size oil painting of a handsome blond man in Air Force blue, with stars on his shoulders.

"Van," said Pike almost reverently. "Hoyt Vandenberg."

"Of course," McDowell murmured.

General Vandenberg, he recalled, had been someone very big in the Air Force many years ago.

"Mr. Sussman said you had a proposition you thought might interest me," Pike said. "I must say he was rather closed-mouthed about the details, for Sussman."

He glanced disdainfully at Sussman as he said it. Sussman appeared unperturbed, sprawling on the couch with his hands in his pockets. The least Sussman could do while they were trying to recruit Pike was to avoid antagonizing him, McDowell thought. He gave Sussman a disapproving look, and Sussman sat up.

"That is because it is my proposition, not his," McDowell said.

"So he said," Pike replied. "Which is the only reason I agreed to see you."

He should not be too devious with Pike, McDowell thought. The man was direct and would wish to be dealt with in the same fashion.

"Colonel," he said, "how do you feel about buried treasure? On public property?"

"That would depend on a number of things," Pike said. "If you're asking for a contribution to a research project, I'm afraid—"

McDowell cut him off with a shake of his head.

"I've located such a treasure and am well on my way to it," McDowell said. "And it is not a research project."

Pike did not try to conceal his interest. A point in the colonel's favor, McDowell thought. The colonel was a man with whom he could be frank.

"What is it?" Pike said. "Where is it, and why are you telling me about it?"

"First of all, I'd like your word that whether you agree to my proposition or not, you will keep what I tell you in strictest confidence."

"That goes without saying, Professor McDowell."

McDowell told him the whole story, beginning with the Diego del C. letter but minimizing Sussman's role, letting it appear that Sussman, though a partner, had been recruited only for his expertise.

"Fascinating," Pike said, his eyes shining. "Question. Why have you come to me?"

"It's taken more time and money than I anticipated."

"Again I ask, why me?"

"Frankly, Sussman suggested you."

Pike's expression grew wary.

"I wanted someone completely discreet, someone absolutely trustworthy, someone who could hold up his end of the load," McDowell said. "Mr. Sussman said you were all those things. And in addition had a thirst for adventure. And, perhaps more to the point, had personal experience with clandestine tunneling in the course of a long and distinguished military career."

Pike's expression changed to one of mild surprise.

"Sussman said all that about me?" he asked.

"Yes. He was also quite frank about a difference between you. He said that while it was the product of a misunderstanding, he may have behaved rather badly."

Sussman appeared verging on a denial, and McDowell silenced him with a look.

Pike rose and walked to the portrait of General Vandenberg. He looked at it with his back to McDowell, his feet apart, his hands clasped behind him, in the position known as parade rest. After a moment he turned to face McDowell.

"What's the proposition?" he said briskly.

"A small investment. Full-time participation in the actual work. For a return of twenty thousand dollars or two percent of the find, whichever is the greater."

"Two percent? Come now, Professor."

"You're coming in toward the end, colonel. I made the find; the bulk of the work is completed. Now it's merely a matter of finishing the job."

"If it were that simple, you wouldn't be letting me in. An equal share. One-third."

"Out of the question, I'm afraid. Taking the preliminaries into account, we've already done two-thirds of the work. An equal share for helping with only the final third? I don't think so."

"But I obviously have something you want and need. Twenty-five percent."

No, McDowell thought. No one was going to hold them up even if it meant a second mortgage on the house and working nights and weekends until Christmas.

"Sussman gave me the impression you were as fair as you were reliable," he said coldly. "It seems he was wrong."

That appeared to sting the colonel.

"My investment," he said. "What would it be, exactly?"

"Seventy-five hundred dollars," McDowell replied. They needed perhaps twenty-five hundred dollars for a new van, another twelve hundred dollars for rent if they ran over into October, though with three men working that was unlikely, a couple of thousand for emergencies and something left over for him and Sussman. They were both running low on funds.

"Fair enough," Pike said. "You say a third of the job remains to be done. I accept your estimate of that."

"Thank you," said McDowell.

"So in effect, I would be doing one-third of a third of the work. Correct?"

"Correct."

"Eleven percent of whatever we find. A third of a third."

"It's a deal," McDowell said.

Eleven percent seemed like a great deal after all they had been through, but they needed a man like Pike. And it would still mean less than six percent less to each of them. It did not seem right not to confer with Sussman before accepting Pike's terms, but it would not do to let Pike know Sussman shared in decisions. Pike might back out if he knew Sussman was an equal partner in every respect.

"Not quite yet," Pike said. "Please don't take this as a reflection on your personal integrity, McDowell, but as a matter of principle I must see certain things for myself."

"Anything you wish," McDowell said.

"The letter, the eight-escudo piece and, of course, the tunnel itself."

"I'm afraid I don't have the coin. I sold it."

"You sold it?"

"We needed the money. I might add, the price I got for it left no doubt of its authenticity."

"I accept that explanation, Professor."

"Thank you. And the name's Arthur."

"Very well. Arthur it is. Call me William or Bill, whichever you prefer." A smile, a surprisingly winning one, touched Pike's lips. "In Korea, my men called me Big Bad Bill. Not to my face, naturally. The 'Big,' of course, was purely honorary."

"I'm sure it was a reference to what was inside the man," McDowell murmured.

"Be that as it may," Pike said, businesslike again.

"Here's the letter," McDowell said, taking it from his inside jacket pocket.

"Just let me get Henrietta in here," Pike said, taking it from him.

"Hold on a minute," McDowell protested. "This entire matter is in strictest confidence."

"My daughter and I have no secrets," Pike said with a significant glance at Sussman. "Henrietta knows Spanish. My languages are German and French."

He said it without boastfulness. A strange man, McDowell thought, more complex than he had first appeared. He liked the colonel.

Pike opened a drawer in his desk and spoke to it. "Henrietta, could you step in here for a minute?"

Miss Pike's voice came out of nowhere. "I'll be right in, Father."

Sussman smiled at her when she entered. She ignored him. Pike and McDowell rose when she came into the room. McDowell saw from Pike's expression his little act of courtesy had pleased the colonel. Sussman got to his feet, also, but belatedly, after seeing McDowell do so. Sussman was of another generation entirely, McDowell thought.

"Will you read this letter for us, my dear?" Pike said.

Miss Pike took his place behind the desk. Pike smiled fondly as she read, as if enjoying her performance and welcoming the opportunity to show her off. He was the very picture of a proud father. No wonder he detested Sussman, McDowell thought.

Miss Pike translated fluently and with great accuracy, her accent Spanish rather than Mexican. She was, McDowell could see, a very bright young woman.

"Thank you," Pike said when she had finished.

"You did that extremely well, Miss Pike," McDowell said. "Where did you study?"

"A little bit of everywhere," she said, friendlier than she had been at the door. "And we were stationed in Spain. Is there anything else, Father?"

"Nothing, thanks, Henrietta. I'll tell you what it's about later."

184

"All right, then. Good night, Father. Good night, Professor McDowell."

She left without a glance at Sussman. Sussman looked at McDowell and shrugged.

"And now," said Pike. "The tunnel."

"You mean tonight?" McDowell said.

"Once a man decides upon a course of action he should follow through without delay, don't you think?"

"Absolutely," said McDowell.

They drove to North Spring Street in Pike's Lincoln, McDowell in the front seat and Sussman in back.

"I saw the movie," McDowell said. *"The Great Escape.* How much like the real thing was it?"

"For one thing, there were no Americans involved in the real thing," Pike said. "It was from the North Compound at Stalag Luft Three. The British compound."

It seemed that Sussman had been wrong about Pike's participation in that particular tunnel. The colonel had been involved in several other tunnels, however, all from the South Compound, one of several American compounds. They had all been discovered before completion.

"I hope your luck's changed since then," McDowell said.

"The goons had experts whose only duty was to find our tunnels," Pike said with a chuckle. "I expect the circumstances are a bit different now."

In the basement, Pike looked distastefully at the clutter.

"I don't see how you managed to get anything done working from here," he said.

They found him a pair of clean coveralls and gave him Sussman's hard hat. Despite the fact that the coveralls swallowed him and the rim of the hard hat came almost to the bridge of his nose, the colonel somehow retained his dignity.

The only light in the tunnel was at the far end. McDowell gave him a four-cell flashlight with which to inspect the entire length of the tunnel and sent him on his way in the electric car. Colonel Pike, he noted, was a better size for the tunnel than either himself or Sussman. The colonel was in the tunnel for almost half an hour.

"Snotty little bastard," Sussman said while they waited.

"I thought he was all right," McDowell replied. "And his daughter, too."

"Whose side are you on?" Sussman demanded.

"There aren't any sides, Steve. We're all in this together now, and don't you forget it."

Sussman clicked his heels and threw a salute. "Yes, sir, General," he said. "Just watch out for the little colonel. He's gonna try to outrank you."

When Pike rejoined them in the basement, McDowell was unable to read anything in his expression. Pike removed the coveralls, shook them free of dirt over the entrance pit, folded them neatly and handed coveralls and hard hat to McDowell.

"A fairly competent job, considering your engineer," he said grudgingly with a look at Sussman. Turning back to McDowell, he said, "Would you prefer cash or a check?"

14

FLORENCE did not think McDowell had struck much of a bargain.

"You and Steven have finished practically all the hard work," she said. "Where does he get off thinking he deserves eleven percent?"

"It figures out," McDowell said. "A third of a third."

"I still think it's too much."

"Florence, sweetheart. Nobody's asking your opinion."

That startled Florence. McDowell was not one to take criticism lying down, but he was almost never sarcastic with her.

"And another thing," McDowell continued. "Pike and Steve don't get along. So we're letting him think I've been running the show and Steve's only in it because he happens to have the technical knowledge. So don't say any different."

186

The phone rang.

"Will you get it, Arthur?" Florence said. "It's been ringing all evening, and every time I answer they hang up without a word."

"Without even any obscene proposals?"

"Not even any heavy breathing."

McDowell answered the phone. The female voice that replied was somewhat familiar but not immediately identifiable.

"Mac," it said, "you finally answered yourself. Can you talk?"

"Who is this?" McDowell demanded.

Florence was watching attentively.

"You're a rat fink," the voice said with a laugh. "Not to know. Ball 'em and forget 'em, right?"

Then he knew. It was Gloria Stavros. What the hell did she mean, calling him at home? And why? His irritation turned to uneasiness when he looked up and saw Florence's quizzical expression.

"Who is it?" she whispered.

McDowell put his hand over the mouthpiece.

"In a minute," he said.

He needed time to collect his thoughts.

"It's Gloria," the voice was saying. "The Golden Greek."

"Yes?" McDowell said guardedly.

"Oh, you can't talk, right?"

"Yes."

"Who is it?" Florence demanded, louder.

McDowell covered the mouthpiece again.

"Gloria Stavros," he said.

In his confusion he could think of no acceptable lie.

"Gloria Stavros? What does she want?"

"That's what I'm trying to find out, for God's sake!" McDowell snapped.

"Your old lady's right there, right?" Gloria said. "You want to go to a phone booth and call me back? My number's—"

"No," McDowell interrupted.

"Just, you know, like listen, then. Did you know I broke up with Steve?"

"More or less," McDowell said, looking at Florence and shrugging.

187

"I moved. Out to the Valley. Sometimes I get a little lonesome way out here. Like, you know, in the shower. You ever get lonesome in the shower, big Mac?"

"Not exactly," McDowell said uncomfortably.

He hoped his flush was not too noticeable. He'd long ago stopped using the sun lamp intended to make Florence think he was working outdoors and was not normally pink anymore.

"Don't shit me, baby," Gloria said, laughing. "You think about the Golden Greek. Even if you do know the gold's out of a bottle. Look, you can listen even if you can't talk, can't you?"

"I suppose so."

"I'm not doing anything Saturday. Can you get out of jail for a while? We could, you know, talk about California history or something."

"I don't know," McDowell said, looking at Florence.

He could see she was growing impatient. It was only impatience so far, he thought gratefully. Not suspicion.

"Just in case, here's my phone number," Gloria said. "Got a pencil?"

"No."

"Memorize it, then. It ought not to be hard for a professor."

She gave him the phone number. It burned into his brain along with recollections of feverish thrashing about in Sussman's shower.

"Got it?" she asked.

"Yes."

"You will try to make it, won't you? Hey, I've got an all-over dye job now. Wait'll you see it. You'll just die."

"I'll do what I can," McDowell said, trying to sound cool and impersonal.

He hung up, his stomach fluttering.

"What did she want?" Florence said. "What did you mean, you'd do what you could?"

"It's like this," McDowell said, stalling for time. "She, uh, Steve dropped her, she said."

"Wise Steven. She wants you to talk to him, doesn't she? Isn't that what she wants?"

"How did you know?" McDowell said, relieved.

"It's obvious. Why else would she call? It must have been her calling all those times. She wouldn't talk to me because she knew she wouldn't get any sympathy from me. But you're such an easy mark. Don't you say a thing to Steven, Arthur. Promise me."

"I promise."

McDowell spent a restless night thinking about Gloria Stavros, his relief at enlisting Pike forgotten. He would not be going to see her Saturday, of course, but he could not resist fantasizing about what would happen if he did. He wondered if an all-over dye job was what he thought it was. The Golden Greek she'd called herself. What a sensual, evocative description.

The next day was Thursday. Pike brought seventy-five hundred dollars in cash to North Spring Street, as McDowell had requested. No more dealing through the James Ferguson account now that Ulrich knew about it. Pike had also brought along tailored flight coveralls and a hard hat that fit. McDowell counted out twenty-five hundred dollars and sent Sussman off to buy a van, being a little bossy with Sussman for Pike's benefit.

"He wrecked ours yesterday," McDowell told Pike after Sussman left.

"I can see now why you wanted an investor in such a hurry," Pike said with a smile. "I could have made a more advantageous deal, couldn't I?"

"No. As it was, you got yourself a larger percentage than I intended. You did very well for yourself, Bill."

McDowell explained the routine, how they alternated in the tunnel and took turns going to Mulholland, thinking Mulholland was halfway to the Valley, home of Gloria the Golden Greek.

"Now that they're three of us, we won't lose any time disposing of the material," he said. "We'll always have two men here to dig and clear."

"We'll need a duty roster," said Pike.

"A what?"

"A duty roster. So we'll know who should be doing what, when."

"We know that."

"That was when there were only two of you. There

are three now. More efficient with a duty roster. And prevents arguments."

"We never have arguments."

Not about the work, at any rate. They may have grown short-tempered in the grueling weeks and had words from time to time, but never about either scamping on his share of the work.

"Very well," Pike said reluctantly. "Broken down into half hour periods as you've been working, a complete duty roster would be cumbersome, at that. But we should have enough to indicate the cycle."

"The cycle?"

"One man digs; one boxes material; the other drives. I propose we rotate daily. One of us begins his day driving, another digging, the third boxing. Alternately."

"Good idea," McDowell said, though he did not think so. There were only three of them. They wouldn't need anything in writing to remember who had done what the day before. But he thought it best to humor Pike this early in their relationship.

Pike got a sheet of yellow legal paper from the pad on which Sussman did calculations and ruled it off in squares headed by the days of the week. Horizontal columns he marked Drive, Dig, Box. He put an initial in each square. M, P, and S, for McDowell, Pike and Sussman. McDowell watched impatiently, anxious to get to work. He smiled inwardly. Pike's duty roster was already screwed up. Today no one would start driving in the morning. They wouldn't have the van until later. And Pike would have to miss a couple of turns in the basement to drive to the dump site with someone and learn where it was. He'd take Pike himself, of course. It wouldn't do to put Pike and Sussman together. In the basement, at least, they would usually be separated by the length of the tunnel. Gloria Stavros. The thought of her popped into his head without warning. The Golden Greek. Gold all over now with her new dye job. "Wait until you see it," she'd said. He was not going to, however much desire pulled him. He would never deceive Florence again, and besides, he could not afford to be sidetracked now. He had to devote all his time and energy to the tunnel.

". . . line it up?" Pike was saying.

"What?" McDowell asked.

"How do you keep your tunnel lined up? You've got quite a distance to go and a small target area."

"Sussman uses a transit."

"Lucky you. We used pegs and a string. We got the string by unraveling the rope that came around crates of Red Cross parcels."

Come on, McDowell thought. Let's get on with it. But Pike settled himself comfortably on the workbench and kept talking.

"You should be farther along with all your advantages," he said. "Unlimited lumber, power saw, electric cart, electric hammer. A van to take away the tunnel material. Getting rid of the dirt was our chief problem, next to keeping the goons from finding us out. Men in blue coveralls were always popping in unexpectedly and poking around the rooms with long screwdrivers."

Oh, God, McDowell thought, his belly knotting with impatience and boredom. We took him in so we could make better progress. Had Sussman sold him a lemon?

"Ferrets, we called them," Pike said reminiscently. "And then the goons with dogs to sniff us out. *Hundführers*. Dog leaders."

"I know," said McDowell, trying to hide his impatience.

"Oh, you know something about life in the POW camps?"

"No. Just enough German to translate *Hundführer*."

"I see," said Pike, sounding pleased that McDowell knew nothing about POW camps.

He lit a cigarette and established himself more comfortably on the workbench. McDowell squirmed but said nothing. In the beginning, at least, he must maintain cordial relations with the colonel. Pike looked around uncertainly.

"Where's the asktray?" he said.

"The ashtray?" McDowell replied incredulously.

Where there were no heaps of lumber, ducting or other supplies, the basement floor was covered with sand, pebbles and sawdust. Sussman threw his matches and cigar butts on the floor.

191

"We don't have one," McDowell said.

"We'll have to do something about that," said Pike, looking distastefully at the litter as he had the night before. "For shoring," he continued, as if McDowell had asked, "we used bed boards from our bunks. In their place we strung the bunks with rope from the parcel crates. What we did, we took an iron rod we'd liberated from the goons and got it red-hot in the stove. At cooking periods. We had a regular issue of charcoal briquets for the purpose. And for heating the room in winter."

"Doesn't sound too bad," McDowell said, regretting the comment immediately. It could lead only to further reminiscences.

"Have you any idea how cold it was in Upper Silesia in winter?" Pike said with a smile. "Eighteen below, at times. And never enough briquets. As I was saying, we bored holes for the ropes with the red-hot rod. And getting air down there when the tunnel got well along. We solved that by making a duct with Klim tins fitted end to end."

McDowell knew better than to ask what Klim tins were. No wonder Sussman had dropped Henrietta Pike. He probably had to listen to this every time he took her out. McDowell looked longingly at the tunnel entrance. He had never thought he could be so anxious to get in there and slave away. Pike, if he saw the look at all, ignored it. The curt military man was gone. In his place was someone boyish and enthusiastic. He probably looked back on those days as the best years of his life, McDowell thought.

". . . a hand-operated pump," Pike was saying, "Similar to that gadget over there."

"That's a vacuum pump," McDowell said, to show he knew something Pike did not. "A squirrel-cage vacuum pump."

Pike flicked cigarette ashes into a cupped hand.

"Getting back to the material from the tunnel," he said, again as if McDowell had asked. "We put it in bags and concealed it under our greatcoats. Bottom up, with drawstrings at the opening. Then we would stroll around the parade ground and let the sand trickle out. The soil was sandy at Stalag Luft Three.

Easy digging, but it took a lot of shoring. We would shuffle our feet to mix the sand into the ground with our boots. The fresh soil was different from the hard-packed stuff on the parade ground, you see."

McDowell did not even nod in acknowledgment.

"The last one, we had almost reached the wire when they marched us out ahead of the advancing Russkies one night. We were crushed, I can tell you that."

Pike shook his head at the memory, gave a comfortable sigh, brushed the ashes in his palm onto a scrap of paper, tore the wrapping from the butt and dropped wrapping and shreds of tobacco onto the paper.

"Shall we get cracking?" he said, getting to his feet.

"Fine," said McDowell. At last. "Why don't I take the first trick in the tunnel? It's miserable going, and you should work into it. You stay in the pit, and I'll send the material out to you for boxing."

"I'd like to take the tunnel first, if you don't mind," Pike said in a tone indicating he intended doing so even if McDowell did mind.

"Whatever you say, Bill. Just don't overdo it at first. You do too much before you're used to it, you won't be worth a darn for a few days."

"Let me be the judge of that," said Pike.

Pike climbed on the electric car and disappeared into the tunnel. Having nothing to do until the car returned with a load of material, McDowell sat down on the edge of the pit with legs dangling and thought about Gloria Stavros. If only Florence weren't such a wonderful woman, he would almost consider going out to see her Saturday.

He wondered why she had called him. He was years older than she was and certainly not handsome. Florence's opinion to the contrary. Mature and interesting-looking, perhaps, but not handsome. And a nice physique from all that work in the tunnel. But nothing to make a sensational-looking girl like Gloria Stavros chase after him. It had to be her way of getting back at Sussman. Sussman had dumped her, and he was Sussman's best friend. She might even intend telling Sussman about it later. All the more reason for not sneaking off to the Valley Saturday.

A load of sand and cobbles came out. McDowell put it in a box and carried the box to the back of the basement. After a while another box came out. Pike was as indefatigable a worker as he was a talker. At the end of twenty-five minutes, when he did not emerge, McDowell called him on the walkie-talkie.

"Are you coming out?" he asked. "You've done your trick."

"I've just started getting into the swing of it," Pike said, breathing heavily but sounding chipper. "Carries me back to the old days. I'll be out shortly."

He was in the tunnel forty minutes, emerging sweat-drenched and weary but in high spirits.

"How great to be doing something again," he said. "Feel like I'm back in my twenties again."

McDowell measured when he went into the tunnel. Pike had dug almost a foot and a half. If he could keep that up, they could count on ten feet a day. Sussman had come up with a winner after all. If only they could keep him from reminiscing.

Sussman returned at midday. The all went out to inspect the new van. McDowell stopped in the office to introduce Pike to Florence. Pike bent slightly from the waist, almost a bow, when he acknowledged the introduction.

"If you had told me Mrs. McDowell was so lovely you might have found me easier to deal with," he said. "You didn't tell me your wife was involved," he said when they were outside. "Do you think it's wise?"

"I'm sure my wife is as discreet as your daughter," McDowell said with a trace of heat.

"No offense, Art. I'm sure she is. It's merely that it seems unusual for a woman to be involved in something like this."

"We needed someone in the office. It was beginning to attract notice we were always closed."

"Of course."

Sussman had said nothing. He seemed bent on not creating any friction.

"If Mrs. McDowell finds it interferes with her home duties, I'm sure Henrietta would be happy to take over for her here," Pike said.

Sussman shook his head in a silent no.

"She enjoys it," McDowell said quickly. "She's the kind of woman who likes to be involved."

"Wonderful trait. You're a fortunate man. My late wife. . . ." Pike did not finish. "I'm blessed Henrietta takes after my side."

It was a fine van, McDowell thought, air-conditioned cab and a radio. Pike examined it painstakingly, looking under the hood, checking the tires, getting down to view the underside. He had a catalogue of complaints. The battery terminals were corroded, the left front tire had a bulge he did not like, one side had a patch of color that did not quite match the rest of the paint, indicating the van could have been wrecked, and there was evidence of an oil leak.

"It's three years old, for Christ's sake," Sussman said, unable at last to hold his peace. "And it's not much of a leak. I looked where it had been parked. No fresh oil on the ground."

"They have a way of shifting them around to deceive you," Pike said. "It's likely they parked the van in a different spot every day."

"It looks fine to me," McDowell said before Sussman could counter.

He could see he was going to have his hands full acting as a buffer between them.

McDowell drove Pike to Mulholland with the boxes from Wednesday. On the way, Pike entertained him with stories of Stalag Luft III and combat missions over Korea, where Pike was a squadron commander. When they reached the site, Pike said, "It's such a long way from the tunnel. Couldn't you have found something closer?"

"We looked," McDowell said evenly. "It's not easy to find an out-of-the-way place. And the farther away we dump, the less chance there is of being connected to North Spring Street."

"It is a point," Pike conceded.

They began tipping the contents of the boxes into the ravine.

"This isn't too efficient," said Pike. "When we get back, I'll build a flume with some of those two-by-tens I saw in the basement. Easier to empty the boxes into

195

a trough and let the stuff slide down than muscling them out over the side of the ravine."

It was a good idea, McDowell thought. Sussman should have thought of that. Everything considered, Pike was proving to be a welcome addition.

Pike faded a bit as the day wore on but insisted on taking his full turn in the tunnel.

"Only way to work myself in is to keep at it," he said. "It's been thirty years since I've done this. Art, I'm actually enjoying it."

"Found your niche, have you?" Sussman said.

McDowell shot him a warning glance. The last thing they needed was for Sussman to get cute with Pike.

Despite their late start, they did eight feet that day. They left the last vanload of material in the basement. The man scheduled to take the first load out in the morning would do so while the other two worked the tunnel. McDowell wished they'd had Pike from the beginning. They would be almost to the Avila gold by now.

When they stopped work, Pike seated himself on the workbench, lit a cigarette and said, "I think we should have a staff meeting, men."

Sussman and McDowell exchanged looks. Sussman's said plainly, "I warned you, didn't I?"

Pike took a small notebook from the knee pocket of his flight coveralls. He flipped it open and looked at McDowell and Sussman. At the moment Sussman was examining his five o'clock shadow in the mirror they had hung on the wall to check for telltale dirt and goggle marks before leaving the basement.

"I'd like everyone's undivided attention, if you don't mind," Pike said. "You planning on entering a beauty contest, Sussman?"

"Nope," said Sussman. "Judging one."

He was really going to have to talk to Sussman about this atitude he was developing, McDowell thought. Sussman came over and joined them.

"I've made a few notes," Pike said. "You've conducted a nice operation, Art, considering your inexperience, but there's always room for improvement, isn't there?"

Sussman gave McDowell another "I told you so" look.

"Let's begin at the beginning," said Pike.

"That's reasonable," Sussman said, straight-faced.

Pike ignored that.

"First thing tomorrow we police up this basement. It's raunchy. A man can't do his best work in such dirt and disorder." Pike flicked his ashes into a tin can he had nailed to the side of the workbench. "I'd appreciate if you'd use the can for your cigar butts and ashes in the future, Sussman," he said.

"You won't mind me mixing 'em with your cigarette butts, Colonel?" Sussman said. "Shouldn't there be a separate one for us enlisted men?"

"Would you speak to your man?" Pike said. "I don't think he understands what we're after."

He sounded like an officer giving instructions to his sergeant. McDowell recalled Sussman's warning. "He'll try to outrank you." Let him, McDowell thought, if it keeps things running smoothly.

"Cool it, Steve," he said.

"I don't know how much more of his shit I can take," Sussman said in Spanish.

"Shall we speak in English?" Pike said. "So when there are jokes, everyone will understand. I have as good a sense of humor as the next man."

"We clean up the basement," McDowell said calmly. "What else?"

"The access hole. It's too cramped. Should have been a minimum of eight by eight."

"We haven't found it a handicap."

"That's because you're not aware of how much easier it would be with more room."

Which freely translated means it's because we don't know any better, McDowell thought.

"Of course," Pike continued with a faraway look in his eyes, "at Stalag Luft Three it was another story. The entrance to our most ambitious tunnel was only two by two. Under the stove. But that's another story. I'll tell you about it one day."

I can't wait, McDowell thought.

"While we're enlarging the hole, we'll build a ramp out of it," Pike said. "We're wasting time and energy

197

climbing in and out and lifting up boxes of material."

That's because it's such a long climb for you, you sawed-off martinet, McDowell thought, hoping his face did not betray the irritation Sussman's did.

"It need be only two and a half feet wide by six feet long," Pike said.

While Pike was explaining how such a ramp would enable them to use a simple roller conveyor belt for getting material out of the hole, McDowell was thinking about how hard it had been to break through the concrete. It might take a couple of days to make the changes Pike wanted. It was not worth it.

"Too much work for too little saved," Sussman said.

"Negative," Pike snapped.

McDowell wished Sussman had kept his mouth shut. Now, when he gave his decision, he would appear to be taking sides, which he would rather not do on Pike's first day.

"Let's think about it," he said.

Sussman gave him a disgusted look.

"When there's work to be done, do it," Pike said.

"No," said McDowell. "We'll think about it."

Pike appeared more startled than angered by such insubordination but merely compressed his lips and studied his notes.

"Lighting," he said. "Our only light is at the end of the tunnel."

"Only place we need a light," Sussman said. "There's hardly any traffic to speak of."

"We should have lights at regular intervals," Pike said, pointedly addressing himself only to McDowell. "To maintain continuous surveillance of the entire length of the tunnel. Never know when we might detect an incipient cave-in."

"We check regularly with a flashlight," McDowell said. "But we'll put lighting on the agenda with the ramp."

Pike frowned.

"I'll come in Saturday and do it myself," he said. "If there are no objections."

"No objections. In fact, thanks."

McDowell wondered if Pike would be in any condition to come in Saturday after another full day in the tunnel, but that was Pike's problem.

"The flume for dumping the material I've already discussed with you, Art. We'll knock it together before we leave today."

McDowell was weary and anxious to get into a hot shower. When he thought of the shower, he thought of Gloria Stavros. He shook his head to rid himself of the notion.

"Why not?" Pike demanded, apparently taking the gesture as an objection.

"What?" said McDowell. "Oh. We're all tired, Bill. The man with the least to do in the morning can do it."

"Very well," Pike said agreeably. "My last item. The air duct. I don't like the way it's secured to the spreaders. Sloppy. Sags so in places it's in the way. Should be snug against the roof of the tunnel."

"You can do that Saturday while you're fixing the lights," Sussman said.

"I intend to."

"Is that everything?" McDowell asked, taking pains to be civil.

"For the present. I'll make further suggestions as I identify our needs."

"Bill, you've made some extremely valuable suggestions. I want you to know we appreciate it. Right, Steve?"

"Right," said Sussman.

"All you needed was someone with a little sense of organization," Pike said graciously.

That night he called McDowell at home. Florence answered.

"It's Colonel Pike," she said. "He's such a dear man, isn't he, Arthur?"

"Absolutely," McDowell said, getting up to come to the phone.

"He's so . . . what's the word, so gallant," Florence said. "And such old fashioned good manners."

McDowell picked up the phone.

"Why don't you ask him to dinner?" Florence said. "Wednesday would be a good night, if you're all not

199

too tired. And Steven, too. Now that his evenings are free. They really should patch things up."

"Hello, Bill," McDowell said. "You bearing up all right? You really did a heck of a lot of work for the first day."

"Never better," Pike said heartily. "Oh, a twinge here and there, but I'll work them out."

"Good."

"I'll get right to the point. I've been thinking about our problem child."

"Yes?" McDowell said warily.

"Sussman's a disruptive element, isn't he?"

"I wouldn't go so far as to say that."

"I've always prided myself on my patience, Art. But it doesn't compare with yours, I must say. The way you've managed to put up with him all these weeks."

"Steve Sussman happens to be one of my best friends," McDowell said stiffly.

"No accounting for tastes, is there, old boy? No offense, Art. My thought is this. We put him on permanent driving detail. He'd be out of the way, and we could get on with it without so much pointless wrangling." Pike chuckled. "In the old days I'd have transferred him out of the outfit. But I don't suppose we could do that, could we?"

"No, we couldn't. And I don't think Steve would like doing nothing but drive the van to the dump. He's the kind of person who wants to do his full share of the hard work."

"Does it really matter what Sussman likes or doesn't like?"

"Yes, it does."

"Pity. But keep an open mind. Perhaps you'll come around to my way of thinking. You know, Art, it puzzles me that a man of your caliber could accept someone like Sussman as a close friend. I'll see you tomorrow then."

McDowell hung up the phone flushed with anger.

"Is he coming to dinner Wednesday?" Florence asked when McDowell returned.

"No," said McDowell. "He can't make it."

15

FRIDAY morning Pike was still feeling the effect of his previous day's toil, but he did not complain and did his share of the work. Sussman obviously enjoyed Pike's manfully controlled distress but held his tongue. There was, in fact, little friction between them all day. McDowell had ordered Sussman to keep his mouth shut. He did not, of course, tell him about Pike's phone call.

McDowell had to moderate but a single incident. When all three of them chanced to be in the basement at midmorning, which seldom happened because one or another was usually in the tunnel or off to Mulholland, Pike looked with annoyance at the radio. As usual, it was blasting away with country music.

"What the devil is that?" he demanded.

"A radio," Sussman said innocently.

"Do you call that music? And must it be so loud?" Pike turned the radio off.

"Now just a fucking minute," Sussman said.

"Watch your language, young man," Pike said with a cool, challenging look.

"It was a little too loud, Steve," McDowell said quickly. "Keep it down, will you?"

Sussman sighed heavily. McDowell could see he was holding himself in only with great effort.

"Okay," Sussman said at last.

"If we must have the blasted thing on, let's have some decent music or a news station," Pike said.

"Suppose the man on the boxing detail does the selecting?" McDowell said with a warning glance at Sussman. "He's normally the only one out here to listen to it."

The logic of that was inescapable, and both Pike and Sussman agreed.

They dug ten feet that day, leaving two hundred to go. Twenty working days if they could maintain the pace. They would reach the chest well before the beginning of the fall quarter.

Saturday morning Florence served McDowell breakfast in bed.

"You deserve it," she said. "You've been working so hard. But it must be such a joy to have Colonel Pike working with you now."

"Oh, it is, it is."

"I've a lot of things to do this morning. And I'm having lunch with Emily Carter. Why don't you just lie around all day and take it easy?"

"I might just do that," McDowell said, thinking it sounded like an invitation to go calling on Gloria Stavros.

But he was determined not to. He was doing exactly as Florence suggested and loafing around the house all day. He might even finish rereading the California section of *Two Years Before the Mast* interrupted so long ago by that fateful telephone call from Chet Heaps in Special Collections.

Around ten thirty, Robert came home from wherever he had been and asked McDowell to take him and a friend to the Griffith Park Observatory. McDowell considered doing so. All morning he had been resisting an impulse to phone Gloria, and if he went off with his son, it would put temptation behind him. But, on the other hand, he did not much like the idea of driving all the way to the observatory and standing around while Robert and his friend pored over the too-familiar displays. And afterward Robert certainly would want to visit the zoo. McDowell could not face all that. He begged off, giving Robert a few dollars for a model kit. Robert seemed satisfied with the compromise.

Half an hour later McDowell had a call from Sussman.

"Trouble," Sussman said anxiously. "Ulrich phoned. He asked for James Ferguson, but he has to know it's my number."

"How did he——?" McDowell cried, alarmed. "I'll be right over."

McDowell did not bother to change from the baggy shorts and shapeless sports shirt which were his favorite leisure wear around the house on warm days. Sussman met him at the door with a can of cold beer.

"I wonder if he came here and checked the mailboxes?" McDowell said.

"He could have. Or got the phone number from the city directory."

"Does he know you're James Ferguson?"

"Probably. I told him Ferguson wasn't in and I didn't know when he'd be back, but I don't think he bought it."

"Well," said McDowell, sitting down heavily and holding the cold beer can against his cheek, "what else did he say? And what did you say?"

"He made the same old pitch. If James Ferguson, or *anybody,* had more coins, he was still in the market."

McDowell sighed. He thought Sussman's letter had ended it. Why was Ulrich so persistent? But that really was not so hard to guess. He'd aroused Ulrich's suspicion and interest by his manner when he sold the coin. And now Ulrich must be doubly suspicious because he'd learned there was no James Ferguson. Ulrich was an intelligent man. He would have to think there was something highly irregular.

"What do we do?" Sussman asked.

"Nothing. If he keeps calling, just keep stalling him until he gets tired of wasting his time. And if he calls me, I'll tell him exactly what I told him before. After all, what can he do?"

"Nothing, I guess," Sussman said, brightening. "You know something, Mac, I'll say this for that little bastard Pike, this is the first Saturday I haven't felt like something drug through a knothole."

"He does pitch in. I'll say that for him. Florence thinks he's a joy."

"Jesus! Say, how about a couple sets of tennis? Like old times. Only I think I've seen the day when I could run your ass off."

"Tennis? After five days in the hole? You can't be serious."

When they were finished with the tunnel though, he wanted to start playing tennis with Sussman again. Maybe even on his own court. He'd be able to afford one. Sussman was right about one thing. He felt as if he could run all day now.

"I guess not," Sussman said. "I guess we ought to save our energy for weekdays." He grinned. "The little colonel was hurting yesterday, wasn't he? Did my heart good to see how he bit back the groans. I'll bet he changed his mind about stringing those lights today."

On the way home, McDowell saw a phone booth outside a service station. Acting on impulse, he parked beside the booth and, after a moment's hesitation, got out of his car and went into the booth. He called the number Gloria Stavros had given him.

"Big Mac," she said, sounding pleased. "I'd about given up on you. Have trouble getting out of jail? Where are you? Can you talk?"

"I can talk."

"You gonna fall by? It's so quiet out here in the Valley I'm biting my nails."

"How do I get to your place?"

McDowell hoped his nervousness did not show in his voice.

Gloria lived in Sherman Oaks. She told him to take the San Diego Freeway to the Ventura Boulevard off ramp and gave him the directions to her apartment. After he hung up, McDowell regretted what he had done. The last thing he needed right now was to get mixed up with a kookie girl. But everything had worked out to make it so easy. Florence going off for the day, Sussman getting him out of the house. Just call it fate, he thought. He looked down at his baggy shorts, wishing he was dressed more presentably. He considered going home and changing. But what if for some reason Florence had returned earlier than expected?

He found the apartment house without difficulty. He took a deep breath before ringing Gloria's bell. He was as nervous as he had been on his first date, and no more sure he'd know what to say. He was not accustomed to this sort of thing. Not after seventeen years of marriage. Just be calm and natural, he told himself. You're a grown man and have had your share of women. Well, almost his share. He heard footsteps coming across the room inside. He wished he had gone home and changed clothes.

The door opened, and there she stood, smiling. She wore a tank shirt and minuscule shorts and, apparently, nothing else.

"Hi, there," she said. "Come on in."

"I hope you don't mind the way I'm dressed," McDowell said, closing the door behind him. "I just happened to be out and thought I'd call."

"You look perfect," Gloria said. "Nobody dresses in Sherman Oaks."

And then McDowell grabbed her. He could not help himself. There was just too much on display and available in that tank shirt and those nothing shorts. Taken by surprise, she took a backward step, then stood her ground and put her arms around his waist. McDowell knew he was not kissing her properly because his lust was so suffocating he had trouble breathing. Gloria trembled in his arms. She's anxious, too, he thought gratefully. And then he realized she was giggling. He dropped his arms, embarrassed.

"Wow!" said Gloria. "You are one horny dude."

"Sorry," McDowell mumbled sheepishly.

"I'm not complaining. I like a dude that knows what he wants."

McDowell grabbed her again, fumbling with the tank shirt.

"Hey, big Mac," she said, laughing again. "Cool it a sec. I've got a bed, you know. Or are you hung up on making it standing up?"

"Not particularly," McDowell said, releasing her.

In the bedroom, she was out of her tank shirt and shorts quickly, but instead of turning to McDowell she looked at herself for a moment in a full-length mirror fastened to the door. Then she turned and flung out her arms. Her public hair was the same color as the hair on her head.

"What do you think?" she said. "Does it look natural?"

"Supernatural."

She was even more nimble and enthusiastic in the conventional arena of a queen-size bed than she had been in Sussman's shower. And she proved to be satiable. McDowell was pleased with himself for having gratified and exhausted so adept and energetic a creature. Gloria lay beside him smiling at the ceiling, her hands folded on her perspiration-slick stomach.

"You are some kind of a bad animal, big Mac," she said approvingly.

"You're pretty great yourself."

"I know. Ain't you glad?"

"Overwhelmed."

"I got a job," she said. "What've you been doing to keep busy?"

"Nothing much. Reading a lot."

"I'd rather do this than waste time reading. Wouldn't you?"

"Since you put it that way, yes."

"You still seeing a lot of Steve Sussman?"

All self-satisfaction fled. He had been right thinking it wasn't really him she was interested in. Gloria had just wanted to get back at Sussman.

"Yes," he said flatly.

Gloria propped herself up on an elbow and looked into his face, one finely turned breast resting on his upper arm.

"Hey, man," she said. "Pull in your lip. That's all over. Shot in the ass."

"Why did you bring him up then?"

"I was remembering how the first time I saw you you raped me in his shower."

"Raped you?"

"That's the way you come on, like a mad rapist."

McDowell had thought he was rather gentle, after the first sortie, at any rate.

"Am I really like that?" he said. "Sorry. I'll try to—"

"Don't change," she interrupted. "Action's more important than hype."

"Beg pardon?"

"I mean foreplay is fun, but what counts is the main event. Dig?"

"I dig," said McDowell, the word awkward on his lips.

"What are you two dudes up to, the way you hang out together all the time? If I didn't know you both so well, I'd figure you for a couple of switch hitters."

206

She laughed in delight. "Wouldn't that be a gas? You two making it with me and each other."

"That's sick," McDowell said indignantly.

Then he understood she was only trying to get a rise out of him. The double entendre occurred to him, and he grinned.

"You think it's funny, too, huh?" she said. "For a minute there I thought you were really pissed off at me. Really, what are you dudes up to? Something heavy, I know. Some nights Steve was too tired to say hello."

McDowell did not like her talking about Sussman when she was lying there naked with him. It made him feel as if she didn't care about the men she went to bed with, just about screwing them. He approved of women's liberation, but this was too much. Just minutes earlier she'd had him believing he was someone special.

"Let's not talk about Sussman if you don't mind," he said, trying not to sound sulky.

"Big Mac is jealous," she said incredulously. "Would you dig that?" She put her mouth on his and gave him a leisurely caress from neck to groin. "I don't give shit about Steve Sussman. He's not the man you are, baby. And that's no hype."

"You're just saying that," McDowell protested.

"I mean it. If you weren't married, I'd make you move in. You save Saturdays for me and I won't say a word about what's his name? Deal?"

"I'll try."

"You're some trier," Gloria said, biting his shoulder. "I'll say that for you." She had sharp teeth, and it hurt. "Hey, I'm starving. Soon's I can get myself together, let's go have some lunch, I know this restaurant on Ventura."

McDowell was embarrassed. He had only two or three dollars in his wallet. He'd given the rest to Robert for the model kit. And he did not want to go anywhere he might be seen with Gloria. He and Florence didn't know anyone in Sherman Oaks but you never knew who you might run across.

"I'd rather not," he said.

"Oh. Big Mac don't want to get caught with his Golden Greek."

"It's not exactly that. It's just that I. . . ."

"Don't try to shit me, baby. I don't care. I'm not out to break up your happy home. All I want is my share." She took a playful handful. "You didn't bring a bun for this, did you?"

"You're terrible," McDowell said, laughing. "There's another reason. I didn't bring but a couple of bucks."

"Why didn't you say so? I'd make us lunch if I had anything here. Hey, I know. How about Big Macs? And fries. You can go out and get 'em. And then maybe we'll have the real big Mac for dessert."

Which they did.

Driving home, McDowell did not at first feel as apprehensive about facing Florence as he had the first time he'd been with Gloria. It was, he supposed, because he had in effect lost a kind of virginity that first time and now he no longer attached such exaggerated importance to fidelity. The only problem was what to do if Florence was amorous that night, as she almost always was on Saturdays now that he was so tired during the week. He began feeling less confident about facing her.

But Florence still had not come home when he got home. His confidence returned. She would not be asking where he'd been.

She seemed a little preoccupied when she did come home, carrying several packages.

"I bought you some slacks in the Village," she said. "Now that you've lost so much weight you don't have a thing that really fits. I want you to try them on."

"Maybe later," McDowell said. "My back doesn't feel right." That was a sudden inspiration. "I think I twisted it getting out of the hammock." If he had a bad back, he couldn't do anything tonight.

"You poor dear." She put down her packages and said, with her back to him, "You'll never guess who I ran into in the Village. William Pike. I'd just left Emily and—"

"He said he was going to do some work in the tunnel," McDowell said. "I suppose he wasn't up to it."

"But he did," Florence said, turning to face him. "He said he'd been up since five this morning. The poor man looked utterly exhausted. But he insisted I have a sundae at Swenson's with him. That's why I'm so late."

She waited, as if expecting McDowell to comment, but he said nothing. If Pike had no more sense than to wander around Westwood Village instead of resting up for Monday, it was his problem.

"The devil," Florence said, smiling. "Telling them to put on extra nuts and whipped cream. There must have been a thousand calories in that sundae."

"You look good filled out," McDowell said, thinking there was not an unnecessary ounce on Gloria's slim, muscular body.

"That's what William said. The devil. He's such a darling, Arthur. I do wish he and Steven were better friends. Couldn't you—?"

"You know I would if I could."

"I think you ought to get right in bed with a heating pad," Florence said.

"What?"

"For your back."

"Oh, yeah. Maybe so. I've got to be in condition to work Monday."

Because of his condition, Florence made no overtures that night. McDowell slept soundly from ten o'clock until after eight the next morning.

"My back feels fine," he told Florence. "I'm glad I took your advice."

In the afternoon he and Florence took Robert to the observatory and the zoo. McDowell would have liked to phone Gloria just to say hello but had no opportunity to slip away. He was already thinking about next Saturday.

Monday morning he found that Pike had strung bulbs every thirty feet or so in the tunnel, expertly cutting sockets into the line.

"Had to come in yesterday to finish the job," Pike said. "Dropped by first thing after church."

"Where do you go?" Sussman asked. "The Little Chapel of Our Lady of the Wild Blue Yonder?"

"Shut up, Steve," said McDowell. "We appreciate your coming in on your own time like that, Bill."

"No such thing as our own time. Way I see it, we're all on call twenty-four hours a day, seven days a week. If the occasion demands. By the way, I ran into Florence Saturday. In Westwood Village."

"She told me. She said you forced a thousand calories on her."

Pike chuckled.

"That nonsense about being on a diet," he said. "She looks marvelous just as she is, don't you think?"

"I keep telling her, but she doesn't believe me."

Having lights the length of the tunnel made a great deal of difference to McDowell. He had never been completely comfortable in the dark journey to the end. With the lights he no longer felt so underground.

Pike had also secured the sagging sections of the air duct. The colonel's devotion to his work went a long way toward compensating for his officiousness, McDowell thought. And Pike was good for Florence's morale, too. If only he could curb Sussman's tongue, they'd have a great team.

During the lunch break, Pike said, "I suppose Florence told you we discussed Henrietta alternating with her in the office."

Sussman looked up attentively.

"No, she didn't," said McDowell.

"In any case, she thought it an excellent idea. Henrietta's to start next week."

Sussman grimaced.

For lunch, McDowell and Sussman had the usual iced tea and sandwiches prepared by Florence. Pike had a variety of crackers, three kinds of cheese and cut segments of peaches, pears and nectarines done up neatly in plastic wrappings. He ate so fastidiously McDowell found himself watching.

Noticing, Pike said, "Henrietta put it up for me. Marvelous cook, too. Knows the cuisine of every place we've been stationed. French, Spanish, Japanese."

"She sounds like quite a girl," McDowell said with a sidelong look at Sussman, who was studiedly indifferent.

"Must have you and Florence over for dinner,"

Pike said. "Make an evening of it. You, Florence and Henrietta's new young man."

"Thanks. We'd like that."

Was Sussman scowling just a little? McDowell wondered.

Florence was delighted with Pike's invitation.

"We're free every night," she said. "But I suppose a Saturday would be best. You're always so tired weeknights."

"I'll tell him. Oh, Bill said Henrietta's to share the office chore with you. You forgot to tell me."

"Isn't that sweet of her, Arthur? She must be as nice as her father."

"Pike'll probably want to make a duty roster for you," McDowell said dryly.

"What's a duty roster?"

"So you'll always know whose turn it is."

"Oh, we'll know. One week I'm Monday, Wednesday and Friday and the next week Tuesday and Thursday. William worked it out."

Pike said Saturday night was excellent for dinner.

"Dress comfortably," he said. "No tie, if you'd rather not. And Florence can even wear slacks if she prefers. Our small dinner parties are very informal."

That week they dug forty-nine feet, putting them well across North Main Street and just under the rear of the Pelanconi House on the near side of Olvera Street. Though it still left a hundred and fifty feet to go, actually reaching Olvera Street made McDowell feel as if the chest were almost in their grasp. Only three more weeks, he thought.

He pictured the chest waiting for them deep in the earth behind the Avila Adobe, waiting as it had for almost a hundred and thirty years, and could see clearly in his mind the hoard of gold coins it contained. Hooked neck eagle eight-escudo pieces, two-, six- and eight-escudo coins of even older vintage, some of them perhaps even more rare and valuable than the one they had brought up. A million dollars might even be a conservative estimate. After deducting Pike's eleven percent, he and Sussman still might share as much as they had hoped for before they took him in.

He could put Gloria up in a more conveniently located apartment, if that was what he wanted. He could not make up his mind about that. It was one thing to see her on the occasional Saturday but quite another to have her as a permanent mistress. He was not sure he was the type to cope with the problems of a full-time mistress. Nor was he sure he wanted Gloria permanently. How long could sheer sex hold its charm? And how long could he hide a permanent arrangement from Florence? Now that he was going to be rich, nothing must keep Florence from enjoying it with him fully. Gloria was not the woman she was except, of course, in bed, where Gloria was peerless, but how much of his time could a man of mature years and interests spend in bed? He would be like Sussman and cross that bridge when he came to it. And meanwhile, he would have his Saturdays with his Golden Greek.

Saturday morning McDowell put on his new slacks and a good sports shirt and told Florence he was off to Olvera Street to make some measurements. Robert wanted to go with him. McDowell said he would like to take him but had things to do afterward that would be no fun for him. McDowell felt bad about that. It was even worse than lying to Florence. A father should be with his son every chance he got because children grew up so fast and then were gone before you knew it.

This time he was less precipitous with Gloria, and they sat and talked for almost ten minutes before getting into bed. Under her sexuality and irreverence she was a bright girl, he thought. She wanted to know all about his work at UCLA and if he balled his students, as Sussman did.

"Oh," she said, pretending to be contrite. "I wasn't supposed to mention what's his name, was I?"

"That's all right," McDowell said. "I'm over that. And the answer is no, I don't. I told you I'd never been unfaithful to my wife until—"

"But I didn't believe you."

"Do you now?"

She made a little "yes and no" gesture with her hand.

"Maybe it's like more yes than no," she said. "Could

be why you turn me on. No other chick had what it took to turn you on."

"I don't understand it," he said. "I'm married, I'm not that good-looking, and I'm a real square. What do you want with me?"

"Same thing you want with me, big Mac."

"A girl with your looks can get anybody she wants."

"Maybe I'm hung up on married squares who're not too good-looking."

"And maybe you're getting back at Steve Sussman."

"Oh, shit," Gloria said with a grimace. "Last week you got all uptight because I mentioned that dude, and now you're bringing him up. Look, man, you turn me on. Don't fight it. Just relax and enjoy."

She was feeling venturesome and conducted him through several unfamiliar maneuvers, one or two of which he found a little shocking, sending her into gales of laughter. She had laid in beer and cold cuts, so he did not have to go out to get their lunch. It was the same brand of beer Sussman kept in his refrigerator, he noted, but he said nothing.

"You have another hard week?" Gloria asked while they were eating.

"What makes you think I have hard weeks? This is my summer break."

"I know you and what's his name have been working your asses off at something. What's so mysterious about it?"

"I don't want to talk about it."

Gloria pouted. McDowell did not like that. He had never seen her any other way than merry or wanton. If she was like that, he certainly did not want her as a permanent mistress.

"You don't want to talk about it," she said. "All you want to do is ball me until my eyes pop."

"I thought that's what you wanted, too," McDowell said stiffly.

"It was. Maybe you're getting to me, you horny old professor." She laughed, her usual self again. "Don't look so grouchy. I promise to keep my mouth shut. Except when it's more fun to have it open. Okay, big Mac?"

McDowell felt flattered but uneasy. It was good that

213

she had feelings for him outside of bed, but wouldn't it complicate things too much? It was better just to enjoy each other and not get entangled. Perhaps this should be his last Saturday in Sherman Oaks.

"I want your advice," she said. "I'm thinking about going natural. All over. What do you think?"

"I like you the way you are. Golden Greek all over."

Who was he trying to kid? he thought. He would be back next Saturday.

16

HENRIETTA PIKE'S new young man was six feet four, quiet and unable to take his eyes off her. He was, Pike told McDowell and Florence, a captain in the Air Force recently assigned to the Office of the Secretary of Air Force in the Federal Building across from the VA cemetery on Wilshire.

Dinner at the Pikes' was pleasanter than McDowell had anticipated. Though Pike told a few of his war stories for the captain's benefit, most of his conversation was devoted to compliments for Florence and amusing anecdotes, which he told well, about his peacetime service in various places. He also displayed a considerable knowledge of literature, music and the theater. Nor was he a bad listener, especially when Florence was speaking.

The food, prepared by Henrietta, was superb. There were no hors d'oeuvres, Pike explaining he thought it criminal to overload the stomach and dull the appetite before one of his daughter's exquisite dinners, but there was jellied consommé, which McDowell detested because of the texture, and radishes. McDowell noticed that the Pikes put butter on their radishes.

"A habit we picked up in France," Henrietta said with a smile. "You should try it."

Then there was a spinach salad and a tremendous paella with a great variety of ingredients.

"And you did all this yourself, Henrietta?" Florence

214

asked, impressed. "I absolutely must have your recipe."

"I'm afraid there isn't one," Henrietta said. "I keep adding things until it seems to be right. But I'll be happy to show you if you'd like."

With the meal, Pike served a Spanish white wine quite unlike the ninety-nine-cent variety McDowell sometimes picked up at Akron or the Bargain Circus.

"It is a decent little blanco," Pike said when McDowell accepted a third glass. "Discovered it during our tour in Spain. You did a tour in Spain, didn't you?" he asked the captain.

"Yes, sir," the captain said.

It was one of the few times he opened his mouth all evening.

For dessert there was flan, also prepared by Henrietta, and later, in the living room, Fundador brandy, with Manila cigars for the men. McDowell did not smoke cigars, but he took one and put it in his pocket for Sussman. He felt a little guilty about Sussman's not being there.

"What an absolutely beautiful evening," Florence said on the way home. "Isn't William a charming host? And Henrietta is a simply darling girl. So poised. And such a marvelous cook. I don't think she really cares much for Harry, though."

"Harry?"

"Where were you all evening? Her young man."

McDowell had missed the name when they were introduced and, as nearly as he could recall, had not heard Henrietta's new young man referred to by name again the rest of the evening.

"She practically ignored him the entire evening. While he sat there looking at her with absolutely doglike devotion. I'm sure it was William's idea."

"What was William's idea?"

"Having Harry to dinner. Another Air Force man. He should have invited Steven."

"I told you, Steve and Pike don't get along."

"But Henrietta's perfect for Steven. I'm surprised at William. Now that you're all working together, you'd think he'd have Steven over when he had us."

"To tell the truth, Henrietta's the reason Steve and Pike don't get along."

"What?"

"Steve used to go with her. And it seems she was more serious than he was. So he ran."

"He should be ashamed of himself! She's so attractive, and such a perfect lady. Not like that . . . oh, what was her name, Arthur?"

"Who?"

"That blond girl. The one who practically seduced Steven right in front of our eyes."

"Oh," said McDowell. "That girl. What *was* her name?"

While they were getting ready for bed, Florence said, "Do you think next Saturday would be rushing things?"

"What things?"

"To have them over for dinner. William and Henrietta. And Steven. I'm sure I could straighten things out between them. But Saturday may be too soon," she added thoughtfully. "William might think they had to have us back right away. I'll make it Saturday a week. And that'll give you time to work on Steven."

Instead of joining Florence in bed, he put on his slippers and said, "I think I'll read awhile. I'm not sleepy."

"I'm not either," said Florence. "Come to bed."

"My back's starting to act up again. Maybe I should lie on the heating pad."

"I'll be your heating pad. Come to bed."

Now I'm in for it, McDowell thought. I won't be able to do anything, and she'll wonder why. Reluctantly, he climbed into bed. After a while Florence said, "What is it, Arthur? Are you worried about something?"

"Not exactly."

"Yes, you are. Now that you're getting close, you're afraid something might go wrong, aren't you?"

"To tell the truth, yes," McDowell said, grateful she had once more provided him with an answer.

"Nothing is going to go wrong. You just relax. I'll help you forget all about the tunnel and anything going wrong."

216

To his relief, Florence's ministrations stimulated him enough to give a performance.

"There," Florence said. "Don't you feel better, now?"

"Lots," McDowell replied truthfully. "And I think you even adjusted my back."

Tuesday, Sussman came into the basement with a black look on his face after returning from a trip to Mulholland. Pike was in the tunnel.

"What the hell's Hennie doing up there?" he demanded.

"You knew she was going to take turns with Florence," McDowell replied. "What's the matter, did she make you an indecent proposal or something?"

"Some joke. It's bad enough working down here with her old man without having her up there freezing my ass off every time I walk through."

"Wear a sweater."

"Fuck you," said Sussman.

"I'll have Pike make a new duty roster. You can drive only on the days Florence is in the office."

"Forget it. I'm not gonna let that bitch get to me."

The following Thursday Sussman appeared greatly concerned when he arrived to begin work but said nothing. It couldn't be Henrietta Pike, McDowell thought, because she would not have come in yet. Before entering the tunnel, Sussman took McDowell aside and told him to call him on the walkie-talkie as soon as Pike left for Mulholland.

"What's this all about?" McDowell asked.

"Later. When we're alone."

"Is it about Pike?"

Sussman shook his head.

McDowell called him on the walkie-talkie when Pike left. Sussman came out of the tunnel.

"I think somebody followed me here this morning," he said.

"What!" McDowell exclaimed. "Who? Ulrich?"

"I don't know who it was, but it wasn't him."

"Are you sure you were followed?"

"When I drove out in the van this morning, there was this dude sitting in a blue Mustang across the street from the apartment. When I made my turn to-

217

ward Sunset, he pulled out behind me. I didn't pay much attention. I mean, why should I? So I'm on the San Diego Freeway and I look in the rearview mirror while I'm changing lanes and I see a blue Mustang changing lanes right behind me. So I start watching. When I took the off ramp to the Ventura Freeway, he was right behind me."

"Thousands of people take that route downtown," McDowell said. "We're both jumpy because we're getting close."

"That's not all. When I pulled the van into our loading zone, what goes by but a blue Mustang? With what looked like the same dude in it. How many people come from Brentwood to North Spring Street this time of morning? I mean, it's too early for Chinatown and Olvera Street."

"What did he look like? The driver?"

"I didn't get too good a look. Lots of hair, pretty big. That's about all."

"Did you get the license number?"

"I didn't think about it until he went by me out front. Then he was gone before I had the chance."

"And you're sure it wasn't Ulrich?"

"Not the way you described him to me. This dude was younger and his hair wasn't gray. Maybe Ulrich hired somebody."

"I don't know," McDowell said. "Why would he go to all that trouble? All he knows for sure is that we had a gold coin and for some reason we didn't want him to know our names. Even if he thought we'd stolen it, there'd be no reason for him to think we had more. Not after he virtually offered to fence them and you still said you didn't have any."

"Beats me," said Sussman. "Maybe the dude wasn't following me. Anyway, I didn't want to say anything with Pike around. He'd give us half an hour on the need for evasive action and tighter security."

"And maybe he'd be right."

Sussman returned to work in the tunnel. McDowell pondered their situation as he boxed material and carried it to the foot of the steps. If Sussman had actually been followed, it meant someone, Ulrich probably, was wondering what he was up to and they would have to be doubly careful. And it was not necessarily Ulrich, though he was the likeliest candidate. They had been working in the tunnel for more than two months now and had been seen regularly by any number of people in Sussman's neighborhood as well as around North Spring Street. At the moment, McDowell decided, all they could do was wait and be watchful.

He had the second run to Mulholland that day. As always since being surprised by the highway patrolman, he looked in the rearview mirror before slowing to turn off Mulholland onto the dirt road leading to the dump site. There was a blue car loafing along behind him. It looked like a Mustang to McDowell, but he was not sure. He was not good at identifying makes and models of automobiles. Robert was, but McDowell had never been interested enough to learn. The blue car was too far back for McDowell to read the numbers on the license plate or tell much about the driver, though he did get a distinct impression of bulk and lots of hair.

McDowell turned onto the dirt road and braked quickly. He would get the license number as the blue car continued past on Mulholland. But, with a shriek of rubber, the car accelerated quickly and shot past the intersection. McDowell got only a fleeting glance at a man sitting high behind the wheel and of a full head of light-colored hair. He threw the van in reverse, backed to Mulholland and set off in pursuit. It was a hopeless chase. The blue car had too much of a head start, and the van, loaded with sand and cobbles, lagged farther and farther behind. McDowell gave up when the car vanished around one of Mulholland's many curves.

He drove to the dump site, pensive and disturbed. There was little doubt now that someone was curious about them. And if it was Ulrich, it certainly was not Ulrich himself following them, but someone working for him. But, as he had told Sussman, it did not seem logical that the coin dealer would go to such lengths merely because two men who had sold him a valuable coin did not want their identities known. Yet Ulrich had seemed to be an unusually bright and intuitive man. Something definitely must be done, though what McDowell did not know.

He considered the implications as he let the material slide down the wooden chute into the ravine. An outsider now knew that Sussman went to an address on North Spring Street in the morning and that the van then made a trip to an isolated site off Mulholland Drive. At the moment that outsider probably did not know for what reason. But he had only to return and drive up the dirt road to discover that freshly excavated material was being dumped there. A hell of a lot of freshly excavated material. That still might not tell him anything. Unless Ulrich was behind it all. Ulrich could very easily make the connection between digging and old coins, though he would not know to where they were tunneling. In fact, there was no reason to think he would realize they were tunneling. It was more likely he would think they were merely digging under the premises. His most logical conclusion would be that they had found the eight-escudo piece there and were looking for more. He could not possibly know they had brought it up from behind the Avila Adobe. McDowell took some small comfort from that.

He remained at the dump site for a few minutes after unloading the material on the chance the blue car might return to investigate. When there was no sign of it, he drove away slowly, watching in the rearview mirror until he could no longer see the turnoff point. The blue car did not reappear.

Back at North Spring Street, he put on a cheerful smile for Henrietta, who was looking efficient but delectable in a white blouse and gray skirt, and hurried down to the basement. Pike was in the tunnel. Sussman was sawing planks for shoring. The radio was tuned to KLAC, and loud. McDowell turned it off.

"Hey," Sussman protested. "You're getting like Pike."

"I think the same man followed me to the dump," McDowell said quietly.

He told Sussman what had happened and his conclusions.

"So what do we do?" Sussman said, worried.

"I'm not sure. I suppose the first thing is to try to learn who's following us. If he keeps doing it, we can get his license number. I'll trail you in every morning and someone will have to trail the van when it goes to the dump."

"That's a lot of trouble. And we'll have to tell Pike."

"I intend to. He's got to know. And he may have some ideas."

"You're right, I guess. The little bastard'll probably draw up a 'round-the-clock duty roster for surveillance of the premises."

To McDowell's surprise, Pike appeared more pleased than alarmed by his news. McDowell told him not only about being followed, but all about Franz Ulrich as well. The colonel's eyes gleamed, and the fatigue lines seemed to melt away from his weary face.

"Well now," he said, "that adds a little spice to what's been unmitigated drudgery."

McDowell and Sussman could only stare.

"Rather like ferrets and *Hundführers* all over again, isn't it?" Pike said. "Though in this case I doubt if we need fear going to the cooler. It doesn't sound as if our problem is with minions of the law."

McDowell had not even considered it might be a policeman who had them under surveillance, but now he did so. That highway patrolman, could he have had second thoughts and filed a report? But the man had followed Sussman to North Spring first and had followed him from North Spring to the dump, not vice versa.

"Now, then," Pike said briskly, lighting a cigarette. "Let's consider the other possibilities. Forget Mr. Ulrich for the moment."

"Why?" said Sussman. "It's got to be him."

"Any number of people could have become curious about what is going on here," Pike said, ignoring the interruption. "The local shopkeepers and merchants, for example. Though it could very well be someone in Sussman's neighborhood curious about his comings and goings. Or he could have let something drop."

"I resent that," said Sussman.

"Why were you the one followed here?" Pike said

221

calmly. "But," he continued, "like you, Art, I opt for our friend Ulrich. You appraise him as a man who is bright, intuitive and of a suspicious nature. But why, you ask, would a single coin so arouse his interest even under such unusual circumstances?"

"That's the one thing that puzzles me," McDowell replied.

"If you were a less substantial citizen, it would puzzle me as well," Pike said. "It's obvious Ulrich suspects chicanery of some sort because you took such pains to conceal your identity. But would a man such as you involve himself in a presumably questionable act for such return? Eleven hundred dollars? It is my firm belief he suspects there must be considerably more at stake, and that is why he has been so persistent. Even to the extent of having Sussman followed."

"Bill, I think you're right," McDowell said.

Even Sussman showed grudging admiration for Pike's analysis.

"What do we do about it?" McDowell said.

He did not mind at all deferring to Pike's judgment in this case. It was not the same as Pike's trying to take charge of the tunneling operation.

"At the moment, I don't think we have a good deal to fear from Mr. Ulrich. I quite agree with your conclusion that Ulrich can't know the location of what we're after or its magnitude. It's logical to suppose he suspects we are sifting through the earth under the North Spring Street Vent and Duct Company. Or will when he learns we've been excavating. However, I see no point in attempting to identify the man who followed Sussman."

"Why not?" Sussman demanded.

"Why would he return?" Pike said, speaking to McDowell instead of Sussman. "He's already ascertained that Sussman comes here and that the van goes out Mulholland way. And I'm quite sure that by now he knows why the van goes to Mulholland."

"Makes sense," said McDowell.

"I propose we continue as before," Pike said. "Doing nothing to lead Ulrich to suspect we are aware of his interest. It will be time enough to deal with him when we're ready to bring out the chest."

"I'd like to say again how lucky we are to have you with us," McDowell said, feeling more confident than he had since receiving Sussman's disquieting news that morning. "Steve, don't you agree?"

"I guess," said Sussman.

"It wouldn't hurt for Henrietta and Florence to take a look outside once in a while," McDowell said. "On the chance Ulrich's man might come cruising by. Or even Ulrich himself. He might be keeping an eye on us."

"An excellent suggestion," Pike said. "I doubt if it will have any result, but it will occupy their time and give them an added sense of participation."

Nothing untoward happened Friday. McDowell instructed Florence to look out at the street from time to time through the clear space Sussman had made in the painted window so long ago when he worked with the transit. He told her what to look for.

"What if it isn't who you think?" Florence said, alarmed. "What if it's the police?"

"We haven't done anything to call their attention to us. If we had, I'm sure they'd have been in here with a search warrant."

"Not always," Florence said. "On television, they always stake you out first. Two of them sit in an unmarked car and watch day and night."

"All right. If you see a suspicious-looking blue Mustang, a foxy-looking gray-haired man *or* two men in an unmarked car, let me know."

"It's Friday already, Arthur. Do you want to tell them about a week from tomorrow?"

"Tell who about a week from tomorrow?"

"If it's not history, your memory is like a sieve. Bill and Steven about dinner at our house Saturday a week. And Henrietta."

"I don't think so," McDowell said. "Not Steven and the Pikes together. Never work."

Florence sighed. "I just know the chemistry is there if they'd only let it happen," she said.

They had another forty-nine-foot week putting them, Sussman said, about to the front edge of the

223

shops across from the Avila Adobe. After Pike left for the day, McDowell and Sussman cleaned themselves up as best they could with soap, a washcloth and a pail of water, put on their street clothes and walked to Olvera Street. They entered through the Plaza end, which was closer to the Avila Adobe than the Macy Street end, and Sussman paced off what he estimated was the distance to the tunnel. Olvera Street, as usual, was thronged. Sussman stopped in front of a shop selling the usual Mexican goods—jewelry, embroidered shirts and blouses, serapes and souvenirs.

"About here," he said. "Maybe a few feet inside."

They went inside and stood on the spot twelve feet below which Sussman said the tunnel ended. To McDowell it was stimulating and a little eerie to be standing here among jostling shoppers above the place where only a few minutes earlier he had been grubbing in solitude. And it made him feel a little superior, too, knowing what lay just below and what was waiting behind the Avila Adobe. He peered out the door to see how close they were to the Avila Adobe but not even its roof was visible. The view was blocked by the booths in the center of Olvera.

A salesgirl came to ask if she could be of assistance.

"Just looking," Sussman answered in Spanish.

"Are you looking for anything special?" she replied in the same language.

"Yes," said Sussman, smiling. "Very special."

"For your wife, perhaps?" the girl said.

McDowell got the impression she was trying to find out if Sussman was married. It seemed he had chemistry for every girl except Henrietta Pike.

"How did you guess?" Sussman replied.

The interest died out of the salesgirl's face.

"Do you see it anywhere, dear?" Sussman said to McDowell.

The girl made a grimace of distaste and fled.

"You crazy bastard," said McDowell.

They went outside and stood for a while in front of the Avila Adobe. Behind them were scores of sightseers and booths filled with Mexican artifacts, sweets and clothing.

"Next week we'll be under all that," McDowell said, turning.

"Just what I was thinking," said Sussman. "And the week after that . . . Jesus!"

That night, Florence again broached the subject of having Sussman and the Pikes for dinner together.

"Henrietta is perfect for Steven," she said. "Even if they don't know it themselves. Isn't there some way we can patch things up between them?"

"Let's keep out of it," McDowell said. "I'm just starting to get along with Pike, and I don't want to rock the boat."

"Just starting to get along with Bill? That charming man? Arthur, you're becoming an absolute bear. I think I liked you better when you were plump and good-natured."

"I'm still good-natured, damn it!" McDowell said, piqued.

Then he grinned sheepishly, realizing how his tone belied the words. Florence smiled, put her arms around him and lay her head against his chest.

"But you're my bear," she said.

After that, McDowell thought, how could he go sneaking off to see Gloria Stavros tomorrow?

But in the morning he told Florence he had to see Sussman for a while and then take care of some other things.

"I probably won't be home for lunch," he said.

"Maybe I'll go out for lunch, too, then," Florence said. "Robert's going off somewhere on his bicycle."

McDowell was relieved that she had bought his story so readily. He went by Sussman's, in case Florence might have some reason to call him there. On the way, he stopped at a phone booth and called Gloria. There was no answer. He let the phone ring ten times before hanging up. She could have gone out for a few minutes, he thought. Or be taking a shower. Which reminded him they had never repeated that first experience. Maybe he would today. He waited five minutes and called again. Still no answer. Disappointed, he headed for Sussman's apartment. He'd call her again after he left Sussman. The previous Saturday he'd called her later in the morning and she probably

225

wasn't expecting him this early. Probably out getting something for their lunch.

Sussman was slow in answering his ring. Instead of opening the door, he called out irritably, "Yeah?"

"Steve. It's me."

The door opened. Sussman wore only a towel around his waist.

"What the hell you want this time of morning?" he demanded. "Couldn't you for Christ's sake call first?"

"I didn't know I needed an appointment."

"I've got company," Sussman growled.

McDowell felt sick. That was why Gloria had not answered the phone. She was here. And had probably spent the night.

"Oh," he said. "I'm sorry."

"Who is it, baby?" a voice called from the bedroom.

It was not Gloria's voice. McDowell could have burst into song.

"Nobody you know," Sussman said. "Just wait there like a good little girl. What's on your mind, Mac?"

"It can wait."

"Okay. Come back this afternoon."

"Sure. This afternoon is fine."

McDowell called Gloria again from the nearest phone booth. Still no answer. He did not know whether to keep calling until he got her or to drive on out to Sherman Oaks on the chance she would be back by the time he got there. He decided to go to Sherman Oaks. Why waste time waiting around when they had so few hours together as it was? He stopped at a market on Ventura Boulevard and called again. He let the phone ring fifteen times. Where the hell was she? he thought angrily. She must have been delayed somewhere. Or had to leave and been unable to reach him on the phone. She'd hardly call him at home again. Maybe she had left a note for him, telling him when she would be back. There was no note tucked in her mailbox or in the door to her apartment. He rang the bell, hoping she had come in while he was on the way. There was no sound from within.

She must have expected to be back before now or she would have left a note, he thought. He went back to his car and waited for almost an hour. Where the hell was she? he thought angrily. She knew she was supposed to be there on Saturdays. It was the only day he could get away. He drove home deeply disturbed. It wasn't like Gloria to stand him up. Or was it? All the way to Sussman's his mood kept changing from disappointment to anger to worry that something had happened to her. He should have left a note to tell her he'd been by. He called her once more before reaching Sussman's apartment, still getting no answer. He felt like a fool keeping on trying. The Golden Greek would have some explaining to do, he thought angrily. That was one thing she could be certain of.

Sussman was alone when he got there.

"You could have called a guy first this morning," he said. "Or are you curious about the sordid details of my social life?"

"Sorry if I ruined any plans," McDowell said gruffly.

He did not feel like joking. He wondered where Gloria had gone and why she had not even bothered to leave a note.

"Don't apologize," Sussman said. "I got everything done. What's on your mind?"

They sat down, and Sussman brought out the inevitable beer. McDowell studied the can. Sussman and Gloria drank the same brand. He wondered who had started whom in it, not that it mattered. And what was he to tell Sussman he wanted to talk about?

"You come over here to read labels, or did you want to talk about something?" Sussman demanded.

"Florence wanted to invite you to dinner next Saturday," McDowell said.

"You fell by here twice to tell me that?"

"With the Pikes. Both of 'em."

"Forget it, Mac. Tell her thanks but unh-unh."

"All right," McDowell said, getting up.

"And that's all you wanted?" Sussman asked incredulously.

"Well, I was passing this way anyhow."

"Long's you're here, how about a little tennis? I'm ready. I slept ten hours last night, not counting interruptions."

"I've got some things to do. Maybe tomorrow, if

Florence and Robert haven't already planned my day."

McDowell phoned Gloria from the service station booth, but again there was no answer. He gave up and went home. Florence had not come home from lunch yet. He made a sandwich and ate it moodily. He tried Gloria's number, then went out to the hammock with *Two Years Before the Mast* but could not concentrate. Where the hell was Gloria? He closed his eyes and slept for half an hour. When he awoke he went in the house. Florence was still out. He called Gloria again. The phone was still ringing when he heard the station wagon pull up in the driveway. He hung up and picked a pamphlet at random from the litter on his desk and pretended to be reading it.

"Hi," said Florence from the doorway. "I'm back."
McDowell turned to look at her.
"So I see," he said, conscious his voice was truculent. The last thing he should do was take out his irritation with Gloria on his wife. His tone seemed to startle Florence, and her face grew uncertain.
"What's the matter with you?" she said. "Your face is like a thundercloud. I didn't know you expected me to rush home right after lunch."
"I was just sitting here thinking. You know my forehead always wrinkles like that when I concentrate."
"Oh," said Florence.
She came over and kissed his bald spot.
"What was your day like?" she said.
"My day? Oh, I dropped by Steve's. He said he won't come Saturday night. Not if the Pikes will be here."
"I see I'll have to speak to him myself."
"Good luck," said McDowell.

17

AFTER dinner, McDowell told Florence he was going to the drugstore on San Vicente to get some shaving cream and asked her if she wanted anything. She wanted a copy of *Vogue*.

228

"I never paid any attention to their kind of clothes before," she explained. "But now that I'm going to be able to afford them. . . ."

Robert wanted to go with him. McDowell could think of no reasonable excuse to refuse him and took him along. While Robert was entertaining himself looking at magazines, McDowell phoned Gloria from the booth. She was at home.

"I came by, but you weren't there," he said accusingly.

"You did? You should have called first."

McDowell did not tell her he had done so repeatedly.

"You were supposed to be there," he said. "Where were you?"

"My girlfriend has this, you know, boutique in Venice and she had to go to Torrance for the day," Gloria said. "And I was the only one she could get to watch the store."

"You could have let me know."

"I didn't think you'd want me to call you at home, big Mac."

"Why didn't you leave a note in your door then?"

"I didn't think you'd come by without calling. And I was in such a hassle. She didn't call till the last minute. Are you mad at me, baby?"

"No," McDowell lied. "How about tomorrow?"

He'd find some excuse to get away.

"Shit," said Gloria. "I'm tied up tomorrow. I've got to go to would you believe Disneyland."

"Disneyland?"

"Yeah? Ain't that a drag? She comes all the way from Albuquerque, New Mexico, this aunt of mine, and wants to see Disneyland. At her age."

"Let her go by herself."

"I wish I could, honest. It's gonna be a real bummer. But I promised to take her."

Robert rapped on the phone booth door.

"Dad," he said, "let's go."

McDowell put his hand over the mouthpiece.

"In a minute," he said irritably. "Look at the magazines."

"I've looked at all the good ones."

"Why don't you say something?" Gloria said. "You really are mad at me, aren't you?"

"No," said McDowell. "Be with you in a minute."

He fished in his pocket for some change.

"Buy yourself a Fudgicle or something," he told Robert. Turning back to the phone, he said, "I'm not mad at you. See you Saturday?"

"Cool."

McDowell left the phone booth more cheerful than when he entered it. Robert had an ice-cream bar for himself and another for McDowell.

"Toffee," he said. "Okay?"

"A sensational choice," McDowell said. "Let's go."

"What about Mom's magazine?"

He'd forgotten all about it. And the shaving cream that was his excuse for visiting the drugstore. He bought both.

Sunday morning he played tennis with Sussman. Making a family outing of it, Florence and Robert came along as a gallery. Sussman, being the better player, won three straight sets, but McDowell was breathing evenly after the last and was well satisfied with his performance. Dig a tunnel for health as well as wealth, he thought. Later they went to the Sculpture Garden and ate the picnic lunch Florence had prepared.

"This is the life," Sussman said, stretching out on his back.

"You should have your own," Florence said.

"My own what?" Sussman asked lazily.

"Family."

"What brought that up?"

"You're getting too old to be fooling around all the time."

"Don't you think that's Steve's business?" McDowell said.

"You ought to find a nice girl and settle down," Florence continued, ignoring him. "You're going to have all that money. You could do wonderful things for the right girl instead of wasting it on. . . ."

She did not finish.

"You're right," Sussman said, sitting up. "The problem is finding the right girl. The nymphomaniac whose father owns the chain of liquor stores."

"Seriously," said Florence. "Why did you break up with that darling Pike girl?"

Sussman scowled at McDowell, who shrugged helplessly. Sussman got to his feet, brushed shreds of dried grass from his hairy, muscular legs and called out to Robert, who was contemplating the nude "Maja" his father so admired.

"Hey, Bob," he cried. "How about a ride on the bike?"

Florence looked pensively after Sussman as he and Robert walked across the lawn toward the parked motorcycle.

"He's terribly touchy about her, isn't he?" she said. "She must have hurt him deeply."

"I told you," said McDowell. "It was the other way around. That's why he and Bill Pike don't get along."

"It's not like Steven to be cruel."

"He's not. She wanted to get married, and he didn't. It's simple as that."

"And you don't think that's cruel? You're as bad as he is. Did Bob ask you about San Simeon?"

"San Simeon?"

"He's dying to see the Hearst castle. I told him we'd go if it's all right with you. I thought next weekend."

He couldn't go off for the weekend. He was seeing Gloria Saturday.

"I don't know," he said doubtfully. "I hear San Simeon's a madhouse on weekends."

"That's true," Florence said. "And its a lot to ask of you after you've been working so hard all week."

McDowell was delighted that she had agreed so readily.

"But he is dying to go," she continued. "I could take him during the week. Henrietta could look after the office. Could you take care of yourself if we went one day and came back the next?"

Perfect, McDowell thought. He wouldn't have to wait until Saturday to see Gloria.

"Of course," he said. "If Robert wants to go that much."

231

"You're such a dear," Florence said.

McDowell was consumed with guilt. Florence was so good, and he was such a hypocrite.

It was Florence's week to be in the office Tuesday and Thursday. She said she would go in Monday and Tuesday instead, drive up to San Simeon Wednesday and return Thursday. McDowell said that was a good idea.

Early Monday morning, despite Pike's opinion the man who had followed them had no need to do so again, McDowell drove to Sussman's neighborhood and waited until the van drove away. It was not followed. McDowell was relieved that Pike had been proved correct. It gave weight to Pike's other assumptions.

Florence and Robert left for San Simeon early Wednesday morning. Before leaving, Florence prepared lunches for McDowell and Sussman and told her husband what to have for dinner that night.

"Should I make tomorrow's lunch and leave it in the refrigerator?" she asked.

"We'll have a taco or something," McDowell said.

"Then you're all taken care of except for breakfast tomorrow. Why not have yourself some nice pancakes somewhere? And we'll be home in time for dinner tomorrow night."

"Fine," said McDowell. "Now you drive carefully."

It felt strange coming home to an empty house that evening. And lonely. It would have been depressing were it not for the thought he would be seeing Gloria that night. He took a long shower, thinking about the Golden Greek, prepared and ate the meal Florence had started for him, and phoned her. A man's voice answered. He was so unprepared for that he said, "Gloria?" before he could stop himself.

"Glor," the man's voice called, "how many times do I have to tell you to answer your own fucking phone?"

The voice was deep and infuriatingly virile, but with a hint of a lisp. The "answer" was almost "anther."

McDowell was stunned. Who was that, sounding so at home in Gloria's apartment?

"Hello," Gloria said.

"What was that?" McDowell demanded.

"Big Mac!" Gloria said. "What are you doing calling at night?"

"I asked who that was."

"Just a dude from next door."

"What's he doing there?"

"He just came over to rap. Where are you calling from?"

"Home. She's out of town."

"Oh. So that's it."

"I'm coming over."

"I've got company. You know that."

"Get rid of him."

"Just a fucking minute," Gloria said, her voice changing. "You don't tell me what to do."

McDowell was taken aback. He had expected her to be, if not complaisant, at least apologetic.

"I take it you won't want to see me tonight then," he said stiffly.

"I see you Saturdays. That's the way you wanted it, wasn't it? The only time you could get out. You expect me to be here waiting whenever your wife decides to leave town?"

"Are you sleeping with him, too?"

"What's it to you?"

"You said I was the only one you were seeing."

"On Saturdays. The rest of the week is my own. Dig?"

"Bitch!" McDowell cried, banging down the receiver.

He was trembling with rage, disappointment and humiliation. He'd known she was a tramp, so why should he let himself be so upset? He began to cool off. She was single, wasn't she, and had every right to see anyone she wanted, whenever she wanted. And she had not lied, exactly, about not seeing any other men, just let him believe what he wanted to believe. She could have been more tactful on the phone, but he shouldn't have called her a bitch. He started to call her back and apologize but did not. Her friend might answer again. And even if she answered herself, she might think he was crawling. He would wait until Saturday and talk things out with her.

He spent a troubled night, missing Florence, wondering what Gloria and the man who had answered her phone were doing and if she was as eager and merry tonight as she was on Saturdays. Despite getting little sleep, he was up early and in the tunnel working before either Sussman or Pike arrived.

"You're really hungry for that gold, ain't you, amigo?" Sussman said when he found McDowell shoveling material from the tunnel into a box.

"With Florence out of town . . ." McDowell said, his voice trailing off.

"Yeah. When a dude's been married as long as you have, I guess he really misses his wife."

McDowell had prepared two lunches, but Sussman begged off when the time came to eat.

"Should have told you last night I was eating out but I forgot," he said, getting out of his coveralls.

"Maybe I'll go with you. I'm getting tired of sandwiches every day."

"I've, uh, got a date," Sussman said.

"A date? In the middle of a working day?"

"I won't be long. We're eating in the area."

"Do you think that's smart? With all that's been happening?"

When McDowell saw the disapproving expression on Pike's face, he wished he had not said it.

"No sweat," Sussman said.

He motioned for McDowell to accompany him to the steps.

"It's Henny," he said in a low voice.

"What?" said McDowell.

"Not so loud, for Christ's sake. You want the little colonel to find out?"

McDowell walked part of the way up the steps with him.

"How long has this been going on?" he asked.

"I said hello last week, and she said hello, and what the hell, we started rapping a couple of minutes whenever I walked through for my Mulholland run."

"Why didn't you tell Florence last Sunday? It would have made her day, knowing you and Henrietta were speaking again."

"And have her start ringing wedding bells in Henny's ears? Be a pal and don't tell her, okay?"

"I'll try. But she has a way of sniffing out those things."

The station wagon was in the driveway when McDowell came home. He was surprised at how the sight of it lifted his spirits. He hurried inside and grabbed Florence in a bear hug.

"Careful," she said with a pleased laugh. "You'll break something. You don't know your own strength."

"I missed you," he said, wondering if he would have missed her as much if Gloria had answered her own phone last night.

"And I missed you. But we had a marvelous time. Bob, Daddy's home."

Robert came out of his room wearing a souvenir T-shirt.

"I got a bunch of neat stuff," he said. "Wait'll you see it. Did you save the crossword puzzle?"

"Naturally," said McDowell.

"Neat. That's the only thing I missed."

"You know you missed your father," Florence said.

"Oh, yeah. Him, too."

Though he felt the effects of Wednesday's restless night, McDowell was so pleased to have Florence back home he was more ardent than he'd been since going to work in the tunnel. To hell with Gloria Stavros, he thought. Who needed her when he had a woman of his own like Florence?

"I'll have to take more overnight trips," Florence said.

"Not without me," McDowelll replied.

That week, spurred on by the knowledge their quest was nearing its end, they tunneled fifty-one feet. If Sussman's figures were correct and they were on target, they would reach the Avila gold by the following Friday. They had but fifty more feet to go. If they worked through Saturday and Sunday, McDowell thought, it would guarantee reaching the chest by the end of the week.

"How do you feel about working over the weekend?" he asked Sussman and Pike. "Now that we're so close?"

"Oh, man, I'm beat," Sussman said. "And I've got an important appointment tomorrow."

235

The look he gave McDowell indicated his appointment was with Henrietta Pike.

Pike, though looking drawn and every one of his fifty-two years, said, "Excellent idea, Art. I've got an appointment, too, but I can break it."

He regarded Sussman with thinly veiled contempt.

"Crap," Sussman said disgustedly. "I'll break my fucking date."

"We can manage quite nicely without you," Pike said.

"I haven't missed a day yet, and I'm not about to start at this late date. Maybe you ought to pass, though. You don't look so hot."

"Never felt better in my life," Pike said stiffly. "I'll race you ten laps of the practice track any time you feel up to it."

When McDowell reached home, and before he could tell Florence the chest was almost in their grasp, she said sharply, "Arthur McDowell, you promised never to keep anything from me again."

Oh, God, he thought, she found out about Gloria. The glow he'd felt knowing they would have the Avila gold by this time next week vanished completely.

"Why didn't you tell me Henrietta and Steven are seeing each other again?" she demanded.

The glow returned.

"I just found out the other day myself. And it's nothing serious."

"Henrietta thinks it is."

"How do you know?"

"A woman senses things like that. And I can tell from the way she talked about him."

"Talked about him? When?"

"She called this morning before she went to the office. She wanted to know if I'd had a good trip. She's such a darling girl. So thoughtful and sweet. Like her father."

"Oh, sure."

"You really don't think Steven is serious this time?" Florence said anxiously.

"How should I know, Florence? I don't have your woman's intuition."

"Has he said anything to make you think he's not serious?"

"All he said was not to tell you or Pike."

"Then he's serious."

"How can you say that?" McDowell demanded, adding quickly, "I know, a woman senses things like that. Maybe you won't think it's important in the light of your grand news about the lovebirds, but I think we'll get to the chest next week."

"That's marvelous! And what a wedding present for Henrietta and Steven."

"Wedding present? Oh, for God's sake, Florence. We'll be working Saturday and Sunday, by the way."

"All of you?"

"Even Sussman, if that's what you mean. Henrietta must have told you they were supposed to have a date."

"Yes," Florence said quickly. "Yes, she did."

Pike looked tired when they met in the basement Saturday morning.

"Bill, why don't you take it a little easier today?" McDowell said. "We'll handle things here and you take care of the driving."

Pike bristled, as he always did when McDowell suggested he slow down a bit.

"I know my limits," he said. "And I haven't reached them. Far from it."

As the day wore on, Pike's fatigue deepened noticeably. McDowell could see he was driving himself but said nothing, knowing it would only provoke the colonel. As for himself, McDowell was glad to be working on Saturday, and not only because it was bringing them nearer to the Avila gold. It meant he could not call Gloria or go out to her place even if he were so inclined. And he was not at all sure he could resist the temptation if he had the opportunity.

By midafternoon Pike appeared so exhausted McDowell decided reluctantly to call a halt. He knew Pike would refuse to stop working if he and Sussman continued without him.

"I'm bushed," he said. "Let's call it a day."

"I second the motion," Sussman said.

"We've done less than six feet," Pike objected.

"I promised Florence and Robert dinner and a movie tonight," McDowell said. "If I don't get home and get some rest, I may not be able to make it."

"In that case, I withdraw my objection," Pike said. "I'll not be responsible for disappointing that lovely wife of yours."

And that's probably really the reason Pike was agreeing to stop work, the damn fool, McDowell thought. Not just using it as an excuse to save face.

"And let's start a little later tomorrow," McDowell said, thinking Pike needed all the rest he could get. "How about ten? We're entitled to sleep in one morning after the sort of week we've had."

"Hear, hear," said Sussman.

"If you insist," Pike said.

Pike appeared in somewhat better shape Sunday morning.

"Wonderful night's rest," he said. "Henrietta insisted I take an early dinner and go to bed at eight. I'm never in bed so early, but she had me take a sleeping pill, and the next thing I knew it was eight thirty this morning. Haven't slept twelve hours at a stretch since coming off 'round-the-clock ops in Korea."

The smile that grew on Sussman's face during this recital was strangely smug, McDowell thought. He wondered if Henrietta had taken advantage of her father's long slumber to go out with him.

Shortly after one o'clock, following the lunch break, McDowell was in the pit filling boxes, and Sussman, who had just returned from a haul, was preparing to take his place. Pike was in the tunnel.

The walkie-talkie crackled.

"Art," said Pike's strained voice. "Art, are you there?"

He seemed to be speaking with enormous effort. Sussman, nearest the walkie-talkie, snatched it up.

"What is it, Colonel?" he cried. "What's wrong?"

"Is Art there?" Pike said, every word enunciated carefully but still with great effort.

"Yes. Are you all right?"

"Then put him on, damn it!" Pike snapped, breathing audibly between words.

By then McDowell had scrambled from the pit and snatched the walkie-talkie from Sussman.

"I'm here, Bill," he said. "What is it?"

"I think I'm having a heart attack."

Pike sounded embarrassed.

"Good God!" McDowell cried. "Don't move! I'm coming back."

The electric car moved with agonizing slowness. It was all his fault, McDowell thought. He should never have let Pike push himself so. But Pike had looked in better shape this morning. What if he were to die back there? That's all they needed. Anger welled in McDowell. The stubborn little bastard. Insisting on keeping up with younger men. Ruining everything. They'd have to call an ambulance, and it would be all over. Strangers poking around everywhere. They'd see them all covered with dirt, see the pit and the tunnel entrance, see the lumber and ducting. Everything. Damn Pike to hell.

The colonel was lying flat on his back with his hands folded on his chest. Was he dead? McDowell thought wildly, his anger evaporating. He stopped the car and scrambled the last few feet on hands and knees.

"Terribly sorry, old man," Pike murmured apologetically.

At least he wasn't dead, McDowell thought, relieved.

"Are you sure it's a heart attack?" he said.

"All the symptoms, I'm afraid."

"Why didn't you tell us you had a bad heart, damn it?"

"My last annual physical my EKG was perfect," Pike said heatedly.

"All right, all right. Don't get excited, Bill. It's not good for you."

He picked up the walkie-talkie and called Sussman.

"Steve," he said, "I'm sending him out."

"Do you think we should move him?" Sussman said. "Maybe I better call an ambulance and send a doctor back there to him."

"Are you out of your mind?" McDowell cried. "I'm sending him out in the wagon. You make him as comfortable as you can till I get there. And send the car back for me."

"He could die," Sussman protested. "I'm going next door and phone for help."

"You do and I'll break your fucking back, you son of a bitch! I'm sending him out."

McDowell picked Pike up in his arms and laid him at full length on the car and wagon. It was not difficult even though McDowell was kneeling. Pike did not weigh very much.

"Just relax," McDowell said. "I'll have you out of here in no time."

He started the car toward the basement and crawled after it on hands and knees. The car and its burden slowly lengthened its lead. The bolts holding the guide planking to the shale floor bit into his knees. He tried to crawl straddling the planking, but it was difficult. The empty car returned at last. He stopped it, climbed aboard and started it back out.

Sussman had Pike stretched out on the basement floor and was kneeling at his side.

"Don't try to move," Sussman was saying. "Don't talk. We'll get help as soon as we can."

It sounded to McDowell as if it were something Sussman had been saying again and again. There was that quality of rote in Sussman's tone. Sussman turned to him.

"Now can I call the fucking ambulance?" he said angrily.

"Not yet," said McDowell.

Sussman stared at him incredulously. So did Pike.

18

McDowell looked closely at Pike, who appeared to be in pain but not at death's door.

"How do you feel?" he asked.

"A little better," Pike said, tight-lipped.

"We're taking you home."

Sussman sprang to his feet, his dark eyes ablaze.

"Are you out of your mind?" he demanded.

240

"You understand we can't have anyone coming here, don't you, Bill?" McDowell said, ignoring him.

Pike, teeth clenched, nodded.

"He needs help, and fast," Sussman cried, grabbing McDowell's arm.

McDowell pulled free, saying, "Get into your clothes."

Without waiting for compliance, he began taking off his coveralls. After a moment's hesitation, Sussman did likewise. When McDowell was into his street clothes, he took a pair of shears and began cutting the ends from cardboard boxes.

"What the hell are you doing?" Sussman demanded, slipping on a shirt. "Have you lost your fucking mind?"

McDowell placed three boxes end to end along a two-by-ten plank so that they formed one long, narrow box.

"We'll have you home before you know it," he told Pike, lifting him gently. "Sussman, go up and open all the doors and the back of the van. Then get back down here."

He deposited Pike carefully in the long box he had constructed.

"What the hell do you think you're doing?" Sussman demanded.

"We can't have anyone see us carry him out. Get your ass up there and get those doors open."

"He's a human being, for Christ's sake, not a load of meat!" Sussman cried, boiling.

"You're wasting valuable time."

Sussman threw open the bottom door and pounded up the steps.

"Bill," said McDowell, "I'm going to fold the tops of the boxes over. Don't worry, you'll have plenty of air. We'll take you home and call the UCLA hospital from there. Or would you rather go to a military hospital?"

"Nearest one's Long Beach Naval Station," Pike said through clenched teeth. "Too far."

He did not appear nearly as outraged as Sussman.

McDowell put Pike's street clothes in the box with

241

the colonel and folded down the lids. Sussman came charging down the steps.

"You take the front," McDowell said. "I'll hold the back up so he won't slide off."

With Sussman at one end of the plank and McDowell at the other, they climbed the steps and went out to the van.

"Get him out of the box while I lock the front door," McDowell ordered.

He locked the office door and got in the rear of the van with Pike.

"Let's move," he told Sussman. "But don't break any laws."

"What hospital?" Sussman asked, burning rubber.

"Drive normally, damn it!" McDowell said. "Pike's house. We'll call UCLA Hospital from there."

"We can't spare the time."

"It has to look as if it happened at home," McDowell said. "And we can't be involved. Right, Bill?"

"Right," said Pike, suppressing a groan.

"Are you having trouble breathing?" McDowell asked solicitously.

"I'll manage, thank you."

When they got to Pike's house, McDowell scooped Pike up in his arms while Sussman raced ahead to bang on the door. By the time McDowell got there with Pike, Henrietta was opening the door. She paled when she saw her father.

"Steve, what is it?" she cried. "Father, are you hurt?"

"He had a heart attack," Sussman said grimly as they moved inside.

"A heart attack? And you brought him here?"

"Don't be frightened, Henrietta," Pike said. "That's a good girl. It won't stop a tough old nut like me."

Henrietta, though shaken, did not appear on the verge of panic.

"Put him on the couch," she said. "Have you called an ambulance?"

"You do it now," McDowell said.

"I'll call the fire department emergency ambulance," she said, running for the telephone.

When she came back from phoning to kneel at her

242

father's side, she seemed quite composed. She held fast to his hand.

"It's on the way," she said.

"I'll be all right, my dear," Pike said.

"Don't talk. Don't do anything." She turned to Sussman. "When did it happen?"

"In the tunnel," Sussman replied guiltily. "He was digging and—"

"In the tunnel?" Henrietta interrupted, springing to her feet. "And you brought him all the way here?"

"It was my idea," McDowell said. "Not his."

"You son of a bitch!" Henrietta cried, starting for him, her hands like claws.

McDowell braced himself for the onslaught, not raising his hands to protect his face. He deserved whatever he got, he thought.

"Your language, Henrietta," said Pike.

"I'm sorry, Father," Henrietta said, kneeling by his side and taking his hand again.

"We wouldn't call anyone to the basement," McDowell said apologetically. "Everything would go down the drain."

"It's all right for my father to go down the drain, I suppose," Henrietta said bitterly.

"He was quite right, my dear," said Pike.

"Please, Father, don't talk."

Sussman knelt beside her and put an arm around her. That wasn't wise, McDowell thought. It could bring on another heart attack. But Pike was not looking at them. He was staring at the ceiling. The tough little bastard hadn't closed his eyes once the whole time, McDowell realized.

"When they get here, tell them your father was working in the yard," he said. "It'll explain the dirty flight suit."

"You think of everything, don't you?" Henrietta said, calm but icy.

When they heard the siren, McDowell hustled Sussman into the kitchen. They remained there until the bustle in the living room died down, the front door slammed and the siren signaled the departure of the ambulance.

"We can go out now," McDowell said.

243

"If he dies, you killed him, you know," Sussman said grimly.

"He won't die," McDowell said, hoping it was so. "He's tough as an oak knot."

Disapproval and wonder mingled in Sussman's expression.

"I never knew you were such a callous son of a bitch," he said.

"Neither did I," McDowell replied thoughtfully.

They spoke only once on the way back to the North Main Street lot where McDowell's TR4 was parked.

"Soon as you hear from Henrietta about his condition, let me know," McDowell said.

"What makes you think she'll call me?" Sussman demanded.

"She's certainly not going to call me. You saw the looks she gave me."

"I hope to hell she's still talking to me after this."

"I told her it was my idea. You heard me. And Pike'll tell her you wanted to call an ambulance right away."

"Like hell. He hates my guts."

"But he's fair. If nothing else. And it's my guts he hates now. You can bet on it."

After Sussman dropped him off, McDowell walked across Main to Olvera Street to see how close they were to the Avila Adobe. They had dug only a couple of feet when Pike had his heart attack. With what they had done Saturday, they were only forty feet from the chest.

There were even more sightseers jamming Olvera than on weekdays. The end of the tunnel must be under the booths in the center, McDowell thought. He tried to visualize the sub-structure map and tell which booth but could not. The map did not show surface structures and, standing in the narrow crowded aisle between the booths and the Avila Adobe, he was unable to guess where the direct line from the basement to the old house might be. It could pass under any of three booths as nearly as he could judge. One of them sold Mexican candy. McDowell bought a sack of cactus candy, a favorite of Robert's, and burned milk patties. He munched a patty while he contemplated the Avila Adobe. They would be under it and nearing the chest in another two or three days even without Pike. And then it was just a matter of locating the exact spot. Sussman had said they would probably need a surface reference. He wondered how Sussman was going to do that.

On the way home he thought about what Sussman had said at Pike's home. It was true. He was a callous son of a bitch, gambling with a man's life. A couple of months ago he would not have done it. Could not have done it. He had done a lot of things he wouldn't have before he began chasing the Avila gold. Toiled like a galley slave, lied to Florence, cheated on her, enthusiastically performed sexual acrobatics he once would have thought depraved and kept a shrewd, nosy bastard like Franz Ulrich at bay. In the excitement of the past week he had not thought much about Ulrich. He would have to now. More so now than before. When they stopped going to North Spring Street, Ulrich would assume they had what they were looking for, or come up empty, if he was still checking on them. And he assumed Ulrich was still doing so. When they reached the chest, they would have to be circumspect about bringing it out. Ulrich might have someone watching the place. Not that it would actually do him any good. McDowell could not picture Ulrich resorting to strong-arm methods, but he was certainly capable of using any knowledge he gained to declare himself in.

"You're home early," Florence said when McDowell got home. "I'm glad. Seven days a week is simply too much for . . . everybody."

"It was too much for Bill Pike," McDowell said carefully. "He had a heart attack."

"Oh, my God!" Florence cried. "Is he? Poor, dear Henrietta."

"He's in the hospital. She's with him now."

"What did the doctor say?"

"I don't know."

"You didn't wait to find out?" Florence demanded.

"We didn't go with him. We didn't think it would be wise. Henrietta went with him."

"Henrietta? What was she doing there?"

245

"She wasn't. We took him home," he added reluctantly.

"Took him home?" Florence said incredulously. "Didn't you know he was having a heart attack?"

"We knew. But we couldn't have the place crawling with strangers, could we?"

"Are you telling me you risked that dear man's life merely to—"

"That's enough, Florence," McDowell said firmly. "I did what I had to do. I've had enough of that kind of crap from Steve and Henrietta. I don't want to hear any more."

"Arthur McDowell . . ." Florence began.

"I said that's enough!"

Florence looked at him strangely, biting her lip.

"I don't know you when you're like this," she said at last. "May I at least ask what hospital?"

"UCLA, I think. It's the closest. And he's on the faculty."

"You don't even know that. Don't you even care?"

"Of course I care. How would it help Bill Pike for me to know what hospital, for God's sake?"

"I'm calling right now."

"An excellent idea."

Pike was in intensive care. Henrietta said preliminary reports indicated it had not been a particularly severe heart attack and there did not appear to be extensive damage. It would be a day or two before they could be sure.

"No thanks to you," Florence said when she told him. "It was his superb physical condition."

Sussman phoned later to give him the same information. Henrietta had called him from the hospital.

"I'm picking her up after a while to take her to get her car," Sussman said.

He hadn't screwed up that relationship, at any rate, McDowell thought gratefully. If he had, he'd be in even worse trouble with Florence.

It was bad enough, however. Florence made him sleep on the couch in the library, though when he came creeping back to the bedroom in the middle of the night, she did not send him away. McDowell wondered if Sussman was spending the night at Pike's

246

house, comforting Henrietta. Whether he was or not, Sussman had better be ready to put in a full day's work in the tunnel tomorrow and as many full days after that as it took to get the chest. They were too close now to drag their feet.

He wished now they had not taken Pike in. Pike had only put in three weeks, and he'd damned near wrecked the operation. But they had needed the money. And wanted to be sure of finishing before the fall quarter. Well, they would now, and Pike's money and his three weeks of work with them had helped make it possible. All things considered, perhaps it had not been such a mistake. And it had brought Sussman and Henrietta together again, which made Florence happy.

When he reached the office Monday morning, he found it had been broken into. The street door showed signs of forced entry, drawers were open in the office and papers strewn on the floor. The doors to the basement had not been forced, but McDowell recalled that in the rush to get Pike out he had forgotten to lock them. He looked around the basement for signs the intruder had gone downstairs, but there were so many of his, Pike's and Sussman's footprints he could not tell if any of them had been made by the burglar.

He went back up to wait for Sussman. Could it have been a common burglar or was it someone trying to learn what was going on? Franz Ulrich, for example. If a burglar, he had probably gone down to the basement to look for something to steal. The electric hammer, the electric drill and Sussman's radio were still there, so it did not look like a burglar. It sounded more like Ulrich or someone working for him. But Ulrich wouldn't have bothered with the office. He would have gone directly to the basement. A wino might have ransacked the office and not gone to the basement. But a wino would have taken the typewriter. Perhpas it was too heavy to carry. McDowell hoped it had been a wino too befuddled to look in the basement or, if he had, thought nothing of what he saw there.

Sussman came in looking sleepy.

"I didn't get much sleep last night," he said. "I sat

up with Henrietta until after one. She finally took a pill, and I went home." He paused and looked more closely at McDowell. "What the hell's the matter with you? Guilt finally catch up with you?"

"Someone broke in last night."

"Oh, Jesus! Did he find the tunnel?"

"I don't know."

He went over his speculations with Sussman.

"I hope it was just some wino," Sussman said fervently. "We get a lot of 'em around here."

"So do I, Steve. But we can't afford to assume that. It could have been Ulrich. Or someone working for him."

"But you said he wouldn't have bothered with the office."

"He could have, to try and make it look like an ordinary burglary."

"So what do we do now?"

"Make sure it doesn't happen again. From now on, one of us is spending the night here. We'll take turns."

"Fine with me."

"We'll get a rollaway bed from Abbey Rents. I've got plenty of bedding at home. Have you got a gun?"

"My deer rifle and my twelve gauge are back in Texas with my folks."

"We need a gun. A pistol."

"I'll ask Henrietta. Pike's got weapons all over the place."

"There's one other thing we need," said McDowell. Sussman looked puzzled.

"A chamber pot."

At ten, Florence came down to report on Pike's condition. "He had a good night," she said. "Henrietta says he's doing remarkably well. He can even have visitors tonight. If we don't stay too long."

"I'm invited?" McDowell asked.

"Your name never came up. But I want you to go with me. And try to apologize."

"Whatever you say, sweetheart," McDowell said.

He did not tell her about the break-in. That could wait until he was obliged to explain why he must spend every other night at North Spring Street.

After they returned to work, Sussman came out of

248

the tunnel wearing a serious expression. "Did you lose a button?" he asked.

"A button?" McDowell said blankly.

Sussman held out his hand. Resting in the palm was a flat white button with three holes in the center. There was a tuft of brown thread in one of the holes.

"I don't have buttons on my coveralls," McDowell said. "Just snaps."

"Me, too. Could Pike have lost it, you think?"

"He had zippers."

McDowell took the button between thumb and forefinger and studied it. It was much too clean and shiny to have been in the tunnel very long. He sighed.

"Are you thinking what I'm thinking?" Sussman said.

"I'm afraid so. I suppose that answers our question about whether our visitor found the tunnel."

"I think we both better stay here at night, Mac."

"You're right. We'll get two rollaway beds. One of us goes home, cleans up, has dinner and comes back. Then the other one can do it. That means except for an hour or so there'll be two of us here."

"I'll need some extra time tonight," Sussman said. "I've got to go by the hospital and take Henrietta to dinner."

"No problem. I've got to go there with Florence for a few minutes, too. You go first."

Sussman kicked the side of the workbench in a sudden burst of fury.

"If anybody tries to fuck us up after all we've been through, I'll kill the bastard!" he cried.

McDowell knew exactly how he felt. No one was going to cheat them out of their hard-won treasure. Let them try. He and Sussman would be ready for them.

"Better get two pistols," he said.

McDowel had never fired a pistol in his life but had seen it done enough in films and on television to believe himself capable of handling a gun.

"Do you think Ulrich would try any rough stuff?" Sussman said.

"No. I think he'd be more likely to declare himself in, want to get rid of the coins for us for a healthy percentage. But you never know. And we're not positive it's Ulrich, are we?"

"Who else could it be? If not him. If he wants in, I guess we could learn to live with it."

"We're not sharing with anyone," McDowell said firmly. "Not after all we've been through. If it is Ulrich, I wonder exactly how much he knows now."

"If he found the substructure map, just about everything."

Sussman kept the map on a worktable, rolled up with a rubber band around it. McDowell nodded at it.

"Is that the way you left it?" he asked.

"How should I know? I didn't mark the spot where I put the rubber band or left it on the table."

McDowell slipped off the rubber band and unrolled the map. Every day's progress, except Sunday's, was marked on the line extending from the basement to the rear of the Avila Adobe. There was nothing to indicate the significance of the little circle marking the position of the chest, and certainly not that it was a hoard of gold coins, but it wouldn't take a genius to know it was the end of the line whatever was there. And Ulrich would certainly know the hooked neck eagle was somehow involved, though it was doubtful he suspected it came from the site marked on the map. He wouldn't know how they had managed to bring it up.

If Ulrich had seen the map, he would know where they were heading and approximately how long it would take them to get there. The question was: Would he have them watched so he would know when or would he simply use what he had learned to blackmail them into letting him share the proceeds? Either way, it would be wise to give no indication that they had found anything after they reached the chest. After they got the chest, they would keep on working as if nothing unusual had happened. Meanwhile, they would have taken the chest out in a cardboard box with material from the tunnel and taken it to a safe place. A safety-deposit box in a bank would be best.

"So what do you think?" Sussman asked.

"We'll cope," McDowell said with more confidence

than he felt. "This isn't getting any work done. Let's do some digging."

In the afternoon, on the way back from Mulholland, he rented two rollaway beds and a chamber pot and stopped by his home to pick up pillows and bedding. Robert was home and wanted to know what it was for.

"Charity," McDowell said.

Thanks to the order imposed by Pike, there was room for the beds in the basement. Sussman took the last run to Mulholland. When he returned to relieve McDowell after taking Henrietta to dinner, he brought two pistols with him, a Colt .45 automatic and a World War II Luger.

"I'll show you how to handle them when you get back," he said. "We'll have lots of time on our hands. Oh, yeah, Florence was at the hospital. I told her you'd be a little late."

"Did you tell her why?"

"I thought I'd leave that to you. She said she'd be home in time to fix dinner for you and Robert and go back to the hospital with you."

Dinner was waiting when McDowell got home. Robert had already eaten and was watching television. In the kitchen, McDowell told Florence what had happened and that he and Sussman would be spending their nights in the basement until they brought out the chest.

"But they might kill you!" Florence protested. "For all that money."

"We'll be armed."

"You don't know anything about guns, Arthur! Shouldn't you wait until Billie is better?"

Now it's Billie, McDowell thought. Calling that snappish little bastard Billie. Ludicrous.

"Steve does," he said.

"Couldn't you just hire a watchman instead?"

"And let them kill him instead?" McDowell teased. "Is that what you're saying?"

Florence refused to be humored. "You know very well that's not what I meant," she said. "A watchman is trained for that sort of thing."

"Exactly what would I tell him he's watching?"

Florence made a helpless gesture. "But you don't even have a bathroom," she wailed.

"We've got a potty."

"Promise me one thing," Florence said, defeated. "You'll be careful."

Henrietta and Florence embraced in the hospital corridor. All Henrietta gave McDowell was a curt "Hello."

"Father wants to see you," she said curtly. "I can't imagine why. The nurse says you may stay three minutes."

Pike was in an oxygen tent but, to McDowell's surprise, looked as fit as he had ever seen him.

"Damned nuisance, all this," Pike said, gesturing at the oxygen tent and the accouterments of the room. "And they insist on at least two more days of it."

There were three baskets of flowers in the room. McDowell wished he had sent some. He'd tell Florence to when he went back out. Pike followed his gaze.

"Thanks for the flowers," Pike said. "Very thoughtful of you and Flossie."

Flossie, for God's sake, McDowell thought. He was glad Florence had anticipated him about the flowers.

"Least I could do," he said.

"I've been wanting a word with you," Pike said.

I should think so, McDowell thought. Whatever he says, I deserve it.

"What you did to me was despicable," Pike said.

"I know. I'm sorry."

"But tactically, damned wise. Ruthlessness is one of those rare qualities one finds all too seldom."

"Should you be doing all this talking?" McDowell asked.

"And when I find that quality in a man, I admire it. I admire it. Frankly, Art, I didn't think you had it in you. You weren't in the service, were you?"

"I'm afraid not. Too young for the big one and in college all through Korea."

"Pity," said Pike. "You'd have gone far. They tell me I'll have to stop smoking. Damned if I will."

"Maybe you should."

"Incidentally, I owe you an apology."

"For what?"

252

"For things I said to you about having Steve Sussman for a friend. He's been a trump."

"I tried to tell you."

Pike studied his nails.

"Florence come with you?" he asked.

"Of course."

"Send the dear woman in, will you? You have a jewel there, McDowell, a real jewel. Until you showed what you were made of yesterday I thought she was wasted on you. Now I'm not so sure."

"Thanks," McDowell said dryly.

He went out and sent Florence in. He tried to make conversation with Henrietta but got only short, cold replies. When he left, he said, "Is there anything I can tell Steve for you?"

"Yes," said Henrietta. "Tell him he's in bad company."

19

McDOWELL and Sussman lay on the rollaway beds in the dark basement. There was a new lock on the street door and a sliding bolt on the office side. The doors to the basement were also bolted from the inside. Sussman's cigar glowed in the blackness, and the radio was tuned to the country music station, low. At the moment, Sammi Smith was singing "Help Me Make It Through the Night." McDowell smiled to himself. The song was so appropriate. It was only ten o'clock. After a half hour session of instruction from Sussman on loading and unloading the Luger, the use of the safety and some dry runs clicking the pistol off at the left breast of the September girl on the calendar, there had been nothing to do but retire for the night.

It was almost like camping out, McDowell thought, except that they were indoors and on beds instead of in sleeping bags. He had not done much camping, and now he found it rather pleasant. He had no sense of peril. They were behind three locked doors and Sussman knew how to shoot. And he did not expect anyone to try anything until there were indications he and

Sussman had reached their goal. That was the time to begin worrying.

Then, even if there were no one snapping at their heels they would still have problems. Rare gold coins were not anonymous like currency. They would have to find a way to dispose of the Avila gold without arousing suspicion. There must be ways. Ulrich would know them, of course, but dealing with him was out of the question. He was in a position to demand more than the usual dealer's margin of profit, and would. They could buy a building lot somewhere, or cheap desert acreage, and claim to have found the coins there. He'd have to ask a lawyer about who owned such a find, if the previous owner had any claim. But even if such an arrangement would permit them to sell the coins openly, there was the question of taxes. They would have to look into that as well. It might be better to keep the find secret and sell off the coins gradually around the country. They'd have to do it over a long period of time anyhow and be careful not to make any garish display of suddenly acquired wealth. Or they could sell them out of the country. They might do better and with greater security in Switzerland, Germany and Japan. Florence loved to travel. He'd have to look into those numbered Swiss accounts.

"You're not sleeping, are you, Mac?" Sussman said.

"At this hour? You know, that's a nice song. Some of your country stuff isn't bad."

"Funny how things turn out, isn't it?"

"You mean my conversion to country music?"

"I was thinking about Pike's heart attack. I ought to thank you for being such a horse's ass about it. Now you're the heavy and I'm the man with the white hat."

"I didn't think you gave a damn what Pike thought about you."

"Henrietta did. And now we don't have to sneak around behind his back."

"You serious about her?"

"You sound like Florence."

McDowell laughed. "Pike said you were a trump," he said.

He heard movement in Sussman's bed, as if Sussman were sitting up.

"Hey," said Sussman. "That's cool."

After a while Sussman said, "Are you gonna keep teaching? After we cash in the coins?"

"Have to. Both of us. At least until our contracts are up. And even then we'll have to be careful how we throw money around."

"I know that. I mean after."

"I haven't really thought about it. I suppose I will, though. Maybe with a lighter load. How about you?"

"I'm not sure. I'm really not cut out to be a teacher. I'd like to be a real engineer. With the financing I'll have I could start my own firm."

"You'll miss those hot little co-eds."

"I'm getting too old for that kind of crap, Mac."

So Sussman was serious about Henrietta Pike, McDowell thought. Florence would be glad to hear that. And he was definitely going to point out that it was he, in a sense, who had smoothed the way for it by getting Sussman back in Pike's good graces. She might forgive him for not rushing Pike directly to a hospital. Somehow things had a way of working themselves out.

He thought about Gloria Stavros. Even that had worked itself out. It had been fun while it lasted, and now it was over without any fuss. Sussman knew how to get rid of women, but McDowell did not think he would have been able to do so gracefully if the Golden Greek had really been hung up on him, as she had claimed. After things settled down, he might even look her up again if he felt the urge for hectic action. Now that he knew it was only physical with her there would be no awkward entanglement.

He awoke in the night and reached over to touch Florence. It was some moments before he realized where he was. Sussman was snoring lightly. He wondered if that bothered Henrietta.

At midmorning Tuesday, Sussman looked at the substructure map and said they were under the Avila Adobe.

"If we're on the nose," he said, "we'll be four feet from the chest by late Friday afternoon. Straight down and easy digging. By Friday night we could be up to our ass in gold pieces."

McDowell felt a surge of elation, followed by a wave of doubt. What if the chest was not full of gold coins but held only a few among less valuable objects and they had merely chanced upon the hooked neck eagle amid the dross? He refused to let himself dwell upon the possibility.

"We'll keep digging until we hit it if it takes all night," he said.

"I'm for that," said Sussman.

They worked feverishly the balance of the week. They took away only part of the material they removed from the tunnel. They would need many yards of material to fill in the hole in the basement and to take out to Mulholland to create the illusion they were still digging after they secured the chest and removed it.

A little after three on Friday afternoon Sussman made a measurement and said they were only two feet from the point above the chest. They dug that out together, piling the material in the wagon and along the sides of the tunnel. When they were done there was nothing but solid shale beneath them.

"Shit," said Sussman. "Let's go another couple feet."

Drenched with sweat and panting with exertion, they pressed on doggedly. After two more feet, and then another, they still had not reached the site of the old well.

"That's about as much as we should be off, distance-wise," Sussman said. "We must be off to the side." He shrugged. "Hell, it would have been a miracle to hit it right on the nose. Just a matter of finding which side we're on. What time is it, anyhow?"

"Almost nine," McDowell said.

"Jesus, that late? Time sure flies when you're having fun."

"Florence must be biting her nails wondering what's happened to me."

"Henny, too. We ought to phone 'em."

"I'll call Florence and tell her to call Henrietta. And I'll bring back something to eat. Then we'll decide what to do next."

He called Florence from the Glorious Dragon while he waited for egg rolls and chicken chow mein to take out.

"I was worried sick," Florence said. "Henrietta and I have been calling each other every five minutes since six."

"Sorry," McDowell said contritely. "We got so busy we forgot what time it was."

"I was imagining all sorts of terrible things. When you phoned, I'd just made up my mind to drive down there."

"Tell Henrietta everything's all right. We won't be leaving the place tonight. So don't worry. I'll check in with you first thing in the morning."

"I won't sleep a wink," Florence said.

When McDowell returned with the food, Sussman said, "Chow mein? Of all the stuff on the menu you get chow mein?"

"Next time you go," McDowell said.

"These egg rolls ain't too bad. Not like Lee's Den, but not bad."

"Lee's Den? You mean General Lee's?"

"No. Lee's Den. It's in Houston. Best Chinese food there is."

"Have you tried Chan's Garden in Westwood or Man Fook Low's on San Pedro?"

McDowell began laughing. Sussman joined him.

"Can you imagine?" McDowell said. "Us sitting here talking about Chinese restaurants at a time like this?"

"We're about half hysterical is the reason."

"I know. What's our next move, Professor Sussman?"

"We can go two ways. One's long and hard; the other's short and risky."

"The way I feel, I vote for the short and risky."

The hard way, Sussman explained, was to dig branch tunnels probing for the well site. They could be several feet off to one side or another and it might take a day or two to dig the branches. The quicker way was to get a surface reference point.

"We make a bore straight up and see where it comes out," Sussman explained. "That means going over the wall again."

257

"We did it once. We can do it again."

The auger they had used in locating the chest was in the accumulation of equipment in the basement. Sussman said they would also need a ladder to get over the wall. They made one by nailing lengths of two-by-four crosswise on a long two-by-ten plank.

Sussman suggested that McDowell make the bore and let him go over the wall behind the Avila Adobe to see where it emerged.

"You'd be taking all the risk," McDowell protested.

"But you'd be doing most of the work. And I don't trust you to pinpoint the exit hole on our diagram of the patio. You remember where I put it? The diagram?"

"The last time I saw it was the night we went over the wall. Oh, Lord, don't tell me we'll have to go through the whole business with the metal detector again!"

"Nope. It's around here somewhere."

Sussman found the diagram under the worktable, still on the clipboard.

They climbed into their beds and napped until 1 A.M. They were still very tired when they got up. McDowell helped Sussman carry the heavy improvised ladder out to the van. Sussman took one of the walkie-talkies, a flashlight and the patio diagram with him. McDowell locked and bolted all three doors behind him when he returned to the basement and went into the tunnel with the auger sections.

It was difficult boring straight up. McDowell lay on his back with sand and gravel showering down on him. The goggles prevented the material from getting in his eyes, but he had to stop frequently to clean them off. Sussman had said he would have to bore upward eight feet to reach the surface. He had gone about six when Sussman's voice came over the walkie-talkie. McDowell could not make out what he was saying.

"You'll have to talk louder," McDowell said. "I can't hear you."

"Not so loud!" Sussman said urgently. "Can you hear me now?"

"Just."

"How you doing?"

"About six feet, I think."

"Cool. Tell me when you've done eight and I'll make a fast check with the flashlight."

"Roger," said McDowell, thinking about Pike, sorry the colonel was in a hospital bed but glad he was not around to tell them what they were doing wrong.

He drilled two feet.

"Steve," he said. "Eight feet."

"Nothing yet," Sussman replied after a moment. "Give her a few more turns."

He sounded worried.

McDowell went up another six inches.

"Done," he said.

"Checking," said Sussman. "I see it! I see it! Wow! Just three feet off. Just three feet off, for Christ's sake. Ssssh!"

There was an abrupt silence. What was happening? McDowell wondered in near panic. Had Sussman been caught? He waited. And waited. Sussman's voice came on again.

"I thought I heard somebody at the wall," he said in a low voice. "But if it was anybody, he's gone now."

"Take a good look around before you come out," McDowell warned.

"Naturally," said Sussman. "See you soon."

"And don't forget to cover the auger hole."

"Roger and out."

Sussman must be thinking about Pike, too, McDowell thought. He went up to the office to wait, not turning on any lights. Only three feet off after tunneling four hundred and seventy, he thought. Sussman had really done a job. He stood at the window looking through the hole in the paint until the van pulled into the loading zone. He unbolted the door before Sussman had a chance to knock, and they hurried down to the basement.

"You get my vote for engineer of the year," McDowell said. "What went on out there? When you thought you heard something?"

"Could've been a watchman. But it was all clear when I looked. I was real careful."

"We're both bushed," McDowell said. "Let's get

some sleep and go after the chest in the morning."

"I was hoping you'd say that. I couldn't dig another inch."

They fell into bed, filthy and sweating. Despite his fatigue, McDowell did not fall asleep immediately. He was too excited. In a few hours they would have Don Diego's chest.

When he awoke after eight in the morning, Sussman was still snoring. McDowell turned on the radio and shook him awake.

"Jesus," Sussman complained. "I just closed my eyes."

McDowell went out to phone Florence and bring back coffee and doughnuts. While they were gulping down the hot coffee, he said, "I'm wondering if we ought to knock off for the weekend, just to make it look normal."

"We worked last weekend," Sussman said. "And how can we wait two whole days with the chest just sitting there?"

"You're right."

Sussman took the first shift to get the branch tunnel started at the proper angle. McDowell shoveled material and heaped it at the front of the basement. In the midst of his activities he heard a determined knocking upstairs. Startled, he grabbed the Luger and went up to investigate. He looked out of the hole in the paint into an eye peering within. The eye pulled back. It belonged to Florence. He opened the door for her, and she came in with a bag of sandwiches and a Thermos.

"Have you got it yet?" she said anxiously.

"Not yet. But this afternoon, I think."

Florence clutched her breast.

"Oh, I hope it's there! I'm going to stay right here until you come up and tell me it's really there."

"As long as you're here, you may as well keep an eye on the street. If you see anything out of the ordinary, come down and tell us."

"All right. Why do you keep holding your hand behind you like that?"

Not wanting to alarm Florence, he had been concealing the Luger behind his back. He brought it into view, saying, "I didn't know who was trying to get in."

"Is it loaded?" Florence said apprehensively.

McDowell nodded.

"Be careful with it, Arthur. You could shoot yourself."

McDowell went downstairs and relieved Sussman in the tunnel. Every few inches he probed the floor with an iron rod, encountering only unyielding shale. During his third turn in the tunnel the rod sank into the earth. He had reached the well site. After taking a moment to compose himself, he called Sussman on the walkie-talkie. Sussman came back to join him, bringing shoring material. They dug another two feet to give themselves working room and put in the final shoring.

"Four feet down and we've got it," Sussman said, knocking on the wood of the shoring.

"God, I'm nervous," McDowell said. "What if—"

"Shut up, for Christ's sake! Just dig."

They dug recklessly, letting the material pile up on the tunnel door behind them. They dug until they were gasping and streaming with sweat.

"I've gotta take a break," Sussman panted.

"Get out of my way then," McDowell cried.

His shovel hit something unyielding. That lump in his throat had to be his heart, he thought.

"I think I've hit it," he croaked.

Sussman had installed the last light bulb with several feet of wire to spare. With the light in his hand in its wire cage he crowded next to McDowell.

"You hold it while I dig," he said. "I've got my wind back."

He dug feverishly while McDowell held the light over the hole. Sussman enlarged the hole and brushed the dirt away with his hand, revealing rotting wood and bands of rust which once had been iron straps. There was a hole where the core sample had gone through so long ago.

"Jesus," he whispered. "Jesus."

"Can you get it open?" McDowell asked in the same hushed tone.

"I'll have to dig around to give us a little room."

While he was doing so, the rotted chest burst. Sussman pulled away the moldering wood in chunks.

"Look!" he cried.

There, shining at the bottom of the hole, was a heap of gold coins.

"It's full!" McDowell gasped. "The fucking box is full!"

"Oh God!" said Sussman. "Oh, shit!"

He dug his hands into the mass, raised them and let the coins fall like rain. He straightened and extended his right hand. McDowell shook it solemnly.

"We did it," McDowell said. "We really did it." He breathed deeply to calm himself. "We can't bring them out in the chest. It's falling to pieces. I'll go back and get bags."

They still had the cloth bags they had used for material before they changed to cardboard boxes.

He had to crawl over mounds of sand to reach the electric car. The car seemed never to have moved so slowly. In the basement, he snatched up a handful of bags and, glancing at the bolted door behind which lay the steps, hesitated a moment. He ought to tell Florence. She was up there biting her nails. But Sussman was waiting for him. By the time he returned to the end of the tunnel Sussman had taken out most of the coins and piled them at the edge of the hole. McDowell began stowing them in bags. They were hard and cold in his hands, and he kept pausing to look at them. So many coins, so many different kinds. And all gold.

"Wait till we get 'em in the basement for that," Sussman said impatiently.

When the chest was empty, he asked for the light. He held it close to the crumbling chest.

"Almost missed a couple," he said, handing them to McDowell.

McDowell distributed the coins among three bags. They would have fit into one but were so heavy he did not think the fabric would hold. He took one of the bags out with him and sent the car back for Sussman. He was tempted to pour the coins out on the worktable and examine them while he waited for Sussman but did not because it was something the two of them should do together. Sussman emerged at last. He deposited his bags of gold on the basement floor and climbed out of the entrance pit after them. Wordlessly, he took the bags to the center of the basement and emptied them on the floor. Rivers of gold, round and winking, poured out of the bags. Coins rolled about the basement.

"What the hell are you doing?" McDowell demanded.

"Dump yours, too," Sussman said excitedly.

He sat down and began removing his shoes and socks.

"What the hell are you doing?" McDowell said again.

"Dump your bag, for Christ's sake."

McDowell added his coins to the mound on the floor. Sussman elbowed him aside and began treading on the heap of coins with his bare feet.

"When I was a kid, I wanted to do this through tits," he said. "But this is more fun."

"You're crazy."

"Try it and see."

McDowell took off his shoes and socks and tried it. The hard edges of the coins dug into his feet, but there was ecstasy in the pain.

They scooped the coins up in shovels and put them on the table.

"Better than shoveling sand, huh, amigo?" Sussman said.

Then they went over the floor carefully and picked up the coins that had rolled away.

"Let's see what we've got," McDowell said, his voice trembling.

They stacked them in neat piles according to denomination. There were 1,706 coins of eight-, four- and two-cscudo denomination, Spanish as well as Mexican, 551 eights, including 43 of the hooked neck eagles, 736 fours and 419 twos. The most recent dates was 1835. The oldest 1721. The hoard obviously was the accumulation of generations.

"I make it about sixty-four pounds," said Sussman.

"Sixty-four pounds of minted gold," McDowell

263

said, looking at the stacked coins covering much of the surface of the table. "If the two you priced are any guide, they've got to be worth more than a million dollars."

They'd get a copy of *Gold Coins of the World* and find out. Not the old edition in the research library but a new one like the one Ulrich had. Ulrich. He'd forgotten about Ulrich in all the excitement.

"A lot more," Sussman said. "Five hundred more coins than we figured and some of 'em early eighteenth century. I'll bet it's more like a million and a half. We're fucking millionaires, amigo."

And they were, almost, McDowell thought in disbelief. He had understood the coins would be worth a fortune, but not so large a one, and until they were actually in hand, the fortune had been illusory. What was it going to be like, being so rich?

"I'll run up and get Florence now," he said.

He kept his expression as inscrutable as possible when he fetched her.

"Did you find it?" Florence said, searching his face. "Is it there?"

"Come on," said McDowell.

"Arthur McDowell, don't keep me in suspense like this!"

At the foot of the stairs he said, "Close your eyes."

"Close my eyes?"

"Yes. Are they closed?"

Florence nodded. He led her across the basement to the table.

"Open them," he said.

She opened her eyes.

"Oh," she said in a small voice. "Oh."

"Is that all you can say?" Sussman said, grinning.

McDowell thought she was going to faint. He reached out to support her. She grabbed him and held on tightly.

"I can tell you now," she said. "I couldn't believe they were really there. I thought it was too good to be true."

"How would you like to walk through them barefoot?" McDowell said.

Florence pulled back and stared at him.

"Steve and I did," he said. "What a sensation."

"You're both insane."

"Sudden wealth does that to men of weak character," Sussman said.

Florence turned to the table and, hands on hips, gazed raptly at the gold for a full minute.

"They must be worth hundreds of thousands of dollars," she said.

"Closer to a million and a half, I'd estimate," said McDowell.

"A million and a half dollars!" Florence cried, bursting into tears. "I can't stand it."

McDowell smiled and gave her a fond kiss. "If I'd known being rich was going to affect you this way I wouldn't have gone to all that trouble," he said.

"I can learn to live with it," Florence said wiping her eyes.

"You better go on home now. It's getting close to dinner time, and Robert'll be wondering what happened to you."

"What will we tell him about all this?"

"Nothing, sweetheart."

"We'll have to, eventually. When we have all that money."

"No. He doesn't know if we're rich or poor. He's been getting everything he wants all his life."

"That's not fair and you know it. There's lots of things he hasn't had."

"Sure. A fully equipped chemical lab, a chimp. Get a move on, Florence. I'll come up and lock up after you."

Florence stopped for a final, lingering look at the ranks of stacked coins on the table. When he let her out the front door, she said, "Do you think it's all right to tell Billie? Or would the excitement be too much for him now?"

"Pike get excited? Don't make me laugh."

"You don't really know him, do you, Arthur?"

When he rejoined Sussman in the basement, they put the coins back in the bags and discussed what to do with them. They considered keeping them in the basement until Monday, when the banks were open and they could get a safety-deposit box but neither was comfortable with that. It was better to get the coins away from the premises as quickly as they could without arousing the suspicions of anyone who might be watching the place even though there had been no indication they were under surveillance.

"You take a load of material to Mulholland as if nothing's happened," McDowell said. "Then clean up, go to the hospital and take Henrietta to dinner as usual. When you come back, I'll go, just the way we've been doing all week. Then we'll wait until two or three in the morning and take them to my place. One of us stays, and one comes back here. Tomorrow we'll make a couple of trips out to Mulholland to make it look as if we're still digging. On one of 'em I'll take the coins to the bank and rent a big safety-deposit box."

"Cool," said Sussman.

McDowell locked the street door behind Sussman and remained in the office with the Luger handy. Every time he heard footsteps go past on North Spring Street he took the Luger off safety and held it ready. By the time Sussman returned he was a nervous wreck. He had not realized being rich could be so trying.

He had little appetite for the celebratory dinner Florence prepared and was of no help to Robert with the crossword puzzle. He was too impatient to go to the hospital with Florence, thinking about Sussman being alone. When he rejoined Sussman, they remained in the office, lying down behind the desk and speaking only in whispers.

Around eleven someone tried the door. They snatched up their pistols and waited, holding their breath. McDowell crawled to the window on hands and knees and, as the footsteps moved away, peered cautiously through the hole in the paint. A man in shapeless clothing was walking toward Macy, reeling a bit. McDowell crawled back to Sussman.

"Just a wino," he said.

At two in the morning they went to the basement and put the bags in a cardboard box. McDowell carried the box up the steps, cradling it in his arms so that the heavy bags would not tear through the bottom. Sussman followed close behind him with the .45 in his hand. Sussman unbolted the office door and looked around cautiously before motioning for McDowell to go ahead. The street was deserted. The only sign of life was up at the corner, where an occasional car went by on Macy. Sussman went ahead of him and opened the back of the van. McDowell slid the box in.

"Freeze," said a deep voice from inside the van.

20

McDowell stiffened. At his side, Sussman made a movement.

"Cool it!" the deep voice grated. "I'll blow your fucking head off. That's better. Now step back. Hands on your heads."

McDowell heard Sussman's pistol clatter to the pavement. He put his hands on his head and stepped back. He was numb. They had been so careful, and now at the very end had blundered. He had misjudged Ulrich, thinking he would not resort to violence. He thought of the fortune in gold for which they had sweated and connived. Ulrich was not going to get away with this.

The man came out of the van. He was tall, wearing some sort of a loose coat and a peaked cap. His features were grotesque beneath a stocking pulled down over his face. He gave a low whistle. A figure emerged from the doorway of the Chinese hotel across the street and came toward them. The second man, dressed like the first, was short and slight. Neither of them could be Ulrich. Were they working for him or were they an unknown quantity? McDowell wondered.

"Check 'em out," the big man said.

The small man felt McDowell's body, found the Luger tucked in his waistband and took it.

"The other dude dropped his piece," the big man said. "Find it."

The small man stooped and picked up Sussman's

.45. He put a pistol in each jacket pocket. The weight pulled the jacket down around his hips.

"You," the big man said, gesturing toward McDowell with the short-barreled shotgun he was holding. "Pick up the box and get back inside."

There was something unusual about the way he pronounced "inside." As if he had a slight speech impediment. McDowell had heard that voice before. But where and when?

Sussman unlocked the door, and the two men herded them inside and down the steps to the basement. McDowell wondered if they intended killing them. Somehow he felt no fear, only cold anger.

"Tie 'em up," the big man said, fishing lengths of rope from a jacket pocket. "On your face, assholes."

Again he just missed enunciating the esses properly. McDowell was positive he had heard the voice before. He lay on his face in the dirt, Sussman stretched out beside him cursing in a low, intense voice. The small man tied their wrists behind them and then their ankles.

"See what we've got," the big man ordered.

McDowell craned his head to watch.

The small man folded back the lid of the box. His hands were small and delicate, with long nails. Faggots, McDowell thought with a new surge of rage. They were being ripped off by a couple of faggots. The small man reached into the box and brought out a handful of gold pieces. He gasped. McDowell wanted to vomit.

"Jesus!" the big man said hoarsely.

It was almost "Jethuth."

"Take the gun," the big man said, handing it to the small one.

The small man took it gingerly, as if afraid of it. God, God, God, McDowell thought. To be plundered by someone like that.

The big man picked up the box and started for the steps.

"Come on," he said impatiently.

The small one backed toward him, the wavering muzzle of the shotgun shifting back and forth from McDowell to Sussman.

"Bye, assholes," the big man said.

He went up the steps with long strides. The small man whirled and followed, moving with effeminate grace. And then McDowell knew where he had heard the big man's voice before. It was the voice that had answered the phone the night he called Gloria Stavros. And the small man. It was not a man. It was Gloria. At McDowell's side, Sussman was cursing aloud, kicking and squirming in helpless fury.

It was obvious now. Gloria Stavros had been seeing Sussman throughout the beginning of their venture. He would not have told her what they were doing, but she was bright enough to know it was out of character and clandestine. She had to think it strange that he came to Sussman's apartment to clean up. McDowell wondered if she had known it was him in the shower when she said she thought it was Sussman. When Sussman dumped her, she was still curious about what they were doing, and possibly vindictive as well. She must have called him and asked him to come see her just to question him. Why else would she have gotten in touch with him out of the blue like that? And then dropped him so abruptly. She wasn't the type who had to chase men. She'd probably already had a new boyfriend when she called him, the man who had answered her phone. The man who had tailed Sussman to North Spring Street and him to the dump site. The man who had broken into the office to see what they were up to and explored their tunnel. The man who had done all that when, like fools, they were blaming Ulrich. But how had they known to be there when he and Sussman brought out the Avila gold?

Sussman was still cursing and throwing himself around like a madman.

"Shut up and let's try to get loose," McDowell ordered.

"I won't forget that lisping motherfucker," Sussman raged. "I'll know that voice if I ever hear it again."

"Sit up," McDowell said.

He worked himself into a sitting position while Sussman was doing the same. He bumped over to Sussman and slid his back against Sussman's.

"When I say the word, let's brace against each other and try to stand up," he said.

It took them several attempts before they managed to squirm erect. McDowell hopped toward the work-table. He lost his balance and fell heavily across it on his face. His nose started bleeding. The blood ran down his chin and dropped onto his shirt.

"Jesus," Sussman cried. "Are you all right?"

"I'm all right."

The shears he had used to cut up the boxes in which they had removed Pike were still on the table. Mc-Dowell dragged them toward the edge with his chin, leaving a trail of blood spots the size of two-escudo pieces. He turned around and picked up the shears. Though his wrists were tightly bound, he found he could open and close the shears by using both hands.

"Come over here and turn your back," he told Sussman.

Sussman hopped to him. McDowell groped for his bound wrists, unable to turn his head far enough to see them.

"Tell me if I cut you," he said, working the shears around the rope between Sussman's wrists.

He began opening and closing the shears and moving them with a sawing motion. When he had cut through the rope, Sussman untied his ankles and freed McDowell. Sussman put a wrist to his mouth where the shears had nicked him and spat redly on the floor.

"Those dirty bastards," he said. "Those dirty, dirty bastards." He looked disconsolately around the basement. "After all we went through to get it."

"Come on," said McDowell. "We're wasting time."

He snatched up two lengths of auger pipe and ran for the steps.

"Where the hell you going?" Sussman demanded. "They're long gone."

"Come on," McDowell cried over his shoulder.

Sussman pounded up the steps after him.

"The little one came out of the hotel," Sussman said. "You think they could still be there?"

"No," McDowell said, locking the street door.

"Then where?"

"Give me the keys to the van."

270

He climbed under the wheel while Sussman ran around to the passenger side. He started the engine and headed for Macy Street.

"Where we going?" Sussman demanded.

"Sherman Oaks."

"Sherman Oaks, for Christ's sake? Oh. Is that where Ulrich lives?"

"Ulrich had nothing to do with it."

"How do you know?"

"Call it a hunch."

"Who were they then? You think you know?"

McDowell did not answer. If Gloria and her boyfriend had not gone back to her apartment, he would be telling Sussman about their relationship for nothing. Even in his anger and despair the thought of Sussman's learning he had cheated on Florence disturbed him.

He got on the Hollywood Freeway and, ignoring the speed limit, raced west to Ventura Freeway. When he took the turnoff for Gloria's apartment, Sussman said, "What makes you think they came all the way out here?"

He would have to tell Sussman sooner or later, McDowell realized. It might as well be now.

"It was Gloria Stavros who ripped us off," he said.

Sussman's mouth fell open. "Gloria?" he said. Where'd you get a crazy idea like that?"

"That's all right where I got it. She lives out here. There's a chance they came back to her place. Or his. He lives next door."

"How do you know?"

"I know."

Comprehension dawned on Sussman's face. "You sneaky son of a bitch," he said.

There was the expected censure in his tone, but also a hint of admiration.

"So you fool around, too," he said. "Just like real folks."

"Drop it," McDowell ordered.

Cars were parked solidly on both sides of the street in front of Gloria's apartment building. McDowell double-parked the van and got out. The building's entrance and foyer were brightly illuminated.

271

"Let's go through the underground garage," McDowell said. "There's an elevator."

"You do know your way around here, don't you, amigo?" Sussman said. "Jesus, I hope you're right about 'em."

They went down the gently sloping ramp into the parking area.

"Elevator's over there," said McDowell.

Sussman grabbed his arm.

"Look!" he cried, pointing.

A blue Mustang was parked nose to the wall. The trunk was open and in it was a large cheap three-suiter case and a bulging suit bag.

"That's the car that followed me," he said. "You were right."

"Looks like they're leaving," McDowell said. "And we're just in time."

"That dirty little bitch," Sussman said tightly. "And that big lisping bastard. I'll kill those sons of bitches."

"They're armed," McDowell said soberly. "And all we've got are these."

He handed Sussman one of the two lengths of auger pipe.

"You look awful," Sussman said. "Blood all over your chin and your shirt."

"They're loading up the car," McDowell said, scrubbing his chin with his handkerchief. "They may be down any minute. We'll jump 'em when they step out of the elevator."

The elevator shaft stuck out into the parking area.

"I'll get over there and attract their attention," McDowell said. "You stand around the corner there, and when the big bastard comes for me, rap him with the pipe."

"What if he's carrying that sawed-off double-barrel?" Sussman protested. "You could get yourself killed."

"Not if you move fast."

Sussman took up a position on the far side of the elevator shaft, the length of pipe across a shoulder, poised to swing. McDowell went to a nearby parked car and crouched behind it. There was crusted blood in his nostrils. He picked at it with a finger.

There came the sound of an elevator descending. Sussman peeked around the corner. McDowell wiped his finger on his trousers and rose just enough to look over the hood of the car. He nodded at Sussman. Sussman, grim-faced, shifted his hands on the pipe and nodded back. McDowell got down again and waited until he heard the elevator door open. He stood erect as a tall young man with longish hair came out with a traveling bag in one hand and an aluminum suitcase in the other. The way the suitcase pulled his shoulder down revealed it was unusually heavy. The Avila gold, McDowell thought exultantly. Gloria Stavros was right behind the man, carrying a dress bag and a small case. Neither had seen him yet.

"Going somewhere?" McDowell said.

Sussman stepped around the corner of the elevator shaft behind them as they gaped at McDowell, standing stock-still as if frozen in place. Then Gloria gave a little scream, and the big man dropped his luggage and, crouching, reached for his waistband. Sussman swung the pipe with an easy, snapping motion of his wrists, not getting his shoulders into it. The man straightened just as he did so, and the pipe caught him across the base of his skull. He fell in a heap, as if dropped from a great height. Gloria screamed again, louder.

"Shut her up!" McDowell cried, running toward them.

The pipe fell to the floor with a metallic clatter as Sussman gathered Gloria in from behind, one arm around her chest and a hand clasped over her mouth. Her eyes were wide with terror.

"Get her behind the car," McDowell ordered, bending down and taking her fallen companion under the arms.

Sussman hustled the unresisting girl to the concealment of the car behind which McDowell had hidden. McDowell dragged the man behind the car. They crouched there, waiting to see if Gloria's screams and the ringing of the pipe on the concrete brought someone to investigate. There was only silence. The elevator remained where it was. Sussman kept his hand clapped

273

over Gloria's mouth. Above it her eyes were still wide and terrified.

"Will you be quiet if he lets you go?" McDowell whispered.

Gloria nodded.

"Let her breathe," he said. "If she yells, slug her." Sussman removed his hand.

"You sorry cunt," he said.

"What are you gonna do to me?" Gloria said thinly.

McDowell bent over the recumbent figure of the big man. He grasped an arm and tried to shake him into consciousness. His head lolled unnaturally. McDowell put an ear to his chest. He could not hear any heartbeat. He felt the wrist for a pulse and detected none. Oh, God, he thought. He looked up at Sussman.

"He's dead," he said.

"He can't be!" Sussman cried. "I just tapped him."

"Toby," Gloria gasped. "Oh, no!"

"Shut up!" McDowell said, getting to his feet, fighting mounting terror.

"Are you going to kill me, too?" Gloria whispered, terrified.

He must not panic, McDowell thought. He must remain clearheaded and not panic.

"I haven't decided yet," he said coldly, giving her a menacing look.

She must be kept in a state of passive terror until he could think things through.

Sussman stared at him, dazed and incredulous.

"Look, Mac," he said. "We're in enough trouble already. Let's just get out of here."

"And what do we do about him?"

"I don't know. Jesus, I don't know."

What could they do about the dead man? McDowell wondered, thinking furiously. It had been an accident, but they'd call it murder. The body must be gotten out of sight until he could think of something.

"It was all Toby's idea," Gloria said. "I didn't want to. He made me. That's the God's truth."

"Go get the van," McDowell said, pressing the keys into Sussman's slack hand.

Sussman did not move. He appeared unable to.

"Get the van, God damn it!" McDowell snapped.

Sussman looked down at the body on the floor and walked woodenly toward the exit.

"And hurry," McDowell ordered.

There was the Avila gold to consider, too, he thought. If any of this came out, not only would they be involved in murder, but also a fortune would be snatched from their grasp and they would have gone through all that hell for nothing. McDowell took the Luger from the dead man's waistband.

"Don't hurt me, big Mac," said Gloria. "Please don't hurt me."

"That depends on you," McDowell said.

They could hide the body in the tunnel until he decided what to do next. And what to do about Gloria. There must be a way to ensure her silence without having to harm her.

"I'll do whatever you say," Gloria said, clutching his arm. "Honest to God."

Sussman returned with the van.

"I've been thinking," he said. "Maybe if we call the police and tell them what happened they'll—"

"Are you out of your mind?" McDowell demanded. "Help me get him in the van."

It was a struggle to get the big, inert body into the van, but they managed. McDowell kept Gloria transfixed with a hard stare during the process. She made no gesture toward escape.

"Which luggage is his?" McDowell said.

Gloria nodded dumbly toward the traveling bag.

"Is that all?"

"There's a suit bag in the car," Gloria said eagerly, anxious to cooperate. "The blue Mustang."

"I know which car. Get it, Steve."

McDowell threw the traveling bag into the van and when Sussman returned with the suit bag had him put the bag in with it.

"You stay put and don't make a sound," he told Gloria. "Understand?"

Gloria nodded.

He drew Sussman aside.

"Take him and his bags to North Spring Street," he said in a low voice. "Put him in the tunnel. Well back. His bags, too. Then come back for me."

Sussman looked at Gloria, huddled white-faced and trembling against the wall.

"Jesus, Mac," he whispered. "You're not going to. . . ."

"Don't be stupid. I'm just going to make damn sure she understands she better keep her mouth shut."

"We're in trouble," Sussman said wretchedly. "We're in real trouble."

"Let me worry about that. Be sure nobody sees you taking him into the shop."

"I didn't mean to kill him, Mac. You know that. She knows that. You both saw I didn't hit him that hard. You can both testify to that."

"Testify to whom? Don't argue with me, Sussman. Just do what I told you. When you get there, unlock the door first and leave it open and then get him in there in a hurry. And don't get any funny ideas on the way. You understand what I'm saying?"

"All right," Sussman said reluctantly.

After he left, McDowell got Gloria's bag from the Mustang and closed the trunk. He made Gloria go with him. He put everything, including the aluminum suitcase, in the elevator and went up to Gloria's floor. He sent her out to open her door and hustled everything inside. He shut the door and slid the safety bolt closed. Gloria was still frightened but somewhat more in command of herself.

"He made me do it," she said tentatively.

"Bullshit," McDowell said, choosing the word deliberately.

"You've got to believe me, big Mac."

"And don't call me that."

"What're you gonna do to me?"

"That depends." He dropped his menacing tone and said quietly, "You're in big trouble, Gloria. You know that, don't you?"

"*I'm* in big trouble?" she said. "It wasn't me that—"

She broke off and bit her lip, looking at him closely to see if her response had angered him.

"You don't call armed robbery big trouble?" McDowell said in the same deliberate tone. "And kidnapping?"

"Kidnapping?"

"When you force someone from one place to another, even from room to room, that's kidnapping. Didn't you know that?"

She shook her head.

Then, hopefully, she said, "But you wouldn't tell. You'd have to tell about the gold if you did."

"That's very true. But nobody's going to say anything about anything." He hardened his tone. "If I decide I can trust you."

"Please. I promise." Her voice grew coquettish. "And I'll do anything you want me to. Any time you want."

"That's not enough, sweetheart," McDowell said coldly.

"Right now, if you want to," she said, grabbing his hand and pulling him toward the bedroom. "Before he gets back."

"You're not that good," he said, shaking loose.

He realized with a touch of horror he was tempted. Because she was that good. How could he think about jumping into bed with her when he'd just been involved in a killing, when for all he knew Sussman might do something stupid and be caught with the body?

"You used to like me," Gloria said plaintively.

"Times have changed."

"I didn't want to rip you off. I really liked you. But Toby. . . . You don't know how mean he could get."

"The hell I don't. How did he know to be waiting for us? And start at the beginning."

She told him everything, eagerly and with little prompting. After breaking up with Sussman, she had begun wondering what he and McDowell were doing that was so important and mysterious.

"Toby did, too," she said. "We'd been tight a long time like, you know, off and on."

Toby had made her call him to see what she could worm out of him.

"I didn't want to," she said. "I mean not just to see what I could find out. I really grooved on you, big Mac."

"I told you not to call me that."

He was chagrined to have his suspicions confirmed.

He would have liked to believe Gloria had really been attracted to him, but it was obvious that was not so despite her protestations.

When her efforts failed, Toby had followed Sussman to North Spring Street one morning and then followed the van out to Mulholland. He had returned to the site later and found they were dumping freshly dug sand and gravel. That had made him even more curious and convinced they were doing something worth looking into.

"After he broke in, he dug you were after something big over on Olvera Street," Gloria said. "Can I have a drink of water?"

"No."

"My throat's dry. I'm scared."

"Later."

"He saw it on some kind of map he found down there. And he said you were like getting close."

They had taken a front room in the little Chinese hotel across the street where they could watch the shop.

"Toby wasn't working, and I took my vacation. It was all his idea. I didn't want to. If you can imagine being stuck in a room with Toby all that time."

"I can imagine."

He was not imagining what she intended him to.

They had not even left the room for meals. Toby went out and brought back food, always choosing a time when he would not be seen by anyone at the North Spring Street Vent and Duct Company. When Toby decided they must be reaching their goal, he and Gloria took turns watching nights as well as days.

"Then when Steve went to that place, you know, where he climbed over the wall, Toby followed him."

Toby guessed it meant they had tunneled as far as they were going to and would get whatever they were after the next day. He followed Sussman out to the dump in Gloria's car when Sussman made the trip intended to make anyone watching believe they were still digging. Then he followed Sussman back to Sussman's apartment and looked in the van to make sure nothing was hidden in it. Then, when Sussman came

278

back and parked the van in the shop's loading zone, he had crawled in the back and waited.

"Smart son of a bitch, wasn't he?" McDowell said with grudging admiration.

"I only dig smart dudes," Gloria said. "That's why I dig you."

She was getting too loose and confident, McDowell thought. He'd have to do something about that. If she thought the pressure was off, she might start getting ideas about declaring herself in as the price of silence.

"Sure you do," he said. He fixed her with a baleful look. "You know what a contract is, Gloria?" he demanded.

A small gasp of reborn terror escaped her.

"Yes," she said, almost inaudibly.

She obviously saw the same television shows and movies he did, McDowell thought. He hoped she was frightened enough not to realize a man like himself would not have the foggiest notion how one got in touch with a hit man.

"Wherever you go, whatever you do, there'll be one out on you ready to go if you talk," he said.

"I won't talk. You don't have to worry about that."

"I'm not worrying, Gloria. You're the one who should be worrying. Have you got a photo of yourself?"

"A photo? Why?"

"Just get me one and don't ask questions. You're getting on my nerves."

Gloria went quickly and fetched some snapshots. McDowell selected one with the best view of her face and put it in his pocket.

"So the man will know what you look like," he said ominously.

"You don't have to do that. I won't fink. I promise."

"Then you've got nothing to worry about, have you? I don't want you to leave this apartment until I tell you. And don't make any funny calls. All right?"

"Yes," Gloria said submissively.

"Incidentally, starting when I leave here, you'll be watched twenty-four hours a day. You're costing me a lot of money. You know that."

279

"I'm sorry, big—"

She caught herself.

"Now get to bed," McDowell ordered.

She turned without a word and walked toward the bedroom. She stopped at the door and looked back.

"Aren't you coming?" she said.

"You didn't mourn too long for lover boy, did you?" McDowell demanded. "Shut that door, and keep it shut. And don't come out until I've gone."

Gloria went into the bedroom. The door slammed shut.

McDowell opened the aluminum suitcase. The three bags were there, packed among men's clothing. All the coins seemed to be there. He had a raging thirst. He remembered he hadn't let Gloria have a drink of water. He considered letting her come out for one now but decided she might interpret it as a sign he was weakening. He looked in the refrigerator in the little Pullman kitchen. It was empty except for a six-pack carton with two cans of beer in it. He had ordered Gloria to remain in the apartment until she heard from him. She'd have nothing to eat. It wouldn't hurt her. He'd get back to her before she got too hungry. He took a can of beer and went into the bathroom to wash the dried blood off his face. Then he went back to the living room to wait for Sussman, trying not to think about what would happen if Sussman were caught with Toby's body.

It was a long wait, during which he was prey to agonizing doubts. Strangely, he felt little remorse about Toby's death, only apprehension that it might lead to disaster. And at a time when they should be celebrating their good fortune. He hated Toby for that. Perhaps that was why he felt so little guilt. What good would it do to feel guilt anyhow? It was done. It could not be undone. If only he could be sure Gloria wouldn't talk. And Sussman wouldn't crack. And that they could get rid of Toby's body without a fuss and cover up every trace of their activities in the basement. If they could do that, it would be as if it had never happened.

When he grew too nervous to sit, he got up and paced the room and sat again. He went into the kitchen and got the other can of beer. When he put it to his lips, he felt selfish. Gloria was in there parched. To hell with her. It was all her fault. He drank the beer and looked into the bedroom to see if she was sleeping. The light was still on. She was sitting up in bed, still fully dressed. She looked at him with fear and surmise.

"Change your mind?" she said.

She pulled her shirt off over her head without waiting for an answer. He'd forgotten how truly remarkable those breasts were.

"You're a real bitch, aren't you?" he said.

He went out and shut the door behind him.

21

SUSSMAN was silent and withdrawn when at last he came for McDowell.

"Any trouble?" McDowell said. "Anyone see you?"

Sussman shook his head.

"Where is he?"

"In the tunnel."

"Let's go," McDowell said, picking up the suitcase with the gold in it.

Sussman stared at the bedroom door, then at McDowell. The expression on his face was apprehensive and questioning.

"She's all right," McDowell said. "I just threw a scare into her. You didn't think I'd really harm her, did you?"

"I don't know what you'd do," Sussman said tonelessly. "Anymore."

They got out to the van without seeing anyone or being seen. When they reached the Ventura Freeway feeder street, Sussman turned in the direction of the Ventura West arrow. North Spring Street was east.

"Where do you think you're going?" McDowell said.

"Home," said Sussman. "We're going home, aren't we?"

"No. Back to North Spring Street. We'll have to stay

there until we decide what to do with . . . him. We'll catch a few winks first and then I'll—"

"I couldn't," Sussman interrupted. "Not with him in there."

"All right, Steve," McDowell said gently. "I know how you feel. But someone has to stay there. Take me there, and then go home and get some sleep."

"Sleep," said Sussman bitterly.

He made a U-turn and got on the inbound Ventura Freeway.

"Don't sleep too long, though," McDowell said. "We've got a lot to do. Call Florence for me when you get up. Tell her I'm all right. But don't tell her about any of this. I don't want her ever to know."

"I wish I didn't know."

The darkness was beginning to pale when they reached the shop. Before getting out of the van, Mc-Dowell patted Sussman on the shoulder.

"You'll feel better when you've had a little rest," he said. "And don't forget to call Florence when you get up."

In the basement, McDowell hid the metal suitcase under a pile of lumber. He climbed on the electric car and went into the tunnel to see where Sussman had put the body. It was only fifteen or twenty feet back, as if Sussman had been unable to be around it any longer than necessary. The heap of disheveled clothing that had once been a man made McDowell's flesh crawl. He couldn't blame Sussman for not having moved it farther inside. McDowell had never seen a dead body before except in a casket. Toby's luggage was there, too.

McDowell put the body across the electric car and wagon and pushed it ahead of him, pausing only to catch his breath until he reached the old cistern. He rolled the body off and returned for the luggage.

Back in the basement, he stretched out on a roll-away bed. He felt better knowing the body was almost two hundred feet back in the tunnel instead of just inside. Exhausted as he was, he still could not sleep. There were too many things to be decided. The most pressing was what to do about Toby. Hiding the body was no problem. They could leave it in the tunnel.

But it wasn't like disposing of a piece of old furniture or a bag of trash. Toby was a human being, known to other human beings. When he dropped out of sight, someone might start asking questions. And questions could lead to an investigation. And an investigation could lead, through Gloria, to him and Sussman.

Toby had simply to drop out of sight in such a way no one would ask any embarrassing, unanswerable questions. Tomorrow he would have to find out if Toby had any family in Los Angeles. And any friends who might care enough about him to worry. Gloria could tell him that. Gloria herself was almost as big a problem as Toby. She was too bright a girl to be concerned about being guilty of armed robbery and kidnapping once she had recovered from her terror. She'd realize robbing thieves was not like robbing a bank. But she might believe he was capable of having her killed and that she was being watched. Her fear had been genuine. He had been utterly convincing. Even Sussman had thought him capable of harming her.

He would have to keep Gloria frightened. But that, in itself, would not be enough. She wouldn't remain frightened indefinitely. Eventually she would come to realize she had nothing to fear from him. That didn't meant she would run to the police—if he knew Gloria, she would not want to get mixed up in murder, even as a witness, especially since it came as the result of a crime in which she was involved—but she might get careless and talk about it with someone. Most likely a bed partner.

The only way to ensure her continued silence was to make her share responsibility for Toby's death or at least think she did. That would serve a double purpose. She could be useful in helping him make Toby's disappearance seem natural or at any rate minimize the chances of it being attributed to foul play, and in so doing, she could be made an accomplice after the fact. Once she had helped him, he would be very careful to point that out to her and explain it to her if she did not know about that already.

And he could further involve her by giving her some of the proceeds of their find. Not enough to put a dent in their fortune but enough to make her think she was getting a considerable share. She was a bright girl, but she had never had enough money to know what a lot of money was. Yes, he thought, he could handle Gloria Stavros.

The only other major problem was disengaging from the North Spring Street Vent and Duct Company without leaving any evidence of what had actually been going on there. That should be the simplest thing of all. They would move everything in the basement well back into the tunnel and fill in the first few yards and the entrance pit with the material they had permitted to accumulate in the basement. Then they would cement it over. Sussman should know a way to make the new cement not too different from the rest of the basement floor. And if not, they would cover it with something. The owner would not think that unusual. They had made other improvements. The partitions, for example. But the owner might think it unusual when they left precipitously.

They'd simply tell him they were sorry, they hadn't been able to make a go of the business and were unable to stay out their lease. He wouldn't make any trouble. He had that last month's rent in advance to soothe him. They would simply go out of business and take the office furniture away in the van and dump it somewhere. Better still, sell it to a used furniture dealer. That would make it look normal. When you went broke, you tried to retrieve every penny you could. No one would suspect a couple of unsuccessful businessmen trying to squeeze the last few dollars out of the failure of having a fortune.

They mustn't forget the James Ferguson account. It had been inactive for weeks, but they would have to close it out. It would not do to have statements coming to Sussman's apartment every month.

When he had thought all that through, McDowell felt unburdened. Even the thought of Toby's body back there in the tunnel was not overly oppressive. His was not the first body to be hidden back there. The cistern had already kept its other secret for perhaps a hundred years. It could keep its new secret another hundred.

He fell into a deep sleep, from which he was awakened by a loud knocking upstairs. Opening his eyes reluctantly, tasting the breath foul in his mouth and exploring his long-unbrushed teeth with the tip of his tongue, McDowell looked at his watch. After ten. It must be Sussman. Sussman could not get in because the door was bolted from inside. He went upstairs to let him in, still stiff and weary from his exertions.

Sussman looked as if he had not slept, and there was pain deep in his eyes. They went downstairs in silence. Sussman looked around the basement as if he had never seen it before.

"Did you call Florence?" McDowell asked.

"Yes."

"Get any sleep?"

"Who can sleep? Knowing this'll be hanging over us the rest of our lives. If we're lucky enough not to get caught."

"We won't get caught. I think I've got it all worked out. And don't worry. You'll get over it."

"I killed a man. How do you get over that?"

"You didn't intend to. It was an accident. And it was self-defense. He was reaching for a gun."

"I wish you'd never told me about that fucking letter," Sussman said bitterly. "I wish we'd never found the gold."

"But I did, and we did," McDowell said patiently, soothingly. "Look, Steve. It's done. It can't be undone. We can't let it ruin our lives."

"I'll bet you slept, didn't you? With him back there in the tunnel I bet you slept."

"A little," McDowell admitted.

"I knew it. You're a cold son of a bitch, McDowell. Do you know that?"

"Not really, Steve. I'm just getting practical in my middle years. When I see what I have to do, I do it."

"And you don't call that cold? What do you intend to do about Gloria? She's a miserable fucking tramp, but you leave her alone, hear? If you do anything to her, I'll. . . ."

"I won't harm a hair of her head," McDowell promised. Her dyed golden head, with pubic hair to match. "And don't worry about her saying anything. The

Golden Greek's frightened to death of what will happen to her if she opens her mouth. She wouldn't, anyway. She wants to forget last night as much as we do. And I know how to handle her."

"I guess you do," Sussman said cuttingly. "The Golden Greek. Where'd you get that? How did you get started with her anyhow?"

"None of your fucking business, Sussman. Now pull yourself together and let's talk about what we've got to do."

"All right," Sussman said, squaring his shoulders. "Just business as usual, isn't it? The show must go on."

"Back there at the well. Is there any possibility it might cave in some day?"

"I doubt it. Not with the shoring. But I don't guess it would hurt to fill in back there."

"Good. Get started on it. I've got to go over to Gloria's. I told her not to leave the apartment until I told her. And there's nothing to eat in the place."

"And maybe a little balling on the side?"

"Don't be a goddamn fool. I want to take her some breakfast and give her some instructions."

"I don't know if I can," Sussman said.

"If you can what?"

"Go in the tunnel with him there."

"Oh, Christ!" McDowell groaned. "I'll go with you. She'll just have to wait."

McDowell went to the cistern and sent the electric car back for Sussman. While he was waiting, he covered the body with sand and gravel. There was no point in upsetting Sussman any more than he was already. He had not expected Sussman would still be so shaky after he'd had time to settle down. Worried and remorseful, perhaps, but not shaky. You never really knew about people. Even himself, he thought. Three months ago he would never have dreamed he could have done all this.

Sussman arrived in near panic.

"He's gone!" he cried. "Wasn't he here when you came back? Didn't you look?"

"I moved him back here. He's under there."

Sussman stared at the heaped sand.

"Do you think you can go the rest of the way and fill in the well without me?" McDowell asked.

Sussman shook himself and nodded.

"Send the car back for me," McDowell said. "It's a long crawl to the basement. And I'll return it." He put his hand on Sussman's shoulder. "Cheer up, amigo. It'll all work itself out."

Sussman got in the car and moved off without replying.

McDowell rode the car to the basement and sent it back to the rear. He went to the North Main parking lot where the TR4 had been parked all night and drove home to shave, clean up and have breakfast.

"What's that on your shirt?" Florence demanded.

"I bumped my nose," McDowell replied. "It's nothing."

Robert wanted to know where he had been all night. They had been telling Robert his father had been leaving early every morning, before he was awake. McDowell was too tired to think of an answer.

"Your father had to leave early and help Mr. Sussman with some work," Florence said, coming to his rescue. "You were putting in bookshelves, weren't you, Arthur?"

"Yes," said McDowell.

He soaked in a hot tub for half an hour. Florence prepared a hot breakfast for him while he shaved. He ate in his robe. Florence sat across from him with a cup of coffee. She was using cream and sugar again as in the days before she began worrying about her weight.

"Is everything all right?" she asked.

"Perfect," McDowell relied.

"And that Ulrich man?"

"I'm sure he doesn't know a thing."

"I hope you're right. But you usually are."

McDowell dressed and phoned Gloria from a booth.

"Where've you been all this time?" she demanded. "You said not to leave until I heard from you and I've been sitting here going out of my skull."

"I was held up," McDowell said without apology. She hadn't said anything about being hungry.

"Can I bring you anything?" he asked.

"What could you bring me?" she said bitterly.

"You went out, didn't you?" McDowell said, chancing a guess.

"No," Gloria said quickly. "You told me not to."

"You went out. Didn't I tell you I was having your apartment watched? Where'd you go?"

"But I didn't. I've been here all. . . . I have to eat, don't I? I didn't talk to anybody. Honest. Didn't he tell you that?"

"Yes. He gave me a complete report."

"Does he have a mustache?" Gloria said. "A fat dude with a mustache?"

"I wouldn't know," McDowell said. "They change shifts every eight hours."

He was encouraged by her question. It revealed she believed he was having her watched. She must think everyone who looked at her was working for him. And it was a rare man, indeed, who would not give Gloria Stavros a second glance.

"I'm on my way to your place," he said. "I want to talk to you."

"I want to talk to you, too, big—"

She stopped short, as she had the night before.

Gloria answered the door barefoot and in a robe. She gave him a bright smile.

McDowell did not smile in return.

"Sit down," he said.

Gloria sat down. Her robe fell open, revealing her leg almost to the crotch. McDowell felt a stirring of interest which he stifled. That was what she wanted. The way her mind worked, she would think if she could just get him in bed, she could do anything she wanted with him.

"You can help us," he said. "If you help us, maybe I'll forget about the contract."

"How?" she said eagerly, leaning forward to let the robe fall open and reveal a breast.

"Close the goddamn robe," McDowell said. "It's not getting you anywhere."

"What do you mean?" Gloria said artlessly. "I didn't even notice. What does it matter anyway? You know what I've got."

"Toby. Did he take everything out of his apartment last night?"

She appeared puzzled by his question.

"His apartment. Did he get all his stuff out or did he leave anything?"

"He didn't have his own apartment," Glora said, not looking at him. "I just, you know, told you that. Don't get uptight."

"I'm not getting uptight."

"He moved in with me. Like he didn't have a job and—"

"Is anything else of his still here?" McDowell interrupted.

"I don't think so. We weren't coming back."

"Let's be sure, all right?"

"Okay. But why?"

"When I want you to know something, I'll tell you."

They searched the apartment, including the medicine chest, and found nothing. Nothing at all to indicate Toby or any man had ever lived there, nothing to indicate anyone had ever lived there except the contents of the garbage pail, some discarded clothing of Gloria's and a drawer full of old letters, bills and photographs. McDowell looked through the photographs to see if Toby were in any of them. He was not. Just Gloria alone or Gloria with young, handsome men or other girls.

He sat her down in the living room again.

"Did Toby have any family here?" he said. "Any close friends?"

"What's this all ab—" Gloria began but did not finish. "He's from back East somewhere. I mean he was. I guess he had relatives back there, but he never said anything about 'em. And he had a lot of friends."

"Good enough friends to wonder when they don't see him around?"

"Oh," said Gloria, comprehension dawning. "Who's got that kind of friends in L.A.?"

"Does anyone know he was living with you?"

Gloria shrugged.

"If they did, and asked you about him, what would you say?"

289

"Like how should I know where he was. We had a fight and I threw him out."

"And don't you forget it."

"Mac, what did you do with him?"

McDowell started to tell her it was none of her business but instead said, "You really want to know?"

"No," Gloria said with a shiver.

"His car," McDowell said. "Is it paid for?"

"Where would Toby get the bread to pay for a car?" she replied, bewildered by the question.

"Who has the title to it?"

"The dealer, I guess. Or some finance company. It's on the registration."

"Does he keep it in his car?"

"No. He carries it. Carried it, I mean."

"Oh, Christ!" McDowell groaned.

He had to know to whom Toby had been making payments, so he could have Gloria turn the car back. When the payments stopped coming in, the repossessors would start looking for Toby. It meant he would have to uncover the body, enough of it to find the wallet with the registration in it, at any rate.

"Is something wrong?" Gloria said anxiously.

She feels threatened, and a part of it, McDowell thought, pleased.

"Don't worry," he said. "We're fine."

He said "we" deliberately.

Gloria breathed a sigh of relief.

"I'll find out who holds the title—"

"The pink slip," Gloria interrupted helpfully.

"—the pink slip, and then I want you to do something for me, Gloria."

"I'll do anything," she said quickly. "Anything."

"When I find out, I want you to take the Mustang there and give it back."

"Give it back? Oh, I dig. You don't want 'em to come looking for Toby, right?"

"You're a bright girl, Gloria. Stay bright. Just don't get smart. Tomorrow's Monday. You can take it in then. Don't tell anyone your name. Tell them . . . tell them he left town and wasn't coming back and he asked you to return the car because he couldn't meet the payments and didn't want to get in trouble."

"Part of that's no shit," Gloria said with a laugh, the first time she'd been so at ease with McDowell. "He sure couldn't meet the payments."

It did not disturb McDowell too much that she felt she could be at ease with him now. It was as if she were accepting her role as co-conspirator without question.

"If you handle it right, and I can be sure you'll never give me any trouble, I may do something for you," he said carefully.

"Like what?" Gloria said, just as carefully.

"You have any idea what those coins are worth?"

"A bundle, that's for sure."

McDowell wondered what might be a reasonable figure to tell her. It could not be too low because she was no dunce and even Gloria knew what gold was worth these days. But probably not gold coins. He'd been surprised himself when Sussman first told him the value of the hooked neck eagle.

"About a hundred thousand dollars," he said.

"Wow!"

"That means there could be a little something in it for you. If I like your attitude."

"You'll love my attitude. How much?"

It should be enough to impress her but not enough to make her think he was trying to buy her off, and consequently that he had as much to fear as she did.

"How does twenty-five hundred sound?"

"Twenty-five hundred? Cool!" Then her expression became shrewd. "I mean it's not so special," she said with something like her old impudence. "I mean when you dudes are splitting a hundred thousand."

McDowell walked to her, smiling. He reached out as if to caress her shoulder. Gloria looked surprised, then held up her face to receive his kiss. He dug his fingers into her upper arm. He had to make himself do it. Even after what she had done, brutalizing a woman was not easy. But he had to convince her he was as ruthless as she had believed him to be last night.

"Oh!" she gasped, her eyes bulging. "Please, big Mac."

"I told you not to call me that," he said coldly. "I may not give you anything. If you don't straighten out,

291

I just might apply the twenty-five hundred on that contract I was talking about."

"I'm sorry, Mac. Honest. Look, I could sure use the bread."

McDowell sat down again.

"We'll see," he said, holding her eyes with his. "But that'll be the end of it. Understand? If you ever ask for another dime. . . ."

"I won't! I promise!"

"It's settled then," McDowell said, getting up. "I'll call you tomorrow and tell you where to take the car. It'll be awhile before you get the money. We've got to melt the gold down before we can sell it."

"Thanks. I really mean it."

"I don't know why I'm giving you anything," McDowell said. "After all your lies, and then ripping us off. I suppose I had a soft spot in my heart for you."

"You really did dig me, didn't you?" Gloria said, brightening. "Do you have to go right now?"

"The spot's not that soft, baby."

When he got to the door, he turned and said, "You can go out if you want to. Just don't forget you're still being watched."

"I never knew you were so fucking cold-blooded," Gloria said angrily.

You and the rest of us, McDowell thought.

22

WHEN McDowell returned to North Spring Street, he found Sussman sitting in the office.

"I couldn't stay down there," Sussman said.

"Did you fill in the well?" McDowell asked.

Sussman nodded.

"We've done enough today," said McDowell. "We're both out on our feet. Let's go home and get some rest and start fresh in the morning."

"I can't sleep," Sussman said wretchedly. "I close my eyes and I see. . . ."

"Take something then. A good night's sleep will do wonders for you."

"Yeah. That'll solve everything, won't it? A good night's sleep."

After Sussman left, McDowell went back to the cistern and raked away sand until he uncovered part of Toby's torso. The wallet was in his hip pocket. The registration slip was in it. McDowell felt queasy touching the body. He wished Sussman were there to see that he, too, was affected by what had happened. He covered the body again and got out of the tunnel as quickly as he could.

He got the three bags of coins from under the lumber and threw the metal suitcase as far back into the tunnel as he could. He put the bags in a box and took them out to his car. When he got home, he put them under the soiled clothes in the laundry hamper.

"You look so tired," Florence said. "Why don't you lie down until dinnertime?"

He fell into bed, got up a couple of hours later to have dinner, then went to bed again. He awoke in the middle of the night and had a moment of sheer funk thinking about the body in the tunnel and Gloria Stavros being a witness to the killing. But it passed. No one would ever find the body, and Gloria was no longer a problem. She was in it too deep herself now ever to talk about Toby or the coins. She was participating in the cover-up and sharing in the money. She wouldn't want anything to come out any more than he did.

Monday morning he rose early, refreshed.

"I'll get up and make your breakfast," Florence said sleepily.

"Stay in bed," McDowell said. "I'll get something on the way."

"Shall I come in at ten, as usual?"

"No. I'm coming back after the bank opens. I want you to stay home until then. To keep the laundry company."

"The laundry? Oh. Arthur, I hardly slept a wink last night thinking about all that money in there. I'll be so glad when it's out of the house."

"Don't worry, sweetheart. It won't be here much longer."

Sussman was waiting in the office when he arrived at North Spring Street. He seemed rested and more composed but was not very communicative.

"Sleep all right?" McDowell asked as they went down the steps.

"Henny gave me a pill," Sussman said curtly.

They began moving things into the tunnel. Lumber, ducting, tools, even the electric saw and hammer and the squirrel-cage vacuum pump. They had to saw the table and the workbench in pieces to get them into the tunnel. As they worked, McDowell had a sense of something missing. There was no music, he realized. Usually, Sussman flipped on the radio as soon as he came in. This morning he hadn't done it.

At nine thirty McDowell said, "I've got to knock off and take the coins to the bank. Will you be all right here by yourself?"

"Does it make any difference to you?"

"Of course it does. If you don't want to be down here alone, wait for me upstairs until I get back. Or go out for coffee or something."

"I'll stay."

"Stout fella."

"Fuck you, McDowell," said Sussman.

Why the hell was Sussman so angry with him? McDowell wondered. Sussman was the one who had actually delivered the fatal blow, and he was saving Sussman's neck as well as his own. Sussman should be grateful. But he wouldn't press the point. Sooner or later Sussman would realize that for himself.

He went upstairs and unlocked the door. When he opened it, a man in a tan cord suit was standing there, his hand poised in the act of knocking. McDowell drew back, suppressing a gasp.

"Sorry if I startled you," the man said. "Walter Burke. Department of Building and Safety."

"What?" said McDowell, shrinking inside.

"Department of Building and Safety," Burke said patiently, as if addressing a simpleton. "You've heard of the Los Angeles Department of Building and Safety?"

"Uh, yes," McDowell stammered.

"I've got to inspect the premises," Burke said. "We've had some complaints about these old buildings."

"I don't know," was all McDowell could think to answer.

He could not allow this man to go down in the basement and see all the material from the tunnel, and the lumber and ducting, the entrance pit and the tunnel itself.

"What do you mean you don't know?" Burke said, pushing his way inside.

"I'm, I'm the plumber," McDowell said. "I don't think the owner would like it if I let somebody in. He's closed while I'm doing some work."

"I don't care what he'd like," Burke said. "I'm an inspector, and I've got a job to do."

He looked around the office and at the partition closing off the rear.

"What's back there?"

"I don't know," McDowell said. "I'm just the plumber."

"Let's have a look then," Burke said.

He threw open the door in the partition and went in back. He came out immediately.

"Nothing's back there," he said. "It's none of my business, but why all that unused space?"

"I told you. I'm just the plumber. I never been here before Saturday afternoon."

"What's down there?" Burke said, nodding at the door to the stairs.

"The basement," McDowell said, his bowels in a knot.

He couldn't let this man go down there. If the inspector saw the freshly dug material and the entrance pit, he'd know something strange was going on. He'd look in the tunnel and find Toby's body.

I might have to kill him, McDowell thought wildly. But I couldn't.

"I know it's the basement," Burke said sarcastically. "What's in it? I've got to inspect the walls, the foundation and the fixtures."

He started for the door. McDowell took him by the sleeve.

"What's bugging you?" Burke demanded, shaking free. "You know something I don't? They got some improvements down there without no city permit?"

"I wouldn't know," McDowell said, fighting to conceal his panic. "I never seen the basement before Saturday. But it's in one helluva mess. When they called me Saturday, it was ass deep in water. Busted pipe. I had to dig up part of the floor to get at it."

"Faulty pipes, huh?"

"That one sure as hell was. Ass-bustin' work, I can tell you. I got the water pumped out and got a temporary seal on the pipe, but it's still in a helluva mess. I don't think the owner'd like it if I let you down there. Like it is now. And you'd get all dirty down there. Still a lot of mud and crud."

The inspector rubbed his chin.

"Could you come back next week?" McDowell said. "I'm finishing up today. Then he'll need somebody in to straighten things out. He ought to have everything all straightened up down there by next week."

"All cruddy down there, huh?" the inspector said, looking down thoughtfully at his shoes and immaculate trousers.

McDowell was glad his own shoes and clothing bore evidence of a mess downstairs.

"You bet your ass," he said. "Look at me."

"All right. You tell him I'll be back next week."

McDowell locked the door behind the inspector and sat down. He closed his eyes and took a deep breath. He opened them and looked at his hand. It was trembling. Nothing to get panicky about, he told himself. By next week, when the inspector returned, the floor would be cemented over and everything moved out. It shouldn't make the inspector suspicious. The man believed he was just a plumber called in to repair a broken pipe and wouldn't have known the firm was going out of business. Even if he went down to the basement, he would find nothing to indicate anything out of the ordinary had been going on.

It took McDowell a few minutes to pull himself together. He left without telling Sussman about their

296

visitor. Sussman already had more than enough on his mind.

At home he showered and got into a suit and tie. He put one bag of gold coins in his briefcase and the other two into the overnight bag he used on short trips.

"I won't draw a relaxed breath until I know they're where no one can take them away from us," Florence said. "Will you call me from the bank when they're safely put away?"

"Of course," McDowell said.

"After you call me, I'll go to the office. You still want me there, don't you?"

McDowell thought about the building and safety inspector. They should continue to have someone in the office until the entrance pit was cemented over and they were ready to move out the office furniture.

"Yes," he said. "And you can take Sussman some lunch. None for me. I've got things to do and won't get back until later."

There were safety-deposit boxes available at the bank big enough easily to contain the three bags. When he rented one, he mentioned casually it was for some of the more valuable items from his collection.

"The way my personal property floater's going up I can't afford to keep them at home anymore," he said. "Some of them are documents I consult frequently, darn it. I wouldn't be surprised if I spend as much time here as in my own library."

If he had to dispose of the coins a few at a time he did not want anyone getting curious about the frequency of his visits to the vault.

"We're always glad to see you, Dr. McDowell," the custodian said. "Did you and Mrs. McDowell have a good summer?"

"Superb," said McDowell.

He called Florence from the pay telephone in the bank and told her everything had gone smoothly and she could leave for North Spring Street. As soon as he hung up, he called Gloria. She answered in the middle of the second ring, as if she had been waiting for his call.

"I'm bringing over the registration slip," he said.

"Do you think I could have my bread by next

week?" Gloria said. "I'm due back at work but I'd rather go to like Acapulco for a few days. To you know, quiet my nerves. And maybe you could—"

"Plan on going back to work," McDowell interrupted. "I told you, it'll take time. And for the next few weeks you've got to stick to your normal routine."

As if her routine had ever been normal, McDowell thought. Or even routine.

"Shit," said Gloria. "You're no fun at all."

"And don't you forget it."

He took her the registration slip and made her repeat to him his instructions about what to say and do. She had no trouble remembering but was nervous.

"You can't go in there like that," he said.

"I can't help it if I'm uptight. Wouldn't you be, too?" She looked at him thoughtfully and said, "I guess you wouldn't, you cold-hearted bastard."

"Take a tranquilizer," McDowell said.

"Haven't got any. What would really tranquilize me . . . . You were so much more fun when you were horny, big Mac."

He let her call him that without objection. By now she knew where she stood with him.

"You'll have to find another way," he said. "If you go to the dealer's this nervous, they'll start wondering."

"Hey, I do have something."

She went to her bedroom and returned with a small cloth tobacco sack from which she produced cigarette papers and some brown shreds mottled with green and gold. She rolled a joint deftly and, looking up at him said, "One for you?"

McDowell shook his head.

"I didn't think so," she said.

She relaxed noticeably as she smoked the joint. When she returned from flushing the roach down the toilet, she said gaily, "Ready when you are, big Mac."

He followed her to the car dealer's and waited for her a block away.

"How'd it go?" he asked her when she slid into the seat beside him.

"Slick as owl shit."

She must have learned that phrase from Sussman, McDowell thought.

"He thanked me for being so nice," she said. "And wanted to know if there was anything he could do to show his appreciation. Like, you know, taking me to dinner tonight."

"You didn't . . ." McDowell began.

Gloria laughed.

"I told him I was already getting as much as I could handle."

McDowell laughed, too.

"You sound like old times," Gloria said.

"It'll never be like old times again. And don't you forget it. By the way," he added casually, "I'm calling off the watchdogs."

"Cool. Now if you'd just come up with the bread. . . ."

"You know what you are now, don't you, Gloria? An accessory after the fact."

"After what fact?"

He explained to her that by returning Toby's car and concealing what she knew she was as deeply involved as either he or Sussman. She was unperturbed by the information.

"I already knew I was in up to my ass," she said. "So what's new?"

When he let her out at her apartment, he cautioned her about trying to get in touch with him.

"You try, and you won't get a cent," he said. "I promise you you'll get your money out of the first proceeds."

"That's good enough for me. One thing you never did was lie to me."

Florence looked troubled when he got back to the office.

"Steven hasn't been fighting with Henrietta, has he?" she said anxiously. "He seems so down in the dumps."

"I don't think so," he said. "I suppose it's a natural letdown after working so hard for so long."

"You're not let-down. I'm not let-down. I've been feeling a little drunk since I first saw all those gold coins."

"Different people react differently," McDowell said.

Sussman had made great inroads in the heaps of equipment. He must have been working steadily, McDowell thought, anxious to put as big a barrier as possible between himself and Toby's body.

"Good work, Steve," he said.

Sussman did not respond.

McDowell changed into his coveralls and began helping him move the rest of the equipment into the tunnel. They worked the rest of the afternoon and most of the following morning. McDowell kept out only the walkie-talkies. Robert would like them.

"Now we'll fill in the first few yards of the tunnel and the entrance pit," McDowell said. "When we cement it over, can you make it look like the rest of the basement floor?"

"I can dirty it up some, but it still won't match," Sussman said.

"We'll have to put a layer of new cement over the whole floor then."

"You any idea how much it would take? And how long it would take?"

"What'll we do then?"

"You're the mastermind," Sussman said curtly. "You figure it out."

"Why are you so mad at me, Steve?" McDowell demanded. "All I've done is save your neck, and the Avila gold."

"Thanks."

"What about that floor tile I've seen on television?" McDowell said. "The kind you cut to shape with scissors and stick down."

"It would work down here, I guess."

"That's what we'll do, then. We'll fill in the pit, cement it over and get rid of the leftover tunnel material. Then put down floor tile to cover the whole basement."

They began shoveling material into the tunnel. It was strange putting it in instead of taking it out, stranger still to be working side by side with so uncommunicative and sullen a Steve Sussman. McDowell turned on the radio in an attempt to recapture some of the old atmosphere of camaraderie.

Sussman turned it off, saying, "I'm in no mood for music, if you don't mind."

They filled in the tunnel to about twenty feet back, then the entrance pit, tamping down the sand and gravel by treading on it. It took them until Wednesday morning to do so. McDowell got a list of necessary supplies from Sussman and took the van to buy cement, sand, a hoe and trowel. He had little left of his share of the money from Pike but did not ask Sussman to contribute. It seemed so petty now that they had seventeen hundred gold coins stashed away in a safety-deposit box.

Wednesday afternoon they mixed the cement on the basement floor, using water from a pail, and Sussman covered the hole with a layer of cement. When he had done so, he strewed sweepings from the floor over it, but as he had predicted, the cement still looked fresh and contrasted with the rest of the floor.

In the morning, Sussman hauled away the tunnel material that remained after filling in the entrance pit.

"Get the floor tile on the way back," McDowell said. "Get a kind that wouldn't be out of place in a basement. A solid color, dark brown or dark green."

Sussman nodded. He was still not saying much.

"Got enough money?" McDowell asked.

"Yes," said Sussman.

After he left, McDowell looked around the empty basement. The basement that had looked so cramped to him the first time he saw it now appeared spacious without its familiar clutter. And, except for the patch of fresh cement and the hole in the window where the vacuum pump duct had been, and the cleanliness, unchanged. No one would be able to draw any inference from the hole in the window glass, McDowell thought.

They put down the dark, institutional type floor tiles Thursday. It was not as easy as it appeared on the television commercials, but thanks to Sussman's handiness, the work went swiftly.

"Let's not forget to tell the landlord we're moving," McDowell said as they worked. "And to close out the James Ferguson account."

"Already closed it," Sussman replied. "Weeks ago when it went dry."

They had started laying the tile at the front of the basement. Sussman had said they should wait until the last minute to cover the fresh cement to give it as much time as possible to dry. They were two-thirds done when Florence came pelting down the steps, much agitated.

"Arthur," she said. "There's a man upstairs who wants to see you. He says he's Franz Ulrich."

"Ulrich!" McDowell cried.

He and Sussman stared at each other. Sussman's usually dark skin was shades paler.

"How did he . . ." Sussman began.

"Lock up after me," McDowell said, starting for the steps with Florence tagging behind him.

When he got to the office, Ulrich had the door in the partition open and was looking into the empty rear section. He looked at McDowell unabashed.

"A pleasure to see you again, Professor McDowell," he said.

"What do you want?" McDowell demanded.

"Might we have a private word?" Ulrich said with a glance at Florence.

Her face was fearfully defiant.

"Why don't you go out for coffee?" McDowell said.

"I will not," Florence replied.

Ulrich looked surprised. He had no idea Florence was his wife, McDowell realized, and probably thought she was a secretary.

"I said go out for coffee," McDowell said firmly.

Florence got her purse and left, slamming the door behind her.

"Now," said McDowell, "what's on your mind?"

Ulrich sat down and crossed his legs. He took out a cigarette and lit it. "I think you know," he said at last.

"I haven't the faintest idea."

"I'm thinking about having my shop air-conditioned," Ulrich said with the faintest of smiles. "I'd like an estimate on the ductwork."

"I'm busy," said McDowell. "I haven't got all day."

"I'd like to handle whatever you've found for you," Ulrich said.

"What's that supposed to mean?" McDowell said,

302

wondering how Ulrich had connected him with the North Spring Street Vent and Duct Company and exactly how much he knew.

"Shall we dispense with this sparring?" Ulrich said matter-of-factly. "I know you've been sifting the ground under here for gold coins. And you must have been finding them, to have kept at it so long."

"I don't know what you're talking about."

"Please, Professor. I'm not a moron. And neither are you."

McDowell felt a little more at ease. Ulrich did not know about the tunnel and therefore that he had a whole chest of gold coins. And that there was a body hidden between the basement and the Avila Adobe. But he was still anxious to know how Ulrich had found him and unsure how he would handle the man.

"How did you trace me here?" he asked carefully.

"It's rather a long story."

"I have all the time in the world."

"Everything was so bizarre," Ulrich said, looking around for an ashtray.

"Use the floor."

Ulrich flicked the ash from his cigarette.

"Your behavior when you sold me the coin. Your associate employing an alias. Your evasiveness in general. I could only assume there was something questionable about your possession of the coin. And I certainly did not believe a man in your position would go to such lengths and risk his reputation for a few hundred dollars."

So Pike had been right, McDowell thought.

"One of my regulars is a private detective. I asked him to follow Mr. Ferguson-Sussman as a favor to me."

McDowell felt mounting horror. Not only Ulrich but also a private detective knew about this place. And perhaps also about the body in the tunnel.

"I told him your associate owed me money and had been avoiding me," Ulrich was saying. "And I wanted to know where I might find him when he refused to answer at home."

"How long has he been watching Mr. Sussman?"

McDowell said, hiding his inner turmoil as best he could.

"It's been some time since he did so. And then only for a few hours. I wasn't paying him for his time, you see. He was doing it as a friend. He followed Mr. Sussman here one morning. And later saw him come out all sand from head to foot."

That goddamn Sussman. They were supposed to brush off all traces of sand before they left the place.

"It made me more curious than ever. Covered with sand. And driving a van. Seemingly employed at so unlikely an establishment. A qualified engineer and college teacher."

How ironic, McDowell thought. Two different men had followed Sussman, but he had noticed only one of them. But it was reasonable to expect that an experienced private detective would not let himself be seen.

"I put two and two together," Ulrich said comfortably. "An old coin. Surreptitious activities. Mr. Sussman obviously doing a bit of digging in the earth. And down here near the heart of old Los Angeles."

"You're too damned clever," McDowell said.

"I consider that a compliment," Ulrich said.

"How much of this did you tell your detective friend?"

"None of it, of course," Ulrich said, looking at McDowell as if insulted by his question. "It's a private matter between the two of us. And Mr. Sussman. My friend doesn't even know you are involved."

"Well," said McDowell, "that's something to be grateful for."

"I take it then you're amenable to my proposal."

"I suppose."

Ulrich's smile was self-satisfied. "How many coins have you recovered thus far?" he said.

"We've finished," McDowell said. "Just yesterday. We've sifted every inch down there."

"How many?" Ulrich said, excited.

"Almost a hundred. Ninety-six."

"So many!" Ulrich exclaimed, springing to his feet. "What were they like? When may I see them?"

"You'll give us a fair deal, won't you?" McDowell said anxiously.

"That goes without saying, my friend."

"Two or three were like the one I brought in. And some of them were even older. They should be worth more, shouldn't they?"

"Age is not the sole criterion. Rarity is the most important consideration. I'll be able to tell you more when I've seen them. When may I do that?"

"Next week. I've got things to do here first."

"I don't think I can wait that long. I'm bursting with impatience. This is exciting, Professor McDowell. Positively exciting."

"You'll have to," McDowell said, thinking it was time to take a firmer line with Ulrich.

"Very well. You won't mention our dealings with anyone? I may want to dispose of them through, shall we say, unconventional channels."

"Next week," McDowell said, taking Ulrich by the elbow and leading him toward the door.

"Yes," said Ulrich. "Next week."

Florence popped in immediately after he left, obviously having been waiting not too far away.

"What did he want?" she said tensely.

"He thinks we've been sifting under here for coins. I told him we'd found ninety-six."

"Did he believe you?"

"He thought it was just peachy. I'm letting him handle them for us."

Florence sighed with relief. "Arthur," she said. "You've grown so clever."

Sussman was waiting for him at the foot of the steps. Sussman must have come to meet him when he heard him coming down. He looked anxiously at McDowell. McDowell told him all that had been said. Sussman was as relieved as Florence but did not unbend. They finished putting down the tiles in silence. McDowell went upstairs and brought some sweepings to scatter over the tiles so they would not seem quite so new. He had Sussman shuffle around the floor with him to spread the dust and grind it in, remembering what Pike had told him about mixing tunnel sand with the harder earth of the prison camp parade ground.

Florence came down and found them at it, her expression one of amused wonder. When McDowell explained what they were doing, she joined them.

"You know what this makes me think of, Arthur?" she said. "How long it's been since you took me dancing."

After she went home to Robert, McDowell said, "All that remains to be done now is move out the office furniture and call the landlord. You'll take care of him, won't you?"

Sussman nodded.

Friday they took the office furniture to a dealer in two trips. After loading up for the second time, McDowell went down for a last look at the basement. Sussman refused to accompany him. The tiles were dusty and scuffed and looked as if they had been much walked on. He went upstairs and regarded the bare office. It was as if they had never been there, except that it was so much cleaner than the day they rented it. He went out and locked the door behind him. He gave the keys to Sussman.

"Mail both sets to the landlord," he said. "We changed his lock."

The dealer gave them next to nothing for the office furniture. McDowell made a pretense of bargaining.

When Sussman took him back for his car, McDowell said, "We won't need the van anymore. What will you do with it?"

"Sell it, I guess. Don't worry. You'll get your half."

"I wish you wouldn't be like this, Steve. We should be going out tonight and celebrating."

"Celebrating what?"

"It's all over."

"Not for me. It'll never be."

"You'll get over it."

"I'm moving back to Houston."

"Moving to Houston? What about your teaching contract?"

"I'm asking out. I'm giving up teaching."

"I wish you weren't. I thought one day we'd be enjoying our ill-gotten gains together."

"You thought wrong."

"I'll miss you, Steve. But we'll keep in touch. Per-

306

haps when it's time for your first share of the proceeds. Florence and I can bring it to you and have a nice visit."

"Florence I'd like to see again. You I won't miss."

"I'm sorry, Steve. After you've had time to think it over, you'll change your mind. You'll agree I only did what had to be done. I had no choice."

He got out of the van and watched Sussman drive away.

"Good-bye, amigo," he said to himself.

He felt an aching sense of loss.

23

THAT night, after a quiet dinner at home, McDowell went to the hospital with Florence to visit Pike. The colonel was long out of intensive care and impatient to go home.

"My heart's ninety percent sound," he said. "Good for another fifty years, my doctor told me. Isn't that what he said, Henrietta?"

"Yes, Father," said Henrietta. "Do you mind if I leave early tonight? I promised Steve."

"Of course, my dear. I have Flossie here to keep me company. Art, it's been almost worth my heart attack to see so much of her."

"I'll just walk to the elevator with Henrietta," Florence said.

When they left, Pike called McDowell closer. "What's been bothering Steve?" he asked. "He was quiet when he came to tell me the good news Sunday night. Should have been jumping with joy."

"Can't stand prosperity, I suppose," McDowell replied.

"Tell me, what's it worth?"

"I'll have a better idea after I get my hands on a new edition of *Gold Coins of the World*. But I'd guess a million and a half or more."

Pike whistled. "That much? You know, I really can't hold you to eleven percent. I didn't go the route."

"Act of God, Bill. You'll get your full share."

"I can't accept. Not in good conscience."

Florence came in and said, "What are you two arguing about?"

She seemed a little edgy to McDowell.

"Bill doesn't want the share we agreed on. He says he didn't help as much as he was supposed to. But we want him to have it, don't we?"

"We certainly do," Florence said, seeming much more relaxed. "And we don't want to hear another word about it, Billie."

Billie. Calling that martinet Billie, McDowell thought. Probably the only one who'd done it since he was a child, if then. He could not even picture Pike as a child.

"I bow to your decision, my dear," Pike said, smiling. "Shall we call it a dowry for Henrietta? Though I shouldn't think Steve needs a rich wife now."

"Wife?" said McDowell.

"Didn't Steven tell you they're getting married?" Florence said.

"No," said McDowell.

The son of a bitch, he thought. Not even enough decency to tell him that. As if he were some stranger. They had been the closest of friends and had been through trying times together.

"Isn't it perfect how everything worked out?" Florence said happily. "We have what you all worked so hard for, and Steven and Henrietta have each other."

"Almost perfect," Pike said with what McDowell interpreted as an undertone of melancholy.

Probably because he was losing his daughter and would be all alone, McDowell thought, wondering if Pike knew Sussman was taking her all the way to Houston, Texas. Probably did, though. Sussman was not one to keep such things to himself. Except with his former best friend. Or maybe Pike was thinking about his heart attack.

"What the hell, Bill," he said. "You could have had that heart attack working in your garden. And you said yourself you're good for another fifty years."

That night he made love to Florence for the first time in days. He had been too weary and preoccupied

308

to think about conjugal sex. Even Gloria had been unable to tempt him. Florence seemed strangely passive at first, responding only in the latter stages.

When McDowell fell asleep, he had his old nightmare about being buried alive. It was different from the other times. Instead of being in a coffin, he was in the cistern. Sharp objects were pressing into him from below and a heavy weight pressed down on him from above. In his dream he groped beneath him. Bones. Bare bones were digging into him. The skeleton. Somehow he was buried with that ancient skeleton. In terror, he tried to push away the weight pressing down upon him. He felt cloth. His hands moved across the rough material. Skin. And above skin, hair. Long hair. He was sandwiched between the old skeleton and the new corpse they had hidden there. How did he come to be here? The tunnel was closed with stacks of lumber and yards of earth, the entrance cemented over. He struggled to free himself from his suffocating burden. It would not budge. Somewhere a woman was laughing. Gloria Stavros. He called to her for help, but no sound emerged from his lips.

He awakened trembling and gasping for breath. He was home safe in his own bed. It was all a dream. Relief flooded every nerve like a narcotic. He reached over and touched Florence to reassure himself he was really where he was.

"What is it?" Florence asked sleepily. "Really, Arthur, don't be a glutton."

"I had a bad dream."

"Oh. Is that all? Go back to sleep."

"Don't you want to hear about it? It was awful."

He wouldn't tell her the whole thing, not about being buried with the corpse of a man they had killed. Florence must never know about that. It was a burden she should not have to share.

"Not particularly," Florence said.

"Now that's a hell of an attitude."

Florence sat up with her back against the headboard. "As long as we're wide awake I think we should talk," she said.

"Talk? About what?"

"You've been very ugly to me at times lately, Arthur."

"I know. I'm sorry. I was under a strain."

"Billie asked me to leave you."

"That little horse's ass?" McDowell said with an incredulous laugh.

Who would have thought Pike had it in him?

"He's a very charming man," Florence said calmly. "I was tempted."

"What?" McDowell demanded, sitting up.

This was crazy.

"I was tempted," Florence said again. "I've grown very fond of him. If you weren't so wrapped up in your own schemes, you'd have noticed."

"Fond of him? How the hell could you be fond of him?"

"I find him very attractive."

"Attractive, for God's sake? Attractive how?"

"Physically," Florence said coolly.

"Physically?" McDowell echoed, an incredible suspicion dawning. The Saturdays she'd been late. Other little things.

"Do you have to repeat everything I say, Arthur?"

"Are you trying to tell me you and that little son of a bitch ever . . . ?"

He could not finish the question.

"You'll never know, will you, darling?"

"Now, just a fucking minute! Let's get to the bottom of this."

"Please don't be so Victorian. It's perfectly all right for you to fool around but not for me. Is that it?"

"What do you mean, for me to fool around? You know I don't do that."

"I'm not stupid, Arthur. Those Saturdays you had so many mysterious things to do and wouldn't take Bob with you. And came home reeking of women and guilt. Do you really think I didn't know you were seeing someone?"

McDowell felt cold all over.

"If you fool around, why shouldn't I?" she said.

He really couldn't answer that, McDowell realized. But with Pike, that little old bastard. Maybe she had just said that to get even with him for being unfaithful.

Or maybe she had really been fooling around with someone, not Pike but someone he didn't even know. He'd neglected her a lot the past few months. And she was an amorous woman. And more than once he had been short and sarcastic with her, something she was not accustomed to from him. He would have to believe she had not and was just getting back at him. Why now, of all times? Could she have been biding her time until they'd finished the tunnel and brought out the Avila gold? Florence just wasn't that calculating. Or was she? How well did he really know her, this wife of seventeen years?

"Look," he said carefully, "I'm not admitting a damn thing about what you said. And I'm never going to ask you about Pike again. All right?"

"If that's what you want."

"We'll just forget everything that's been said or done up to now and start over tomorrow exactly the way we were before I ever learned about the goddamn gold."

"Exactly the way we were," Florence said comfortably. "Only richer."